I0783920

The Black Bow

A.R. Bender

THE BLACK BOW

Written by A.R. Bender

All rights reserved

No part of this book may be reproduced or transmitted in any form or by any means, electronic or mechanical, including photocopying, recording, or any information storage and retrieval system, without written permission from the author, except for the inclusion of brief quotations in a review. For permission requests, write to the publisher at the email address below, with the subject of A.R. Bender.

aramb.pub@gmail.com

https://arambender.com/

Copyright © September 2024 by A.R. Bender

First Edition Printed 2024

IBSN 979-8-9888086-1-9

X – Twitter: @arambender

Bluesky - https://bsky.app/profile/arambender.bsky.social

Cover Design by Nada Orlic

Acknowledgements / Permissions

I want to thank my friends and family, including those in my writer's groups, for their support, encouragement, feedback, and suggestions.

To Matthew Bennett and staff at the Cascade Editors Collective, whose critiques have made this a better story.

To Harper Collins Publishers for granting permissions to use excerpts written in THE SPIRAL DANCE: A Rebirth of Ancient Religion of the Great Goddess by Starhawk (the 10th anniversary edition published 1989), used in this book's Yule and Eostar (Spring) ceremonies.

To Morgan

Table of Contents

BOOK TWO

BOOK ONE

Prologue

Erich had always believed that his ancestral home was far removed from the tumult and destruction that had ravaged the realm for so long.

He gazed at his chateau while sitting beside Gunther, the family servant, in the shade of pine trees. They had been resting and enjoying bread and sausages after working most of the morning pulling stumps in the northern pasture with their team of horses. He handed Gunther a skein of water and flexed his knee as he shifted his position.

"How's the leg?" Gunther asked as he chomped on a sausage.

"Better. Should be healed soon."

The chateau stood amid an array of birch trees on a rise of land south of the Danube and the town of Ulm. His mother, Agatha, and brother, Peter, chatted on the covered front porch, facing east. He smiled when his daughter, Anna, shouted for joy as his wife, Catherine, pushed her on a swing hung from one of the birches. Horses roamed the fenced western pasture, which included a barn and several smaller structures for the goats, cows, chickens, sheep, and pigs. A small river ran alongside the pasture, flowing into the Danube. The colts and fillies he'd bred romped playfully in the field. His horse, a Bavarian Warmblood and Andalusian cross named Baldur, grazed peacefully on the grass. He noted that Baldur looked as fit and strong as when he first broke him almost ten years ago.

A thick plume of smoke rose behind the chateau from the southern part of the estate, which sloped down to a lowland area where a scattering of wooden huts stood, inhabited by peasants tending the cultivated fields. The smoke emanated from a large covered fire pit they used as a communal kitchen for preparing and cooking meals.

Gunther glanced up the field, where a burly man was chopping one of several fallen trees. "Looks like Thomas will be working on those for a good fortnight. I'll help if my back holds up. We're running low on firewood."

"I'll get Cort to help too. He's old enough to swing a big ax now."

"That he is."

They resumed work after the break. He maintained a firm grip on the reins of his two workhorses, waiting for Gunther to loop and tighten a thick rope beneath the base of a partially uprooted stump. After Gunther stepped back and nodded, he led the horses forward until the rope, connected to a wagon harness, was taut. He pulled the reins and urged the team onward. After much bending and cracking, the stump broke free from the root ball and dragged along the ground until he halted the team.

"Ach," Gunther exclaimed, stooping slightly and holding his lower back. "Such a stubborn one. Didn't want to leave this earth yet."

"Some are like that. Only one more left."

A supply wagon driven by two men captured his attention as it turned off the main road onto the smaller one leading to their estate. A heavy canvas covered a box-shaped object secured to the bed. They directed the wagon past the entry gate and toward the house.

Both men appeared to be soldiers in his trained eye. One sat next to a crossbow, with a quiver of arrows attached to his belt. The other was dressed in musketeer attire and equipment. The musketeer's hat resembled those worn by the Swedish soldiers he had once served alongside. He felt a growing concern about their presence and contemplated what lay beneath the canvas, the size and shape reminiscent of what he had witnessed in the aftermath of battles. They halted the wagon and approached the house. Agatha and Peter greeted the men, who doffed their hats as they spoke.

"What do they want?" Gunther asked.

"I'll find out."

He was about halfway there when Agatha suddenly covered her mouth with one hand and collapsed to the ground.

————

The two men were Protestant soldiers, one a member of the Swedish Yellow Brigade. The casket in the wagon contained the body of his father, Richard, who had been killed in the Battle of Lützen the previous month. A heroic death, they said, fighting against the Imperial Catholic forces under Count Wallenstein. Due to Richard's accomplishments during the battle, the Protestant command sent two soldiers to return the body to his home and the family's most cherished possession, the Black Bow, which he'd taken with him on the campaign.

He tried to dissuade his father from joining the fight. After all, he was over fifty years old at the time and had last served as a Protestant officer more than twenty years earlier. Richard made up his mind to re-enlist after the family learned that Imperial forces had massacred more than 20,000 civilians at Magdeburg, where his daughter, Beata, resided with her husband and two children. They never found their bodies. He beseeched his father to wait for his injured leg to heal so he could go instead, but Richard would not alter his decision.

It was Richard's dying wish, the soldiers told the family, to be buried on his estate with a view of the chateau.

1.

Atop the Tower

A soaring thunderhead churned across a stark gray sky, dumping torrents of rain onto the forested countryside of rolling hills and meadows.

He rested Baldur at the top of a ridge while observing the thunderhead on the northern horizon beyond the Danube. Bolts of lightning flashed. Distant thunder rumbled. Dark sheets of rain loomed. He wrapped a scarf around his neck as a chilly breeze wafted up the slope. A thin blanket of snow from an early-season storm still covered a desolate landscape of barren trees and grasses, but the road to Ulm appeared dry and in good riding condition. A wide band of sunlight from a break in the clouds in the south rolled across the terrain toward him. He squinted against the sudden brightness and savored the brief warmth until it passed.

Baldur clopped one hoof to the ground, ready to run. He guided the horse down the slope and flicked the reins when they reached the road. The horse snorted, reared up, and plunged into a full gallop. Leaning forward, he jerked the reins again. Baldur then kicked into a run at top speed.

He continued riding at this rapid clip as Baldur's pounding hooves shook the earth, sending dirt and mud spraying with every step. These solitary rides to town from his farm always filled him with exhilaration and took his mind off the troubles and misfortunes that had befallen him and his family in recent years. Moreover, they reminded him of the time he rode Baldur into raging battles at such a pace almost eight years before, feeling invincible on the horse's back.

He halted at a crossroads south of Ulm, which overlooked his ancestral home. Two men sat on the front porch, part of the family who had moved in after the local Catholic authorities evicted his family from the estate two years earlier. It always angered him to see others living there, but at least they maintained the property instead of allowing it to fall into disrepair. He usually rode past the estate, but today, he had a task to attend to on the grounds.

He proceeded toward the northern pasture, noting the men on the porch who watched him closely as they talked. He stopped in front of a tall gravestone and dismounted. It had been some time since he had visited his father's grave, so he took out one of Peter's sharpest carving tools and began to prune the shrubs around the site.

After paying his respects, he turned toward the chateau. He glanced down at a depression in the ground ahead, created, he recalled, when he and Gunther uprooted a tree stump at that spot three years earlier, when that wagon carrying his father's casket entered the property.

Things were never the same for the family after that.

———

He galloped Baldur swiftly away from the estate but slowed to a trot as he approached Ulm. The town had become an unwelcoming place for him. He crossed the bridge over the Danube and entered Ulm through one of the gates along the fortified town walls.

He emerged from the livery after stabling Baldur, turned up the collar of his long, thick deerskin coat, and trudged along Steingasse Road, stamping his wooden staff on the ground with every other step. The vendors in the Münsterplatz market were already closing their stalls on this dark and dreary December afternoon. He was heading to the Krone Inn for a drink of ale before starting his shift at the prison. He preferred working nights since the gruesome interrogations occurred during the day, but it was only a temporary duty to cover for another guard who had fallen ill. Three men stood near the inn entrance engaged in a lively discussion. One of them he recognized all too well was Klaus, the local Catholic League leader.

Klaus gestured for the other men to be quiet and glared at him contemptuously as he entered.

———

He sat in a far corner of the room, clutching a mug of ale. Sipping the brew often led him down a brooding path, but today it wasn't the loss of his ancestral land that troubled him. He had recently learned that a woman in a nearby town named Irmgard was being held by the authorities due to suspected witchcraft activities. He worried about who she might implicate under the duress of interrogations since she used to be a member of his mother's coven.

He took another swig and tried to dismiss his concerns, but soon, other disturbing thoughts about his family came to the forefront. He had been aware for some time of how the behavior of some of them had changed since they moved to the relative isolation of their farm. Catherine had fallen into dark and moody spells that sometimes lasted for days. Eva, his sister-in-law, had become more fearful of strangers and seldom ventured into town. His teenage son, Cort, was spending less time with the family and more time in the woods with his new friends—the wolves.

A group of town officials, including Jacob, the Town Sheriff, sat together near the entrance. Jacob was a staunch Catholic but not militant, and he had maintained good relations with the family since childhood. Nearby, another man was asleep—or possibly passed out—at a table, his head resting on his forearms. A small dog curled up at his feet. Men played cards at the gambling table on one side of the room. A bystander observed the game while smoking tobacco from a curved pipe, the soothing aroma of the smoke drifting throughout the room. Other patrons occupied the counter, including one of the local strumpets, who joked with an elderly man while gently tugging on his long white beard. At the other end, a man wearing a broad-brimmed hat slouched against the wall. Above him, a calendar hung, depicting the year 1635 and the month of December, with half the days marked off. It was a relatively quiet night at the inn.

He strode to the counter, his empty mug in hand. Jacob approached him, holding his own mug.

"Ah. Good day, Erich," Jacob said. "Why not join us at our table for the next round?"

Erich glanced at the table, recognizing one of the officials who'd voted to evict him. "Perhaps another time. Leaving for work soon."

"I've been thinking," Jacob said. "We should go hunting after Yule if the weather holds. It's been too long. Young Cort can come with us. Don't you think?"

"Yes. We often go together. He's learning fast."

"To The Hunt!" Jacob exclaimed.

They both raised and clashed their mugs. "To The Hunt!" Erich repeated.

After a healthy swig, Jacob's mood turned serious. "One of Klaus's men asked about the Bow yesterday."

He nodded in acknowledgment as it had happened before.

"This time he wanted to see it," Jacob said. "To make sure we still had it, he said. Of course, I refused."

"Who was it?"

"Lothar."

His hand tightened into a fist. "Let me know if he tries again."

It had been two years since Catholic authorities ordered him to give the Black Bow to the sheriff's office, as they claimed it had been used as a weapon against them during the War. The Bow had been in his family's possession for nearly 400 years, dating back to the Holy Wars, and the decision to part with it still pained him. However, he reluctantly complied to avoid the trouble that would arise from refusal. The fact that the Bow would be in Jacob's trusted hands made it easier, as did the assurance that it would be returned to him after the War. Nonetheless, the bloody conflict between Catholics and Protestants had been raging for over seventeen years with no sign of a truce.

Erich leaned back in his chair and fixed his gaze on the gambling table. Three of the four gamblers were vendors from the marketplace. The other man, a rough-looking stranger with wild red hair, had the most coins. Erich recognized him as one of those who had spoken to Klaus before he entered. They were playing a version of Karnöffel. Each player took turns drawing cards from a deck in the middle of the table before discarding cards from their hand. After a brief deliberation, they added more coins and proceeded to the next draw. The stranger moved his hands and arms in an odd manner as the men examined their hands, prompting Erich to approach them.

One of the gamblers slapped his cards down, shaking his head as he muttered oaths of frustration. The others tossed in more coins and drew from the deck. The stranger twisted his wrist in a similar manner and tucked two fingers into his long-sleeved shirt.

Erich had witnessed that trick in taverns during the War. He slammed his hand down on the stranger's wrist and twisted it upwards, revealing the edge of a card tucked beneath his sleeve.

The stranger glared at him with shocked and bulging eyes and reached for a knife on his belt. Erich pounded his fist into the stranger's jaw before he could grasp it, knocking him to the floor. He staggered up, enraged, and pulled out the knife. The other gamblers and onlookers retreated from the table, but Erich stood his ground. The stranger thrust his blade at him, but Erich grabbed the hand holding it and smashed his jaw again. He fell back, dropped the knife, and groggily crawled toward it. He stepped hard on the stranger's arm with one foot, hesitated momentarily, and stomped much harder onto his hand with his other foot, grinding into the floor. He bellowed in pain and writhed in agony.

The other gamblers approached Erich, who was still glaring at the stranger.

"Ha! He's a slick one," Herbert said.

"He won't be dealing false cards with that hand anymore," Georg added.

"Now we get our coins back!" Dieter said, grinning.

He drained his ale and donned his coat. He nodded respectfully at Jacob, who had just finished tying the stranger's hands, as he walked to the door.

———

Once outside on the misty night, he made his way down Steingasse Road. The only light source now came from the torch-lit lamps lining the street. He paused at the entrance to an alley, where a pack of snarling dogs feasted with a vicious frenzy on something against the wall, nipping and snapping for dominance. One of the dogs growled and lunged at him. He thumped his staff. The dog retreated into the shadows.

At last, he approached his destination—the town prison. Its tall, dark tower loomed over the other buildings. Flickering candlelight filtered through the shutters on the ground floor. He lowered his head and walked toward it.

He paused at the door, reluctant to enter. He shuffled around the building and entered through a back entrance. The muffled voices of the other guards, whose presence he found hard to endure due to their bloodlust during the interrogations, were faintly audible behind the wall. He ascended a winding stairway, pushed open the trapdoor, and climbed onto the roof. Leaning over the chest-high wall atop the tower, he gazed out over the town.

He had visited this place numerous times before, usually during the daytime. It was one of Ulm's tallest and oldest buildings, originally constructed as a watchtower. Only a few people crossed the torch-lit Marktplatz square. Not long ago, Ulm thrived with activity for hours after sunset. These days, however, most people retreated early into the safety of their homes and shelters. The climate of fear and hatred among the people had worsened over the years. Friends became enemies and enemies became friends, all depending on one's faith: a believer in the teachings of Luther or a traditional Catholic. The repression of one faith toward the other grew increasingly severe. Yet, the people, like cowards, allowed this to occur, which only increased the power of the oppressive fanatics. A wave of disgust washed over him as he realized his complicity, the worst of which had occurred within the tower's walls.

He gazed at the Ulm Cathedral to the west. The torchlight lamps illuminated much of the massive base, while the dark silhouette of the giant steeple rose into the sky. In moments like this, his desire to oppose the injustices he had witnessed over the years grew strongest. He took such a stand when he fought in the War as a Protestant officer, yet it wasn't enough. While recovering from a leg injury, he believed the hostilities would end after the decisive victories by the Imperial forces under Wallenstein. His optimism surged when Gustavus Adolphus's Swedish troops joined the conflict and shifted the momentum in favor of the Protestants. He resigned from his commission after his father's death to care for and protect his family. Meanwhile, the Habsburgs reconstituted the Imperial army and won subsequent battles after Gustavus fell at Lützen, prolonging the War with no resolution in sight.

A woman's scream pierced the still night air. He scanned the square and streets but couldn't discern its source, as his hearing had never fully recovered from being so close to cannon fire during the battles. A man stood in the street, staring down an alley, perhaps the origin of the scream. The townsfolk seldom ventured into those "beggar's alleys," as they referred to them, and never at night.

More shrieks echoed from the area. Erich pounded his fist on the railing—the same one that had smashed the gambler at the inn. He felt great satisfaction as he did so, yet the gambler was merely a small and petty man. No, he harbored stronger desires to exact more severe retribution on those responsible for the hardships endured by his family and community. Such as the newly appointed officials of the Ulm town council who'd evicted them from their estate. Also, the members of the Catholic League and their leader, Klaus, who ruthlessly enforced the newfound powers of the Church upon the Protestant citizens of Ulm. Then there were those like Duke Maximilian in München and the Habsburgs in Vienna, whose decisions prolonged the War for so long.

He cared little about the consequences of such retributions for himself, but he did, above all, care about the consequences for his family. So once more, he resigned himself to the harsh reality that he had to live his life like many others: retreating into themselves and their families, hoping the War would end soon, yet feeling powerless to do anything about it.

This time, he pounded his fist much harder. He turned and shuffled to the trapdoor to start his shift.

———

The following day, he donned his coat and departed as three other guards joked about the upcoming interrogations. Once outside the prison gloom, people bumped and jostled him as they rushed toward the central marketplace.

A loud, exuberant crowd gathered in the town square where the public executions and tortures took place. He slowed down and caught a glimpse of someone in the stocks again. He immediately recognized the victim by his wild shock of red hair—the cheating gambler from the inn. The townsfolk took great delight in mocking and humiliating him. The more enthusiastic citizens threw pieces of rotten food and dung from the horse stables at him.

Such spectacles angered him initially, but he became inured to them over the years. Still, he avoided the punishments for those found guilty of the more serious crimes: the floggings by the whip and birch branch; those being tarred and feathered; the dismemberments of hands and feet; the slow deaths on the wheel; and the burnings at the stake.

He took a shortcut through one of the beggar's alleys on his way to a shop on the north side of town to see if Albrecht—a soldier he once served with—still lived there with his wife and child. He had given Albrecht odd jobs on his farm and knew he resided in one of these shelters.

The eviscerated carcass of a dog sprawled against a wall at the head of the alley—the exact spot where snarling dogs had fought the night before. Most habitats were empty, but in some of them, people gaped at him with hopeless, vacant expressions as he walked by. The tall buildings on each side blocked much daylight, except along a narrow corridor. He covered his nose as he passed a flimsy structure that served as an outhouse.

He couldn't find Albrecht and wondered how anyone could live in such conditions. Many of them, like Albrecht and his family, had fled the countryside after troops on both sides of the conflict had razed their homes and villages, and later, highwaymen had robbed them of their remaining possessions. At least in the town, they had some safety in numbers and a means to scrape by, although feebly.

He emerged from the alley and walked along a side street until he approached a noisy, bustling marketplace. He recognized some vendors from his childhood visits to the market with his family. Everything felt more casual and relaxed during those years, and people always took the time to tell stories and share about their families. Now, they seldom interacted, constantly in a hurry and desperate to buy and sell the essentials needed to survive these turbulent and rapidly changing times. Such a contrast to the people in the alley, who had given up hope and were consumed by the shifting circumstances.

Finally, he arrived at the candle shop. It was time to stock up for the long winter nights. After selecting a bulk of the longest-burning candles and a sack of flints, he browsed through the store, searching for a gift for his mother's birthday. He settled on a glistening, ornate candle holder.

On his way to the livery, a brawl broke out between three men in front of a money changer's stall. Two men fought against one, but the lone fighter gained the upper hand. He knocked one man down and had a chokehold on the other. The crowd cheered him on. He often witnessed fights around these stalls by people who believed the money changers shortchanged them when they exchanged their old silver and paper currencies for the newly minted ones. Many also mistrusted them due to their unusual appearance and different religion and customs.

Two strong, burly men burst out near the moneychanger's stall and set upon the single man. They pummeled him to the ground with their clubs and continued the beating after he'd been subdued.

Erich stepped out from the crowd toward the fight.

The two enforcers stopped when he loomed above them with a staff in hand.

"That's enough," Erich said.

"Go away, peasant, unless you want some of this too," one of the enforcers snarled.

He was about to strike the beaten man again when Erich knocked the club from his hand with a swift swing of his staff. With an opposing swing, he hit the other end against the enforcer's skull. The second enforcer charged at him with his club, but Erich cracked his staff into the enforcer's knee, sending him sprawling to the ground. Both enforcers lay on the ground, moaning. Two other men assisted the beaten man to his feet, nodding to Erich as they did so.

He stamped his staff and walked away.

2.

Abduction

A horse-drawn carriage raced along a country road outside the village of Ballendorf, north of Ulm. Two women sat inside, bundled up against the cold breeze whistling through the door cracks. One of them, stout and middle-aged, had been dozing since their departure, her head bobbing up and down from the bumpy ride. The other woman was younger, with long dark hair. Her arms rested on a satchel in her lap as she gazed thoughtfully at the passing countryside through the narrow window slats. The carriage stopped by a small farmhouse. A man and two young children waited for them in the doorway.

"Trude, I'm so glad you made it," the man whispered to the older woman, gripping his hands in worry. He shot a hopeful glance at the other woman. "The apothecary is inside."

They stood at the entrance to a back room, where a woman lay in bed, groaning in agony. The apothecary sat beside her, applying leeches to her forehead, but paused when he saw them.

"My name is Mara," the woman with the satchel said. "I have come to help."

He glared at her. "There's nothing you can do."

Mara entered the room and pulled back the covers, revealing the woman's distended belly.

"Her contractions started this morning," Trude said.

Immediately, Mara recognized the source of her suffering by the shape of her belly. She verified it by placing her hands on the area.

"I must give this woman a potion to calm her disposition and ease her pain. Then move the baby's head so she can have a proper birth."

"That will do more harm than good," he said. "She's in God's hands now."

"Yes, and God has sent me to help. If we act now—"

"Blasphemy!" he shouted and stomped out of the room.

"I fear Mathilda might not last the night," Trude said.

"We'll work together as we did in Ballendorf. First, I'll remove these dreadful leeches."

"I'll fetch more towels and blankets," Trude said.

Mara sat cross-legged in front of a small table next to the bed, her eyes lowered as she meditated on techniques to alleviate Mathilda's distress. She placed a candle, a stick of incense, and a small water bowl on the table, transforming it into a shrine. She had assisted with several such procedures before, but only once on her own, and she hoped there wouldn't be any complications.

She stood over Mathilda, whose moans had diminished—the potion had taken effect. She gestured for Trude, seated on a chair at the foot of the bed, to join her. She pinned back her hair and leaned down to Mathilda.

"The baby is crooked in your stomach," Mara whispered. "I'll help straighten the head so you can give birth. I'll try to be gentle, but you may have some discomfort. Do you understand?"

Mathilda grimaced and nodded.

She massaged Mathilda's belly while Trude applied a cool compress to her forehead. Mathilda groaned occasionally, prompting Mara to pause, but each time, Mathilda urged her to continue, her lips pressed together and eyes closed. With one hand, she eased the head toward the center of her belly while guiding the feet in the opposite direction with the other. Soon, Mathilda exhaled deeply and began to breathe at regular intervals. The baby appeared to be centered.

She and Trude exchanged hopeful smiles.

A short time later, the baby's head emerged from the birth canal. Mara completed the procedures she'd done many times before. It was a boy. She picked the infant up by the feet, slapped it on the rump—and out came a cry! She cut the umbilical cord and placed the newborn on the mother's breast.

The husband entered the room and smiled at seeing a healthy baby. A young boy and girl joined them at the bedside as the infant nursed.

Mara sat in the kitchen with her grateful husband, Joseph, Trude, and the children, enjoying a simple meal of bread and soup. Mathilda rested in the bedroom with the newborn.

"So now I have a brother!" Hans said. "I can't wait to play with him!"

"Papa, when will I have a sister?" Lora asked.

"Ah, maybe next time."

"Where will you be going now?" Trude asked Mara.

"I'm traveling with two other midwives. We'll follow the road south to another village as soon as we—"

A loud banging shook the door. Before Joseph could respond, three men burst into the room, led by the apothecary.

"That's her!" the apothecary said, pointing to Mara.

The other two grabbed her by each arm and lifted her from the chair. "What are you doing?" she asked, shocked at the sudden intrusion while struggling to free herself.

"Stop!" Joseph commanded, rising from his chair. "Who are you?"

"She's been accused of witchcraft in Setzingen," another man said. "We're taking her to the authorities."

Joseph stepped forward to block the door, but the apothecary pushed him aside. He advanced toward them but retreated after hearing his children whimpering in the corner of the room. Trude handed Mara her coat with a pained and helpless expression.

Wordlessly, they carried Mara out the door and toward a makeshift prison cart.

3.

Ceremony

The forest stood frozen in time that night. Silvery moonlight filtered through the trunks and branches of the trees, casting shadows on the snow-covered ground. A sudden gust of wind shook the long branches of a pine tree, sending clumps of snow crashing down. Fresh deer tracks cut through a broad clearing and along the fences surrounding a barn. A lynx crept along the forest's edge and stopped beside a growth of willow bushes. She'd been on the trail of a small roe deer most of the night, driven by hunger and the need to feed her kittens, who were still helpless in the den. She stared ahead at the vast expanse of exposed terrain before creeping across it, crouching all the way.

Just beyond the clearing, a wisp of smoke rose from the chimney of a spacious farmhouse. A faint light flickered at the edges of the shutters covering the front and side windows.

———

Inside the farmhouse, Agatha huddled by the fireplace. She tucked back her long gray hair and placed a log onto the flames. She rubbed her feet along the floor in the new woolen socks that her daughter-in-law, Eva, had knitted for her. Nothing felt as comforting as thick, warm socks on a cold winter night.

As usual, she was the last one still up in the household. She picked up a candle, shuffled toward the kitchen stove, and paused to admire the holder, a gift from her son. It was as heavy as iron and coated with polished silver, so shiny that her reflection appeared on the rounded surface.

She poured a brew made from dandelion roots, goldenrod, and assorted grasses and herbs from the forest that she had gathered earlier in the year. The mixture always gave her a pleasant and soothing feeling at the end of the day. Sitting before the fireplace, she sipped the brew while contemplating her upcoming journey. Her cat, Bertina, padded in from another room and curled up beside her.

She had traveled to the woodcutter's house before but never during winter. The road was bumpy and rough in places, but Gunther and Thomas would be with her to clear it if necessary. It was a shame they had to journey so far from town to participate in the Yule ceremony again this year, but it was a necessary precaution to ensure their safety. She looked forward to being among her companions in the coven. For her and all those who still worshiped in the old ways, Yule was a meaningful ceremony: the rebirth of another year and a time of hope and promise when darkness gives way to light.

Ever since the summer, however, she had begun to think that this Yule would be different from the others due to her recurring dreams and visions. The central image in her vision was a crude and massive wooden wheel, reminiscent of a wagon wheel. Within these visions, she sensed significant events unfolding in the coming year that would turn the wheel away from the darkness of their times and toward the light. Despite her daily meditations, a clearer understanding of the vision seemed to elude her. She hoped the answers would reveal themselves with greater clarity during the ceremony.

The constant barking outside from Max, the family dog, interrupted her musings. She remained alert for any signs of danger as the barking continued. A sudden noise from the kitchen startled her for a moment.

"Oh, I didn't think you were up," Erich said. He poured himself some brew and stood beside her. "Is it wolves again?"

"No. Something else."

For some time, they stared into the flames as Max barked.

Peter came into the room, still half-asleep. "Shall I awaken Gunther?" he said to his brother.

"Not yet. I'll check outside first."

Agatha and Peter joined him on the porch. Soon, Max's barking stopped.

Erich and Agatha settled by the fireplace. Peter returned to bed.

"You should get some sleep now," he said to her. "For the journey tomorrow."

"And you, for your early ride to town."

He nodded and lingered by the fire.

Agatha glanced up at him and noticed his troubled demeanor; his prison work had been weighing on him more lately.

"Any news about Irmgard?" he asked.

"Nothing since they took her. I hope to learn more tomorrow."

"Goodnight, mother," he said, patting her shoulder.

She stirred the fire with a poker, comforted by her thoughts. So much had been taken from her: her childhood home and family estate; her daughter and grandchildren, lost to pillaging troops; her loving husband claimed by battle; and her livelihood as a midwife. Yet the one thing they could never take away was her abiding belief in the almighty spirit of God. The spirit evident in all of nature's creations, from the earth and sky to the stars and moon, and from the trees, streams, plants, and stones—a celebration of God unburdened by the formalities of organized religion or the rule of law. She had sensed this spiritual connection to the natural world when she worshiped in church during her youth. Despite all her hardships, she rediscovered this spirit among the kindred souls in her coven. Because of this, she possessed a deeper faith that gave each day greater meaning, strength to continue, and the belief that things would improve.

———

Agatha woke with the first light and peered out from the shutters. Thomas and Gunther were hitching the horses to the carriage. To her relief, no fresh snow had fallen and the sky was clear.

She crept out of the room, careful not to awaken Anna and Rudi, the two children inside. Peter was asleep in the next room with Eva and their infant daughter, Heloise. Cort shared another room with Thomas and Gunther. She passed by Erich and Catherine's bedroom before entering the kitchen.

After eating some porridge, she packed the items for the trip in a bag: a heavy blanket, cloth wraps, and two loaves of bread she had baked as a humble offering for the celebration. She also included cheese and sausages for Gunther and Thomas. If all went well, she expected to arrive at the woodcutter's house by midday.

When she stepped outside, the men had finished preparing the carriage. Thomas loaded her supplies, and off they went. As they traveled, they passed several other farms. She recalled one where she had assisted in delivering twins while working as a midwife. They would be nine or ten now. Around that time, the persecution of midwives began, forcing her to limit those activities to families within her coven.

Later that morning, five men on horseback approached them. The leader signaled for Gunther to stop. Four of them wore soldiers' uniforms, while one was dressed in the black robes of a Jesuit monk. One of the soldiers circled the wagon, inspecting its contents.

"Where are you going?" the monk asked Gunther.

"To a family gathering," Agatha interjected. "Not far away."

The monk eyed her suspiciously without responding.

"There have been reports of highwaymen in the area," a soldier said. "Proceed with caution."

The monk glared at Agatha as he galloped away with the soldiers.

After crossing a bridge over a gully, Agatha searched for the landmarks she recalled. They passed a series of large rock formations and arrived at the narrow side road leading to the woodcutter's house. She tapped Gunther's shoulder and pointed to the spot. He nodded and directed the carriage onto it.

They passed several isolated huts nestled deep in the woods, all appearing abandoned except for one, from which smoke was rising from the chimney. Three horses were in a makeshift barn near the hut. She glanced back several times to make sure they weren't being followed.

The road meandered alongside a stream until they reached a cultivated field where the woodcutter Karl's house stood before a dense stand of trees. A few horses and carriages were corralled next to the barn. Karl's exuberant son, Pauli, waved at them when they came near the house. Their shepherd dog beside him also greeted them with loud and friendly barks.

———

Agatha sat by the fireplace, sipping hot apple cider. About thirty people were gathered in the room, including some children, all engaging in cheerful banter. She recalled a time not long ago when many more people attended the ceremony in much larger quarters closer to town. Each year, fewer people came as the repression from the Church authorities grew stronger. They had all witnessed the burnings and the tortures in the public square and heard about what occurred inside the prison for those accused of worshiping in the old ways.

She asked about Irmgard during this time. No one knew about her situation, but they all wore grave expressions when discussing it. Now, each knock on the door could mean the worst, even after her outcome was decided.

Agatha was speaking with another midwife when an older woman entered the house. The woman stood alone, bundled up in layers, with a small pack slung over her shoulder. She placed her walking stick down and pulled back the hood from her head. Now she recognized

Klara, who lived alone in a cottage deep in the forest between their farm and Ulm. Agatha hadn't seen Klara since the last Yule ceremony and sometimes wondered how she was faring.

"Ah, Klara. So glad you could make it," Agatha said, embracing her. "How did you get here?"

"I walked," she answered in a raspy voice.

"All this way?"

"I've done so before."

"My, and in this weather. We'll give you a ride back."

"You shouldn't trouble yourself."

"It is nothing," Agatha said, still holding her smile.

She tried to mask her concern about Klara's frail appearance: her unkempt, whitish hair and watery, pale blue eyes revealed a sorrowful resignation. She sensed that Klara had something significant to share with her, perhaps the reason she pushed herself so hard to be there.

"You must be tired from such a long walk. Let's sit down to talk and sip hot cider before the meal."

She learned during the talk that Klara had similar visions to hers, including one about The Wheel turning from darkness to light. Klara's vision, however, was much more distinct because it featured the figure of a man, which hers lacked. They both possessed the gift of Seeing, which they were careful to share only amongst themselves or with a select few in the coven.

Agatha reflected more on her vision as Klara slept in a chair:

A man emerged from a multitude of people carrying a long, bent rod in one hand, walking alone toward a huge rounded object shaped like a wheel. When the man reached out to the wheel with the hand holding the bent rod, others from the multitude followed him. And then the wheel slowly turned in the opposite direction—toward the light and away from the darkness of the times.

Klara's vision was both an enlightening and unsettling realization for Agatha, as it seemed to touch her deeply. Nevertheless, she remained uncertain about its exact significance and hoped that events would unfold to confirm her intuition on the subject.

Karl placed the Yule log on the fireplace's hearth; the ceremony was about to begin. Agatha tapped Klara's shoulder, and together they joined the worshipers. They formed a circle, sitting with their heads lowered in meditation.

Agatha spoke first. "This is the night of the Winter Solstice, the year's longest night. Darkness now triumphs. Yet soon, darkness gives way to light. The Dark King will give way to Infant Light. Tonight we'll call the sun from the womb of night. We'll watch for the coming dawn when the Great Mother gives birth to the divine Sun Child again."

"To die and be reborn," Karl said. "What will you lose tonight?"

"Fear," the worshipers answered in unison.

"Fear will be lost tonight!" Karl added. "To die and be reborn! What will you lose tonight?"

"Fear will be lost tonight!" they responded in louder voices. "To die and be reborn!"

After a moment of silence, another worshipper spoke. "The Wheel is about to turn. We're entering a space of perfect harmony. The time just before birth."

"Sleep the sleep of a newborn," another one whispered.

Upon hearing those words, everyone lowered their heads and drifted into meditation.

One by one, they raised their heads and opened their eyes.

An older man spoke. "We are awake in the night. We turn the Wheel to bring the light. We call the sun to bring the light."

"Who is that who goes down in the darkness?" Agatha asked, staring at Klara. "Whose eyes are bright? Whose face is shining? Who is that?"

"The Child of Promise," Klara answered with liquid eyes. "The Renewer."

"Morning's hope," another said. "The Sun Child."

"The Winter-born King," said one more.

"Oh bright and golden sun," Pauli exclaimed. "Light the earth! The skies! The waters! Light the fires!"

He sprang to the altar, lit a candle, and hopped toward the hearth. The others followed suit, standing by the hearth with their candles in hand. As the host, Karl lit the kindling for the Yule log first, and then the others joined in. Afterward, they gazed into the fire, watching the log burn.

"I, who have died, am alive again today," a worshipper said. "We are born again. We shall live again."

They responded together with a chant. "We are born again. We shall live again."

"The Dark God has passed the gate," Agatha said. "He's been reborn through the Mother. With him, we are each reborn."

"The tide will turn," Karl concluded. "The light will come again. In a new dawn. On a new day. The sun will rise!"

They embraced one another, and soon, laughter and joy filled the room. One of the men played a tune on a flute. Some danced with their partners, including Gunther with another woman. Thomas, grinning broadly and merrily from the ale, pranced to the tune by himself. Others gathered around the banquet table to eat and drink their fill. The shepherd dog barked excitedly amid the sudden activity.

Agatha bought a plate of food for Klara. They ate in a corner of the room, talking about the ceremony and more about their lives.

———

The next morning, Agatha and a few worshipers huddled by the hearth while others, like Klara, slept in chairs. Some food remained on the table from the evening feast: remnants of roasted boar, bread and cheeses, chicken bones, apples, and a scattering of walnuts. Karl entered the house and motioned for everyone to join him outside. They bundled up, nudging some of the children awake. Agatha roused Klara, and they both went outside.

They sat in small groups on benches on the spacious porch, which offered an unobstructed view of the eastern horizon for miles. A band of bluish light glowed above the distant hills.

Agatha reflected on how familiar the scene looked: the broad vista of the dark landscape, the muted hues of light, and the arrangement of the stars. It reminded her of a time she had spent with a group of people from another coven near Heidelberg nearly twenty years earlier. Although it was for a different ceremony, they had sat together at dawn to await the day. That was when they witnessed the remarkable sight of what appeared to be a star falling from the heavens. Its long, bright tail lit up the sky. She gasped in awe at the spectacle, as did everyone in the group.

They discussed what it might have meant after the event. Some from the university in Heidelberg offered academic explanations, while others considered it more in spiritual terms. Agatha suspended her judgment, stating that time would reveal what this could signify. Years later, she was astonished to discover a drawing on a pamphlet, based on a woodcut, of the same event she had seen, titled: *The Angry Star.*

The blue band of light on the lower skyline brightened into a rich purple hue. Several children chatted among themselves while their elders whispered for them to be quiet. The few clouds stood out as silhouettes against the ever-brighter sky. Agatha began to feel a deep connection with those around her. She grasped Klara's hand.

The horizon shimmered with fiery hues of yellow, orange, and indigo blue. And then the sight they'd all been waiting for—the glowing orb of the sun burst above the hills, sending waves of light across the firmament!

At that moment, Agatha felt closer to the almighty spirit of God than at any other time in her life.

4.

Interrogation

The rising sun illuminated the distant snow-capped Alps to the south and the forest-covered hills west of Ulm. Inside the town, the first beams of sunlight shone on the giant steeple of the cathedral and the tallest buildings. The streets remained in shadows, but the townsfolk were already on the move: bundled up against the cold, crisp air, going in and out of stores and buildings on foot and horseback, pushing carts, carrying bags, some in gathering groups and others wandering by themselves. Soon, more people emerged onto the streets and the squares where vendors set up stalls and opened their shops. Church bells harkened to the beginning of another day.

———

Erich stood alone in the dark corridors of the prison later that morning, gripping his staff. He glanced up at the high ceiling, where a narrow beam of sunlight filtered through the only window in the corridor's upper reaches. The all-too-familiar voice of the Inquisitor resonated with a deep and solemn tone from a nearby cell, followed by the sound of a rod cracking against flesh and a woman's pitiful screams. This evoked a response in him that he couldn't recall experiencing during other interrogations—he flinched.

Most of those screams were the pleading and desperate ones who'd say and do anything to stop the torture. Others were the angry, defiant screamers who usually confessed early. Some victims managed to repress their cries, emitting short grunts, perhaps not wanting to reveal the extent of their suffering. They often held out the longest but eventually broke down and confessed. Then there was the young woman who came in a fortnight before, with long red hair, and accused of enticing and bewitching certain married men in the community. Her reactions to the inflictions were ones of shrieking, hideous laughter as if taunting the Inquisitor during the ordeal. She was one of the few who didn't break, thus condemned to be burned alive at the stake.

The woman in the cell now was different. Her name was Magda. Her deep, heartfelt wailing evoked sympathy not only for her own plight but also for the terrible sufferings he imagined many others had endured since the War began.

Magda lay bound by thin leather straps to a wooden table. Razor cuts marred her shaven head. A crude, sack-like piece of heavy canvas dropped down to her knees, with holes cut out for her head and arms. Welts covered the soles of her feet.

One of the guards, Otto, stocky and brutish, lashed the rod against her soles. She screamed again at a higher pitch. He delivered another blow. This time, her screams were fainter and muffled. Her eyelids fluttered, and her breathing grew shallow and rapid.

The Inquisitor studied her latest reaction and motioned for the guard to halt. The bastinado torture, which he had learned about while touring the Italian monarchies, was the most effective method for breaking a subject. Nevertheless, experience taught him that it needed to be applied with some restraint. He stepped aside, adjusted his coat collar, and brushed the dust off his sleeves.

On the opposite side of the cell, a monk sat at a table with a quill in hand, writing on parchment. Klaus stood beside him, smartly dressed as the Inquisitor. He stroked his trimmed goatee and stared intently at Magda with piercing blue eyes.

The Inquisitor nodded to Otto, who struck her again. This time, she showed little reaction to the blow. Otto hit her once more. She barely flinched and stared up at the ceiling, unblinking, in a kind of trance, breathing more deeply. He recalled such reactions before, though rarely, from others he had interrogated. She seemed to be one of those rare individuals who had reached a point where they couldn't feel pain anymore, so strong was the Devil's power over them. He shook his head in disappointment. She had been taking far too long to break. He had other matters to attend to later in the day. He paced back and forth and leaned over her.

"Shall we continue?" he asked.

"No . . ." she pleaded.

"Then tell us the names of those you have conspired with." He scowled before continuing. "You've already confessed to being a witch! But you must give us names! Or your soul will suffer in eternal damnation!"

His clean-shaven face reddened as he awaited her reaction. She looked up at him, opened her mouth to speak, then turned her head away. Tears streamed down her cheeks.

The Inquisitor stepped back and tried to maintain his composure. He pulled a cylindrical object from his vest and examined the intricate gears and sharp plates. He purchased the device, called The Pear of Anguish, from a monk while traveling through Ingolstadt, intrigued by its ingenuity and ability to cause excruciating pain when applied to interrogation subjects. He stroked the smooth, round surface of The Pear, trying to decide whether to use it on her. He'd only used it once on a woman such as this who'd been so strong in the Devil's grip. He recalled with much disgust how he almost retched from the smell when he inserted The Pear inside the putrid orifice between her legs, then turned the handle to expand the sharpened plates. What repulsed him the most was not her horrific screams when he pulled it out, but the blood flowing out onto his hands. He scrubbed his hands with the strongest lye for days to remove all traces of her filthy blood, but sometimes, when he examined his hands in a certain light, he imagined her blood still on them. No, he would not sully himself in such a manner this time.

After recalling the incident, he stuffed The Pear inside his coat with growing anger. He focused on a rack of torture implements on the wall behind her.

"Satan has put an evil spell on you. So we'll rip him from your flesh by force."

He turned to Willy, another guard. "The Claw."

"But your Excellency, what if—"

The Inquisitor raised his hand. Short and stout, Willy retreated to the wall and selected the one with a long pole featuring five metallic prong-like fingers bolted together at one end, each curved downward and sharpened at the tips.

Magda's eyes widened in terror. "No! Not that! No!"

"Release her from the table and lash her to the cross," he commanded. "Then tear off her garment!"

Once freed, she summoned her last reserves of strength to escape the guard's grip. She collapsed and crawled to the Inquisitor's feet, sobbing between her words.

"No! Please! No more!"

She wrapped her arms around his legs as the guards attempted to pull her away. The Inquisitor gestured for them to halt.

"Now, do you have more to confess?"

She hesitated for a moment but broke down. "Yes," she uttered while sobbing. "I consorted with others. And will give you names."

He rested his hand on her head, a cruel and twisted smile on his face.

"Your soul will thus be purified. God will look with favor on your confession. The ending will be merciful."

Magda continued to sob at his feet out of relief by knowing the torture had ended, but also out of shame because of what she'd be forced to disclose.

Willy slammed the door open as Otto struggled to lift and drag Magda from the cell. Klaus and the Inquisitor sat together, sharing a loaf of bread and cheese. The Inquisitor took a long swig of water and walked over to the monk, who continued writing on the parchment.

"How many names did she give? I could barely understand any words during her incoherent wailing and babbling."

"Four."

The Inquisitor pondered the statement. Not as many as he had hoped for, but better than none. This would demonstrate to the Church authorities that he was progressing in purging the town of evil, satanic influences.

"Anything of value from her?"

The monk uncovered another parchment and glided his finger along the page as he read.

"She's a widow with two children. One is near Augsburg, and the other is in München. She lives alone."

"She has property?"

"Yes, left to her by her husband."

"How has she been supporting herself?"

"Unknown. Perhaps from her children."

"We'll have to question them. They'll be the ones to pay the costs of our service. And her property will be redeemed to the Church."

"Of course," the monk added with a scowl.

The Inquisitor noted the disdain in the monk's expression, but it troubled him little. He would allocate some proceeds to the Church as required, but most would go into his accounts. After all, he was doing important work for them and deserved a reward.

"Is the next one ready?" the Inquisitor asked.

"Yes," Klaus answered, "but this one will differ. The Bull."

"Ah. The one who killed three of our soldiers in a rage. Clearly, a man possessed by the Devil."

"He has enormous strength," Klaus said with a glint of awe in his eye. "And might take some time to break."

"Perhaps not. I've seen the strongest of men confess in moments. Whereas others, like that frail woman, sometimes take many days. It depends on the spell cast on them. Women are the weakest and cling most eagerly to the Devil's powers. They resist the longest. Men are not so weak and have the strength to turn away from the Devil sooner."

"I can't understand why they don't all confess sooner. Their suffering is so great."

"Because, good Klaus, some want to die before they do so. That is Satan's wish. So he can possess their cursed souls for all eternity."

"And your skill is such," he responded admiringly, "that you push their pain to the highest pitch and withdraw it before they expire. This way, most confess as this woman did. I've learned so much by watching you."

"One thing you must never forget is that we are doing God's work," the Inquisitor said, raising his index finger. "For all the pain we inflict on their bodies, we must always show compassion for their souls. That is why we do this. Those who confess their sins will be grateful to us in the end. This is what you, as leader of the Catholic League, should communicate to all you deal with."

"Of course. You are so correct. As always."

The two guards dragged Magda down the corridor and past Erich, who remained unblinking and morose in the shadows. They threw her into the cell, slammed the door shut, and moved on to the next one. Otto unlocked the door, and both entered, each carrying a club.

After a loud commotion, they emerged from the cell, struggling to keep hold of a prisoner with a shaved head and a heavy, muscular build. Although he was shackled in leg irons, he still managed to throw Willy off while Otto held him around the waist. Willy called out to Erich for help.

He had been watching the struggle with mild indifference. First, he loosened his leather headband, brushed back his shoulder-length hair, and ambled toward them. The prisoner swung at him, but he blocked it with his forearm, grabbed the prisoner's wrist, and pinned his arm behind his back. Just as quickly, he slipped his other arm underneath the prisoner's armpit and forced his head down. Now in a headlock, the prisoner snorted angrily, like a bull, as he pushed him down the corridor. Otto and Willy followed.

He stopped before the interrogation cell as the Bull struggled to get loose. He tightened his grip.

"Listen to me. Relent and confess. Your death will be less painful."

The Bull stopped struggling and nodded. Erich loosened his grip and guided him into the cell with one hand on his shoulder. The Inquisitor pointed toward a chair in the corner of the room. After the Bull sat down, the guards strapped him in place. The Inquisitor watched Erich as he walked away, but said nothing. Klaus followed Erich out the door.

"Why not stay this time?" Klaus asked in a mocking tone.

"There is no need."

"*No need*, you say, to help us do God's work on this wretched soul?" They glared at each other from across the threshold of the door.

"Stay close in case we call you," Klaus sneered.

He slammed the door in Erich's face.

———

Erich whittled a long piece of wood in the guard's quarters, shaping it to a point. As he worked, he reflected on how difficult it had become for him to continue laboring in the prison and being around men like Klaus and others from the Catholic League, who had taken so much from his family during the War. He decided to talk to Jacob to see if there were other job opportunities in town.

He paused as the Bull's bellowing screams echoed through the corridors. He resumed whittling, this time with faster, harder strokes.

5.

Banished

Erich strode away from the prison toward the market, passing gauntlets of beggars along the way. Afterward, he went to the livery, where a boy combed Baldur's mane with a simple, crude brush. He gave the boy a copper coin before he loaded up and rode away.

About halfway home, he stopped by a stream, tightened the strap around the saddle, and waited for Baldur to finish drinking. He gazed out at the horizon, leaning against his staff. The thin layer of snow on the ground blended in hue with the light gray cloud cover. A faraway cawing from a raven echoed across the landscape, and an occasional breeze whistled through the bare branches of nearby trees. The solitude of the place brought forth the distressing thoughts and feelings he pushed aside when working in the prison. Knowing he'd soon be back with his family was the only thing lifting his spirits. He'd plunge into the darkest of despair if not for them.

A distant rattle of wagon wheels interrupted his reverie. A horse-drawn carriage rounded a bend in the road ahead. He recognized it as yet another prison wagon approaching, a familiar sight since the Catholics had taken control of the region. He stepped off the road as it sped by.

Before he turned back, a woman with long, dark hair observed him from behind the barred rear window.

———

He rode down a slope leading to his farm while his family performed chores around the grounds. Gunther guided a team of horses to harvest potatoes and cabbages from the field. Although Gunther was getting up in years, he worked as hard as ever and showed few signs of aging, except for an occasional sore back. Thomas, Catherine's younger brother, carried two buckets of water he had fetched from the stream. Cort chopped a log in a shed by the barn. Soon, he'd need to remind his son to use soap and a razor, considering the wisps of hair beginning to grow above his lips and chin. Peter sat on the porch, carving a piece of wood. Beside him, Eva knitted the beginnings of a sweater. Their young son, Rudi, played on the makeshift swing near the house.

The family had been working hard ever since they moved to the farm after being banished by the Catholics two years earlier. Right away, they all pitched in to improve the place by renovating the living quarters and adding several more rooms, patching up the barn, clearing the field of stumps, and building a corral for the horses. Soon after, they purchased goats, cows, a rooster, and chickens. By the first spring, they planted crops. Despite the hardships, they seldom complained about their situation and diligently performed daily chores.

Max spotted him first and raced from the porch to greet him, yelping all the way. Cort acknowledged him with a nod as he chopped wood. As Erich dismounted, the door flew open, and out came little Anna, shouting for joy with arms outstretched before she hugged him.

"Mama put a new ribbon in my hair!" she said as she pulled back her long blond hair. "It's like a horse's tail. Oh, Papa, when will I have a horse?"

"Maybe in the next year. You're almost old enough now."

"Goodie! Now for a ride! Race me faster this time!"

Thus commanded, he lifted her onto his shoulders and ran from the house to the barn, along the corral, and back to the house again, with Anna laughing all the while. The family paused their work and observed with bemused expressions.

"One more time! Please?"

"Oh no. You're getting *way* too big for that."

"Any surprises for me?"

"Only food today."

"Mmm. I can't wait. I'll tell Mama now."

Catherine greeted him at the door with a warm embrace.

"You haven't worn this dress in some time," he said. "And with a dirndl."

"You like it?"

"Very much so."

———

The family sat together around a table in the main room, eating the midday meal. Peter had just finished telling them a funny story.

They all smiled and laughed, little Anna the loudest.

"You tell such good stories," Eva said.

"You've always had that gift," Agatha said. "Even as a boy, you told tales with the best of them."

"I remember some of those," Gunther said. "Like those little people you said you saw in the forest. Made me believe it."

"I wish I could tell tales like you," Thomas said.

"I wish I were as big and strong as you," Peter said.

Thomas grinned and emitted a goofy chuckle, prompting the family to laugh, except for Erich, who remained silent while eating. One by one, they observed his glum demeanor.

"How's your foot?" Gunther asked.

"Better," Erich answered.

"You're not the skater you used to be," Peter said. "With a little more practice—" He stopped short, aware he was in no mood for levity.

Catherine understood the reason for his gloom; he'd had another troubling day at the prison. "I wish you would stop working in that dreadful place. What goes on there is—"

"I cannot. The work puts bread on the table." He lifted a loaf. "The bread we're eating now!"

He tossed a scrap of food to the dog and continued eating, head bent. The family fell silent for a while.

"Maybe you could work in Peter's store," Catherine said.

"Business is slow this time of the year," Peter said.

Thomas scratched his head. "We could sell some chickens at the market. Or the goat."

"And then what, Thomas?" Cort yelled. "Then we'll have no eggs or milk." He slammed his cup on the table and stomped out of the room.

"Cort!" Catherine shouted. "Come back and sit down!"

He paused briefly before storming out of the house.

"I don't understand what's wrong with him," she said. "He's always angry lately or off somewhere. Sometimes, he doesn't do his chores."

"I'll speak to him when he's in a better temper," Erich said.

"He's changed so much," she went on. "He used to listen to me. But look, like now. He turns away. He'd rather be talking to those animals in the woods. If someone sees him—"

"I don't think we should worry about that," Agatha said.

Catherine faced her. "I think we should. And about other things as well." She paused before continuing. "I'm sorry, but what worries me most are the people you consort with in the coven. We all know what could happen if they catch even one of them. They won't just take away our home like last time."

She stopped herself, aware of everyone's disturbed expressions.

"Will we get in trouble?" Anna asked her father.

"No, Anna. We'll be safe as long as the family stays together."

———

Erich climbed a hill in dense woods, adjusting the bow strap over his shoulder. Cort shouted in the distance, followed by a muffled growling sound, but that did not concern him. He stood beside a tree and watched Cort playing with a large gray wolf, gripping a stick with one hand as the wolf attempted to pull it away.

As soon as he stepped out, the wolf released the stick and glared at him before it ambled off into the forest.

"I don't think he likes me," Erich said.

"He would if you spent time with him." He threw a rock against a tree. "Grandmother is right. If you show no fear and respect them, they'll do the same for you. They're good animals."

"You should still take care around them."

"Why? They won't hurt me."

"I'm not talking about the wolves hurting you. I'm talking about other people. It might cause problems if anyone sees you."

"Aww. No one ever comes here anyway."

"I know. But be careful."

"Let's shoot now!"

Erich handed him the bow and quiver.

"Oh, another thing. You need to pay more attention to what your mother says. We all have chores to do."

"I will. But sometimes I feel . . . more at home in the woods."

Cort nocked an arrow onto the bowstring and turned toward a tree with a circular target etched into its trunk. He stamped his feet, aimed, and released the arrow. It struck the trunk but missed the target. He shook his head and handed the bow to his father.

"You rushed it." He pulled out another one from the quiver and aimed. "You should think of every shot you take as important." He took in a breath. "Try to gauge the wind. And when you *feel* the moment is right—shoot!"

His arrow hit the middle of the target.

"You never miss."

"What I said about feeling," Erich said as they walked together to the tree, "is the main thing, not just in your arms but in your whole body. Everything else is easy. You must learn to become one with the bow. This will take time, but you should start thinking that way now. You're of age."

"Do you always feel that way when you shoot?"

"Always," he answered as he pulled out the arrows. "It was easier to do when I fought in battles with my life at stake. Other times, like now, it takes longer. Each person is different. It also depends on the type of bow. Some are stronger than others."

"Like the Black Bow. l remember when you and Grandfather shot it. Did he teach you how?"

"Yes. When I was your age, but it took me years to understand what he taught me," he added, reflecting on those early years. "And then one day . . . it just came to me."

"When will you teach me to shoot it?"

"Perhaps next year, when—"

"I know. When the War is over. Well, I don't think it will ever be over! Why can't we take the Bow back now? It's ours!"

"We can't. And I've told you this before. It's part of our agreement with the Catholics when we moved. They think of it as a weapon because we used it against them in battle. Taking it back might cause trouble."

"What kind of trouble?"

"Trouble we don't want."

"I still don't understand. It's only a bow. So what if we used it against them?"

Erich tried to be patient. They'd had similar talks about this, so he took a different approach.

"Yes, but people think differently about it now."

"What do you mean?"

"As you know, there are stories about it. Some true. Others not. Before the War, both sides regarded the Bow as part of our common folklore. Now the followers of Luther look at it in one way and the Catholics another."

"How?"

He sighed, trying to find the right words. "I think it has to do with what it stands for in people's minds. To the Protestants, it isn't so much a weapon but more of a symbol of the poor fighting the rich and power-ful oppressors. They think of the Bow as an object that gives them the courage to fight for what they believe in. The Catholics didn't like the idea of the Bow being in our hands, so they took it away. But not for themselves because the Protestants would've rebelled. So they made a truce. Neither could have it. They agreed to return it once peace is signed between both sides."

"Is it against the law if we take it?"

"No, nothing is written."

"Then we *can* take it back!"

"It's not that simple."

"They've taken so much from us! We should start taking back what's ours! The Black Bow! Our old house and land!"

This time, his son's words and righteous indignation made him change his outlook on the subject.

"You may be right. I'll think about what you've said." He glanced up to the darkening sky. "We should go home now."

About halfway back, they spotted a deer grazing in the distance.

They crouched down behind a bush.

"Let's get closer," Erich whispered. "It's too far for this bow."

The deer bounded away as they approached a tree. Erich shook his head and slung the bow back over his shoulder.

They walked silently the rest of the way home, both disappointed at the missed chance to shoot the deer. During the walk, Erich pondered more about the Black Bow and whether he should take it back. Tomorrow? In a week or more? He concluded he'd recognize the best time to retrieve it when the right circumstances arose.

6.

Trial

A large and restless crowd milled in front of the Ulm courthouse building, waiting for another witchcraft trial to begin. A light snow had been falling and they were bundled up to stave off the cold. As usual, they exchanged lively tales about those rumored to be on trial. On this day, the discussion was even more fanciful due to one of the accused; a captured witch of haunting beauty who practiced her dark arts in a nearby town. Her supernatural powers were so immense that she could turn grown men into toads and cast spells on others, all accomplished with just a glance or a wave of her magic wand.

Klaus stood near the front door among six of his henchmen, pleased at the sight of so many enthusiastic people. The trials were achieving their desired effect. Order was restored in the town. The Protestant dissenters who had previously spoken out against Catholic rule were now silenced. Some of them left for the north, heading toward Saxony and Westphalia. Those remaining in the community kept quiet.

A guard opened the courthouse door as the crowd surged forward. Two of Klaus's younger henchmen stood at the entrance, permitting entry only to those who offered them coins.

————

Erich stood in front of the loud and boisterous gallery, while Klaus and his henchmen sat across the room sharing a bag of walnuts and joking among themselves. Lothar, who had been with Klaus the longest and had fought alongside him in the War, was the most ruthless henchman, carrying out the Catholic League's orders without mercy against those who stepped out of line. Sigi had served Klaus for almost as long. He disgusted Erich not only because of his appearance—tall and thin, with a weak chin and unkempt, greasy hair—but also because he enforced his authority over the elderly and afflicted townsfolk. Ernst and Horst sat behind them. They once operated food and craft stalls in the marketplace but joined the League to earn more money.

One of the younger henchmen handed Klaus a pouch of coins from the entry collection. It amused Erich that he wore the same colored shirt as the other henchmen, as if they were part of a military unit. Most days, they donned dark blue or brown shirts, but today, they wore gray shirts—except for Lothar, who never adhered to this practice.

Some in the audience shouted their disapproval above the noise, impatient for the trial to begin. They quieted down when Judge Heinrich, an elderly, thin man with a wispy layer of white hair encircling a bald crown, entered the room. He walked with a limp, hunched over, as two court officials assisted him to the bench. Heinrich had served as their judge for as long as most could remember. Some town council members encouraged him to retire due to his failing health, but he vigorously declined. It was his duty, he said, to perform this sacred task until the day he died.

A court official handed Heinrich several written parchments. He reached into a vest pocket, pulled out his pince-nez reading glasses, and placed them unsteadily over the bridge of his nose. He squinted in an attempt to decipher the writing. The other official pointed to sections of the document and leaned in to whisper to him as he did so.

Some merchants and officials who made up the jury, including Jacob the Sheriff, were seated on one side of the bench. The Inquisitor and a monk occupied a table on the other side. Erich stood by his post next to the gallery.

As usual, the Inquisitor was dressed in the finest attire. His dark blue pants were tucked into shiny black boots, and his crimson robe and scarf were crafted from the finest materials. A broad white collar adorned his pale blue shirt. His hair was neatly trimmed, revealing some gray at the temples.

Heinrich banged his gavel. "Let the trials begin," he declared in a gravelly voice. "Bring in the first accused."

All eyes turned to see who the guards, Otto and Willy, were escorting into the room. Some in the audience groaned in disappointment as a haggard-looking old woman appeared. They led her to the chair in front of the bench. Willy motioned for her to sit. She stood frozen in a dumbfounded pose, her eyes seeming to search for someone in the crowd she recognized. A noticeable tremor shook her hands and head.

"Sit down, dummkopf!" Willy exclaimed as he pushed her down onto the chair

"Margarete Stump," Heinrich said while reading from the parchment, "from the village of Rammingen, you are accused of certain detestable acts of witchcraft and sorceries, wickedly and feloniously used, practiced, and exercised on the children and citizens within that good community. And of consorting with the Devil. What say you to this?"

"What? Say to what?" she asked while cupping one ear.

"Of practicing witchcraft and consorting with the Devil!"

"Oh no. I live alone. My Joseph died years ago."

The gallery erupted in peals of derisive laughter. She tried to force a smile as she stared at the audience. The Inquisitor rose from the table and approached her from behind. When she turned back, the Inquisitor's baleful countenance, so close, made her jump in fright, which provoked even more laughter.

The Inquisitor didn't take long to break down the fragile Margarete. He revealed how she had caused "grievous harm" to the village children by "luring them" into her home and feeding them the cakes and pies she baked. When some of the children became sick afterward, rumors spread that she had been using recipes "concocted by the Devil" to poison their minds and spirits. In the end, the Inquisitor demanded that she confess to being under Satan's spell, "or your soul will burn for all eternity in hell!" Confused and broken, she haltingly admitted her guilt. The gallery erupted into cheers.

During the questioning, Erich recalled that Agatha occasionally traveled to Rammingen to visit members of another coven. Now, he had another concern about whom Margarete might implicate during the interrogations.

"Unless there are questions from the jury," Heinrich said, "I will pronounce the sentence."

The jury remained silent, with some—like Jacob—shaking their heads.

"Margarete Stump," Heinrich proclaimed. "Due to the intolerable and wicked acts that you have admitted to, I hereby sentence you to be strangled by the neck until you die. Your body will then be consumed by flames so people will learn the consequences of such vile acts."

Once more, she cupped her ears during the sentencing. She waved her hand at the rowdy audience as Otto led her away, believing she would soon be free for agreeing with the accusations.

Two additional individuals were presented to the court for lesser offenses. One was a young man named Gumprecht, approximately the same age as Cort, who faced charges for assaulting boys from upper-class families and for terrifying his neighbors by howling like a wolf at night. After the interrogation and questions from the jury, Heinrich sentenced him to be flogged in the town square.

"Bring in the last accused," Heinrich proclaimed.

Once again, all eyes turned toward the entrance. Otto and Willy brought in a woman with raven-black hair framing a face of exquisite beauty. A palpable silence settled over the audience. The rumors of her mysterious arrival were true. She looked around the court with expressive, full eyes, absorbing her new surroundings. She wore a long gray dress and walked with such an even gait that it seemed she floated along the floor, enhancing her enchanting allure.

Erich noticed her high cheekbones and olive complexion, leading him to guess that her heritage was from a distant land.

Klaus and his henchman watched her with leering grins as she sat in the chair. More whispers came from the gallery. Heinrich and the Inquisitor regarded her with suspicion.

"And so," Heinrich began, "we have little information about you. Family name unknown. Place of residence unknown. First, tell the court your name."

"My name is Mara."

Heinrich waited for her to continue. "And your family name?" he asked.

"I believe that's all you need to know."

"The court looks with much disfavor at your answer to such a simple question," he said, peering at her above his glasses with a scowl. "Perhaps you have no family. Tell the court where you are from then— woman who calls herself Mara."

"From the north."

"Where in the north?"

"In a monastery near Rüdeshiem named Eibingen."

He appeared perplexed at the response. One of his aides whispered in his ear.

"It's a small town on the Rhein across from Bingen," she added.

"I know where it is!" He regained his composure and continued. "And so, woman who calls herself Mara, from near the town of Bingen. You are accused of certain detestable acts of witchcraft and sorceries, wickedly and feloniously used and exercised within our communities, and of consorting with the Devil. What say you to this?"

"To what?"

"Is everyone so afflicted on this day? Of consorting with the Devil and practicing witchcraft!"

"I do not consort with the Devil. Only with people in villages I help with my cures and advice. And of practicing witchcraft? That is untrue."

And so you are from the north," the Inquisitor said.

"Were you born there?"

"No."

"Where then?"

"In the south."

"Where in the south?"

"I don't know," she said, staring directly at him.

Murmurs of disapproval arose from the gallery. The Inquisitor backed away from her gaze.

"My people traveled a lot. Always on the move."

"Your people?"

"My family."

"Perhaps you don't know because you have no family." He suppressed a smile before continuing. "Or if you do, your upbringing is not one of a Christian offspring. But more of one from a . . . satanic association."

"They were kind and loving people!" she shouted.

"*Were?* You mean they no longer exist?"

Her eyes narrowed and then relaxed. "That's all I have to say."

He glanced at the gallery, taking note of their troubled, suspicious expressions. Her angry outburst provided the effect he desired.

"I must agree with the judge. Your answers to our simple questions have been most unsatisfactory." He took a step toward her but halted. "I hope at least you'll tell us why you've been wandering around the countryside and spreading evil over the land."

"I've been healing people wherever I go."

"You've told the court that you don't *practice* witchcraft," he said in a slow, deliberate tone. "But is it something you *believe* in?"

She paused before answering. "I believe there is a spirit in all life on Earth. In the air we breathe, the sky, the moon, the stars, and the sun. In the seas and rivers, the trees, the stones, and the animals. If we embrace these things, we can become closer to our true nature and to God."

"To God, you say? What about the God of the Holy Mother Church and of Jesus Christ almighty? Where is He in everything you *believe in* so dearly?"

"He is there."

"And of the blessed Virgin Mary?" he asked while gesturing to a painting of the Virgin Mary hanging on the wall behind the Judge.

She stared at it before answering.

"In her as well. And most of all."

"And within the mud and the rocks and the trees and the lowly animals you worship?"

"Yes. He is the creator of all things."

"Well, thankfully," the Inquisitor said as he turned to the gallery, "the civilized people of this community and throughout our lands do not *believe in* or practice such a base form of worship."

"What I believe and practice is much the same as the teachings written by Saint Francis. Especially the—"

"I will not debate matters of orthodoxy with you here!" he interjected. "It's clear where the dark powers you've used on the poor folk of Setzingen come from."

Mara recalled her time in Setzingen, where she stayed for a week and assisted other midwives with two childbirths. Two days later, Trude returned and asked her to help with Mathilda's childbirth, during which they snatched her.

"I was in the village when they called me to help a woman give birth. I gave her some roots and plants, which relieved her stress."

"Roots and plants? Raw from the earth? A sinful and vile practice! Instead of the admonitions from a wise apothecary."

"The child and mother lived. Both are doing well."

"The husband of another woman you say you *helped* in Setzingen testified that you put a spell on him and appeared to him at night in the shape of a she-wolf, holding him down in bed so he couldn't breathe."

"Those were thoughts from his mind alone."

"He said you raised the newborn in an offering to Satan."

"Nonsense. I showed the child to their family."

He turned to Heinrich. "The man she put a spell on is in the audience, and I ask, with your permission, that he be allowed to tell the court what happened, in his own words."

"You may proceed."

The Inquisitor faced the gallery. "I ask Georg Müller to stand and testify."

A short, stout man with a thick black beard and bushy eyebrows rose to his feet. As Willy guided him to the witness chair, Mara remembered how Georg hovered in the corners of the room, following her wherever she went, yet never speaking to her.

"I understand you've been in poor health," the Inquisitor said.

"Yes, but I'm better now," he answered in a high-pitched voice that belied his dark and swarthy appearance.

Some townsfolk stifled laughter after hearing him speak.

"When did your symptoms begin?"

Müller shot a nervous glance at Mara. "After *she* came, I wanted to stay with my wife, but she told me to leave. That's when my suffering began." He struggled to gain his composure.

Mara recalled how far from the truth this was. He'd been the one who left the room during the most difficult time of childbirth.

"I couldn't sleep for weeks due to visions haunting me at night. Terrible visions. Which put me in dire confusion. I couldn't eat the food before me."

"All the symptoms of someone under a spell," the Inquisitor said.

"Such bad times for me."

"But you're well now, you say."

"Yes. I recite my prayers daily and have gotten better."

The Inquisitor rested his hand on Müller's shoulder. "Your prayers have been answered. He has cleansed your mind and body of those evil influences."

"I never should've doubted Him," Müller uttered in a weepy voice. "And never will again."

"How are your wife and child now?"

"Both well. We attend church every week. The singing fills me with great joy. I feel protected by His spirit. We hope to have more children."

"What say you to this?" the Inquisitor asked Mara.

"I cast no spell on him. Perhaps his lack of sleep was due to the infant being up and crying at night. Such things often happen to people with their firstborn."

He scoffed at her response but realized she would not be so easy to break as the others.

"Fortunately, the authorities in Setzingen caught you before you caused more harm."

"I did not harm those people. They were grateful for the aid I offered."

"No harm, you say? How do you explain the fact that soon after you arrived, many of the villagers in the area reported the most extraordinary and fearful sights? Witches riding on broomsticks across the moon at night. Trees and plants that crawled. The faces of their neighbors shifting into gruesome shapes. Their pets turning into hideous monsters."

"There were poor folk in those villages. The grain of their bread had not been properly harvested or stored. Eating such grain sometimes causes fanciful sights. It passed, and they suffer no more."

"Admit that you used potions written by the Devil and put them in their food and drink! Potions you devised caused the frightful apparitions from the victims of your black magic!"

"I did nothing of the kind."

"We've heard reports from other communities since well before Yule that suffered the same way. From disease and sickness and famine. Places you surely visited. It seems like wherever you go, such troubles and suffering follow."

"I've been here less than a fortnight."

"Or so you say. More likely, you have indeed been to all those places. Not just in Setzingen," the Inquisitor went on with a louder voice. "You poisoned their bodies and minds with potions and superstitions from your witchcraft! You are the most evil of witches! Confess to your treachery!"

"I do not know what you mean by witchcraft," she replied in the same calm tone that contrasted with the Inquisitor's growing agitation. "I travel to villages and towns to assist mothers during childbirth. I also help those suffering from ailments with my roots and herbs. What I do is no different from practices that have been followed for many years." She turned to the gallery. "A practice that, perhaps, some in this very room have also experienced. Before these . . . these burning times have descended upon us."

Erich grew increasingly impressed by her manner and words, which resembled those often spoken by his mother.

He resumed his attack with renewed anger. "And you will indeed burn for your heinous crimes!"

"You've decided this already? Then why the trial?"

"So you can confess!" The Inquisitor declared in a frenzied voice as he moved closer to her. "Before the people! And before God! This is the only way you can purify your soul and free yourself from the Devil's hold on you! Confess to being a witch! Confess to being possessed by the Devil!"

He held his angry, contorted face close to hers.

Mara stared at him calmly but then narrowed her eyes, adopting a much more severe demeanor. He trembled with agitation; his rage shifted into profound fear, yet he remained unmoving as if paralyzed.

"You are the one possessed," she said in a low, deep voice. "Speaking with such hateful venom. God is not with you. You are like a mad beast—your skin and eyes—a mad beast."

The Inquisitor staggered back, clutching his chest and breathing erratically. He stumbled to his table. "I turn away from you," he stammered. "I turn away from your evil eye and the spell you attempt to cast on me."

He collapsed into his chair. The gallery erupted. The monk offered him water.

Heinrich banged the gavel several times before the audience quieted down.

"Never have I witnessed such an outrage!" he rasped. "Spells cast in this honored court!" He faced Mara. "You! Woman who calls herself Mara and who came here from the north to diabolically hex those towns. You speak with an eloquence and guile that only one under the guidance of Satan could perform. I give you one more chance to confess to the charges. What say you?"

The courtroom waited in rapt silence for her answer.

"I will not confess to that."

The gallery arose in shouts and clamor again. Heinrich raised his hand, and they quieted down, waiting for him to speak.

"So be it." He glanced at the jury. "I thus sentence you to further examination within our prison walls. There, your confession will surely be extracted."

He banged his gavel one last time. Mara lowered her head in sorrow.

As Otto and Willy led Mara away, she went by Erich. Their eyes met briefly, eliciting a flash of recognition in her expression.

Erich followed the guards as they escorted her to the prison building. Upon arriving in front of her cell, they opened the door, and Willy forcefully pushed her to the floor. They laughed as they made their way to the guards' quarters.

Erich watched them from a distance with seething, helpless anger. The staff shook in his hand. He turned and walked away.

7.

The Bow Retrieved

"**G**od bless the Inquisitor!" Willy declared to Otto and Klaus's henchmen while stuffing his mouth with bread and sausages in the guard's quarters. "My purse is full from all this work."

"And your fat belly," Lothar said.

The others in the room laughed, except for Erich, who sat and ate apart from them with Manfred, another guard.

"How long will he stay?" Willy asked Klaus.

"When the Church decrees Ulm is cleansed of evil spirits. Perhaps a fortnight or more. Then he'll perform God's work in another town. There are souls everywhere needing to be freed from Satan's grip."

"Like the witch in yesterday's trial," Otto said.

"You should've seen the spell she tried to put on the Inquisitor," Sigi told Dieter and Joachim, the two younger henchmen.

"The judge too," Horst said.

"But they both remained firm and resolute," Klaus said. "Their faith is strong."

"All the stories about her are true then," Willy said.

"There must be others like her," Otto said. "We need to kill them before they do more harm."

"Ah, but before that, we must make them confess," Klaus said, raising his index finger. "That's why we do this. For their souls. They'll thank us regardless of what we do to them beforehand. Our actions are viewed favorably by the community. And in the eyes of God."

They nodded solemnly in agreement.

"I wonder if she'll confess," Otto asked. "If her evil is so strong."

"She might be one of those few who will not. If so, she'll burn in hell for her sinful crimes."

"I can't wait to watch her squirm," Willy mumbled with a mouthful of food. "When will the interrogations begin?"

"Soon. The Inquisitor has some pressing matters to attend to in Augsburg."

"Pressing matters?" Lothar joked. "You mean he's going to use the press on some poor sinner there?"

"I heard from others," Manfred said, "that his health suffered at the trial, and he went to Augsburg for a cure."

"Rumors and gossip only," Klaus said, giving Erich and Manfred a suspicious glance. "There's nothing wrong with him."

"Maybe we can soften her up first," Willy said.

"Yes," Klaus said with a smile. "To ensure she'll be in the proper state of *humility* for the interrogations."

This provoked more laughter from the guards. Erich continued to eat, pretending not to listen. Klaus noticed his discomfort.

"Erich. Perhaps you can take a turn with her too. After we're done, of course."

Erich glared at him. "You're a pig, Klaus."

Momentarily shaken, he responded with a sneer. "Oh, is that so? Spoken like such a nobleman to all his subjects. But you aren't so noble now, are you?"

Erich ignored him, and so he prodded on.

"How is it now for you? Unable to give orders to us anymore."

"I think you'd better stop," Manfred said, "or else—"

"His words mean nothing to me," Erich said. "I've gotten used to his senseless babbling for no reason."

"Senseless, you say?"

"That's right! Your mind is vexed. Perhaps leeches on your head will cure you."

"I don't need that to remember how things were with my family. All our hardships and sufferings. Things you've forgotten. I think you're the one whose mind is vexed."

"I've forgotten nothing."

"Oh, but you have," Klaus said in a subdued voice as if recollecting painful memories.

For a moment, Erich noticed something in him that he hadn't observed in many years: a hurt and vulnerable expression reminiscent of Klaus in his youth, when they were friends playing together in the woods. This also stirred a vague memory that he couldn't quite place.

"We treated you well."

"Or so you think," Klaus said, reverting to his harsh tone. "But how would you know? So far removed from us in your big, grand house high on the hill. While we lived in huts on the muddy ground below. Freezing in the winter! Burning in the summer!"

"You and everyone else on our land lived better than other farmers. We never forced you to pay your share during the bad times. And how we helped the children attend school and learn to read."

"We learned that mostly on our own. And when we tried to improve our condition, you threw us out."

"The town authorities did that, not us."

"Your family was a part of it! All conspiring against us!"

"Your father went too far. The men he led attacked members of the council."

"He was only defending himself! And we ended up with nothing, living like beggars."

"You twist the truth," Erich said as he tried to finish his meal between the words.

"The truth is that now *your* family isn't doing so well." He waited for Erich's reaction. "The only reason you have *anything* left is because of your few friends in town. But that will change. And when that happens, I'll ensure you and your family have *nothing* left. Then what will you do?"

Erich grabbed his staff and strode towards him.

"What do you mean, Klaus? Are you threatening my family?"

Klaus stepped back and grasped his sword. Horst obstructed Erich's path, but Erich shoved him aside. Manfred approached from behind and restrained him.

"Stop," Manfred said. "This is what he wants. So he can accuse you."

He began to free himself from Manfred's hold but halted, recalling a recent talk with his son.

Now was the time.

"You're right. He's not worth the effort."

Erich turned and walked away, while Klaus kept a hand on his sword, leaning against the wall.

"If doing God's work so displeases you," Klaus said, "just leave and don't come back. And stay on your little farm with the rest of your brood."

Erich halted for a moment before walking out of the room.

Manfred shook his head after he'd left. "You shouldn't have threatened his family."

"I can say what I want to him."

"They say he fought in many battles," Willy said. "And that no man can beat him with his staff."

"I fought in those battles against those cursed unbelievers!" Klaus said. "I have no fear of him! Soon, he'll be gone. He, and all his kind."

"I think we should let people worship the way they want," Manfred said. "That's why we're in this damnable War."

"The problems with Erich and I go much further back. And men like him are the cause of why we're at war. There is only one true God and faith. That's the way it was and the way it should always be!"

————

Erich strode through the town, pounding his staff with each step. He stopped in front of a familiar old building he had visited many times with his father during his youth when they went to see the sheriff. No, the building had not changed since those days. Some of the wood looked weathered, and at the very least, the front needed a new coat of paint.

He opened the door and entered, still troubled by what had occurred in the prison while he waited. Jacob came in from another room.

"Well, good day, Erich. I haven't seen you here for some time."

"It's been too long. How's your family?"

"Giselle was ill for a week but now is better. And yours?"

"The same. All in good health."

"You're not in trouble, are you?"

He shook his head.

"If it's about the prison, I could look into it."

"It would do no good. They do what they want."

"There are still reasonable men on the council of both faiths who can intervene if things become too . . . extreme. Let me know."

"I will. One reason I came here is to find out if there's other work in town."

"I'll inquire tomorrow." He noted Erich's still-troubled demeanor. "Is there something else?"

Erich stared intently at him. "I want to take back the Black Bow."

"You want to take the Bow, you say?" he asked, surprised by the request.

"Yes. I've thought much about this."

"Just to check the condition? Or—"

"I want to take it with me. Away from here. To my home."

"Are you sure? It's safe here."

"I know. Cort needs to learn to shoot it. He's of age."

"Some will think differently about this. Like Klaus and his bunch from the Catholic League. Why not think about this for a day or two and return if you feel the same?"

"I've made up my mind."

"I don't think you should, the way things are here now. For you or your family. Again, I must object—"

"My father would've wanted it so."

Jacob tightened his expression and nodded. "Yes, he would've." He took out a set of keys from his desk drawer. "Follow me."

He walked to the back room and opened a door to a stairway leading to the cellar. He picked up a lantern before going down.

"I haven't been down here since my childhood," Erich said, taking in the surroundings. "So many more things in here now."

"From those who left because of the persecutions. I hope some will return and fetch them."

They stopped near the back wall, where Jacob shined the lantern on a group of trunks.

"Do you recognize any of them?"

"The biggest one in the back."

Jacob pulled the trunk out, opened it, and reached inside. He lifted the long, ornate sheath and handed it to Erich.

Erich removed the Black Bow, unwrapped the oilskin around it, and held it aloft. The dark sheen on its surface glimmered in the pulsating lantern light.

"Here," Jacob said, handing him a quiver of arrows.

Erich focused on the two sets of fletchings on the arrows. The lighter fletchings were easier to create, while the darker ones required more effort to replace, as they were made with a stronger shaft and a harder stone. He last used them in battle, knowing they could pierce the chainmail vests of his adversaries.

"I'll need your help to string it," he said.

As Jacob bent the bow, Erich slid the knotted end of the string into a narrow slot. He initially pulled back the string a little to detect any signs of strain and then pulled it further back, feeling his spine straighten and a surge of energy and strength within his body. He then slipped it back into the sheath.

"I'll go now," Erich said. "And I thank you for retrieving this."

He burst out of the building, striding through the town with determination. A few townsfolk noticed the large sheath slung over his shoulder as he passed, but most paid it no mind.

———

Max excitedly barked to announce his arrival as he rode down to the farm, causing everyone to pause their chores when they recognized the Bow. Cort buried his axe in a log and ran up to him.

"The family bow!"

Thomas dropped a stack of kindling and headed toward him. Peter stepped off the porch, Rudi at his side. Gunther approached them from the barn. He dismounted and handed the sheath to Peter, who displayed it to Thomas and Gunther.

The sudden hush over the yard lured the women out of the house. Catherine wrapped her arms tightly around her waist when she noticed the Bow.

"What is this?" she said. "Why bring that here?"

"It's time I teach Cort to shoot it."

Cort's eyes lit up with admiration.

"For how long do you intend to keep it?"

"We'll see," Erich said, aware of her concern.

"Can we shoot now?" Cort asked. "I'll finish cutting the wood afterward."

"All right. Come on."

He placed an arm around his son and headed into the woods. Catherine and Eva returned to the house while the others resumed their work.

Agatha watched them from the porch as they walked away, lost in the memory of when her Richard had taught young Erich to shoot the Bow for the first time.

————

They entered a meadow and sat on a log by a small creek. Erich handed him the Bow.

"I remember holding this and watching you and Grandfather with it," Cort mused. "But it feels different now."

"How so?"

He pondered the question before responding. "It feels . . . strong."

Erich smiled. "I felt the same at your age."

"I also remember both of you telling stories about it. And about a man named Mathias."

"The Bow has been in the family since the time of the wars against the Mohamedans in the Holy Land, over 400 years ago. Its history is written on the parchments your grandmother keeps in a trunk by her bedside. Mathias was the first holder. He acquired it during his time as a soldier there."

"A teacher in school talked about those times. Except he said we fought the *infidels*. Why did he call them that?"

"Because the Mohamedans were of a different faith. And didn't believe in Jesus Christ."

"Did they not believe in God?"

"They do, but a different God. They lived in the Holy Land of Christ's birth. Christian men like Mathias went on missions to free the land from the infidels' control."

"Did they win?"

"Yes. Until the Mohamedans drove them out again."

"Hmm. All that fighting because they were of a different faith. It sounds like—"

"What?"

"Like the reason we're fighting the Catholics."

"That's one reason. But I didn't come here to talk about that. I want to tell you more about the Bow."

"How come it's so much bigger than the ones now?" Cort asked.

"They called them longbows. Most of them were crafted in those times. There are only a few left here. But none like this. With such a wide face."

Cort examined the Bow again. "These marks on the surface have animal shapes."

"The first holders inscribed them to honor the animals they felt closest to in spirit—their *geisttieren*. Some are easy to recognize," he said while pointing to the etchings on the face. "See, there's a deer . . . a horse . . . a wolf . . . and some birds. Others I am not sure about. One could be a bear."

"This one's like a cat," Cort said.

"More likely a lynx."

"Remember the time we saw one on a hunt last year?"

"Of course. A magnificent animal. But we seldom see them anymore."

"Why not?"

"People hunt them for their pelt. But also out of fear."

"People fear wolves and hunt them too. But there's more of them, it seems."

"Wolves are a different kind of animal. They live together in packs. Lynxes are solitary creatures. Most of them live deep in the woods and far away from people."

Erich contemplated the lynx etching, recalling a youthful memory. "I never told you this, but when I was your age I went on a deer hunt with your grandfather and others. Soon we came upon a lynx, and the dogs chased it up a tree." He paused before continuing. "We could have left it there. But no, the men decided to make a game and shoot it down. It didn't take them long. One arrow knocked the lynx out of the tree, and it tried to run away, still wounded. The dogs got on it right away. We watched them tear it up. No one said anything. I remember how I wanted to scream about how stupid this was. How *wrong* this was! But kept my silence."

Cort shook his head and turned his attention to the Bow. "There's more room on the edge. We can make our animal shape on it."

"Don't have to. Mine's there."

"The horse," Cort said as he touched an etching.

"Yours too," Erich said.

Cort slid his fingers to another spot on the Bow. "The wolf!" He stared at it for a while. "I wonder if this was Mathias's spirit animal."

Erich could tell he was beginning to forge a deeper connection to his past and ancestry through it—the same way he'd done when his father told him about the Bow.

Cort ran his fingertips over the middle of the surface. "This shape is different. It's like a cross of some sort."

"When Mathias returned from the Holy Wars, he settled west of the Rhein in the Frankish lands. Our scrolls show that his descendants belonged to an order of knights. The cross was their symbol. But they had to flee. The holder of the Bow during those times resettled on the land that became our family farm and estate."

"What about those stones around it?" Cort asked.

"Those we're not sure about. The craftsmen who built it might have put them on. Or later, by those who belonged to the order of knights. I've read words in our parchments about them. One says that the stones get so bright in battle that they blind the enemy when you aim at them. And can make the arrow go farther and faster."

"Is that true?"

"Some of it is just a tale. I think they go farther because of the wood."

"Why is it so dark?"

"It could be from the oils they first used on it. It's been told that the wood came from a tree growing along the banks of a great river in the African region near the Holy Land."

"Africa! The place with all the strange animals. I remember drawings of them in the school library. Giant animals with long noses and others with long necks. Horses with stripes. Someday, I want to go there."

"Back in the days of Mathias, these bows were weapons most used in warfare. Now, it's mostly cannons and muskets. Some soldiers use crossbows. But they're small and only effective at short range. This Bow can shoot farther than any."

"Show me!"

"You first."

Cort nocked the arrow and pulled it back.

"Aim for that one," Erich said, pointing to a nearby pine tree.

Cort pulled the string back, but when the Bow began to shake, he released some tension and shot. The arrow flew weakly past the tree. He shook his head.

"My first shot was the same. You'll get stronger with practice. It takes years to shoot well. Later I'll teach you how to keep it in good condition. That's very important. You'll learn how to polish and oil the wood. And how to restring it and what kind of fiber to use. You'll also learn how to make arrows and what stones to use for the tips."

Erich nocked the arrow and aimed the Bow. "See the tree on the other side of the meadow with the crooked branches?"

"Way over there?"

"Watch me," he said while pulling the string back.

"Can you bend it more?"

Erich pulled it back further. The Bow's renewed powers, which he hadn't felt in years, returned to him. He steadied himself, paused for a moment, and released the shot. The arrow emitted a high-pitched whistle across the meadow and struck the target with a loud crack. The impact sent pine cones and needles tumbling to the ground like a light rain squall. A murder of crows perched in the tree took flight, cawing madly as they fled.

Cort stood there, stunned. Erich lowered the Bow. He took a few wobbly steps and then hunched over, holding his knees.

"What is the matter?" Cort asked.

"I forgot to tell you this. The power of the Bow . . . sometimes weakens the holder afterward for a short time." He took a deep breath. "When you pull it far back. Don't worry. I'll be fine soon. I've pulled it much further than this."

Cort watched him intently as they walked across the meadow to retrieve the arrows.

"Are you sure you're alright?"

"Ha!" Erich answered, clenching his fists. "I'm fine now! But that's enough for today. We'll shoot again soon."

———

Cort had just finished the evening meal and waited impatiently while the rest of the family ate slowly and leisurely. He glanced over at the Black Bow propped against the wall, aware that his father had placed it there for a reason.

"It was cold today," Thomas said as he took a bite of bread. "Cold enough to snow."

"We're due for some," Gunther said. "We haven't had much since before Yule."

"It's been a warm winter so far," Peter said.

"Does it mean we'll have a cool spring?" Gunther asked Agatha.

"It's too soon to tell. Sometimes mild winters can bring about cooler springs. The balance of nature is a little late or early in some years. Other times, the cycle is off for a year or more."

Erich took a long swig of water and reached back for the Bow. He handed it to Gunther.

"Gunther will show you how to oil and polish the Bow," he said to Cort.

"Like your father and I taught you," Gunther said. He gave it to Thomas, overcome with emotion.

Thomas waved it up and down with a grin. "Yup, that's it," he said, passing it to Peter.

"It's good to hold the Bow again," Peter said. "I want to shoot it too."

Rudi glided his little fingers along the face of it.

Catherine and Eva finished their work in the kitchen and sat at the table. Catherine folded her arms across her chest again as they talked.

"Can I go with you, father?" Rudi asked.

"Of course!"

"We'll all go out and shoot tomorrow," Erich said.

"And so," Catherine said. "We'll return it the next day after everyone takes their turn. Am I right?"

"No need so soon," Erich answered.

"I'm afraid there is. They'll *make us* take it back."

"They will not. Only the sheriff knows of this."

"Oh, I bet the whole town knows by now. Someone must have seen you with it. People talk."

"I think Father did the right thing," Cort said. "We can't always be so scared of everything. I think we should keep it."

"I know what *you* think," she said dismissively. "What about everyone else? This affects all of us."

Erich tried to hide his impatience with her questions, even though he understood she was asking out of concern for the family.

Gunther placed his fist on the table. "It will stay!"

"I agree," Peter said. "This is where the Bow belongs."

Eva huddled closer to Peter. "The family is safe here now. We don't need it for anything. I think it should go back to avoid problems."

Thomas gaped at the Bow with a sheepish expression. "Ah, I think it should go back, too."

"Oh, Thomas!" Cort blurted out.

All eyes fell upon Agatha since her words carried much weight.

"I remember when your father first showed you how to use the Bow," she said to Erich. "And later to you, Peter. It seems like such a short time ago, but also a long time ago. These are different times. There are more things to consider." She took a sip of tea. "Everyone has had a chance to speak about this, but the decision should be left to you, Erich."

Erich contemplated her words before speaking.

"Yes, these are different times. I know how the Catholics regard the Bow now. And agree that the word will spread that I've taken it. But the Bow is ours, and I believe it's important for us to have it. Not only for Cort but for all of us. It represents the spirit of our family." He cleared his throat. "For those reasons . . . I say the Bow stays with us." He took note of Catherine's disappointment. "But if any trouble comes from having it here, I'll consider returning it. But only as a last resort."

Catherine smiled softly at him.

He was pleased that his words relieved her worries and acknowledged that her concerns were valid. He would likely find out soon if his actions had any repercussions.

8.

Encounter in the Cell

Erich and Manfred sat together in the guard's quarters, pondering their moves above a chessboard. Manfred slid a bishop and captured one of Erich's pawns.

"I understand this game better now."

"Understand this," Erich replied.

He made a quick move and took the bishop.

"What? You can't do that!"

"The knight," he said as he held up a wooden figure shaped like a horse's head. "Remember? Two squares one way, one square another."

He shook his head. "How did you learn this?"

"My father taught me. I played some at the university in Wittenburg."

"Ah. My regiment was stationed in Leipzig, near there. Before that, I apprenticed as a baker. Can you believe it? But look at me now."

"I think you'd be a fine baker."

"I love my food," he said, tapping his ample girth. "But the War stopped that for me. Now, all I can do is fight. And not so well at that."

Willy entered the room, grinning.

"Otto will be done with her soon. You ought to try her. She hardly struggles."

They ignored him.

"I don't understand you two. She's the best we've had. Not like the hags we usually get."

"We'd sure like to, Willy," Manfred said. "But we don't want her to put a spell on us like she did to the Inquisitor."

"I don't believe you. Klaus said he's fine." He laughed nervously. "I feel better than ever!"

"Maybe so," Manfred said with a straight face, "but your skin is kind of *whitish*. Don't you think, Erich?"

Erich stared at Willy and nodded with mock concern. "Yes. It's much paler than usual. But also . . . a light green."

"You're right," Manfred said. "His face is turning green."

Willy dropped his smile. "You're lying!" He rolled up his sleeves and examined his hands and arms. "My skin is normal. You're trying to scare me!"

"We're only telling you what we see," Manfred said. "This witch has great powers. You must've heard the stories about how she turns men into snakes and toads."

"I'm not a snake or toad! I'm a man. Still a man!"

"Sometimes, these spells take days or a fortnight to finish," Erich added. "And one morning, you'll wake up, and people will scream in terror, so gruesome will be your appearance."

"I'm afraid he's right," Manfred said. "The greenish color on your face shows that the spell has already begun."

Willy's hands shook. "No, no—"

"I hope your fun in there was worth it," Erich said.

Otto burst into the room. "I'm hungry," he said to Willy. "Come on. Don't just stand there like a dumb ox."

He staggered toward Otto, still panting.

"What's the matter?" Otto asked. "Say, you don't look so good."

Willy broke down into a quivering mass of tears. "Oh no! You see it too! We're doomed! Doomed!"

"What say you? Come on, a few cups of ale will cure you." He put his arm on Willy's shoulder as they walked out. "Such crazy talk."

"The stupid fools," Erich said.

They tried to concentrate on the chess game.

"I don't know how long I can work here," Manfred said. "Every time I go into the torture cell—"

A faint chanting emanated through the corridors. They exchanged glances, both recognizing Mara's voice.

"I'll check on her," Erich said.

He peered through the cell door's viewing window. She sat cross-legged, chanting with her eyes closed, hands resting palms up on her knees. A beam of light from a barred opening near the ceiling shone down on her. He watched, transfixed, for some time before returning to the quarters.

He took out some cheese and bread from his satchel and placed them on the table. Manfred brought out a skein of ale to share. They ate in contemplative silence while listening to her chanting.

Willy and Otto stumbled back from the inn, drunken and noisy. Willy soon fell asleep on a bunk, snoring loudly. Otto sat next to him, whittling on a piece of wood.

"You sure scared Willy today," Otto said. "It took three cups of brew before I convinced him it was all a joke."

"We just told him he didn't look well after he came out of the witch's cell," Manfred said. "You said the same thing."

"You said more than that!" He raised his knife menacingly. "You said she put a spell on him, and he believed it. Well, such talk doesn't scare me. And I don't want to hear any more about it!"

"If that's what you want," Manfred said. "We won't say anything if we see any changes in *your* appearance." He took a quick swig of water. "Others might, though."

Otto glared at him but went back to his whittling.

Soon, the familiar sound of a clanging cup echoed from the corridor. Someone wanted water.

Otto sighed and rose.

"Water," a voice pleaded from one of the cells.

"It sounds like the one you were with this morning," Manfred said.

Otto tried to cover up his fear and settled back on the chair. "I went last time."

Erich stood. "I'll go."

He fetched a bucket and dipped it into the barrel.

"You're a brave man, Erich," Manfred said as he departed. "Venturing forth in there alone. Take care not to look into her eyes, though."

Otto glared at him again.

————

Mara sat on a narrow wooden platform and snapped her head up in fright when he entered, until she recognized him. She brushed her hair back and looped the torn straps of her dress over her shoulder. He knelt, dipped her cup into the bucket, and handed it to her.

"Thank you," she said with a faint smile. "I've seen you before."

"In the courtroom."

"And before that. On a road outside the town."

"When?"

"I was in a prison cart and saw you standing beside a horse. About a fortnight past Yule. You looked . . . much troubled."

It took him a moment to recollect it. "I think I remember."

He stared at the bruises on her wrists, grasped her hands, and examined the welts with a pained expression.

Deeply touched by the gesture, she observed his hands until he let go of her grip.

"Fear not. There is no pain. May I see your hands a little closer?"

He nodded, still kneeling at her feet.

"Here, sit next to me," she said, patting the bench.

He extended his hands, palms up, while she gently stretched his fingers down and occasionally pressed with her thumb. As she continued, a faint tingling sensation radiated upward from his arms and inward to his chest, followed by a sense of calm and peace.

She faced him with confidence after she finished.

"You possess a strong destiny."

He stared at her in surprise. "What do you mean?"

"You will soon affect the lives of many others. But your path is fraught with danger and—"

"How do you know this?" he said, pulling away from her.

She detected his apprehension and took a lighter tone. "I'm a witch, you know. Aren't you afraid?"

"So-called witches are just people who believe in things not in favor anymore. In my own family—" He stopped and changed the subject. "You should confess when the Inquisitor arrives. Otherwise—"

"What's your name?"

"Erich."

"Ah, Erich. I'm ready to meet my fate. The chanting prepares my soul for the journey to the next world. I'll say a prayer for *your* journey in this life."

A wave of disturbing, conflicted emotions struck him, as if a deep-seated truth had just been uncovered, but so suddenly that he couldn't comprehend it. He wanted to say more but couldn't find the words. He grasped the bucket and stood.

"I must go now."

————

He walked through the town square on his way to the livery, reflecting on his encounter in the cell: the tone of her voice and the nuances of her expressions. However, the way her hands held his affected him the most. What did she mean by his destiny?

He had been so absorbed in thought that he hadn't noticed Klaus and four henchmen approaching until they stopped before him, blocking his path. Each of them pulled out a club.

Klaus stepped out from behind them. "You've taken something from the sheriff's office."

"That's none of your concern."

"Oh, but it is. I represent the Catholic League and watch for signs of rebellion. You must give back the Bow at once."

"I obey the sheriff and the mayor. No one else."

"It's a weapon," he said in a louder voice, "that can be used against the peaceful citizens of this town."

A crowd gathered around them.

Erich assessed the henchmen. He had seen Sigi in action before: tall and slender, a wild, uncontrollable fighter. Lothar, the seasoned cavalry veteran, was tough and ruthless but hampered by a bad leg. The two younger men, Dieter and Joachim, were both fit and muscular, yet fear lingered in their eyes.

"It will stay in my home."

"You must return it to the sheriff today!"

"Your words mean nothing to me."

Erich attempted to walk past them, but Lothar pushed him back. Sigi raised his club, but Erich swung his staff into Sigi's ribs, knocking him down. The younger henchmen came at Erich from behind. Dieter wrapped his arms around Erich's neck as Joachim struck his torso. Erich spun away and took Dieter down with a hard shot to his leg, but Lothar clubbed him on the head. He fell, dazed, to his knees and reached for his staff, but Klaus kicked it away.

Dieter and Joachim lifted Erich by his shoulders.

"This is what happens," Klaus said in a haughty tone, "when you resist our laws. You'll get more of this unless you return the Bow."

He signaled Lothar, who punched him in the stomach.

He struggled to break free, still groggy from the blow to the head. "So now you force us to take it from your home. Then we'll see what else we can take."

Erich trembled with rage. He broke free from the younger henchmen and struck Sigi in the jaw, sending him to the ground again. He seized his staff just in time to deflect a blow from Lothar's club.

The crowd dispersed as the fight approached them.

He struck Dieter on the head with his staff and knocked down Joachim with blows to his ribs. Lothar hit his shoulder, but Erich countered with a punch to his torso. Lothar drew his knife and lunged at him. Erich took him down mid-stride with a swing to his leg.

Erich turned to Klaus. They squared off as Klaus drew his sword.

"Now it's your turn," Erich said through gritted teeth.

Klaus took a swing that Erich deflected with his staff. They charged each other and fought at close quarters, punching and kicking until

Erich struck him with a fierce blow to his midsection. Klaus staggered back and swung wildly at him but missed, losing his balance. Erich pushed his staff forward, but Klaus stumbled into it as he tried to duck away. The tip of the staff landed with a sharp crunch directly into his eye socket. He dropped his sword, screaming, while covering his eye.

Dieter and Joachim staggered forward to confront Erich as Jacob and two deputies pushed through the crowd.

"Stop now!" Jacob shouted.

Jacob surveyed the scene while the deputies subdued the two younger henchmen. Lothar and Sigi remained on the ground, struggling to stand. Klaus covered his injured eye with a cloth, and Erich had gashes on his forehead and cheeks, along with cuts on his arm.

"What's the cause of this?" Jacob asked.

"They wouldn't let me pass," Erich answered, panting.

"He took the Black Bow," Klaus said, his face contorted in pain. "He must return it. That's the law."

"No," Jacob declared. "The Edict doesn't apply to personal property such as this. He can keep it as long as it stays in his home. That's my decision."

"You're wrong!" Klaus screamed. "There are higher laws. The laws of the kingdom! And the laws of God!" He dabbed his eye with the cloth and grimaced from the touch. "I'll go to München to report this act of *defiance* to Duke Maximilian's court."

"I would think twice about that," Jacob said. "You know the penalty for false accusations."

Erich turned to leave.

"And you, Erich," Klaus said. "You and your Protestant vermin will pay for this."

Erich plunged toward him. Klaus dropped the cloth and reached for his sword. Jacob blocked his path, halting the charge.

"You speak so bravely to someone's back," Erich said. "Yet when they turn to face you, your tongue is tied."

Some townsfolk laughed. Klaus glared at them. The laughter ceased. Now, Klaus's grotesquely swollen and bleeding eye was visible to all. Sigi handed him the cloth. He dabbed it over his eye with a scowl.

Erich turned and left the scene. The crowd parted as he walked through. Some maintained their distance, arms crossed with expressions of disapproval. Others patted him on the shoulder as he strode by.

Klaus watched him walk away in a silent rage.

———

Erich rode through the town, realizing that even though he had won the fight, the consequences could be serious. Jacob and a few of his supporters on the council could only do so much to protect his family from the growing power and influence of the Catholic League in the region. He passed by the prison along the way and stopped in front of the grim stone edifice. He wanted to meet and talk to her again and ask what she meant by the reading of his hands. He stared at his hands for some time and again sensed her touch.

At that moment, a flood of thoughts emerged, still unclear yet powerful. Then it struck him. The prison, long a source of suffering for him due to *what* had transpired within, had now become a beacon of hope and salvation because of *who* was present. He shook his head in disbelief at the sheer simplicity and purity of this sudden realization. He urged Baldur to move forward.

He crossed the bridge and rode into the countryside, unaware of the sounds and movements surrounding him. The ideas that arose in his mind before the prison started taking form.

He stopped by a small, half-frozen lake to reflect on everything that had happened that day: the encounter in the cell, the fight, and, most of all, those emerging thoughts since he had left town. The distant ringing of the town's church bells seemed to bring everything into focus.

He urged Baldur on again quickly. He wanted to tell his family about a very important decision he'd made.

9.

Departure

Erich washed the cut areas around his face, arms, and chest with a wet cloth in the back room of the house. The worst was a swollen gash on his forehead from Lothar's club. Catherine entered and was shocked at the sight of all those bruises and welts on his body.

"Mein Gott!" she exclaimed. "What happened?"

"A disagreement in town."

She reached for another cloth and pressed it on the cuts on his back, causing him to flinch. "Sorry, I'll be more careful." She dabbed it again. "What kind of disagreement?"

"I need to speak to the family. Please ring the porch bell and bring everyone together."

———

An uneasy tension filled the room as they sat around the table, sharing a loaf of bread and waiting for Erich to speak. Catherine understood that sometimes he needed gentle coaxing to express his thoughts, so she touched his hand. "You can tell us what happened now."

He looked up, blinking as if startled from a trance. "Klaus and his men attacked me, but I fought them off."

"Did it have something to do with the Bow?" Catherine asked.

"I bet they wanted you to take it back," Cort said. "But you wouldn't let them."

He nodded.

"I knew this would happen," Catherine said. "I fear for what they'll do next."

"The sheriff told Klaus we can keep the Bow if it stays here."

"The sheriff? He won't be able to protect us if they come after us. And you know who *they* are."

She waited for him to respond as he ate.

"I'm afraid she's right," Agatha said. "Jacob is an honorable man, but he's losing his power and authority to others."

"That damnable Klaus," Peter said. "Things were fine here until those bullies joined him. Those cursed black robes are the ones who started all this."

"I wish I could've been there today," Gunther said with a clenched fist. "I would've knocked some of those fellows down."

"Me too," Thomas chimed in, raising his fist.

"And me!" Rudi said as he thrust out a little fist, too.

"You men," Catherine said. "We can't fight them all. There's only one thing to do now. We know what that is."

No one responded in support, not even Eva, who clutched Peter's arm.

"You said you'd take it back if it causes trouble for the family," Catherine said, sensing his seething anger. "Well, this is trouble."

"No!" Erich bellowed, slamming his fist on the table. "We will not return the Bow! They've taken enough!" He composed himself and turned to Agatha. "Mother, you're right about the sheriff. He can only do so much. Klaus is the problem." He took a swig of water. "He vowed to go to München and address Duke Maximilian about this."

Catherine gasped.

"Does he have grounds for such an action?" Agatha asked.

"According to the Edict, no," Erich answered.

"That's what we thought," Peter interjected, "before they took away our rightful land."

"I know." He cleared his throat. "Because of what happened today, I've decided we must move from here. And from Bayern."

His words stunned the family.

"This is all because of the Bow," Catherine said.

"No. We would've had to leave eventually. The Catholics are too strong here. You've seen what's happening to our fellow Protestants. The longer we stay, the less safe we are."

"Where will we go?" Gunther asked.

"Leipzig."

Once again, his answer rendered everyone speechless.

"Leipzig? Why so far?" Peter asked.

"We have family there," he said, turning to his wife. "They'll help us resettle."

"But we can't impose on them," Catherine said.

"Families help each other during these times. Do they still have those other properties in town?"

"I haven't heard otherwise."

"We can move in one of them," he said, trying to calm them. "We have savings, and some of us can find work there. Then return when the War is over."

"Leipzig," Gunther said. "The journey might take over a month. Or more, depending on the weather."

"Not again," Catherine said while wiping away tears with a handkerchief. "When will it end? Moving. Running. Hiding."

"We must be brave and strong," Agatha said. "We'll survive these times. This is sudden and unexpected, but I think Erich has made the right decision. As he said, we've seen others run out of the town with little or nothing on their backs. And we're so defenseless here. At least we'll have a chance to carry what we need."

"Mother?" Anna asked, about to cry. "Is something going to happen to us?"

Catherine shook her head, too distraught to answer.

"No dear," Agatha answered. "We're moving to another place. Where you'll find other girls to play with."

"I want to make new friends too," Rudi said.

Cort remained silent in the corner of the room with furrowed brows.

"Is Leipzig safe?" Eva asked.

"It's a well-fortified town. The Elector is a Protestant as are most of the people."

"We thought Magdeburg was so safe too when—" Catherine said before realizing that this touched upon a sore subject for the family.

"Those were different times," Erich said, shaken by the memory. "When the War was at its peak."

"I tell you what," Peter said, "if the Catholics keep grinding their heels into our necks, the War will start up again. People can only take so much!"

"What about the animals?" Thomas asked. His innocent but practical concern calmed the adults and brought them back to the matter at hand.

"You and Gunther can go into town," Erich said, "and sell them tomorrow."

"Why so soon?" Peter asked.

"Because—" he hesitated before continuing, "we must leave in two days. That will give us a full day to pack after Gunther and Thomas return."

Once again, the family stared at him in dismay.

"Why the rush?" Peter asked.

"Yes, Father. Why?"

"The sooner, the better."

"I'm puzzled by this also," Agatha said as she stroked Bertina on her lap. "It's a two-day ride to München. Then he'd have to petition the Duke for an audience, which might take many days. And another two days back."

She let the statement hang and waited for him to answer, as did the rest of the family.

"There are events in town that I must deal with. We should be gone from here when I do. That's all I'll say for now. We'll leave the morning after tomorrow. That's my decision."

Catherine sobbed next to Eva. Agatha placed a hand on her shoulder. "Think about it, my dear," Agatha said. "It's a long journey, but soon you'll be closer to your family. And in a safer place." Catherine nodded, soothed by her words.

The women went to the kitchen, and the men headed outside to finish their chores. Cort followed his father to the porch, frustrated by how little he'd explained.

"Father, I know you can't tell the women everything, to worry them. But tell me why we must leave so soon."

"Son, I have a lot to think about. I'll explain later."

He strode off toward the barn, leaving Cort stunned and angry.

———

After the evening meal, Erich entered a small room in the corner of the house where Agatha sat with Eva. Heloise crawled on the floor, trying to follow the cat.

Agatha sensed the reason for his visit. "We need to talk alone now," she said to Eva.

"More about the fight?" she asked, noticing his disturbed countenance and struggle for words. It always seemed that the deeper his feelings, the harder it became to express himself.

"It's about someone I met in prison. A condemned witch."

"Catherine is right. You should stop working there. The injustices you witness are terrible. But there's nothing you can do about it."

"Oh, but there is!"

"What are you going to do?" she asked, now sensing his answer.

"I'm going to rescue her!"

She looked at him with concern before replying. "I'm sure you understand the consequences for both you and the family."

"That's why I want you to leave so soon. I'll give you a day's head start and go into town the next day and free her." Now his words flowed forth. "You should take the north road and catch the Günzburg ferry. Then travel to Donauworth and head to Nürnberg. I'll make it easy for them to follow us to the Iller. They'll lose our trail after we cross."

"But when will you join us?"

"I might have to guide her back part of the way to where she's from, near Mainz, until she's safe. I can't leave her too soon. They might snatch her again."

"So it might be some time before we see you again."

"Sometime after you've settled in Leipzig."

Agatha shook her head, thinking about how this would affect the family and Catherine most of all.

"Another thing," he said, taking a deep breath. "I want to talk to you about things she told me."

"Go on."

"It happened after I gave her water. She took my hands and studied them for a long time. She seemed to be looking at the lines in my palm and pressed down on them. I felt strange when she did it. Do you know of people who do this?"

"I've seen people practice it, but many years ago. Now, it's considered a form of witchcraft. Are you worried she put a spell on you?"

"Not at all. It's what she said afterward. That I have a *strong destiny*. Can such things be seen through hands?"

Something within Agatha stirred, but she chose to block it out. "This can be said about anyone. Don't you think? We all have certain destinies in life. It's an old carnival trick to make people feel better about themselves."

"She wasn't trying to flatter me. Almost the opposite. She seemed reluctant to tell me."

"Did she say more about this?"

He paused to recall her words. "She said that I'll affect the lives of many others soon—"

"And?"

"The path I'll travel on will be dangerous."

"What else?"

"She wanted to say more, but I interrupted her. Perhaps she detected my fear and changed the subject."

Agatha shut her eyes and rested her head on one hand. The same feeling surfaced again, but this time it was much stronger and connected to her conversations with Klara during Yule.

"So," she said after opening her eyes, "you had a fear when she spoke to you?"

"At the time, yes, but not anymore. It's *how* she spoke. I sensed a truth in them. And her hands, when they touched mine." He held out his hands. "I feel them now."

"Tell me more about this woman. What did they accuse her of?"

"The usual. They turned her in for practicing midwifery and concocted more tales against her. But she isn't like other midwives I've seen. For one thing, she's younger than me. Also, I must admit, she has a rare beauty."

"Perhaps that's what influenced you the most."

"Oh, it's more than that. It's her entire bearing and countenance. They tried to break her, but, if anything, she broke the Inquisitor. Her words bespoke of one with a high education."

"I know of no one of that description here."

"She's from the north. And grew up in a monastery near Mainz at a place called Eibingen."

This sparked Agatha's interest even more. "You say she spoke like one with some intelligence?"

"Not only the individual words but the thoughts behind them. With so much wisdom."

"There's a small convent in Eibingen that I passed by during the trip. I visited another larger one in the town of Bingen, which follows the teachings of Hildegard. A convent of the highest order protected by the Bishops at Mainz. Perhaps she studied there." She paused to stretch. "All I can say about her reading of your hands is that there might be some truth to it. Sometimes, people's destinies cross each other, causing them to take different life paths. I know the decision wasn't easy. But you should follow your heart in the matter since you feel so strongly about it."

————

She reflected on her conversation with Erich and other recent events while resting in bed. After years of relative peace, so much had happened in the past few days. She wished she had time to consult an astrologer in her coven. Surely, some significant realignment of the planets must have occurred for such a sudden shift in fortunes to happen, which all began, by chance, when he retrieved the Bow. All this seemed connected to other aspects of his past, which were now coming to fruition.

The key to it all was the woman in prison who foresaw his destiny by reading his hands.

————

The family spent the next day packing, all somber but resigned to the fact that they would soon embark on a long journey.

The move was hardest for Catherine, as she had grown most attached to certain possessions they couldn't take. She had worked hard to create a warm and restful home there, and they had accumulated many items that brought comfort and stability to their lives.

During this time, Erich regretted his decision and worried about the hardships and dangers on the roads to Leipzig. It became so difficult for him that he changed his mind and began unpacking, only to change it again.

Cort ventured into the woods searching for the wolf but returned dejected and unable to find it.

Others in the family also spent some time alone. Agatha meditated in her room in the morning. Peter gathered his carving tools and chose which pieces of unfinished wood to take. Thomas swept the barn even after all the animals had left. He seemed to miss the cow most of all. Gunther worked the field with a spading fork, searching for the last ripe potatoes and turnips. Rudi helped him pick the vegetables and place them in the sacks. Anna took a few breaks from assisting her mother pack by going on the tall rope swing that Erich had built for her and Rudi. Eva joined her, and they took turns pushing each other. Max sat on the porch, watching the activities as if sensing the upcoming move. Bertina stayed close to Agatha's side, even more than usual.

Much to his relief, the family seemed to have adjusted to the situation during the last evening meal. Because of the children, they spoke only positively about the future: how they would be safer in Leipzig, meet more people, and make new friends. Cort, however, remained silent, only speaking when asking for more food.

After the meal, Erich pulled Peter aside to discuss his plans. They sat down in a corner of the house used as the pantry.

"Are you sure you can do this on your own?" Peter asked.

"Freeing her will be easy. Those fools guarding her won't be a problem. The hardest part will be to reach the Iller as fast as possible."

"What provisions will you have?"

"I'll bring shelter material, plenty of warm clothes, some weapons and hunting gear, and enough food to last until we come to the first town."

Cort barged into the room.

"Peter and I have been talking about the trip," Erich said. "He'll be in charge when I'm gone for a few days." He could tell Cort wasn't convinced. "We'll talk about this more later. Goodnight."

Cort gave him a short nod and stomped away.

———

Erich lay in bed while Catherine brushed her hair in front of the dresser mirror, a routine she followed every evening before they turned in for the night. He gazed at her features as she brushed: her slender arms, smooth white skin around her neck, long, light brown hair, and the profile of her face highlighted by those bright blue eyes sparkling in the candlelight. Her mind seemed distant from the realities of their situation.

He struggled with whether to reveal the full extent of his plans to her. She had a right to know, and withholding the truth would deny her the respect she deserved. However, as he contemplated it further, he realized it might be too much for her to handle. If it were only a matter of taking justice into his own hands in a different way, she'd likely try to understand; nevertheless, he concluded it would be better for the family to inform her later since it involved another woman.

"Time for bed," he said. "Tomorrow, we rise at dawn."

She turned and offered him a warm, radiant smile that she always wore when she was at her happiest. He felt his desire for her intensify. This would be their last night together for a while.

At first, she tried to tell him that the timing for making love was not quite right; however, she couldn't resist his ardor and surrendered to both their desires. Afterward, they fell asleep in each other's arms.

———

The family sat in gloomy silence during the morning meal, but Catherine wore a dreamy expression as she ate, reflecting on their time together at night. Her eyes darted to him with a broader smile. He forced a returning smile but couldn't maintain it.

Peter and Gunther picked at their food. Neither of them had slept much; both were worried about the long journey ahead. Thomas ate his fill without a care in the world. Eva huddled close to Peter. Rudi pushed his food around in the bowl. Anna didn't have much of an appetite either. Agatha remained calm and serene as usual. Cort ate with his head down at the far corner of the table.

"Is everything packed and ready?" Erich asked Peter.

"Except for a few crates on the porch."

"And the horses?" Erich asked Gunther.

"All fed and cinched to the wagons."

"There's one more thing I remembered last night." His expression tightened. "I have unfinished business to attend to in the town. So I won't join you on the first part of the journey."

"What business?" Catherine asked him. "You never told me."

"I thought about it after you fell asleep. I must ensure the papers are written about our farm so it'll be in our name when we return."

"Is that all, Father?" Cort asked with a riveting stare.

"That's one of the reasons," Erich answered. He hated lying to his family and to Cort most of all.

"What other reasons?" Cort asked.

Before he could answer, Catherine broke in. "I don't understand why we can't wait here until your business is finished."

"I'm concerned about what Klaus might do because of the fight. That's why we must leave now. They could come for us any day."

He turned to Cort. "That's the other reason. I must talk to the sheriff to ensure Klaus is kept in line. At least before he petitions the duke."

"When will you meet us?" Catherine asked.

"It should only take a few days. I'll catch up with you after the ferry crossing."

"Oh, *after* the crossing," Catherine said. She shook her head and sighed.

It took all his willpower to keep a calm appearance. He wanted to tell them the truth but realized it would be more difficult for them to accept.

After the meal, Gunther and Thomas loaded the last of the crates.

Erich shook hands with Peter and then with Gunther and Thomas.

Anna began to cry. He embraced Agatha and Eva, then gave Anna a long hug. She wouldn't let go of his arm as she sobbed. Rudy broke down, too, until Peter comforted him.

"Come now, Anna," he said. "Be brave like Cort."

She hugged him once more, trying to stifle tears, and shuffled to the wagon with Eva.

He turned to his son, leaning against the back wagon.

"Don't be so glum. I know you miss the wolves, but you'll make new friends in Leipzig."

"That's not it," Cort replied.

"I'll tell you more when I return. Then you'll understand." He extended his hand.

"Sure," Cort said. He gave him a quick shake and climbed on.

He went to Catherine, who couldn't hide her hurt feelings even after they embraced.

"I'll miss you," she said. "I know it won't be long, but I always feel lost without you."

After she settled into the wagon, her concerns intensified. The tone of his voice and behavior hinted that he had been concealing something from her. After exchanging farewells, she turned away, overwhelmed by emotion.

Thomas and Gunther sat in the lead wagon, which held most of the foodstuffs, supplies, and furnishings, including a small coop for the best egg-laying hens. Max was wedged between them. Gunther jerked the reins and set off. Peter guided the other wagon, equipped with bunks and living quarters. They exchanged waves one last time.

Agatha watched Erich, standing ramrod straight and clutching his staff, as they rode away. Off on another quest, she mused. So much like her Richard and other holders of the Bow before him who plunged into the unknown to fight against injustices, their lives incomplete until they did so.

He stood there long after the wagons had disappeared down the road. Torn by emotion, he took a step forward but halted. He remained rooted to the spot, knowing that a run would follow the next step, and he wouldn't stop until he reached them.

After some time, he considered the next day and all the tasks he needed to complete to prepare for the escape. He trudged back to the house.

10

Escape

Erich rode into Ulm to purchase food and supplies for the journey and visit the sheriff. As usual, they talked about their families until the conversation shifted to the fight with Klaus.

"I doubt he'll come after you because of that," Jacob said. "It's all talk and bluster from him. Besides, I'm told he's still under the care of an apothecary for his eye."

"I fear he will when he gets the chance." He shook his head. "Because of that . . . I'm making plans to leave and move to Leipzig. Catherine has relatives there."

His words stung Jacob. "These times. So many people are leaving. All good members of the community. I hope you'll reconsider."

"I've thought much about this, but we've already started."

"I'm sorry to hear that," he said, unable to disguise his disappointment.

"We plan to come back after the War. When it's safer. I also worry about the Inquisitor. Have you heard any news about him?"

"Only that he went to Augsburg and is due back soon."

That's what he needed to know; her interrogation hadn't begun yet. After discussing their families further, he bade farewell to his old friend.

———

He arose before dawn. He planned to leave Baldur outside of town, south of the bridge, to avoid attracting attention from the townsfolk. He found an old hooded coat in the barn for her to wear after the rescue. Then, he would return to Baldur, ride to the farm, load the horse, and head to the Iller.

He led Baldur to a thicket off the road near an abandoned mill house. He opened the feed bag and poured some onto the ground. As Baldur fed, he once again began to doubt his course of action—he knew it wasn't too late to change his mind—but he pushed those thoughts aside. He patted Baldur twice on the neck, a sign that he would return soon, slung the bag over his shoulder, and marched into town.

———

When he arrived, the streets were nearly empty; only a few shops and vendor stalls had opened. After entering the prison, he was surprised to find that Manfred, instead of Willy, was sitting with Otto.

"What are you doing here?" Manfred asked.

"I'll take over for you. Go now."

"I was just going for food at the market because —"

"Don't bother."

Manfred eyed him suspiciously as he left.

"Klaus is going to get you," Otto said, grinning.

"I think not," Erich said. He set down his staff, pulled out a knife, and held it to Otto's chest. "Walk to the cells!"

Otto rose but quickly moved to knock the knife from Erich's hand. Before Erich could recover, Otto threw a punch at him. Erich blocked it, grabbed his staff, and slammed it down onto Otto's head. The force of the blow made Otto's head crash against the wall, causing him to slump to the ground, unconscious. Erich took the keys from the wall and rushed to Mara's cell.

She stood in surprise as he came in.

He reached into the bag and handed her the hooded coat. "Hurry! Put this on."

She now realized his intentions and backed away. "You shouldn't do this."

"I've knocked out the guard."

"That will bring you trouble. But not as much as this. You have a greater destiny to fulfill. This will set you back."

He placed a hand on her shoulder. "Perhaps this destiny of mine is meant to be fulfilled together with you. On this *dangerous* journey, as you mentioned."

Her demeanor shifted. She nodded and donned the coat.

As they walked away, he noticed she only wore socks. "Where are your shoes?"

"They took them and my other belongings."

"Wait here."

He strode down the corridor and opened another cell door. The youth Gumprecht from the trial cowered against the wall after Erich entered.

"You're free to go!" he exclaimed.

Gumprecht stared at him in disbelief.

"Come on! This isn't a trick!"

Gumprecht dashed to the door, looked both ways, flashed Erich a wild-eyed grin, and then ran off.

"Why him?" she asked.

"He might not survive his sentence. I have a son his age."

In the guard's quarters, he pulled off Otto's socks and boots and handed them to her. They were far too large, even with the heavy socks.

"They'll do for now," he said. "I'll get you another pair."

Halfway down the corridor, he remembered that he had forgotten to drag Otto into the cell, but the front door swung open just as he turned back. Manfred entered with a bag of food slung over his shoulder.

"Aha!" Manfred exclaimed. "I thought something was up."

"Manfred. Walk away and say you know nothing of this. Or we'll have to fight."

He drew out his sword and rushed toward Erich.

"Behind you!" Manfred shouted.

Otto charged at Erich with a raised sword. He lunged out of the way just as it crashed onto the stone floor. As Otto was about to strike again, Manfred blocked Otto's swing with his own sword. Otto swung wildly at him and missed, but before he could recover, Manfred plunged his sword into Otto's midsection. Otto slumped to the ground, groaning.

"Now what?" Manfred mumbled, staring down at Otto.

Erich tried to gather his thoughts. "You can come with us. You can't stay here now."

"But where?"

"I'll tell you later. Go to your room and pack all your clothes and blankets. And any food you have. Did you get another horse?"

"Still have the same one."

"It'll have to do. After you pack, take the south road out of town. We'll wait for you just past the old mill house."

He rushed down the hall and out of the prison.

Mara pulled the hood over her head and followed Erich as he stopped to check outside the door, signaling for her to follow. They did their best to remain inconspicuous as they walked together.

They quickened their pace after crossing the bridge over the Danube. She stumbled a few times in her boots, trying to keep up. When they returned to Baldur, she sat down to catch her breath. He scanned the road for Manfred. As he waited, he couldn't help but recall being at this spot earlier in the morning, when he still had the choice to perform the rescue. But that was no longer the case. The deed was done.

At last, Manfred rode toward them. He guided Baldur out of the thicket to meet him.

"Can you ride?" he asked as he helped her up to the saddle.

"I grew up riding horses."

As they galloped along, she attempted to comprehend the sudden turn of events while trying to maintain a firm grip on his strong shoulders.

Manfred's horse was panting heavily when they arrived at the farm.

"Wait here while I pack more supplies," Erich said.

Manfred and Mara sat on opposite ends of a bench on the porch.

"How long have you known him?" she asked.

"About a year. But we didn't talk much at first. It looks like," he said with a laugh, "we'll be getting to know each other a lot more soon."

Inside the house, Erich gathered all the items he had prepared the night before and placed them in a pile by the door: blankets, changes of clothes, shelter materials, rope, cooking supplies, flint, and the Black Bow. He also found old clothing the family had left behind, including worn-out shoes and boots.

He walked outside, carrying a pair of boots, and knelt before her. "These were my mother's, but we bought her a new pair."

She noted his features as he fitted them on: his wavy brown hair parted in the middle and held back with a leather band, his close-cropped beard, and, most importantly, his strong arms and hands. After all the hardships she'd endured, this man had suddenly entered her life, now kneeling before her as he had in the prison cell.

"Stand and see how they fit."

She stamped her feet and took a few steps forward and back. "They're perfect!"

Her eyes clouded with emotion as he cinched up the boots. "This is all happening so fast. You should be with your family."

"They're going to Leipzig. We couldn't have stayed much longer anyway. Our beliefs are not in favor here."

"You can leave me at the next town. And then I'll go back to Eibingen."

"They'll snatch you again. These are bad times for women traveling alone. Besides, you have no means."

"I'll find a way. I got careless last time."

"I'll take you to your destination. Or part of the way. The roads are full of danger. You'll never make it on your own."

"I agree that the next town might be unsafe, but Eibingen is too far."

"We'll see how things go. I've gathered some old clothes. You can change in the back room while we load the horses."

"You think your horse can make it?" Erich asked Manfred as they loaded Baldur.

"I hope so."

"We're going through some rough country with steep climbs past the Iller."

"I'll push it as best I can."

After they finished loading, Mara came out wearing the clothes, which were quite a mismatch coming from the adults in his family.

"What do you think?" she asked, extending her arms out from a bulky old coat.

"As long as they keep you warm for now. I'll get newer ones in the first town."

"Not to bother. These are fine."

"The next two days will be hard," Erich said. "We can't stop until we reach the river and must walk through the night. We'll take turns riding."

They paused briefly after climbing a rise in the land above the farm. Erich reached into a saddlebag, pulled out Otto's boots, and placed them on the ground.

"What are you doing?" Manfred asked. "They'll find them and—"

"I want them to. So they won't go after the family."

He clutched Baldur's stirrup, and the three of them headed into the forest.

11

Pursuit

Klaus, the Inquisitor, and Willy stood over Otto's body with grim expressions. He adjusted a patch over his injured eye, secured to a leather cord around his head, and knelt beside him.

"You said he was dead," Klaus said to Willy after he placed his hand on Otto's forehead. "He still has warmth." He slid his hand over his nose and mouth. "And breath!"

Willy felt utterly mortified by Klaus's glare, which was more forbidding now with the eyepatch. "He looked dead. With so much blood and his face so white."

"Fetch some water and a cloth!" Klaus demanded.

Klaus dabbed the wet cloth on Otto's head. He groaned and opened his eyes.

"Can you talk? What happened? Who did this to you?"

"My stomach," Otto whispered, wincing in pain.

"Who else was with him?" Klaus asked Willy.

"Only Manfred. He took my place."

"Manfred? Did he do this to you?"

"I tried to stop them," Otto sputtered.

"*Them?*"

Otto's eyes fluttered to a close, so Klaus spread the wet cloth over his forehead. He bent over closer to his ear.

"You said *them*. Who else?"

"Erich."

"Erich!" Klaus growled, glancing up at the Inquisitor.

"Have you checked the cells?" the Inquisitor asked Willy.

"No, I didn't think—"

"Do so now!" Klaus commanded.

He was about to grab the keys, now absent from the post against the wall. He glanced sheepishly at where they should be and rushed away.

"I fear the worst," the Inquisitor muttered.

"Rest now, good man," Klaus said to Otto. We'll get the best apothecary for you. You performed your duties bravely."

Willy returned holding a set of keys. "The witch's cell is empty. And the one with the boy."

"Diabolical treachery!" the Inquisitor charged. "She's in league with the Devil! You must capture them at once."

"I'll get word to hunters with dogs today. We'll leave with the first morning light. And check his farm first. The sheriff can't protect him now."

"What about the other one?" the Inquisitor asked.

"What other one?"

"The boy."

"He's no threat compared to Erich and the witch. Don't you agree?"

The Inquisitor hesitated as if confused by the question.

As Klaus waited for a response, he couldn't help but notice, once again, the overall change in the Inquisitor's countenance: the stooped posture, disheveled hair, glassy eyes, and wrinkled face, which seemed to *sag* on one side. His clothes hung loosely on him as if he had lost considerable weight. This made him wonder if he had indeed suffered a health setback after the trial or, worse, if the cause was a spell cast upon him by the witch.

"Of course," the Inquisitor finally answered. "He's unleashed a demon back into the world. We must find them before more harm is done."

"Well then," Klaus said. "The Sheriff can chase the *boy*. I will hunt the *man*."

The Inquisitor nodded. "May God be with you in the pursuit."

After he left, Klaus lifted the eyepatch and removed the cloth underneath it. He examined the yellowish-red stains and put the clean side over his eye.

————

Erich led Baldur through the woods and stopped beside a stream. He took a length of sausage from his saddlebag, broke off a piece, and offered each of them a portion.

"We'll eat along the way. We can't stop to rest for long. Stay close to me."

That night, Erich pulled Baldur through a clearing, cutting through the underbrush with his sword. Manfred walked alongside him, holding a makeshift torch. Suddenly, his horse reared up, and Baldur became agitated as well. Erich stopped him.

"What is it?" she whispered.

"I'm not sure . . . listen."

Manfred and Mara shook their heads.

"Better dismount," Erich said to her. "I'll hold Baldur."

They had only gone a short distance when Manfred's horse reared again. Some nearby bushes rustled, followed by snorting sounds.

"Boar," Manfred warned.

They huddled closer together and plunged on.

———

The next morning, Klaus inspected the nearly empty rooms of the farmhouse with Lothar and Sigi.

"Only a few things worth taking," Sigi said.

"We'll load a wagon for them after the hunt," Lothar added.

"And capture," Klaus said. "Rolfe's dogs are the best in Bayern."

They stepped outside onto the porch. Six of his henchmen—including Horst, Ernst, Dieter, and Joachim—scoured the barn.

Klaus scanned the horizon; still no sign of the hunters. He'd hoped they would've found Erich's trail by now.

Some raucous crows perched in a nearby tree. Their incessant squawking irritated him, prompting him to throw a rock at them. It landed with a thud against the trunk, and the crows took flight. He detested the very sight of those wretched birds.

This all started in his youth when he tossed a rock at one of their nests, sending a fledgling tumbling to the ground. The mother crow and others swooped down and attacked him, forcing him to run away, both angry and frightened. After that, those pesky birds seemed to have it in for him. Fortnights, and even years later, they squawked and hovered above him whenever he approached. It became so bad that his friends called him *Krähenjunge* with mischievous glee whenever he tried to chase them away.

The hunters emerged from the forest and rode swiftly toward him. As he stepped out to meet them, a dark shape in another tree caught his attention—a raven. He glared at the raven until it flew away when the hunters rumbled closer.

Rolfe and another hunter halted beside Klaus. The other henchmen joined them.

"We found his trail," Rolfe said. "Heading west."

"What about his family?" Klaus asked.

"We spotted wagon tracks right away leading north to Günzburg," Rolfe said. "But they looked several days old. Meaning they left before the escape."

"We might catch them if we start now," Lothar said.

Klaus pondered the situation. "Choose three men and do so. But don't waste time following them across the river. They could go any direction from there." He turned to the others. "The rest of us will follow the witch's trail."

Rolfe guided them to a vantage point overlooking the farm. Four hunters stood ready for them, holding barking and yelping hunting dogs on leashes.

"Are you sure this is it?" Klaus asked Rolfe.

"Oh yes. From the scent of his old clothes in the house. And from the boots they left here. Rather careless of them, I think."

"Those are Otto's boots," Sigi said.

"No one else has such giant feet," Ernst added.

"How many horses do they have?" Klaus asked.

"Only two."

"But three sets of footprints," another hunter said.

"Ha! Three, you say."

"So Manfred is with them on his horse," Sigi said.

"Three people, two horses, loaded down with supplies, which is why they came here first," Klaus said. "That will slow them down. When will we capture them?"

"They have a day start on us," the other hunter said. "But they couldn't have traveled far at night. If we can stay on their trail, we might get them by the end of the day."

"Once my dogs grab a scent, they never lose it," Rolfe said.

———

Early the next morning, Mara rode slumped over Baldur, barely awake. They had just completed a tough climb and stopped at the top of a ridge, overlooking a valley. In the distance, a river flowed northward.

"Is that the Iller?" Manfred asked.

"Yes," Erich answered. "We'll rest here to eat and feed the horses." Erich examined Baldur's legs and hoofs as they ate.

"How long have you had the horse?" she asked.

"Almost twelve years. We've been through much together."

"What's his name?"

"Baldur."

"He reminds me of one I had in my childhood. The same color and tail." She glanced at Manfred's horse. "What's the name of your horse, Manfred?"

"Lucky."

"What a wonderful name!"

"I won him in a game of dice. But I think age is catching up with him."

"Let's go," Erich said. "We'll rest again after we cross the river."

Both men clutched their horses' bridles and went down a slope.

————

The family was nearing the Danube, but the numerous muddy patches on the road had hindered their progress. Cort sat hunched in the back of the rear wagon, gazing at the land they passed by. He had taken turns guiding the horses and performing tasks around the camp, but spoke little to anyone. They all understood that he missed his father and the wolves and hoped his sorrow would soon pass.

"Are we getting close to the ferry?" Anna asked her mother.

"I hope so," Catherine answered.

"We'll be there today if the road stays clear," Peter said.

"I'll feel so much safer when we do," Eva said.

They had traveled with another group of wagons the day before, which gave them a sense of security. However, that group took a different road in the morning, leaving them alone once again.

Thomas urged the horses forward at a brisk pace. As they rounded a bend, a peg-legged man appeared walking with a crutch and a bag slung over his shoulder. He turned to face them and raised his hand as they approached. Thomas slowed to a stop.

"No, Thomas," Peter muttered. "Don't stop here."

"What are you doing?" Gunther asked.

"Just seeing what he wants."

The man, a scruffy figure clad in tattered peasant rags, forced a smile, exposing his crooked and missing teeth.

"Thank you, good people," he said fawningly. "Can you give a poor soldier a ride to town?"

Max growled at him while Gunther scanned the area and nodded curtly.

The peg-leg reached out his hand to Gunther. "Just need help to get up."

As Gunther gripped his hand, the peg-leg jerked Gunther's arm, sending him tumbling to the ground. Just then, four men charged out from behind a thicket. Two of them ran to the lead wagon, and two went to the other.

The peg-leg pulled out a knife and attempted to stab Gunther, but Gunther kicked the crutch away, causing the peg-leg to topple. Gunther got to his feet, but a robber wearing a headscarf grabbed him around the shoulders. Another robber, large and strong, charged at Gunther with a raised club. Max bit down on his ankle. Annoyed by this, he tried to shake Max off. Thomas stayed on the wagon, slow to react as usual. The peg-leg crawled away from the fight.

Peter reached for a musket, but it was too late. A robber with a dirty gray beard lunged at him, brandishing a knife. Peter quickly grabbed a stick and fended him off with it.

"Father!" Rudi screamed.

Agatha climbed inside to be with the children. Catherine screamed as the graybeard attacked Peter. Anna cried in fright. All this roused Cort from his nap. Another robber, around Cort's age, tried to sneak in through the back, holding a crude sword.

"Behind you!" Agatha yelled.

Cort turned to face the young robber. They glared at each other for a moment, both filled with fear and surprise. He resembled a boy Cort had gone fishing with years ago, but now he looked much shabbier. Cort snatched a nearby pitchfork and thrust it at the robber, who took a step back.

Peter knocked the graybeard down. "Stay in the wagon," he said to Cort, "and protect the women! Take a crate to block the back! Guard the front!"

Cort pushed a crate to the back, blocking the rear entrance.

Gunther engaged in close combat with the robber wearing a scarf, throwing punches and delivering kicks. The larger assailant managed to strike Max, causing the dog to yelp and retreat. He then hit Gunther in the back. Stunned, Gunther turned to confront him but was struck squarely on the head again. He fell to the ground.

Thomas finally faced the situation when Gunther fell and jumped off.

Peter brought down the graybeard and struck him with a stick, but the young one grabbed him from behind. As Peter tried to shake him off, the graybeard landed punches to his gut and head.

Cort watched the fight with increasing concern. Gunther was down, and two men were approaching Thomas. Peter struggled to fend off the other two. He grabbed his bow to help Peter.

The scarfed robber swung at Thomas but missed. Thomas punched him down, but the larger one struck Thomas on the shoulder and head, momentarily stunning him. The wounded Gunther picked up the knife dropped by the peg-leg and crawled toward the scarfed robber, who was about to stab the dazed Thomas with his sword. He plunged the blade into the robber's leg, causing him to bellow and drop his sword. The big one marched over to Gunther and bashed him on the head. Gunther collapsed in a heap.

Thomas, more enraged than ever, charged the big robber, growling, with arms outstretched and fingers flexing.

During this, Max barked furiously at the attackers from a distance.

Cort snuck up behind the young robber, who still had Peter in his grips while the graybeard punched him. He shot the arrow and hit him in the midsection. He groaned and fell.

"Father, help me," he pleaded to the graybeard.

The big one swung at Thomas, who blocked the strike with his arm. Thomas grabbed his neck, still growling, and choked him. He let out a muffled scream as Thomas shook him by the neck. After Thomas dropped his lifeless body, he turned to face the scarfed robber, still sprawled on the ground from the knife wound. He managed to stand and raise his sword, mortified, as Thomas strode toward him.

The graybeard saw his son fall while fighting Peter. He sprang up, wrestled Cort to the ground, and punched him. Peter was still too groggy to help.

Seeing this, Agatha grabbed the pitchfork and sneaked up behind them. She lunged at him with the pitchfork, drove it into his back, and staggered back. The graybeard screamed and turned to her with bulging eyes and a reddened face as he tried to pull it out. He fell on his stomach with a thud next to Cort, gasping for breath. Peter rose, holding his head.

Agatha left to check on Gunther. Nearby, Thomas clubbed the scarfed robber's head again and again, sending spurts of blood into the air. He stopped when he realized he was dead and trudged toward the wagons. He passed by Agatha, staring straight ahead as if in a trance, and then proceeded to club the young robber.

The graybeard watched Thomas pummel his son with a helpless, pitiful resignation. He turned away as the beating continued and offered no resistance when Thomas came to him. Thomas pounded him a few times and pulled out the pitchfork. He hit him again and gaped at the body in a daze.

"He's dead, Thomas," Cort said, breathing heavily. "They're all dead."

Thomas dropped the club and shuffled toward Agatha, kneeling over Gunther.

Eva cradled Heloise and rushed to Peter, who was cut and bruised, with one eye swollen shut. They embraced, and she gently dabbed his wounds with tear-filled eyes. Rudi hugged his father. Catherine remained in the wagon, holding the whimpering Anna, both of them in shock from the violence.

"I thought this was the end of us," Eva said. "I'll cleanse your wounds."

"Let's see how Gunther is first."

Agatha looked up at them and shook her head. Blood flowed from a deep gash in his head, staining his gray hair. She lifted his hand and gazed at the silver wristband that Richard had given Gunther before he went off to battle. Overcome with emotion, she lowered his hand.

"I shouldn't have stopped," Thomas cried. "He told me not to."

"It's not your fault," Peter said. "They might have attacked us anyway."

"Hey," Cort said, "where is he?"

"Who?" Peter asked.

"The man with the crutch."

They spotted it on the ground, but there was no sign of the peg-leg. Max pricked up his ears, limped toward a thicket by the road, and barked fiercely. Thomas strode over and found him cowering in the bushes. He dragged him to the family and dropped him down. They all gathered around him.

The peg-leg squinted up at them with a piteous gaze. "Mercy!" he begged. "We're poor folk with no money or food."

"I'll finish him the same way," Thomas said, raising his club.

"Wait!" Agatha said. "Leave him be. There's been enough killing today."

"Look what he did to Gunther!" Cort exclaimed.

"Not by his hand. No. Let him be among his dead friends and dwell upon his condition. Maybe he'll realize the error of his ways before departing to the next world."

"Yes," the peg-leg pleaded. "I'll pray to God for forgiveness. I will."

"What about Gunther?" Peter asked.

"We'll give him a proper burial somewhere across the river," Agatha said. "Find a spot for him in the front wagon."

The peg-leg hobbled down the road in the opposite direction.

———

The hunters and their dogs were the best that Klaus had ever seen. The pack followed whichever lead dog had the scent; if that dog lost it, the others weaved around until one of them picked up the scent again—a sequence repeated many times without delay during the pursuit.

In the early afternoon, the men dismounted by a small stream to take in some water and food.

"How close are we?" Klaus asked Rolfe.

"I'd say we've made up half a day on them. If they stopped to rest at night, we might catch them by the end of the day."

"But if they didn't," another hunter said, "they might be able to cross the Iller before us. Then we'd have trouble picking up their trail. I bet that's their plan."

"You'll have to make sure it doesn't happen."

"I'll get them back on the trail now," Rolfe said.

———

A group of riders with a small supply wagon approached the family quickly from behind as they entered the outskirts of Günzburg. The riders slowed down as they rode alongside their wagons. One of them, wearing a local constable badge, signaled for Thomas to stop.

"Why are you stopping us?" Peter asked.

"We picked up a man along the road who said people in wagons attacked him," the constable said.

"What man?"

"In our wagon."

Peter and Cort recognized the peg-leg right away.

"What!" Cort shouted. "The dirty liar! They're the ones who attacked us!"

"What say you?" the constable asked the peg-leg.

"I told you what happened," the peg-leg rasped weakly.

"Do you believe him?" Peter asked.

"No. We took him because he matched the description of highwaymen robbing people here. We weren't sure until now. You said they attacked you?"

"This morning!" Cort interjected. "Four others! We killed them all! They killed one of us, too!"

"That's true," Peter answered, trying to remain calm. "It was them or us."

The constable eyed the cuts and bruises on Peter's face and arms and the rest of the family. "It looks like you were in quite a fight."

"They caught us by surprise. Were it not for our Thomas," Peter said, pointing ahead to him, "they would've taken us."

The constable shot a glance at Thomas. "Where are the others?"

"We dragged them off the road not far from here. Just past a stream and on the west side of the road."

"You've done the community a great favor. We've been trying to nab this bunch for over a fortnight. We might be able to reward you."

"But we have to catch the next ferry."

"You'll have to wait until tomorrow," another rider said. "The last one today just left."

Peter pondered the situation. "There is something you can do for us. Can we talk in private?"

The constable dismounted and followed Peter to the edge of the woods.

"We could use some help burying a member of our family here."

"Of course. I know the undertaker. A cemetery is close by."

"One more thing." He hesitated momentarily, but his concern about staying another day before crossing drove him to speak. "We're leaving because of our religious beliefs. And we might be pursued by some who will harm us. Can you and your men protect us until we cross tomorrow?"

The constable shook his head. "We've seen many like you come through here in the past few years for the same reason. It angers and saddens me to see this. Yes, we'll protect your family if needed."

———

When they arrived at the Iller, Erich recalled the fateful fishing trip from his youth with his friends, Leo and Klaus. Near the end of the day, Leo fell into the river and gashed his head on a rock, prompting Erich to dive in to save him. They were both swept downstream and stranded on a large flat rock all night in the middle of the raging river. He had never experienced such a fearful night beside the dying Leo as the waters rose, ready to engulf them. He was also confused and angry at Klaus's behavior. Klaus left them "to get help from others," he sneered. That was the beginning of his troubles with him, or perhaps it started earlier. It became far worse later on.

"This is where we're going to make them lose our trail," he said. "Manfred and I will guide the horses across." He turned to Mara. "You stay on Baldur until the other side. And then we'll head downstream along the bank. At some point, we'll walk inland and return to the river."

"A good plan," Manfred said. "Leave a false trail and escape farther downstream."

"Not quite," Erich said. "From there, we go back *upstream*. In the water so they won't see our tracks. And past this spot."

Mara and Manfred exchanged concerned glances.

"They'll track us with hunting dogs and capture us within a day if they find our trail after we cross. I doubt they'll go upstream first. This will be hard, but we'll rest afterward."

Neither of them complained. He was impressed by the way they both held up.

Both men took hold of their horses and started across. After a few steps, Lucky reared up and nearly sent Manfred into the water. "Whoa, boy," Manfred said as he tried to steady him. Once settled, he pulled on the reins, but Lucky wouldn't budge. "Come on, boy. You can do it."

Erich pulled Baldur back as Manfred continued to struggle with Lucky.

"There's nothing you can do. We have to leave him here."

Manfred stared forlornly at Lucky and nodded.

"We'll take the supplies off and onto Baldur."

After they finished, Manfred glanced back at Lucky, still standing at the bank.

"You take one side of the bridle," he said to Manfred, "and I'll take the other."

Both men guided Baldur across the river, with Mara in the saddle. Erich used his staff for balance and to measure the water's depth, while Manfred held a stick he'd found for the same purpose. The river flowed swiftly, yet the water never rose above their knees.

As they crossed, memories of being stranded on the rock surged back in Erich's mind. He fought to stave off a growing panic. Manfred nearly slipped several times, maintaining his grip on the bridle to regain his balance. Erich also stumbled but steadied himself with his staff. They paused on the other side.

You'll have to walk from now on," Erich said to her. "There's too much weight on Baldur now."

They headed downstream along the bank until they stopped to rest at an area where the forest was denser.

"Both of you go for a short distance and come back," Erich instructed. "Try to step on the same footprints. Meaning you'll have to walk backward for a while. I'll wait here."

Erich took out another piece of sausage. After a few bites, he began to doze off.

When they returned, he was asleep with his head down. Manfred nudged him to wake up. Mara took out more bread and sausage, and the three of them ate silently together.

They moved upstream, sloshing forward against the current. Erich took the lead, pulling Baldur by the reins. Mara gripped the bridle for support while Manfred walked behind her, holding onto the sad-dle horn. Soon, they passed the crossing point where Lucky clopped around in a circle on the other side.

Manfred shook his head and plunged forth, head down. He lost his patience a few times as they slogged along, muttering. Mara labored with each step.

Ahead, the river curved to the east.

"We'll go on land after we pass by the bend ahead," he said.

They staggered up the bank and stopped to rest, too exhausted to eat or drink.

"We'll make camp when we reach higher ground," he said. Wordlessly, they followed as he led Baldur up a woodsy slope. Mara halted when a distant sound sent a chill up her spine—barking dogs. Manfred nodded at her, hearing the same thing.

Erich continued to lead Baldur without indicating that he had heard this.

———

Klaus had been driving his men and the hunters all day, aware they were getting closer because of the dog's increased agitation. Near dusk, the barking and yelping grew louder, followed by the sound of a horse in distress. It had to be one of *their* horses!

When he rushed to the scene, two hunters were pulling the dogs away from an old horse that was cornered against a thicket of shrubs, kicking feebly at the dogs. The horse's flanks were streaked with blood where the dogs had savaged them. He rode over to Rolfe and another hunter.

"Any sign of them?" Klaus asked.

"No," Rolfe answered. "We found tracks leading to the river. They made it across but left this horse behind."

"They can't be too far ahead," the other hunter said. He glanced up to the sky. "Too dark to follow them now."

"We'll camp here tonight," Klaus said, "and resume the search by the first morning light."

"Our men and dogs are spent but not as much as those we're track-ing," Rolfe said. "They must've traveled the whole night without rest. We'll get them tomorrow."

"What about their horse?" the other hunter said.

Sigi rubbed his stomach with a grin. "Horse meat isn't so bad."

"Something for the dogs too," Rolfe said.

"Kill it," Klaus said.

———

The sound of a musket firing echoed from the valley below as they trudged up the slope. Mara and Manfred exchanged glances, but Erich kept walking once more.

Finally, they reached a flat stretch of ground. While waiting for the others to catch up, Erich noticed a nearby grove of trees.

"We'll camp here tonight," he said.

They followed him through the dim light to the campsite. Erich poured feed for Baldur while Manfred took out some sausage and cheese from his saddlebag for everyone.

"At least it hasn't snowed," she said.

"I almost hope it will," Erich said. "The snow will cover our trail."

"You were right about the dogs," Manfred said to Erich.

"What do you mean?"

"Didn't you hear them?"

He shook his head. "My hearing has been poor since the battles. That means they've reached the river."

"What about the musket fire?" Mara asked.

He shook his head again. "Maybe they were shooting at some game."

"Or—" Manfred began to say, then hit with a disturbing thought.

"Should we keep watch tonight?" Mara asked.

"No. They couldn't have picked up our trail yet. We all need sleep."

———

The family camped near the ferry landing to be first in line the next morning. Two of the constables' deputies stayed with them. After settling in, they gave Gunther a proper burial. The undertaker crafted a casket, etched Gunther's name on a rough stone marker, and enlisted other townsfolk to dig the grave in what served as the local cemetery. Everyone shared a few words in his memory. Agatha was the most affected by his death. Gunther and Richard had always been close, and his presence provided a connection to Richard for her.

Cort watched Peter talking to Thomas in hushed tones away from the rest of the family. They were keeping the truth from him again!

Peter stopped when Cort stormed toward them. "What are you talking about?" Cort demanded.

"About the trip ahead," Peter said.

"I don't believe you! You're hiding something from me."

Peter now realized that this deception couldn't go on. "Cort and I need to talk," he said to Thomas. He guided him farther away from the wagons.

"I was going to tell you this later, but I'll do it now. You mustn't tell your mother." He paused to gather his thoughts. "Some bad things are going on in the town and prison. People hurting each other—"

"I know. The tortures. The burnings. Father told me about it. But not everything."

"A woman in one of those trials must've greatly affected him. She's accused of being a witch and was about to be tortured and burned."

"So?"

"He's going to rescue her."

Cort struggled to understand. "Why would he do that?"

"I think everything he's seen in the prison finally got to him."

"What if they caught him?"

"No," said Peter. "He said freeing her would be easy with only one or two guards on duty. He'll cross the Iller river so they'd lose his trail. And then continue north to a town on the Rhein near Mainz, called Bingen, where the witch—I mean the woman—is from."

"How long will he be gone?"

"He figured it would be sometime after we arrive in Leipzig." He nodded at him. "So now you know."

"Yes, now I know."

————

Klaus couldn't sleep, troubled by the fact that he hadn't caught Erich yet. He stepped out of his tent several times and scanned the hills across the river for the unlikely sight of a campfire, tormented by the thought of returning to town empty-handed. But then he recalled his vow in the square to petition Duke Maximilian, which now carried more weight after Erich freed the witch. He began to formulate a plan, believing that if he wrote his petition in a certain way, he might find himself in a situation that could significantly increase his power in the community. Yes, that would ease the sting of not having caught him yet.

When he emerged from his tent in the morning, the slaughtered carcass of the horse lay near the campfire. He hadn't had horse meat in a long time, but it made for a filling meal. After eating more, he walked toward the hunters by the riverbank.

"What are our chances of finding them?" Klaus asked.

"It'll be hard in this cold weather, but at least it hasn't snowed," Rolfe answered. "They probably went downstream, so we'll try there first."

"I want him found today," he said. "As you said, he has to be close."

Klaus's hopes soared when they reached the other side, and the dogs immediately picked up the trail.

————

As the ferry approached, the family felt a mix of emotions about what lay ahead. The river served as a boundary between the familiar area around their home and the unknown roads to Leipzig.

Two oarsmen maneuvered the ferry between the wooden posts submerged in the water before the landing. Thomas and Peter guided their wagons onto it while the rest of the family got out of the wagons to stretch their legs.

Cort crept to the rear wagon, hidden from the family. After the last passenger boarded, he reached inside for a bag of supplies and food he had been filling the day and night before. Bertina crouched in front of the bag, staring at him. He pushed the cat away and grabbed it, then placed a small folded parchment in its place.

After the captain pushed off from the landing with a long pole, Cort tossed his bag onto the dock. As the ferry drifted away, he gripped his bow and leaped off.

"Ho boy! What are you doing?" the captain bellowed.

Catherine turned and saw Cort on the landing.

"Cort!" Catherine screamed. "Why is he not on?" she asked the captain.

"The crazy boy jumped off!"

"What? No! Turn around!"

"I cannot!" the captain answered.

The current pulled the ferry farther away. The oarsmen used all their effort to keep it on a straight course.

The rest of the family rushed to the back as Cort strode away. Catherine began to sob.

"Cort!" Peter yelled. "What are—?" But then it hit him.

"Why?" Catherine moaned.

"He wants to be with his father," Peter answered.

"But he'll be with us soon. Why couldn't he wait?"

He couldn't think of an answer.

His silence upset her even more. "Something else is going on!"

Agatha visualized Cort in the wilderness to meet his father and sensed he wouldn't make it alone—and then it came to her. She cupped her hands to her mouth and shouted to him.

"Cort! Cort!"

He turned around on the rise of land to face them.

"Go with the wolf!" The wind blew off a clasp holding her hair in place. Cort shook his head and cupped one ear.

"Go with the wolf!" she shouted louder as the wind blew her hair. Cort nodded and waved.

The family observed him from an ever-increasing distance until he was out of sight. Agatha went to check on Bertina.

"Can we come back for him?" Thomas asked.

"Not a good idea," Peter answered. "There might be danger on that side."

"What do you mean?" Catherine asked.

"I mean, more highwaymen."

"They'll get him!"

"They won't bother with one person."

"I can go back," Thomas said.

"We need you here with us."

"But he can't survive alone," Catherine pleaded.

"If anyone can, he can," Peter said. "He knows much about surviving in the woods. Erich taught him well. We'll see them both soon."

"Why, oh why," she said, shaking her head. "And where is he going?"

Agatha returned holding a parchment.

"This is from him," Agatha said, handing it to Catherine. "He wrote for us not to worry. He's going back to meet his father, like Peter said. They'll come back together and join us on the way to Leipzig."

Catherine still wasn't convinced. "But he's still a boy."

"He's not a boy anymore," Agatha said. "Not ever again."

———

The hunting party moved downstream until they reached a spot where the dogs dashed into the forest. The hunters trailed them until the dogs surrounded an area, sniffing the ground. Rolfe examined the footprints, noticing that they were considerably deeper at the toe than at the heel.

"Well?" Klaus asked.

"He's a smart one," Rolfe said. "They led us up a false trail, reversed it, and returned to the river. We'll get them soon, though."

The dogs hadn't found the scent as the day wore on, so Rolfe rode back to Klaus.

"Bad luck, sir, but we need to head back before nightfall. They couldn't have traveled this far downstream. I fear they might've gone back upstream in the water to trick us. Like I said, he's a smart one. Tomorrow, we'll search upriver."

"Tomorrow?" Klaus asked, "Why not today? We search until dark."

He reluctantly obliged.

Klaus and his henchmen waited for the hunters to catch up at the crossing point.

"We're going to the camp," Klaus said to Rolfe. "If you find the trail, mark the spot and go after them in the morning."

Rolfe glanced at his tired, panting dogs and headed upstream. He noticed rocks in the water that looked to have been recently dislodged a couple of times. He urged his men onward but stopped when he spotted snow clouds beginning to form. Ahead, the river curved to the east, and he pondered whether to continue. His men were exhausted from being on horseback all day, but more importantly, his dogs were spent. He signaled for them to turn back.

Klaus was disappointed but not surprised that they returned with the bad news.

"I found signs that they might have gone upstream," Rolfe said. "If so we'll have a good chance of finding their trail again."

————

The three of them sat on logs around their campsite, eating their rations and exhausted from climbing up and down hilly terrain. Erich had pushed them all day, knowing they needed to put more distance between themselves and their pursuers.

"Hear anything today?" Erich asked.

"Not I," Mara said.

Manfred shook his head but said nothing.

"Tomorrow, we'll make a fire."

"I shouldn't have taken him," Manfred said.

"If not for Lucky," Erich said, "we wouldn't have made it to the river in time."

"He served us well up to the end," Mara added.

Manfred nodded, wiping his eyes.

It started to snow just before dusk. They stayed sheltered from most of it within a dense grove of trees.

"No reason for a watch tonight," Erich said.

They crawled into their shelters and bundled up in their blankets.

———

Klaus gazed at the thin blanket of snow covering the ground the next morning with grim resignation. He strode toward the hunters huddled around the campfire. The hunters watched him warily as he approached, most of them aware of Klaus's hatred for Erich and uncertain how far he would push them and for how long.

"We'll head back right away," he said to them. "I don't want to get caught in a bigger storm out here."

"A wise decision, sir," Rolfe said with much relief.

This pursuit was over, but all night, he'd been working on his plan, which could make him wealthier and more powerful and provide him with the means to take revenge on Erich and his family. His failure to find them, along with the snowfall, turned out to be fortunate for him. God was surely on his side and had greater plans for him.

12.

Separate Ways

Cort trudged along the road, head down, absorbed in thought. He couldn't shake the memory of his family drifting away on the ferry, their troubled and helpless faces and his mother in tears. He hoped the note would ease their concerns.

He stopped to rest and stared down the bleak, barren road. He hadn't seen anyone all day. He untied the crude wooden frame cinched around his waist, which held his heavy leather supply sack. He made the frame right after leaving town by cutting and lashing several wooden branches together to loop the sack onto it. After eating cheese and sausage, he pounded down a walking stick he had found along the way and set off again. He recalled the words his grandmother had shouted to him about the wolf. As he trudged on, he wondered how, and if, he'd find it.

The first flakes of snow began to fall late in the afternoon. He was glad he wore such a sturdy pair of leather boots, which his father had made for him by the best shoemaker in town. With the two pairs of socks, his feet were warm and dry. His trousers, shirt, and sweater were crafted from the thickest fabric. He buttoned up his long deerskin coat, wrapped a scarf around his neck, and adjusted the woolen cap over his ears.

Later, the snow fell even heavier. At dusk, he set up camp in a thicket by the road. He chopped down a few branches, dug holes for them, drove the ends into the ground, and draped an old canvas sheet he had brought over the sticks—a simple shelter, just as his father had taught him to build. He spread cut tree branches over the canvas and crawled inside.

He peered out of the shelter, huddled in the blankets, watching the snow fall while chewing a piece of bread. As he ate, he thought more about the journey ahead. He had enough food for a week at most, but he'd have to rely on his hunting skills afterward. He possessed a bow, a knife, an axe, a few coins he'd been saving, and some flints. Fire. This realization made him understand that he needed to begin scraping the moss off tree trunks and place it in a separate small bag to dry. His father taught him how to start a fire by striking the flints into dried moss, a process he repeated many times on his own.

When he woke up, the snow had ceased falling. After eating, he gathered his supplies and set out. Soon, the sun broke through the clouds, warming the air. Clumps of melting snow tumbled down from the trees along the way.

A supply wagon rumbled toward him later that morning, the first person he had seen since leaving the town. After it passed, he walked along the tracks, which made the journey easier.

Around midday, four horsemen galloped toward him, churning the slush behind them. He stepped off the road to let them pass. As they drew near, he thought he recognized one of Klaus's men, Lothar. He lowered his head and pulled his hat down as they rumbled by.

Another wagon approached him from the back in the afternoon. He raised his hand, signaling for a lift. The driver, an older man with a full white beard, slowed to a stop.

"Thank you for stopping, Mister," he said. "I sure could use a ride."

"How far are you going?" he asked gruffly.

"To a farm this side of Ulm."

"I'm going to Ulm, so I'll drop you off there."

He climbed to the back of the wagon. "I won't be any trouble. And can share some food if you want."

The driver nodded and urged his horses onward. Once settled, he realized this would give him a chance to rest and likely save him at least three days of walking.

———

Mara gazed up at the multitude of stars in the night sky, marking the first cloudless night since their trek through the endless forest had begun the week before. A faint sliver of moon hung low on the horizon. She had always slept soundly until morning, but not this night. She attempted to settle deeper into her shelter several times to sleep, but her growing concern about their situation kept her awake.

Her worries began the day after the first campfire. They were still deep in the woods, with no path to follow. Sometimes, they traveled down a slope for most of the day, only to find themselves climbing back up to an area with less vegetation. More than once, Manfred admitted that he was lost. Erich reassured them that they were heading in the right direction and would soon encounter a road or village.

Erich's health also worried her. He started coughing after the first snowfall, and it became more frequent and severe in the following days. She made a soup from their rations and added some bark from a tree with healing properties that she had peeled along the way. It helped him through the night, allowing him to sleep restfully.

———

The next day, her spirits lifted when she spotted an eagle soaring above, comparable in wingspan to one she had noticed the day before. She made sure they both saw the eagle and felt encouraged that they were heading in the same direction as its flight. However, they soon took a different path from where the eagle had flown. She tried to suppress her doubts but ultimately spoke up.

"Why are we going this way?" she asked as she stood her ground behind them.

"What do you mean?" Erich asked.

"I think we should keep going here," she said, pointing a different way.

"But why?"

"Because—"

"Ah, the eagle," Erich said with a smile. "I'll tell you what. We'll go to the top of the ridge for a better view."

He scanned the horizon from the crest. One way went along the ridge, and the other dropped into the forest—the direction the eagle took. He decided to heed her advice.

They trudged along until they entered a spacious meadow. About halfway through, Erich fixed his gaze on something on the ground in the distance. They followed him until he stopped in front of a narrow path that barely cut through the vegetation.

"A good sign," Manfred said. "Now which way?"

"You were right earlier today," he said to Mara. "We'll keep going in the same way."

The path became more distinct as they continued. Shortly thereafter, it merged with a larger one. They had to be on the right track now. As the day neared its end, they entered a clearing and came upon a long, wide road marked by recent wagon tracks. The Danube was visible in the distance. A small wooden sign resting on a stack of stones beside them indicated where the path entered the forest. Finally, they were out of the wilderness.

They sat by the road to rest and eat. Fresh clumps of dung were scattered nearby, faintly steaming in the cold air.

"Look," she said, pointing to the clumps, "someone must have just passed by here."

"No doubt," Erich said. "I don't think I've ever been so glad to see a pile of dung."

"All this time in the woods," Manfred said with a hearty laugh. "And the first sign of civilization is this dung."

"A good omen!" she exclaimed.

Erich stood and surveyed the area while stifling a cough. "There should be some towns if we keep going west."

"Too late to travel far today," Manfred said.

"Perhaps we can take shelter there," Mara said, pointing to an old farmhouse across the road.

The building had long been abandoned, with a few pieces of broken furniture left behind. Still, it was better than the conditions they had just endured. Best of all, it had a functioning fireplace. They dismantled the furniture and huddled around the crackling fire. They ate their meager rations, hoping to find a town soon to replenish their food and supplies. Mara held a small ceremony before the meal, giving thanks to the helpful spirits for guiding them out of the wilderness. She offered Erich more of the bark and vegetable brew for his cough. They all slept soundly that night.

Cort bounded down the hillside toward the family farm. Inside the house, he searched for items that might be useful along the way. He found some old sewing needles that he could bend and use as fishing hooks. He also salvaged a few rusted kitchen utensils, more twine, plenty of used flints next to the fireplace, an old blanket, some fabric, torn shirts, and socks.

His father's old shirt made him realize he needed to go into town and visit Jacob to ensure he hadn't been caught. He also had another idea for what to do with the shirt. He left right away since it was only mid-morning. Soon after, he got on the main road and hopped onto a supply wagon heading to Ulm.

He walked through town with his hat pulled down and skirted along buildings so as not to be conspicuous. Whenever someone came toward him, he turned away, always alert for a familiar face to avoid. He dreaded the thought of anyone recognizing him and calling out his name.

He peered through the shutters of the Sheriff's office, where Jacob sat by his desk. He took a deep breath and went in.

It took a moment for Jacob to recognize him. "Cort? My God! What are you doing here?" He sensed Cort's apprehension. "Don't worry, son. You're safe with me. But where's your family?"

"I left them. They're on their way to Leipzig. I came to find out if Father is here."

"They tracked him to the Iller and lost his trail. Did anyone tell you what he did?"

"Peter said he freed a witch from jail."

"He did that and more. He's in much trouble now. There's nothing I can do to help him this time. People are stirred up because of what he did. Some support him, others do not. Tensions have increased. Klaus is going to the Duke in München to bring more soldiers to the town. To restore *order*, he said. Things are getting worse here for the Protestants."

"What did you mean," Cort asked, "when you said *and more*?"

"They stabbed a guard during the escape, who later died. They also freed a youth about your age. The poor boy didn't do anything bad. He fought with other boys and liked to howl like a wolf. We went to his parents' home and found them dead. Their heads bashed in."

Jacob's description of the youth sounded familiar. "Someone about my age, you say?"

"That's right. Did you know him?"

"What's his name?"

"Gumprecht. His family lived south of town."

"Tall? Long black hair with a pointed nose?"

"That describes him pretty well."

He remembered their brief times together and how they had met in the woods. Soon, they started talking and later shared food over a campfire. He liked being called Gumpy. Gumpy sometimes complained about his strict parents, who often beat him, and he always had a wild, distant look in his eyes. He also liked wolves and even imitated their howl, which made Cort laugh. But he hadn't seen him in months.

"What happened to him?"

"We captured him in a cave a few days later and, well, for such a crime, they sentenced him to the wheel."

Cort winced. He'd only seen one victim tortured on the wheel, but that was enough. He'd been walking alone near the market square when he heard someone screaming in pain behind a raucous crowd. He never saw the executioner crush the man's limbs with a heavy bar against the large wheel and then wrap the victim's broken arms and legs around the spokes, but watched them raise the wheel with the victim on it. He couldn't imagine the terrible pain he must've been in, writhing on the wheel, his crushed limbs wrapped around the spokes. It sometimes took all day for people to die after the authorities left them hanging as an example for anyone thinking about committing similar crimes.

"What are you going to do now?" Jacob asked

"I'm going to find my father!"

Jacob recalled the meals with their family when he was a boy, but now on the verge of manhood by the look of it. "You know where he's going?"

Cort bit his lip.

"Keep it to yourself then. He's five or six days ahead of you by now. How do you expect to catch up to him?"

"I can and will."

"What will you do for food and shelter?"

"I can survive on my own."

"It won't be easy this time of the year."

"I have some coins."

"Probably not enough."

Jacob opened a drawer in his desk and handed him a hefty pouch of coins.

"I don't want to get you in trouble."

"Take it!" he bellowed, "or I *will* throw you in jail. For your protection!"

Cort took the pouch, stifling a smile.

"Here's something else," Jacob said. He reached into a cabinet and gave Cort an ample supply of cheese and sausages. "Eat this until you arrive at the next town. Do *not* buy anything here."

"I'll tell my father of your kindness."

"And tell him we'll all go hunting together again when he returns. Now go!"

He wanted to ask one more thing. "Did this woman he went with have a horse, too?"

"No. The hunters later told me they only have one horse, your father's, among the three. So they'll be on foot, which might help your chances of catching up."

"The *three* of them?"

"Yes, a guard named Manfred helped in the escape."

Cort cinched up his pack and took his walking stick. They shook hands.

"Goodbye, Jacob."

"Goodbye, Cort. May God be with you." He pulled down his hat and went outside.

As Cort walked away, Jacob reflected on his time with their family and how much had changed since those days. He had witnessed many families leave the area, but this one was the hardest to bear. After Cort ducked around a corner, Jacob felt that somehow, in some way, he would find his father. He also sensed, with great sadness, that he would never see him, or his father, again.

———

Cort returned to the farm before dark after catching another ride. First, he built a sturdier frame for his backpack. He tried to pack everything as efficiently as possible: the warm blankets, extra sets of clothes, the shelter material, loops for hanging the ax and small bow and arrow, a smaller bag for all the food, and another one for the flints, moss, and other items. He feasted on the sausage and cheese Jacob had given him.

In bed, he recalled how comfortable and safe he felt at night listening to his family shuffling around in the other rooms, their muffled voices resonating in the background. Now, a deathly silence pervaded the place. He wouldn't have even minded Thomas's snoring now. On some nights, another sound filled him with wonder; the far-off howling of a wolf. He listened for it as he tossed and turned under a blanket until he eventually fell asleep.

A distant howling during the night awakened him. Was the wolf close by? He'd find out in the morning.

He woke at first light, invigorated by food and sleep, eager to begin. He had been to the Iller a few times to fish, so he knew the way. He made sure to grab one of his father's torn shirts. As he walked through the pasture, he foraged for potatoes, cabbages, and turnips, tossing them into his bag. He climbed the hill above the farm and made his way to the meadow where he shot arrows with his father and often played with the wolf. Sometimes, it appeared when he least expected it, while at other times, he called it with a whistle. He cupped his hands and whistled, sat down, and waited.

A short time later, he sensed the wolf nearby and turned his attention to an area in the woods—and there it stood! It loped toward him, its ears pricked and eyes fixed on him. He began to feel the same deep connection to the wolf's spirit as it approached. Cort braced himself before the wolf reared up, jumped onto his shoulders, and licked his head and face. Cort returned its licks with some of his own. He lifted its paws and set it down.

"Good to see you, my friend! Were you howling last night?"

The wolf stared intently at him.

Once more, he recalled the words of his grandmother. And then it came to him. "I will go—*and follow*—the wolf," he whispered. The thoughts that occurred to him the night before were now much clearer. "Want to take a trip with me?"

The wolf watched his every movement as he reached inside his pack and pulled out his father's old shirt. He extended it to the wolf.

It briefly sniffed the shirt and looked back up at him, so he exposed a different part.

It sniffed the shirt longer this time, raised its head, and let out a short howl.

"You know the smell!" He made a waving motion with his hand. "Show me!"

The wolf stood, unable to comprehend the command. Cort pushed the shirt under the wolf's nose for it to sniff and repeated the hand gesture. The wolf pricked its ears and ambled away. Initially, it followed the meadow's edge before ducking into the forest, nose to the ground. Cort struggled to keep pace as it navigated the difficult terrain. Eventually, it slowed down and stood beside the remnants of food, bones, and numerous hoof prints.

He tossed some pieces of bread and sausage to the wolf. "I'll give you a name soon. It'll be a good name for a big, strong wolf like you!"

He made the same waving motion with his hand. "Now show me the way!"

The wolf turned and loped away slowly, allowing him to follow more easily.

———

Manfred guided Baldur behind Erich and Mara along the road. Earlier in the day, they passed two abandoned farms and, later, another charred farmhouse with only the chimney left standing. Near the end of the day, they stopped by the remains of a small roadside village, where most buildings were burned or nearly collapsed. Erich had never known that such widespread looting and destruction of the countryside had reached this far south.

The following day, travelers arriving from the opposite direction informed them that the town of Riedlingen, which had a ferry crossing, was just a day's journey away. Mara recognized the town's name, having served as a midwife there the previous year.

In the evening, he and Manfred sat together by a campfire eating the last of their food.

Manfred gnawed on a crust of bread. "I can't wait to have some real food soon."

"We'll have to buy all the provisions Baldur can carry," Erich said, stifling a cough. "I would've brought more if I knew things were this bad."

"We should rest there, too," Manfred said. "Especially Mara." He scanned the campsite. "I wonder where she is."

Erich stood, alarmed, and grabbed his staff. "I warned her not to go off alone!"

Just then, she emerged from the woods. "Where have you been?" he demanded.

"Oh," she answered with surprise, detecting his concern. "I found plants to help your cough. I didn't stray far."

She arranged and cut the plants as they ate.

Before they settled in for the night, she poured steaming water into a cup and dipped a thin cloth pouch filled with herbs and roots.

"This will reduce the cough during the night," she said. "What you need most is to rest in the town tomorrow."

"We needn't stay too long because of that," he said.

"I fear the poison within you has taken hold and gotten deeper. You're getting weaker each day."

Erich cleared his throat. "Perhaps you're right."

"I haven't told you this," she added, "but I've been to Riedlingen. A shop sells roots and plants with healing properties. Some will cleanse your body of the poisons."

She handed him the cup. Erich examined the dark green contents. "I remember this smell. My mother gave me some when I fell ill as a child." He took a few sips.

"These are from the leaves of a thyme plant. It will ease your cough but may not cure you." She poured him more after he finished. "Your mother knows about the healing arts?"

"She has some skill."

"Nature abounds with gifts that can heal many afflictions. But alas they are not used much anymore."

"I tell you what," Manfred said. "I'd rather chew plants than have some apothecary put those leeches on me."

"Such cures are sometimes useful but most often overdone. They should be combined with other remedies, if at all."

"Where did you learn this?" Erich asked.

"Some from other midwives in my travels. And from what I learned in the Bingen convent where I was raised." She shot him a glance. "In the meantime, on our journey together—however long it will be—I'll show you the plants and herbs that will keep you in good spirits and health."

He finished the drink and stifled a cough.

"I'll give you more tomorrow. For now, you should rest."

As he drifted off to sleep, he thought more about their upcoming journey and the words she spoke: *However long it will be.*

———

The family traveled north toward Leipzig alongside other wagons. They had left Nürnberg in the morning, where they stayed for a few days to wait out a snowstorm and for additional wagons to join them. A town official informed Peter that it was unsafe for them to journey alone due to highwaymen preying on small groups along the road.

Catherine lay bundled on a cot for most of the time, despondent that Erich had not yet met them. The family tried to cheer her up, but she still couldn't shake the feeling that Peter and Agatha were hiding something from her. Even worse, she had been experiencing stomach ailments that began before they arrived in Nürnberg. Agatha gave her tea for relief, but she continued to feel sick, often in the mornings.

———

Cort reached the Iller toward the end of the second day. During the trek, he felt safe and protected beside the wolf—especially at night—and realized how fearful it would have been for him otherwise. The wolf had picked up the scent after they left the farm, but at times, it seemed to have lost it. Fortunately, they always managed to find the scent again, reminding him of how dogs performed on hunting trips with his father.

As he scouted for a place to camp, he came across a large, recently burned fire pit, likely left by the men tracking his father. Nearby lay the carcass of a horse, and the wolf tore at the remaining meat on the bones.

He decided to build his first fire inside the pit. He chopped smaller branches and twigs for kindling and thicker ones to place on top. He piled them next to the pit, formed a small circle of rocks, and added the dried moss. After several strikes of flint, the moss ignited, and he blew on the flame. The flame grew as he added more kindling and logs. Soon, he had a crackling blaze. At last, he could boil the potatoes and turnips he foraged from the farm.

He chewed on one of Jacob's sausages as the wolf circled a few spruce trees, marking the territory around the campsite. And then he had an idea. He rubbed the wolf's head after it sat down next to him.

"Maybe that's what I'll call you—Spruce. Yes, Spruce!" he said in a louder voice.

It looked up at him, ears pricked.

"Spruce!" he shouted again.

The wolf now had a name.

He gazed at the embers of the dying fire from beneath the blankets in his shelter, contemplating where to go after crossing the river. He recalled a story his father had told him over a campfire about his time as an officer during the War. He and his men were in a forest, cut off from the rest of their division. As the Imperial troops pursued them, they crossed a river and traveled upstream through difficult terrain. He remembered how his father emphasized the word "upstream." The pursuers lost the trail, and they made it back to their division. That was the lesson his father imparted to him: whenever someone is pursued or tracked, he said, they should always take the hardest route possible, especially when crossing a river.

Cort drifted off to sleep, planning to head upstream the next morning. It was just a hunch, but a strong one.

———

Erich peered down through the shutters of the second-floor window at the bustling streets below. Riedlingen resembled Ulm—a "strong town"—surrounded by walls on all sides. Boats and rafts of various sizes floated along the Danube. He slept well that night but didn't eat much before drifting back to sleep. In the morning, Manfred accompanied Mara to the shop that sold remedies for his illness.

As he rose to pour a cup of water, dizziness overcame him, forcing him to steady himself against the wall. His throat and chest ached from coughing. After taking another sip, he thought about his family for the first time since the pursuit began. He hoped that seeing Peter, Gunther, Thomas, and even Cort would be enough to deter any highwaymen. Although he wanted to go to the stable to check on Baldur, he felt too weak to climb the inn's stairs. A deep chill made him shiver, so he settled back into the bunk and fell asleep instantly.

He awoke to the feeling of a cool, damp cloth on his forehead. Mara looked at him with concern in the candlelight, and Manfred stood behind her.

"You must drink this soup now," she said.

He struggled to sit up and coughed to clear his throat. "I didn't feel this bad before. Just since coming here."

"I fear you wouldn't have lasted much longer on the road," she said. "This rest and food are overdue." She handed him a steaming bowl. "The cold air has trapped poisons in your chest, which must be flushed out. Otherwise, your condition will worsen."

Erich grasped the bowl and examined the contents floating in a brownish-green liquid. He sniffed the steam and jerked his head back. "What's in it?"

"Some common plants used in the kitchen," she said. "Chives, fennel, cabbage leaves, horseradish, and onions. Also, some other medicinal herbs. Drink it now. I'll give you more. You'll have some discomfort in your stomach soon, but it will pass."

After he finished, he slumped back in the bunk.

They stayed up all night tending to his health. During that time, he experienced more stomach cramps, followed by episodes of diarrhea. They took turns sleeping the next day while keeping an eye on his condition. His fever broke in the afternoon. Afterward, they provided him with more fluids before he collapsed from exhaustion.

He slept for over a day and woke up feeling weak but recovered.

———

Cort crouched behind a bush at the edge of the forest and watched a train of wagons on the road ahead. Spruce sat beside him. They had been trekking through the wilderness for three days since leaving the Iller, but now, amid more populated areas, a new concern arose—what to do about Spruce? He needed to find ways to bypass the villages and towns with the wolf.

It didn't take long for Spruce to find the scent after they traveled upstream from the Iller. They had trekked over rough terrain, and several times he lost the scent; however, after discovering a crude path in a meadow, they picked it up again and tracked it to this spot.

He set up the shelter near their vantage point. He devoured the last potato, some stale cheese, and crusty bread. Spruce watched him as he ate.

"Sorry, nothing for you today."

When he woke up, Spruce was gone, but it didn't bother him, as he often wandered away from the campsite for short periods. After he had packed, Spruce still hadn't returned, so he sat on a log waiting for him to come back. Pangs of hunger gnawed at his stomach, and he grew impatient to leave.

As the morning wore on, he realized that the wolf might not return. He remembered how jittery Spruce had been near the road and how hungry he must have felt after many days of living off scraps. Perhaps this was the end of it, he thought. Spruce had led him out of the wilderness but couldn't travel farther with him. Around midday, he reluctantly set out.

Soon afterward, he passed a small village. Most of the buildings were burned, but a few remained intact, so he decided to investigate. There was no sign of life as he walked past them. He entered one of the houses and found some kitchen utensils, clothing, and—best of all— five candles of various lengths. He stuffed them into his pack. After entering another room, he came to a dead stop, covering his nose; a rotting corpse lay on the bed, half-covered with a thin blanket. He scampered out of the building and left the village.

Toward the end of the day, two groups of wagons passed by him. One raced past as he tried to ask for food. The other, a family, stopped and offered him a few crusts of bread out of pity for his condition after he mentioned he was searching for his father. They informed him that the nearest town was a day away.

Just before dark, he stumbled upon an abandoned farmhouse not far from the road and made his way toward it. The rooms were bare except for an old bucksaw, rusted and dull, resting by the fireplace. He spent the night there, shielded from the cold wind, but hungry and feeling lonelier than ever without Spruce.

———

The family gazed at the outskirts of Leipzig across the Pleise River as they waited for the next ferry—the culmination of a long journey. As time passed, the stress of being on the road for so long took its toll on all of them. Peter struggled to keep his spirits up after days of trudging along the muddy paths, constantly alert for danger. Agatha found ways to uplift their morale, reminding them how much worse things could have been and that their situation was only temporary.

The trip had the greatest impact on Catherine. Agatha, Eva, and even Anna were unable to lift her spirits. Her stomach illness per- sisted throughout the journey, sometimes accompanied by vomit- ing. Agatha speculated that the rolling motions of the wagon might be affecting her, but she also considered that it could be something else. She advised Eva to spend more time with Catherine to monitor her condition.

Peter and Thomas guided the wagons on the ferry. Anna huddled between Eva and Catherine. "Aren't you glad we're here, mother?" Anna asked. Catherine barely acknowledged her.

"You and Rudi will make many new friends here," Peter said.

Rudi jumped up and shouted with joy.

"Will Father be there too?" Anna asked.

Catherine turned away and stifled sobs.

The family sat in weary silence as the ferry glided across the river.

13.

An Audience with the Duke

Klaus sat on a wooden bench in an antechamber of Duke Maximilian's court, ramrod straight in his soldier's uniform, staring at the entrance door as if in a trance. Sigi, Horst, and Ernst played a game of cards behind him.

"You think they'll see us today?" Sigi asked, to no one in particular.

Klaus remained silent and unmoved in his position.

Ernst threw his cards down and paced the room. "How soon before they—"

"Be patient," Klaus interjected. "This is a test of our loyalty. We'll wait here all day. And the next if needed."

The three of them rolled their eyes with strained obedience.

He had to remain firm and resolute in front of his men, but he was increasingly concerned that his petition hadn't been taken seriously. He wondered if he should have added more urgent language, even though much of what he wrote was fabricated.

A short time later, the Court Page entered, holding a scroll. He glanced at Klaus and signaled a well-dressed older couple on the other side of the room to follow him.

"Sir, may I ask when the Duke will receive us?" Klaus asked the Page.

"You're next on the list," he replied curtly.

"That's what they said yesterday," Horst whispered to Ernst and Sigi.

As the day wore on, Klaus's men became more impatient.

"I'm hungry," Sigi said. "Why not get some food now?"

"I'm for that," Ernst said.

Klaus turned and glared at them. "We'll stay until they tell us otherwise. I need you with me to show I'm not acting alone."

The Page entered later in the afternoon and acknowledged Klaus. "The Duke will see you now."

He adjusted his eye patch and followed the Page through the door.

———

Two soldiers escorted them as they emerged into the spacious and ornate court adorned with formal paintings, portraits, religious artifacts, and military ornaments hanging from the richly detailed woodwork. Various court attendants, officials, and aristocrats observed them with curiosity. He walked with a confident, proud stride while his men shuffled behind him.

The Duke sat on a throne atop the dais in the main room. Beside him stood a man clad in long black robes, a glittering crucifix hanging from a chain around his neck. Others, likely members of the Duke's family and certainly of noble birth, also occupied the elevated area near him. Klaus focused on the man standing next to the Duke: his Jesuit Confessor. He felt a twinge of regret for the death of his previous Confessor—Adam Contzen—just a few months earlier. As a result, he had forged a friendship with Contzen and gained prominence within the Catholic League. This Confessor, Father Helmut, was younger than Contzen, possessing darker features and a soldier's strong, upright physique. He remembered encountering him after one of Contzen's sermons.

They halted in front of the dais. The Page read from the petition, which requested that Klaus be granted the authority to suppress "acts of rebellion and insurrection in the city of Ulm."

"We have reviewed your petition," Maximilian said, "and became aroused at the word *insurrection*—a serious matter. Why hadn't this been reported before now?"

"Because it has just begun, Your Eminence," Klaus answered. "My men and I tried to stop it, but the mob overtook us."

"What caused this mob to act?" Helmut asked.

"It's not *what* caused them, but *who*. A Protestant who incited the citizens to rebel. Local authorities can document all this."

"When did this occur?" Maximilian asked.

"Almost one month ago."

"Why did you take so long to inform us of this?"

He was about to declare that he had sent the petition three weeks earlier but noticed a concern in Helmut's expression. He sensed that the delay might have been tied to Helmut's handling of such petitions and opted to shift the blame away from him.

He tried to maintain his composure. "You are correct, Your Eminence. I should've drafted it right away, considering the seriousness of the situation. But I'd been in the care of an apothecary since the fight with the mob. This same man broke into the local prison, cut down one of my men and freed all the criminals, including a notorious witch. He and another guard absconded with her. We tracked them for three days but lost their trail in the snow."

"The delay in your petition is understandable," Helmut said.

Klaus noted a slight smile on Helmut's otherwise cold expression. He sensed he had gained considerable support from Helmut by taking the blame for the delay onto himself.

"We've heard of incidents in the area but nothing like this," Maximilian said with renewed interest and concern. "Who is the man responsible for it?"

"His name is in the petition," Klaus answered. "He comes from a Protestant family that's previously taken up arms against the Empire."

Helmut gave the petition to Maximilian and indicated a spot on it.

"I know this family," Maximilian said while reading it. "The man's father—Richard—was an assistant to the Elector in Ulm."

"He's a traitor to the Empire," Helmut said, his anger rising. "A man of lower nobility who fought beside the infidel Adolphus. His son also fought in the wars, and now his heinous actions have disrupted the peace in the town. This is what I've been saying all along. The Edict and Peace didn't go far enough and did nothing but appease the unbelievers." He turned to Klaus. "Tell us more of what this man did."

Helmut's enthusiasm fueled his confidence, and he proceeded with renewed assurance. "He brandished a banned weapon, a bow, before the crowd, inciting them to take up arms so they could free themselves from the yoke, as he stated, of the *oppressors in Vienna.*"

Klaus took pleasure in hearing the audience's groans of disapproval. The words he had rehearsed many times had drawn the desired response.

"How can a simple bow be a banned weapon?" Maximillian asked.

"It's more than just a simple bow. It's a longbow that's been with their family for centuries. They used it in battles against the Holy Alliance."

"A long black bow?" Maximilian asked.

"Yes."

"Interesting." The court waited for him to continue. "I remember seeing his father, Richard, use it in an archery contest years ago. He beat our best man with a remarkable shot."

"Some say the bow has magical powers," Klaus said, again recalling the words he'd rehearsed. "But it's only the Protestants who've fallen under the sway of this false idol."

"This is precisely why such things are so dangerous!" Helmut declared while stroking his crucifix with increased agitation. "It's not so much the damage they do in warfare but how they poison the people's minds like all satanic objects and artifacts. They must be eradicated! And all those who use them to foment rebellion against the Church."

"There is no peace in Ulm anymore," Klaus said. "The citizens are divided between those who support him and those who do not. That's why I seek the authority to put down the rebellion and establish order in the town."

Helmut turned and spoke to the Duke. "Your Eminence, we can use the incident to our advantage. This would justify retrieving the lands taken from us by the Peace."

"A call to arms?" Maximilian questioned. "To break the truce we've negotiated with them?"

Helmut pressed on. "But this and other reported incidents have already broken the agreement. The Protestants are becoming increasingly rebellious! We must respond firmly before the rebellion escalates and restore what we possessed before the cataclysm caused by the treacherous Luther!"

Helmut could tell Maximilian wasn't convinced, so he bent down and whispered in his ear. "The salvation of your very soul in the eyes of God depends on how you defend the true faith from the unbelievers." He stepped back and waited for a response.

The Duke shut his eyes, thinking. Gradually, he assumed his authoritative pose.

"Our records show that you rose to the rank of sergeant in our service," Maximilian stated while reading the petition.

Klaus stiffened his posture. "I fought with Wallenstein at Dessau and Stralsund and Frankfurt. And with Tilly at Potsdam and Magdeburg."

"Magdeburg?" Helmut asked.

"Yes. I served with faith and honor for the great general."

Helmut faced the dignitaries in the audience. "*Honor* is not a word I would use to describe the campaign in Magdeburg."

Klaus realized that he might've blundered. The atrocities by the Imperial forces against the defenseless Protestant population were a painful subject for many.

"And yet *fidelity*," Helmut said, "is a virtue becoming more difficult to maintain in these troubled times. When far too often people shift their alliances in the face of danger to save their skin. People whom we thought could be trusted." He noted the discomfort from some in the Court with grim satisfaction. He faced Klaus. "But you've been unwavering in your support in defense of the Empire. Your actions and wounds speak for themselves. As guardians of the Catholic League, we look favorably upon your petition." He turned to Maximilian.

"Your service should be rewarded and used as an example for all to follow," Maximillian told Klaus. He motioned to a scribe sitting next to him, holding a quill. "Based on your experience and exemplary record, I will sign an Order promoting you to the rank of Captain. The Court will draft a Letter of Appointment before you leave tomorrow. You will present this Letter to the authorities in Ulm. It will give you the authority and access to whatever funds are necessary to conscript a company of men. You will use them to restore peace in Ulm and other regional towns. You'll receive orders to join a larger force later."

Helmut nodded his approval.

Klaus bowed. "I thank Your Eminence for this honor."

With a wave of Maximilian's hand, the soldiers escorted Klaus back through the Court. Sigi, Ernst, and Horst trailed behind, now regarding Klaus with renewed awe.

14.

Across the Danube

Baldur's hooves cracked through a thin layer of ice of a stream as Manfred pulled him across. Erich and Mara walked together ahead of him. Ever since they had left Riedlingen and crossed the Danube a few days before, he'd been watching them share their thoughts and observations along the way. She often pointed out things in nature that they passed by on the trail. In turn, Erich told her what to look for when hunting in the forest. At day's end, they discussed them around the campfire. The previous night, she had informed them about the little yellow flowers growing near the streams that stop blood flow from wounds when ground up and applied as a paste. The same flowers would bring a restful sleep if drunk as tea.

As they walked, Manfred realized he had been plodding along aimlessly, living each day without any real thought for the future. Now, with them, he felt a joyful spirit awaken—an emotion that had long been dormant since his time in prison. He planned to leave when they reached the first town, but no more. He had started to respect them and sensed that they felt the same way about him.

He had also been aware of his growing feelings for Mara. He found himself attracted to all the nuances of her appearance and behavior, from the graceful way she walked to her laughter and speech. He understood why she spent more time with Erich; however, he was married. This gave him hope, albeit faint, that his relationship with her might develop as the journey progressed.

On the fourth day from the Danube, they stopped in the small town of Albstadt to replenish their supplies and food. Most residents were simple craftsmen, hunters, or fishermen. Erich studied a travel guide the innkeeper had shown them, indicating one road from Balingen to Horb. The innkeeper also pointed out other roads branching away from Horb, including one heading west toward the Rhein.

———

Cort walked along the road in a forlorn mood because the night before had been the first without Spruce. He missed keeping warm with the wolf on the cold nights and felt less safe since Spruce's markings around the campsites kept other animals away. In the morning, people in a passing wagon told him that Riedlingen was nearby. He figured his father had taken a ferry across the Danube there, but he couldn't be sure. From now on, he would have to rely on his sense of direction and seek help from people along the way.

As dusk approached, he had not yet reached the town and began searching for a campsite. Soon, an odd sensation stirred in his stomach, reminiscent of the times he had hunted with his father just before encountering the animals they had been tracking. He stopped and scanned the area. Everything was still and silent. The skies were gray and darkening. A rustling sound in the woods caught his attention. He turned and noticed movement in the bushes. He reached behind his shoulder and pulled out his bow, never taking his eyes off the spot.

A wolf emerged from the thicket.

"Spruce!"

Spruce loped to him, jumped on Cort's shoulders, and licked his face. Dark red blood stains streaked around his chops.

"So you've been hunting! Come. We'll make camp now!"

They arrived at the outskirts of Riedlingen in the morning. He set up his shelter away from the road and prepared to go into town for food and supplies. Spruce tried to follow him, but Cort led him back. After three attempts, Spruce stayed behind.

Once there, he bought more food, socks, and gloves. He often accompanied his family to the market in Ulm and knew how to strike a bargain with vendors, especially after showing them the silver coins Jacob had given him. Most people had no silver these days, so they eagerly traded their goods for it. When he returned, Spruce was curled up in the shelter, so he rewarded him with a piece of sausage.

———

Cort crouched beside Spruce behind the shrubs on a hill overlooking the Danube, east of Riedlingen. A rope collar and leash hung around Spruce's neck, which Cort had put on when they got close to the town. At first, Spruce resisted the leash but soon grew accustomed to it. Upstream, numerous boats and ferries crossed the river in both directions to and from the town. He couldn't board them with a wolf, so he searched for nearby boats.

A small boat, driven by a single man, approached them, likely a fisherman given the nets and other equipment inside. He told Spruce to stay back before venturing out along the riverbank.

The fisherman eyed Cort suspiciously as he walked toward him. He reached for an oar. "That's close enough," he said, gripping the oar like a weapon. "What do you want?"

Cort halted his advance. "I'm traveling to my father on the other side of the river. Can you give me a ride in your boat?"

"Why not take the ferry?"

"I missed the last one today."

"You'll have to go tomorrow. My family is waiting."

"I can pay but don't have much." He gave him a copper coin.

The fisherman examined it. "This will do if you're in such a hurry. Hop in."

"I need to bring my pet with me. The family dog."

"Where is it?"

He whistled. Spruce emerged from the shrubs and loped toward them.

"My God," the fisherman uttered as he backed up and crouched behind his boat.

"Don't worry, mister," he said as he took hold of the leash. "He won't hurt you."

"That's no dog," he said, still crouched behind the boat. "It's a wolf! The deal's off. Go away!"

He pulled out another coin and showed it to him.

"This is almost all I have left. Please, we need a ride. I'll make sure to stay between you and Spruce in the boat. I—our family—raised him since he was a pup. He likes people."

The fisherman rose. "Spruce, huh? Funny name. Alright. But keep him in the back!"

Once across the river, Cort found the main road leading north. They had to duck into the woods whenever others passed by because of Spruce. Just before dark, his spirits soared when Spruce picked up the trail again, indicated by the loud yelps. He set up camp shortly after and looked forward to a tasty meal, having convinced the fisherman, with another copper coin, to part with two of his fish.

15.

Roadside Companions

Mara poked a sturdy walking stick into the ground as they trekked along a rough, hilly forest road. She found it along the way and used it to relieve pressure on her knees, which grew sore after some days of climbing. She also told Erich that she wanted to learn how to fight and defend herself with it and asked if he'd teach her to do so. He agreed, thinking this would be a passing fancy, but after the first lesson, he realized she took it seriously.

They left Balingen the day before after spending a day there to rest, wash up, and purchase food, and feed for the horse. Just outside the town, Erich used Baldur to pull a wagon stuck in a muddy ditch. The condition of the people reminded him of his own family, although they were much poorer. He couldn't shake off the worry about his family all day.

As Erich waited for Mara and Manfred to catch up, he spotted a man wearing a long cape and a wide-brimmed hat walking along the road far behind them. He had noticed the man earlier in the day and thought nothing of it—but there he was again.

———

At dusk, they sat by the campfire finishing Mara's stew.

"Maybe we could hunt for rabbits tomorrow," Manfred said.

"They're not worth the effort," Erich said.

"I saw one burrowing in the ground yesterday," she said. "A sign it might snow soon."

She picked up a bucket to fetch water from a nearby stream.

A short time later, she let out a piercing scream. Both men rushed to her. A man in a long, dark cape and a wide-brimmed hat crouched behind bushes.

"Step out and show yourself!" Erich demanded.

The man stood, clutching a large bag over his shoulder.

"You've been following us today!" Erich exclaimed. "What do you want?"

"To find out if you were good people. And maybe join you."

"Why not during the day?" Manfred asked.

"I walk slow."

"You can sit with us," Erich said.

The man tilted his hat to shield most of his face while she served him some stew. He gripped his spoon like a child, shoveling it into his mouth.

Manfred stared at the man's features as he ate. "You're welcome to take your hat off in our company."

"I prefer to keep it on."

Manfred continued to stare at him until he lunged forward and tore at his hat off.

His face, illuminated by the firelight, revealed reddish sores with dark black marks on his scalp.

Manfred dropped the hat and backed away. "The plague!"

"Be off with you!" Erich demanded

"No! I don't have the plague!" he said, reaching for his hat.

"Let me see," she said

The man lowered his gaze in shame as she examined the disfigurements.

"Tar," she said. "An evil punishment."

They exchanged glances, not knowing what to say.

"What's your name?" Erich asked.

"I'm . . . a scholar from Freiburg," he answered, averting their eyes. He donned his hat. "I taught at the university and am heading north to the Low Countries."

They waited for him to respond with a name, but none insisted.

"Sorry I treated you so rough," Manfred said.

"I'm used to it."

She handed him a chunk of bread.

"You people are the first I've talked to in over a fortnight." He dipped the bread in the stew and took another bite. "Some people helped me along the way. But most shunned me. Others ran me off with pitchforks or dogs. I can't blame them. Look at me now."

"How did it happen?" Manfred asked. "I mean—"

The Scholar glared at him for a moment, his first eye contact with any of them and lowered his head.

"I made a mistake. I spoke out about things I witnessed." He gazed into the flames. "Now all I want to do is to flee this cursed land."

Erich stirred the fire with his staff. "The next town is two days away. You can come with us."

"I'll get some soaps there to make a salve," she said. "To soften the tar so it can be removed easier."

———

After arriving in Balingen, Cort had a decision to make. The townsfolk told him that two roads led out of the town: one going northeast to Tübingen and the other cutting west towards Horb. His father could have taken either one.

He asked a friendly couple if they had seen anyone matching his father's description recently. They told him that a man with a horse, as he described, had come by a few days prior, but they didn't know which road he took. Then, he had an idea. He figured his father must have stabled Baldur at the livery, so perhaps someone there knew where he had gone.

Two men tended to the horses in the stable.

"Hello, Mister," Cort said to the older man. "I'm looking for the owner of the stable."

"I'm the owner."

"I'm searching for my father. We separated a fortnight ago and need to know if he left his horse here. A large brown one with a white blaze. He's traveling with two other people. Sometimes he carries a long dark bow."

"I do remember them from the horse. It's of a breed I haven't seen in years."

"How many days ago?"

"About two, I think."

"Do you know what road they took out of town?"

"The west road to Horb."

"Are you sure?"

Yes, I'm sure," he answered gruffly. "I gave him directions!"

He slept soundly at night, knowing he was on the same path as his father. And getting closer!

Dark gray clouds gathered the next morning, bringing snow. The first few flakes began to fall around midday, and the snowfall intensified as the day progressed. By late afternoon, it had reached his knees, making each step more challenging. He set up camp in a grove of trees that sheltered him from the accumulating snow. He tried to start a fire but couldn't find enough dry kindling. He huddled beside Spruce under the blanket, peering out from the shelter as the snow continued to fall.

———

Erich quickened their pace when the snow began to fall, allowing them to reach Horb at dusk. After settling Baldur at a livery, they found an inn with only two available rooms. Erich decided that he and Manfred would take one while Mara and the Scholar would take the other. This slightly vexed Manfred because, for a brief moment, he'd imagined sharing a room with Mara.

The snowfall had stopped overnight, so Erich and Manfred went out to try their luck at fishing in the morning. Mara visited a store to buy soap and lye for a salve. The Scholar sat by the fire, reading a book.

Erich and Manfred burst into the inn later that morning with a string of a dozen fish on a line.

"Here," Manfred said to the innkeeper as he cut some fish off the line, "take a few. We can't eat them all."

"Well, that's good of you," the innkeeper said. "Have a drink of ale. How did you manage to catch so many?"

"We wrapped sausage on the hook," Erich said, looking for Mara. "Have you seen the woman who traveled with us?"

"She's in her room. She stirred soaps and powders into some water I heated for her. To treat the other man's condition, she said. Did he do anything wrong?"

"He just joined us but hasn't said much. I think he was punished for speaking out against injustices in his town."

"He caused some people here to talk, so I went a little closer to him." He shook his head. "I've seen people tarred in other towns. But we don't allow it here."

Erich began to develop an affinity for him as they talked. In temperament and manner, he reminded Erich of Jacob the Sheriff. He seemed to be the same age, with a similar body size and beard, except the innkeeper had a longer mustache, twirled at the ends, giving him a merrier appearance.

"I say we cook *all* the fish now," Manfred said as he slid his empty cup to the innkeeper, who filled it up again. "I'm hungry!" He turned to the others in the room. "What about everyone else? Let's have a feast! Come on!"

The snowbound patrons walked to Manfred with cheerful expressions. The innkeeper handed the string of fish to his wife, who took them into the kitchen. He filled everyone's cups with more ale.

———

Mara dipped a cloth into a pot of warm water to soak it. The Scholar sat in a chair with wet towels wrapped around his head. She removed the cloth and squeezed the liquid onto one of the sores on his arm.

"The ones on my scalp are worse."

She lifted one of the towels from his head to examine the sores. "The soaps should soften the tar, but—" she paused to find the right words, "you may have scars after it's gone. Parts of your hair will never grow back."

"I expected that. I'm fortunate to have found you."

"It's my training. And you?"

"I was a professor at the university. I taught all the Fine Arts, but mostly literature. There's much writing of the highest quality now: Descartes, the essays of Montaigne, the lost translations of Plato, and of course the writers from England—Shakespeare, Milton, Donne. I do miss those books."

"I see you brought some along," she said, glancing at three books beside his backpack.

"They're my most cherished possessions. Are you interested in literature?"

"Oh yes. I love to read and listen to good stories."

"I'll recite some passages to you," he said with a faint smile. "But another night. I'm quite tired from the long day."

He shuffled his way to the bunk and collapsed on the bed. She applied the fresh hot towel to his scalp.

"You're so very kind," he muttered and drifted off to sleep.

———

Later that evening, Erich and Manfred sat with the innkeeper at a table by the fire, studying a rough map of the region.

The innkeeper puffed on a pipe as he spoke. "There are three roads out of here," he said, pointing at the map. "This is the river road to Tübingen and Stuttgart. It's a bit longer, but it's the easiest and safest one." He took another puff. "The other road goes northwest through small villages, but I wouldn't recommend it."

"Why not?"

"Because lawless robbers and deserters have taken over the area. Some came here last year, but we beat them back with sticks and axes."

"And pitchforks!" proclaimed a smiling patron with a pointed red hat at the next table.

Erich raised his cup of ale to the man. "That's the way to do it."

"Those were the easy ones to run off," said another older man sitting beside Erich.

"More highwaymen?" Erich asked.

"Not exactly," the man said. He exchanged knowing glances with other townsfolk at the counter.

"We had trouble with other folks who came here last year," the innkeeper said. "They seemed well-intentioned initially and said they wanted to build another church here. We only had one, so we let them do it."

"Trouble is, it was a Catholic church," the older man said.

"They fooled us," the innkeeper said. "No one in town cared what faith you were, and we all got along. But the black robes came and preached things that got people stirred up. I've seen what happens in other places when this starts, so we told them to leave. One of them continued preaching, which was a mistake for him."

"We got together one night," the older man said with a tight smile, "and hung him from a tree."

"We told the other priest that if he comes back with any force, we'd run them off," the innkeeper said.

"With our pitchforks!" the man with the red hat exclaimed.

Erich raised his cup to him again, took a swig, and studied the map. "What about the other road?"

"Ah, yes—well," the innkeeper said in a more measured tone. "That's the shortest route, but it goes through the Black Forest, with few villages along the way. You may go many days without seeing anyone during this time of year."

"Have you been on it?" Manfred asked.

"Only for short hunting trips."

"How many days to the Rhein on it?" Erich asked.

"By foot, almost a month. Parts of the road are steep and hilly, they say."

"We'll take that road." He glanced at Manfred, who nodded in agreement, droopy-eyed from the ale.

————

The weather warmed up the next day, and the snow began to melt. Erich and Manfred bought as much food and feed as they could pack on Baldur. The Scholar also gave them coins to purchase provisions and materials to replace his tattered shelter. Erich checked on Baldur and helped the stable hand put new shoes on him.

Mara took the time for another warm bath and later cared for the Scholar's wounds, pleased that the salve had softened the tar on his skin.

The following day, the snow continued to melt, making the roads passable for travel. While they had their morning meal at the inn, a jovial wainwright they had met the day before sat beside him. He was also heading north but wanted to take the road along the Neckar first.

"What do you say we travel together?" the wainwright asked. "I try not to go alone because things could happen along the way. My strong horse can carry some of your load. I have relatives in Heilbronn where we can rest for a while."

"That's something to consider," Manfred said to Erich. "What do you think?"

"Remember, we decided not to go on that road last night."

Manfred attempted to recall the conversation, his memory clouded by the ale.

"Which one will you take?" the wainwright asked.

"The west road to the Rhein."

"Why would you want to take that one?"

"It's the fastest way to get there," Erich answered.

"*If* you get there."

"What do you mean? The innkeeper said it's safe from highwaymen."

"It is from people, but—" He fumbled for words.

"But not from the forest spirits," Mara said. "Is that what you're trying to tell us?"

"Well, yes. Anyone here will tell you the same. There are stories about people who went that way. Some never came back. Others told of the goblins, ghosts, and witches coming for them at night."

"I'm sure most of those are fables and nothing else," she said. "People's minds play tricks on them."

The wainwright glared at her. "Is that so?"

"Listen," Erich said, "I don't believe in any of those stories either. That's the one we're taking, and you can join us if you want."

The wainwright thought it over and shook his head. "No. I think I'll take the river road. I wish you luck on your journey. Perhaps our paths will cross again."

———

When Cort woke up, the snowfall had stopped, but it had piled up to his knees. Not long after he had walked away, he realized he might get lost since the snow covered most of the road. Reluctantly, he returned to camp.

He was warm and dry in the shelter but felt frustrated that he couldn't travel and catch up with his father. He sensed he was closer, perhaps in the next town, waiting out the snow like him. What a perfect time and place to meet! He munched on his food and drifted in and out of sleep with Spruce beside him.

The next morning, a supply wagon rumbled by, but was going in the opposite direction. After it passed, he bounded to the road. Sure enough, the wagon tracks were visible and easy to follow. He trudged along the tracks as they wound through the woods and meadows in the snow.

———

Two days later, Cort stood atop a small hill overlooking a bridge that spanned the Neckar River, leading to Horb. He had camped deeper in the forest than usual and set out for the town, carrying an empty bag for food.

On his way to the market, he stopped at an inn for a bite to eat. The aroma of warm, cooked food instantly stirred his appetite, prompting him to order a bowl of stew. After finishing, he asked the innkeeper if anyone matching his father's description had passed through.

"Why yes. The man you describe was here with three others. They left yesterday morning. Why do you ask?"

He could barely contain his elation. "I'm his son. I've been following him from Ulm . . . to tell him news about our family."

The innkeeper's wife emerged from the kitchen and stood beside him, listening to Cort. Like her husband, she was somewhat stout, rosy-cheeked, and had her long gray hair pulled back into a single braid.

"From Ulm, you say?" the innkeeper said. "In this weather, too. It must've taken you more than a month on foot. Am I right?"

"I think so. I've lost track of the days. What day and month is it?"

"Tomorrow is the first day of March," the wife answered.

He paused to examine Cort's haggard appearance. "Looks like you could use a rest. And clean up."

"I have to keep going."

"Whatever you say, but I think you should."

She whispered in her husband's ear and turned to Cort with sympathetic eyes. He hesitated to speak until she elbowed him in the ribs.

"Your father gave us all the fish he caught, and we sold much ale that day," he said. "Since you're of his family, we can offer you a free night's lodging and a morning meal."

His wife nodded in approval. "We'll wash your clothes and let you clean up too."

He worried about leaving Spruce at the campsite for the night and falling a day behind his father; however, he couldn't resist the idea of sleeping on a real bed, cleaning up, and having a free meal.

"I think you're right. And thank you."

"My wife will show you to a room."

First, Cort removed his dirty clothes and set them outside the door for her. He washed with the heated water from a pan that she poured for him. While doing so, he stared at his face in a crude mirror hanging on the wall. The innkeeper was right; he looked dirty and downtrodden, with wild, unkempt hair and ragged wisps around his chin and upper lip. He asked her for scissors to trim it all.

Afterward, he went to the market and bought more food, careful not to overspend. When he returned, he ate a little more, plopped down on the soft, clean straw bed, and slept soundly through the night.

The next morning, his clothes lay outside his door, still warm and faintly smelling of soap. His wife served him the biggest and best breakfast he'd had in a long time: sausage and eggs with plenty of potatoes. The innkeeper set a small sack on the table.

"This is a little extra for you. Some old scraps of bread and meat we can't give our customers but still good to eat."

"Thank you so much," Cort said. "Oh. Do you know which road my father took out of town?"

"The one going through the Black Forest. It starts west of the bridge. You can't miss it."

On his way, he bought two fat trout from a man fishing near the bridge.

———

When he arrived, Spruce wasn't at the campsite. He cupped his hands and whistled, then did so again later. Still, no sign of Spruce. As it was getting late, he decided to spend the rest of the day there and leave in the morning, hoping Spruce would return.

He sat by the fire as the fish cooked on a makeshift spit above the flames. Soon, rustling sounds in the forest interrupted his thoughts. Now, he feared a bear had caught the scent of the fish. Nearby, shrubs shook. As he reached for his bow, Spruce burst through the brush, panting, then darted back into the woods. He followed. Not far away, Spruce stood over the partially eviscerated carcass of a small deer.

"Spruce! What a good hunter you are!" He patted him on the shoulders and dragged the deer by its hind legs to the camp.

He added more logs to the fire and prepared pieces of the carcass for cooking. There was plenty of meat to last a long time. He felt Spruce's comforting presence more strongly than ever as it cooked.

————

The innkeeper was right about the road being rarely traveled. On the first day, a supply wagon loaded with crates and boxes passed them. Two days later, a train of wagons arrived from the opposite direction—grim-faced individuals who hardly acknowledged them. After a week, the enormous trees grew closer to the bumpy road each day, making the days seem even shorter in the dimmer light.

On one of those days, a man trudged toward them in the distance, leaning on a cane. When he noticed them, he stopped and quickly retreated, ducking into the forest. They halted at the spot where he'd vanished, peering down a rough footpath that disappeared into the dense gloom of trees.

"I've seen other trails like this," Manfred said. "They might lead to villages where we can get more supplies."

"Only if we run out," Erich said. "Maybe we'll come across a town soon."

In the late afternoon on a cool, gray day, a bearded hunter approached them, dressed in a bearskin coat with a musket slung over his shoulder. He wore a leather hat adorned with a feather on one side. His horse towed a makeshift frame piled high with pelts of various sizes. Rather than continuing on, he stopped to greet them.

"Good day to you," the hunter said in an open, friendly manner.

"And to you," Erich said.

"Been traveling long?" he asked.

"We're going to the Rhein. From there to Mainz."

"It should take you a fortnight to reach it by foot."

"We've only seen a few people on this road," Manfred said. "You're the first who's stopped to talk."

"Not many take it this time of the year. People here keep to themselves."

"Where do they live?" Erich asked.

"In the forest like me. There are some villages, but hard to find."

"Is that where those side paths branch off to?" Mara asked.

"Some do. Others not."

"We thought about going down one of them to see if we could replenish our supplies," Erich said.

The hunter shook his head. "I wouldn't recommend that. Most people are all right. But others don't like strangers."

"We'll stay on this road."

"There's a town three days away by foot. And a good fishing lake not far away. You'll pass by a stream on the west side of the road. Follow it through the woods, and you'll see it."

"We'll be making camp soon," Erich said. "If you want to join us."

The hunter thought about it for a moment. "I thank you, but we're going different ways. And have someone waiting for me."

———

Erich stood on a log extending into the lake, casting a fishing line into the deep green waters that reflected the surrounding trees. He had caught four fish that morning but none since. Manfred fished from another log while watching Mara wash her clothes on the rocky shore. Behind her, the Scholar chopped wood.

They would never have found it without the hunter's directions. They decided to spend an extra day there to rest and clean up. Most importantly for Erich, it also gave Baldur more time to graze in a nearby meadow.

———

They stood facing each other with staffs in hand at a clearing near the campsite.

"Remember what I told you about the footwork," Erich said as he raised his staff. "And always think of the first few moves you'll make."

She took two quick steps toward him, swinging her staff one way and then the other, which he deflected. She swung at him from the opposite direction but missed and then took another swing that he blocked. He checked his swing at her legs since she couldn't block it. She backed away, breathing heavily.

"Your first steps and thrusts were good," he said. "But then you swung wildly and couldn't recover when I attacked. It's all about the balance between your feet and hands. Concentrate more on your feet, and everything else will flow."

"I understand," she said. "To be more grounded."

"It'll take time to learn. We'll do more tomorrow."

"I want to try once more."

"Hurry then. So we can return to eat."

Frustrated by his impatience, she attacked him once again with the same moves. He deflected her first swing with a bit more effort this time. She took another swing, which he blocked, and positioned herself for yet another assault.

"A little better," he said. "Now let's go."

His cavalier attitude only increased her desire. She thrust her staff toward him and swung aggressively, which he deflected. Now, he noticed a rage in her eyes. She came at him in a fury, swinging at his body and head, which he blocked each time. She charged at him again. He gripped his staff with both hands and halted her advance.

The clash stopped momentarily as they pushed their staffs against each other in front of their faces, staring intently into each other's eyes. His gaze fell upon her heaving chest. The top buttons on her blouse snapped off, exposing the smooth white skin below her neck down to the cleavage of her breasts. He lowered his staff and inched his face closer to hers.

She stepped back and fumbled to adjust her torn blouse. "I'm sorry . . ." she said, still out of breath.

"You shouldn't be," he answered, trying to recover his emotions.

"No. I'm sorry for my behavior. I wouldn't blame you if you didn't want to teach me anymore."

"We can continue. But I've never seen you . . . so angry."

"I felt threatened by you. So I had to protect myself. Does that sound foolish?"

"Not so foolish. Maybe it is about why you wanted to learn this."

They continued on the rest of the way in silence along a twig-strewn path.

Manfred was chopping branches by the camp when they emerged from the woods. He stopped upon noticing her partially torn blouse. *So that's why they had been gone so long.* He tried to dismiss these thoughts but couldn't help feeling resentful toward them if it was true. Even if not, seeing them together stirred the desires he'd been feeling for her. He resumed chopping with greater fervor as they passed.

———

That evening, they gathered around the campfire, enjoying fish and potatoes while discussing the upcoming journey. They hoped to reach the town mentioned by the hunter within a day or two. From there, it would take another week to arrive at the Rhein.

"It'll be good to be around people again," Manfred said. "I don't know how anyone can live so far away from everything. These woods give me strange feelings at night."

"People come here for different reasons," she said. "Some by choice. Others by force. The persecuted ones."

The Scholar set down his book. "What do you mean?"

"I've met people during my travels," she said, "who helped those living in forests like this. Some of them would've been imprisoned or killed if they stayed in towns. Because of their beliefs."

"Yes, I know," the Scholar said.

"I went with such a group once," she said. "It took us all morning to reach an old woman living alone for many years. We gave the woman roots and herbs, but we found her dead on our next visit."

Erich recalled his mother sharing similar stories about the times she went with her coven to help those living in the forest.

"I was one of those," the Scholar said. "One of the persecuted ones, as you said, and given refuge."

They all turned to listen, as he seldom spoke much around the campfires. Sometimes, he said a few words about his time at the university, but always stopped when they asked about the students.

"My colleagues guided me to such a place near Rothwell. I suppose they felt guilty about what happened after they did nothing to stop it. They were kind enough to give me books and parchment for writing. I gave them coins for food and started planting vegetables. After a fortnight, my spirits sank. So I left and headed north and found you." His bitter, sad expression changed to one of gratitude. "Thanks to your help, my body is healing. Now I must attend to my soul."

"Talking and sharing your thoughts and feelings are best for that," Mara said.

"No!" he interrupted. "That's a task only I can do. My soul is my own."

"Yes. A person's soul is their own. But it's connected to others. Like what it said in one of the books you read to me in Horb."

"Which book?"

"The one from the English writer you met when teaching. The passage describes how one man's death and suffering affect us all because we're all united in some ways. I think he meant to say that our souls are all connected on a deeper level."

"I remember now. What you said is logical. I'll think more about it."

"You've never told us why you're going to the Low Countries," Manfred said.

"Because it's the only bastion of enlightenment in this realm. With people freed from the yoke of the Spanish oppressors. A place where a man can speak his mind and celebrate his faith without fear of reprisals." His voice turned bitter. "Not like the German states. Where there is no hope. Not in our lifetime. This cursed land."

"I, for one, am getting weary of your *cursed* blustering," Manfred said.

"Why? I speak the truth."

"A half-truth only! Yes, our people are suffering and have come through hard times. But this is *our* land! We should stay and make it a better place! Not run off to some . . . false paradise."

The Scholar glared at him. "That's your choice. Not mine."

He tilted the pages of his book toward the flickering firelight.

Manfred shook his head and went back to his shelter. Erich and Mara followed. She glanced back at the Scholar, turned back, and sat next to him

"Is that the book you showed me in Horb?" she asked.

"This one is different."

"May I see it?"

"It's been so long since I've read one like this," she said while fanning the pages

"Since your days at the monastery?"

"Yes, but they were academic books. There's something almost magical about books of literature. It's like opening up a whole new world of someone else's thoughts and imagination."

"I suppose you're right in a way." He watched her with curious interest as she thumbed through the book. "I've read about the Bingen monastery."

"If you're still with us, you can rest there. I'd be glad to show you our library."

"I'd like that," he said, cracking a rare smile.

"We don't possess many books like these. They're the ones I enjoy the best. Like the book you read to me by the man you met from England."

"John Donne."

"There's so much wisdom in those passages."

"He was a great man. A man of God and the world of letters. I hosted him when he visited Freiburg when he toured the continent. We exchanged thoughts about many things. He invited me to stay with his family if I traveled there. I planned to do so a few years ago but found out that he'd passed."

"I'm sorry."

"He inspired me to speak the truth and to teach and counsel my students to do the same." He scoffed and shook his head. "But look where it got me."

She tried to change the subject. "The cover and binding of your books are well-made."

"I had no book of equal value to give to him, so I gave him some of my wood carvings and a painting from Hans Holbein. Perhaps you've heard of him."

"I studied the lives of both Holbeins. We have paintings by Holbein the Younger in our library. Oh! We also have engravings and woodcuts by Albrecht Dürer, too."

"It sounds like a cultured place. I miss my paintings and my books. I wish I could've carried more. They've given me much comfort and hope for my fellow man. Such noble thoughts from free-thinking men. But none from here. Not in our country anymore."

"There must be some."

"No, there are not. All the composers of music today live elsewhere. In Venice, Florence, and France. And painters? Again, all in other regions, especially Spain and the Low Countries. The same with writers." His voice increased with passion. "Can you imagine that? We Germans invented the movable-type printing press! But the only writings from here these days are on those cheap pamphlets that do nothing but inflame the passions of hate and anger of those reading them. Writing shouldn't do that! Words should ennoble the mind and spirit! But no! Fear and terror have so consumed people's lives now that they can't even *think* of art in any form. This cursed land."

She wanted him to recite more passages from the book but could tell he was retreating within himself again. She handed it back to him.

"Perhaps you can read to me another time."

"Yes, perhaps another time," he murmured, clutching the book.

———

A thin layer of snow blanketed the ground as they entered the town the hunter had mentioned. The townsfolk stopped and gawked at them as they walked along the street. First, Erich stabled Baldur at the livery. A stable hand gave them directions to a place offering food and drink.

Erich carried the Black Bow with him, which drew even more stares from the townsfolk.

When they arrived, no one was at the store counter. Three rough-looking men sat at a table, observing them with vacant eyes as they stood at the entrance. One of the men, with a long protruding jaw, shouted to someone in an adjoining room, "Hey, Hans! You have a customer."

The other men laughed as if sharing a private joke.

An older man with stringy white hair came in from another room. "Hello, good people," he said in a fawning manner. "I hope you haven't been waiting too long. What would you like?"

"Some bread, cheese, and sausage," Erich said.

"Some potatoes, turnips, or onions if you have any," Mara said.

"We have all that, but only a few pieces of sausage, I'm sorry to say. We can get you a chicken or two. And can bake some bread if you can wait."

"We'll take all the bread you can make this morning, and the cheeses, vegetables, and chicken meat."

"Yes, I will, but . . . can you pay?"

Erich placed some coins on the counter.

The storekeeper eyed them greedily. "We'll provide all those things. While you're waiting, we can serve soup from our kitchen. Where are you going, if I may ask?"

"To the Rhein," Manfred said. "And then north."

"We can fix you a room to rest before your journey."

"We'll let you know," Erich said.

"I don't like this town," Manfred said as they sat together at the table waiting for the soup. "Did you see the way they stared at us? Their mouths open as if possessed."

"What do you think?" Erich asked. "Shall we stay the night or go?"

"It doesn't matter to me," Manfred said.

"I could use the rest in a real bed," the Scholar said.

"And I," she said.

"We stay then," he said.

———

The next morning, they paused to watch a short, stout juggler wearing a blue headscarf perform for a crowd on a small makeshift stage in the town square. Mara dropped a copper coin into a hat near the juggler's feet. The juggler acknowledged her with a nod while continuing his performance.

Captivated by her beauty and kindness, he watched as she and the others left town. He became so distracted that he lost focus and dropped one of the balls. He caught it on the bounce and continued juggling. Some children and adults laughed and threw snowballs at him, causing him to drop two more. The crowd hooted in mockery before dispersing. The juggler smiled and bowed in exaggerated deference as he picked up the balls. A few people tossed him coins before walking away.

The juggler placed the balls in a bag, stuffed them into a larger backpack, and hurried across the square to the stable. He emerged, pulling a small horse loaded with supplies. He rode away along the same road they had taken.

The juggler spotted them a short distance ahead.

"Hello!" he called out as he rode toward them, his gear bouncing up and down against the saddle. He halted in front of them and patted his winded horse.

"Thank you for stopping. My little horse is not used to riding so fast. I want to join you if it's not too much trouble, at least until we're out of these woods. The roads aren't safe for people traveling alone here."

"There are highwaymen on this road?" Erich asked.

"Some men in town prey on lone and weak travelers passing through. I was stuck there for a week, waiting for someone to go this way. I carry my food and shelter and can pay for things on the way." He waited for Erich to respond and continued in a mirthful tone. "Oh! My name is Franz. I'm a minstrel and a jester by trade. I can entertain you with the lute, and if you twist my arm a bit, I'll also play the flute. I like to recite poetry and sometimes speak in rhythms and rhymes."

Mara studied his features as he spoke. He might've been Erich's age, with a round, merry face and a rather stout, portly body. His most prominent feature was a long, hooked nose.

"You know poetry?" the Scholar asked. "From the classics? Or ballads from Chaucer or Dante? Or verses from Marlowe or Donne?"

"Not that I know of. Just what comes into my head. Not from anything that I've read."

"Oh," the Scholar remarked disappointedly.

"I speak in rhymes because it makes most people smile. And as you've seen, I also juggle."

"I think it would be wonderful if you joined us!" she said.

Erich and Manfred nodded.

Franz clapped his hands. "If I weren't so tired, I'd dance a little jig for you."

"I'd like to learn to catch the balls as you do," Manfred said.

"If you like, we can start tonight. We'll begin with three and another day with four. And if you're good, we'll even do some more!"

16

Above the Rhein

Cort trudged along a hilly road with a determined stride near the end of another tiring day. He'd been pushing himself hard since leaving Horb the week before, rising with the first light and walking all day with little rest until dark. Each day, he sensed he was getting closer to his father and seldom interacted with anyone on the road. Whenever that happened, Spruce dashed into the woods after a terse command from him. Sometimes, he stopped by a stream to try his luck at fishing but left before catching anything. The need to push on to reach his father was stronger than the desire to catch more fish. Besides, he still had meat from the deer Spruce killed near Horb.

He plodded on until dusk, searching for a place to camp and build a fire without risking a blaze in the dense forest. He halted when he noticed a slight movement in a thicket of shrubs. As soon as he stepped forward, a lynx darted from the underbrush and scampered along a small creek before vanishing into the shadows. The creek appeared to lead to a clearing deeper in the woods, so he made his way toward it.

He followed the creek until he reached a meadow. To his surprise, a series of large stone formations, arranged in a circle, stood around the blackened fire pit in the middle of it. The formations reminded him of those his family had encountered while strolling in the forest during his childhood. Agatha had told them that people worship in such places and that they should be quiet and respectful around them. Now, he wondered if people used this area for the same purpose. But who?

Despite his concern, he made camp. He filled his canteen from the creek and chopped more firewood. Soon, he had a blazing fire. As the deer meat heated up, he dwelt on his location, deep in the Black Forest. He recalled all those stories about the ghosts, goblins, and gremlins that liked to play tricks and torment people who ventured into the area. As always, though, the presence of Spruce allayed his fears.

He didn't sleep well at night because Spruce woke him several times by growling at something in the woods. Spruce had done this before, likely sensing an animal nearby, but this growling was different and interspersed with short yelps. Later, he heard rustling in the bushes and what sounded like garbled whispering, but he dismissed it as mere wind gusts.

The next morning, he became aware of how *quiet and still* everything was as he rekindled the fire; there were no chirping birds or even a breeze. Now, he felt like an intruder who'd disturbed the peace and tranquility of this hidden place and—recalling those whispering sounds at night—sensed that he was being watched. He quickly packed, not even wanting to eat first.

He followed the stream through the forest until he reached the road. He pounded the stick and walked with long, quick strides. Spruce bounded ahead, nose to the ground, searching for his father's scent.

————

Franz played a lively melody on the flute as Manfred guided his little horse along. Erich and Mara walked together beside Baldur. The Scholar trudged behind them, his head down, absorbed in thought. It had rained the night before, and the sun had just broken through the clouds. The sky beyond was dark and cloudy, but the sunlight illuminated the distant trees and glistened on puddles on the road, which stretched across flat and open meadows. A rainbow appeared on the horizon, forming an arch over the road. They stopped to gaze at it while basking in the sun.

"Such a sight makes my feelings strong," Franz said. "And inspires me to play another song."

"A sight that should be painted," the Scholar said. "And captured for eternity."

"I think I dreamt about a rainbow last night," Manfred added.

"I remember some in Bingen," she said. "Over the Rhein."

"I'll always remember one in the War after a battle," Erich mused. "It appeared on the way back to our barracks. Right above the ground where all the dead and wounded lay. A double rainbow. With another small one behind it."

"This could be a sign that we'll have luck the rest of the way," Manfred said.

"Perhaps so," she answered. "Since it's in our direction."

————

That evening, Manfred, Franz, and the Scholar sat by the fire, sharing their rations of fish and bread. Nearby, Erich and Mara practiced their fighting moves with staffs.

After Manfred finished his meal, he picked up three juggling balls. He tossed them into the air and kept them aloft until one bounced off his forehead. The Scholar chuckled.

"Keep trying," Franz said. "One day it'll come to you!"

"How many can you do?" Manfred asked.

"I've done up to seven."

"That I'd like to see," the Scholar said.

"Let's start with five," Franz said.

He reached into his bag and pulled out two more balls.

"Watch my hand motion as I catch them. That's the key. The throwing part is easy."

Soon, he juggled all five balls. Mara and Erich came over and sat down with him. When he finished, she clapped her hands in appreciation.

"I wish I had another coin to give you," she said.

"Ah, but your applause is worth much more than a simple coin," Franz said, bowing to her.

The wind suddenly picked up, sending embers from the fire near them. Thick clouds drifted across the sky, and tree branches swayed with each gust.

"Here comes the rain," Franz said. "I've smelled it since midday."

"With that big nose of yours, no wonder," the Scholar said.

"Good one," Franz said, slapping him on the shoulder.

Halfway through the night, the wind died, but the rain began to pelt their shelter tarps. Soon, it started coming down harder, accompanied by the first flash of lightning and the loud claps of thunder in the area.

Awakened by the thunder, Mara stared into the silent blackness until the sound of footsteps startled her, followed by the dim shape of a hunched figure creeping along. Now alarmed, she listened as the footsteps faded away. Another flash of lightning briefly revealed Erich standing beside Baldur at the edge of the woods, gently stroking his neck.

———

The storm persisted in bursts for two more days, but they pressed on. The road wound along steep hillsides, some of which had been washed out by minor mudslides and rockfalls. Near the end of the second day, they traversed one such hillside when several rocks tumbled down the slope across their path, followed by many more. An ominous rumbling echoed from above.

Erich looked up in alarm and shouted for everyone to run.

Manfred seized Baldur's bit to assist Erich in pulling him forward. Mara dashed alongside them while Franz and the Scholar ran back in the opposite direction.

Baldur reared, startled by the roar of the rockslide. Erich calmed him and moved ahead, but Manfred fell. Massive rocks cascaded down around him. One boulder struck his ankle, making him bellow in pain. They gathered around him once the slide subsided.

"Can you walk?" Erich asked.

He struggled to rise but winced when he put weight on his leg.

"Ride on Baldur for now," Erich said. "We'll check on it when we make camp."

————

Cort realized shortly after arriving that he didn't want to spend much time in town. He tried to remain inconspicuous, yet everyone stared at him. When he asked for directions to a store, an old man pointed across the street to a building and abruptly turned away.

Three gloomy characters sat at a table, observing him as he waited for service in the store.

"Are you lost, sonny boy?" one of the men, with a long jaw, asked.

"No. I want to buy food."

"Hey, Hans," he shouted. "Looks like you have a *customer*." The other two chuckled and resumed drinking.

Hans emerged from another room and couldn't hide his contempt for Cort's bedraggled appearance.

"Go away now! I don't want beggars here!"

"I'm not a beggar! I'm here to buy food. Some cheese and sausage or whatever else you have."

Hans changed his tone. "How much do you need?"

"Enough to last me a fortnight."

"Can you pay?"

He threw down the coin pouch on the counter.

Hans raised his brows. "I'm sure I can get what you want." And louder, "judging by your big, fat purse."

Cort realized the mistake he had made by showing his pouch. "There's not that much in it."

"Looks like enough to me. Do you plan on staying here?"

"Just passing through."

"Are you traveling alone?"

"Why do you ask?" he answered, becoming suspicious.

"You said you wanted food for *yourself.*"

He devised a story as he spoke. "I meant that I want some for my family. Our wagon is stuck in the mud nearby. They sent me—and my brother—back for food."

"We can send men to help," Hans said.

"They can manage."

"Will they be coming into town afterward?"

Cort tried to stifle his impatience. "We passed through yesterday. We're going . . . east."

"That's a hard road up from the Rhein."

"Listen. I'm in a hurry. They're waiting for me."

One of the men at the table slinked out of the store while they haggled over a price. Once outside, he headed east down the road out of town.

———

Cort trudged along with the food bag slung over his shoulder. About halfway back to his campsite, he spotted two men emerging from a bend in the road behind him—the same men he had seen in the store. He quickened his pace. When he glanced back, they were running toward him.

Another man stepped out from behind a tree ahead of him—the third man from the store. He crossed his arms and grinned, revealing most of his missing front teeth except one, which stood out like a fang.

"Don't be in such a hurry. We just want to talk."

The other men rushed in, surrounding him entirely. Cort dropped his bag and raised his walking stick with both hands.

"What do you want?"

"To make sure you have a safe journey," the long-jaw said, catching his breath.

"Of course, it might cost you a little," the other one said, the biggest of the three.

"I don't need your help."

"Oh, I think you do," the long-jaw said.

"My family is up the road. They'll hunt you down if you take anything from me."

"There's no one," the fang-tooth said. "I checked. No fresh wagon tracks either."

"I think you're traveling alone," the long-jaw said. "So give us the pouch, and we'll be gone."

"Your boots too," the fang-tooth added.

"And your coat," the big one said, laughing cruelly.

He wasn't going to allow this to happen without a fight. Now, he thought of Spruce. He cupped one hand against his mouth and whistled twice.

The fang-tooth shook his head. "Crazy boy. No one can hear you."

"Come now," the long-jaw said. "Give it to us now! Otherwise, we'll hurt you." He backed away. "Take him," he said to the others.

Cort plotted his moves as they advanced—advice his father had given him when teaching him how to fight. *Never show fear in a fight, no matter what the odds.* He decided to go after the long-jaw first. If he took him out, he might be able to handle the other two.

"Go on!" the long-jaw demanded.

Never hesitate once you decide on the first move, his father also instructed.

Cort charged past the other two, who swung at him but missed as he flew by. The long-jaw reached for his club, but it was too late. Cort hit the long-jaw's midsection hard with his first swing. He struck him again in the head, causing him to fall to the ground.

The other two lunged toward him. The fang-tooth wrapped his arms around him while the big one slugged Cort in the stomach. He spun free from the grip of the fang-tooth and struck his leg with his staff. He limped away in pain. The big one clubbed his head. He fell stunned from the blow. He jumped on top of Cort, taking swings at his head and body.

Spruce charged out of the woods with a ferocious growl. He leaped across the road, clamped his jaws onto the big robber's arm, and yanked him away. Spruce released his grip, baring his fangs. The large man remained motionless on the ground, his eyes bulging with horror and shock.

Spruce wheeled and charged the fang-tooth, who was limping away. He jumped up and clenched his jaws around his face and neck, causing him to fall, screaming in terror as blood spurted from his head. Spruce shook his head back and forth while maintaining his grip. Soon, the fang-tooth stopped struggling, and the only movements from his body were twitching spasms from his arms and legs.

Spruce raced after the large robber, who was running down the road toward the long-jaw. Spruce caught him and clamped down on his leg. Cort struggled to his feet and whistled at Spruce, who ceased the attack and returned to him. The robber limped down the road, clutching his leg.

Cort gazed down at the fang-tooth. Deep gashes lacerated his head and face, but the worst ones were on his neck. Blood spurted out from them and formed red pools around his head. His breathing was labored and rasping. Ashen-faced, he stared up at Cort, trying to raise his arm, but it fell back. His eyes widened in terror until he lost consciousness. A moment later, he stopped breathing. He dragged the body into the underbrush and returned to his campsite with Spruce.

———

He reached the edge of town at dusk and huddled behind a cluster of trees, trying to figure out which route to take since it was at the base of a steep, narrow valley. He felt fortunate to have avoided detection so far. Once, some horsemen approached, but he dashed behind some shrubs before they saw him.

He tightened his backpack around his waist and trekked up the hillside alongside the town. He paused for a moment to rest. From his viewpoint, he noticed a gathering of townsfolk in the square, some holding torches. A loud voice addressed the crowd, accompanied by the clamor of many other angry, shouting voices. He couldn't discern any words but feared they related to Spruce's earlier incident. The two men who escaped must have informed the authorities about the fight and undoubtedly provided an account that made them seem innocent. Later, some townsfolk mounted their horses and galloped toward his camp.

Once again, he realized how fortunate they were going in opposite directions. However, his advantage would be lost if anyone recognized them. By this time, the townsfolk were probably spreading tales about the evil "wolf boy" prowling the area. Grimly, he recalled Jacob's words about Gumprecht's fate.

A man emerged from behind a building and walked toward them while whistling a light tune. Cort ducked behind some bushes and kept a firm grip on Spruce. The man paused a few trees away on lower ground to relieve himself. The splashing trickle caused Spruce to growl. Cort placed his hand on his muzzle. The man stopped whistling, glared toward them in the dark, and raised his knife. He took a few steps back and ran toward the building.

Cort fled, pulling Spruce's leash. Once he was past the town, he stopped to rest again. He listened for any sign of pursuit: a distant commotion of voices, horses, or, at worst, the sound of hunting dogs. Hearing nothing, he trekked along the steep terrain until he was far away from the town. Finally, he found a flat area to settle in. After a bite to eat, he curled up in his blankets beside Spruce and slept for the rest of the night.

The next morning, he descended to the road, remaining ever-vigilant for anyone coming from either direction. Despite the risk, he knew he had to take action or risk falling farther behind his father.

———

Manfred rode Baldur, guided by Erich as they ascended a steady, gradual slope. Mara examined his leg the evening before and found no fracture, but advised him to avoid putting weight on it for a few days to prevent aggravating the injury. Erich fashioned a simple crutch for him. He could walk on his own on flat terrain with the crutch, but struggled on hills.

At the crest, they halted and stared, transfixed, at the sight ahead.

"Well, look at that," Manfred said.

"At last," Erich said.

Erich greeted them with a smile as the others drew near. They gazed in awe at the horizon. The Rhein meandered northward across the expansive landscape below, stretching as far as their eyes could see.

They rested in the shade of an oak tree while admiring the view of the wide river. Manfred dismounted from Baldur and stood beside them with his crutch. A refreshing breeze wafted from the slope, cooling them after the hot, arduous climb. Baldur's mane rippled in the wind. Boats of all sizes traveled up and down the river. Farms with cultivated fields, villages, and lush meadows lay along the shores beneath forests and cliffs.

Mara had never seen the Rhein from such an expansive view. From this vantage point, she observed how the river nourished the earth and those living around it, like a ribbon of life, in many ways.

"A welcome sight," Franz said.

"That it is," Erich replied.

"So beautiful," she said.

"Our pathway to freedom," the Scholar said.

They gazed at the vista for some time before going down the road.

Halfway down the slope, a medium-sized lake stretched out ahead. Several crude wooden shelters and a dilapidated fence bordered one side of the lake. A few wagons and horses were parked by the shelters, with families camped nearby. It seemed like a good place to rest, so they made their way toward it.

17.

Together Again

The next morning, the men ate fish by one of the shelters while conversing with members of the Richter family. Alfred Richter, the head of the family and a cobbler by trade, described how they had to flee their village near Münster after highwaymen pillaged it. Once again, the Richters reminded Erich of his family and renewed his concern about their situation.

"...and we've been traveling for nearly a fortnight searching for a place to settle along the Rhein," Alfred recounted. "But we haven't found one yet."

"There are fortified towns on the river," Erich said. "Did you try any of them?"

"We stayed in Phillipsburg for a few days," Alfred answered. "But it wasn't safe for a family."

"About a month's ride away," Manfred said, "there's the town of Horb on the Neckar River. It's a peaceful place with law-abiding people."

"I thank you for the advice," he said. "Where are you going?"

"North to Bingen," Erich answered

"You should be on the alert for highwaymen. And some places are infected with the plague."

Erich glanced down the slope, where Mara roamed in a vast meadow. She appeared so happy and carefree that he couldn't help but smile.

She went down the hillside to find a place to meditate and thank the helpful spirits for protecting them on the journey thus far. She spread out a rolled-up piece of leather from her bag, which had evenly spaced markings on its surface surrounding an etched circle. First, she placed a stick in the center and marked where the stick's shadow fell on the circle with a small pin.

Afterward, she absorbed more of her surroundings. She felt exhilarated sitting there: the warm sun and gentle breeze, surrounded by fragrant wildflowers and the bright blue sky, but most of all the vast openness of the terrain, so different from the dark confines of the Black

Forest. She sat for a while listening to the buzzing bees among the colorful wildflowers. Soon, an idea connected to her earlier meditations came to her. She plucked some of the flowers and placed them in a small pouch tied to her belt.

She walked up toward them with a beaming smile.

"We've been talking," Erich said to her. "And want to spend another day or two here. We all need the rest, and the lake has plenty of fish. The horses can graze the fields to regain their strength."

"I like it here too," she said. "We should take the time to cleanse ourselves and wash our clothes. I have soaps for that."

The men fell silent, realizing this would be a bothersome but necessary duty.

"Now that we're all here," she said, "I'd like to conduct a ceremony to celebrate this special day."

"What special day?" Manfred asked.

"The first day of Spring."

"How do you know?" the Scholar asked.

"By looking at the sun's angle and the shadows it creates when falling against certain objects. I have a simple sundial and used it in the meadow."

The Scholar nodded, impressed by her knowledge of the matter.

"Let's begin," she said. "I'll recite a short prayer to commemorate the day."

Before she started, the men waved farewell to the Richter family as they headed toward the Black Forest.

She bowed her head in prayer, as did the others.

"This is the time of the Spring's return. A joyful time and a seed time. When life bursts forth from the earth and the chains of Winter are broken. Light and dark are equal. A time of balance." She took in a deep breath. "When the Prince of the Sun reaches out his hand and the Dark Maiden returns from the land of the dead. Where they step, wildflowers appear. Despair turns to hope. Sorrow to joy. May our hearts be open to the Spring."

She reached into her pouch and placed the flowers on the ground: the red flowers in one group, the blue ones in another, the white ones opposite the red, and the yellow ones across from the blue.

"These flowers represent a direction," she told them. "White is north, red is south, blue is east, and yellow is west. Each of us will choose a flower whose color matches the direction of our freedom."

The men surveyed them, thinking about the decision.

"I'll begin," she said. "I'll take a white flower because my freedom and home reside in the north near Bingen." She cupped the flower in both hands.

The Scholar jumped up next. "I take a yellow one. The west. Where the sun goes! I follow the sun!"

Franz patted the Scholar on his shoulder. "I must remember that for my songs—*to follow the sun.*" He circled the flowers, studying each group. "Those red ones are pretty. I'll take one of those. A white one too. And the blue and yellow ones. To me, it's all the same." He picked one from each group. "I've traveled all over this land and will keep doing so as long as my legs carry me. Wherever the wind doth blow, that's where I will go!"

Erich reached for a blue one. "I take a blue flower. The east. Where my family is." He cupped it in his hands the same way Mara did hers.

Manfred limped to the flowers but hesitated before picking one, unsure of which one to choose. And then it came to him. "I go east with Erich. A blue flower for me."

Erich nodded as they exchanged glances.

————

The next day, Manfred sat on the steps of a shelter, loosening the boot from his bruised ankle. Mara approached him, carrying a bundle of fresh clothes that had been drying in the sun. Erich and Franz were fishing at the lake, and even the Scholar chose to try his luck with them this time.

"I'm almost ready," Manfred said as he struggled to pull off the boot.

She set the bundle beside his foot. "Here. Put your leg on these."

She pulled off his sock and examined his foot. And then began to massage his ankle.

He stared at her as she did so, feeling aroused. He scanned the area; no one else was around. All those feelings he had had for her along the road, which he had tried to suppress, were now bursting forth. He ignored the small stab of pain as she massaged.

"Feel better?" she asked.

He leaned closer to her with an intense and troubled expression, grasped her head, and pressed his lips to hers. Initially, she tried to push him away, but then placed her hands against his chest. A moment later, he broke the kiss and leaned back, breathing heavily.

"I'm sorry," he mumbled. "It's just that . . . you're always with him and—" He became more contrite because of her downcast eyes and furrowed brows. "But you prefer his company to mine."

"It's not what you suspect," she responded with a whisper.

"What am I to think? Always with him. Never with me."

"Manfred. I respect you both very much."

"I don't know what came over me. It won't happen again."

"I believe you, Manfred. I want to say something that might help you understand." She paused to gather her thoughts. "For some time, I've had difficulties being with men. In a certain way."

"Because of what those pigs did to you in prison."

"It started before then in my early womanhood. Soldiers invaded my people's camp and took everything we had. Burnt our wagons. Killed our men. And . . . took advantage of my condition."

"My God."

"I've been fearful of getting close to men after that. Even though part of me desires their company. In many ways, I'm more comfortable with women. It's hard to explain. I've never talked to Erich about this. But I think he senses it."

"I'm glad you told me this."

"And I. Now let me finish attending to your leg. It seems to be healing well!"

That evening, Erich and Mara practiced with their staffs near the campsite. He demonstrated how to plant the staff in the ground with both hands and spin her body around it.

Manfred, Franz, and the Scholar sat by the shelters before dusk, exchanging stories and news with another group of travelers who had come from the Rhein.

"One reason we're leaving," one of them said, "is that there's talk that the War will start again. My family barely survived the last time. I won't go through that hell again."

The travelers had retreated to their wagon when Erich and Mara returned.

"Did you find out where they're from?" Erich asked Manfred.

"Westphalia."

"Where are they going to?"

"They didn't say."

"They didn't say where they were going *to*," the Scholar said. "But they made it clear what they were going *from*."

"What do you mean?" Erich asked.

"They told us the War might begin again. And want to get away while they can."

"Based on what?"

"Just rumors," Manfred said.

"It's more than rumors," the Scholar said.

"Learn anything else?" Erich asked Manfred.

"The same. The lawless and diseased towns. And highwaymen."

This made him realize that the next part of their journey might not be as simple as he had hoped.

"I remember the times of peace before the War," the Scholar said. "When I was a student in Bamberg. That's when it began."

They all listened with rapt attention since he rarely spoke to them about his past.

"At first, we welcomed the trials and executions in the square. Most of them deserved what they got: the thieves, robbers, and murderers. But it continued, becoming more extreme over the years. I moved to Freiberg, but the persecutions began there as well. There is no refuge from such evil in this land! My colleagues and I witnessed people—our neighbors and friends—arrested for crimes they did not commit. We stood by as it intensified over the years." He grimaced before continuing. "Eventually, it became too much. They began taking students—my students! Those who did nothing more than express their opinions. I complained to the authorities. My colleagues supported me until—" He chuckled sarcastically. "Until they seized me from my room at night and threw me into prison. I soon realized what a fool I was for speaking out."

"No!" Erich exclaimed. "You spoke out against those injustices. That took much courage."

"I was a fool to think anyone would support me! No one did, even during the trial." He faced Manfred. "This country *has* become a hellhole! The fear to speak your mind: that's what hell is!"

He picked up his book and shuffled back to the shelter.

————

Cort stood atop the ridge overlooking the Rhein with Spruce in the late afternoon. It was a welcome sight because of the beauty of the vista but also a disappointing one because he'd expected to reach his father before this.

He pushed himself hard since leaving that godforsaken town in the valley. A few times, he encountered people, some on horseback and others in wagons. Each time, he hoped to find his father among the groups, but his hopes were dashed when he realized he wasn't among them.

He worried about what to do with Spruce as he trudged down the slope, since they were approaching an area far from his natural habitat. Halfway down, he spotted wagons and people camped in small shelters by a lake. Several horses grazed in the field. He shaded his eyes from the sun. Even from such a distance, one of them appeared to have the same color and mane as Baldur!

He left Spruce in the woods and walked toward the shelters behind a line of trees and shrubs. He couldn't see his father among the first group of travelers, so he crept to the next one. There, three men chatted around a campfire. Nearby, a man and a woman playfully sparred with their staffs, laughing as they did so. It took him a moment to realize that the man was . . . his father!

Now he felt a pit grow in his stomach and his heart sink into it. *Why was his father cavorting in such a way with that woman? It must be the woman he had rescued.* His confusion took a darker turn. *Did she put a spell on him? Or maybe he wanted to be with her instead of the family.* He crawled away and trudged back to Spruce, more dejected than ever.

He rested against a log, taking in the view of the Rhine. The sun sank behind the hills across the river. Lacking the strength or will to set up a shelter or start a fire, he simply wanted to observe the sunset and think for a while. As dusk fell, he ate sausage and bread, tossed a chunk to Spruce, and settled down for the night, still troubled by what he had witnessed.

Just before he nodded off, he glanced at Spruce staring at him in the fading light.

Later in the night, as Cort slept, Spruce circled him a few times, sniffed his leg and ambled off toward the Black Forest.

When he awoke, Spruce was gone. He reached into his backpack, pulled out some cheese, and gazed down at the valley. Thick clouds gathered on the horizon and raced across the sky. Halfway down the slope, a faint wisp of smoke rose from the campsites. He whistled twice and sat down to wait.

His worry grew throughout the morning. He gazed down the hill—that wisp of smoke had vanished. Had they left yet? Suddenly, it struck him: Spruce wasn't coming back. He had led him to his father and had thus fulfilled his duty. It was best that Spruce left while he slept; the departure would have been much more difficult otherwise. He strapped on his backpack and strode down the hillside with a heightened sense of urgency.

———

They sat around the camp after deciding to spend another day there to stock up on more fish and let Baldur graze in the fields. Franz's little horse, which had grown friendly with Baldur along the way, also benefited from the rest.

Mara examined the washed clothes hanging on a rope between the shelters. Along the way, she noticed someone descending the hill.

"Well," she said to the others whose backs were to the hillside, "Looks like we might have another visitor."

They turned around. A slender man carrying a backpack guiding each step with a walking stick walked toward them.

As he approached them, Erich sensed something familiar about the figure: the clothes, the hair, and how he walked. When he realized he resembled Cort so closely, he stood up in alarm.

The young man raised his hand to greet them. Erich staggered back as the young man approached. The others noted his fearful expression.

"My God," Manfred said to him. "What's the matter? It's like you've seen—"

"No . . . it can't be," he stammered.

"Father, it's me," he said as he walked toward them.

Cort's voice brought him back to his senses. "Cort?" Haltingly, he made his way to him. "How can this be? How?" He placed both hands on Cort's shoulders.

"Have I changed so much? It's like you didn't know me."

"I couldn't believe my eyes!"

"Well, it's me. I'm here."

"Yes, you're here," Erich said as he examined him more closely. His physical appearance had changed; he looked more haggard and thinner than in Ulm. His voice sounded different from what he remembered; however, he sensed something else in how Cort's eyes met his. He no longer displayed that boyish, innocent expression.

"You look thinner," Erich said. "And we need to cut your hair. Otherwise, you seem healthy." His demeanor shifted. "But you're supposed to be with the family! What happened? Are they all right?"

"Yes, when I last saw them."

"Why aren't you with them?"

"I left before we crossed the Danube."

"Why?"

"I was mad at them for not telling me the truth."

"What? With no explanation? My God, they must be worried about you." He wanted to chide Cort about his temper, but this was not the time or place.

"I left them a note," he answered, aware of his father's displeasure.

"How did you find us? Traveling so far and alone."

"I . . . wasn't alone."

"What? With whom?"

"I mean—" He shook his head, too tired to explain.

"Tell me later. Let's eat first! Come meet my companions!"

Cort engaged in friendly banter with everyone during the meal except Mara, who understood the reason for his coldness. He let out a loud burp after finishing his third fish.

"I didn't think I was so hungry," he said. "I hope I didn't have too much."

"Too much?" Erich said with a laugh. "Not at all. Food will be easy to get from now on." He gazed at his son with admiration and curiosity. "Speaking of which, how did you feed yourself all this time? And how, in God's name, did you find us?"

Cort finished a drink of water. "It's a long story, father."

"Give us the short version," Franz said. "We're all ears."

They listened in wonder as he recounted his adventures on the road, beginning when he jumped off the boat, and how he returned to the farm and reunited with the wolf. He also shared the story of the attack near Günzburg and Gunther's death, which his father took very hard. They were captivated as he talked about his experiences with the lone gray wolf he had befriended and how it guided and protected him.

As Cort spoke, Mara observed that he had similar facial features and wavy brown hair as his father. Moreover, she discerned the same strong, innate warrior spirit in him. In addition, his mannerisms were like those she'd known with pronounced artistic natures.

"Where is the wolf now?" she asked.

"The wolf's name is Spruce!" Cort answered. "He left last night. I miss him so much." He clenched his jaw to hold back sobs.

"That's quite an adventure," Manfred said.

"So," Franz said in an upbeat tone, "you made friends with a wolf. You're a lucky young man! I knew someone who did the same after he settled in the woods. Those who saw him said a wolf was always at his side. He seldom returned to town. And why should he? They say a wolf makes the best and most loyal friend a man could ever have."

"What I don't understand," Erich said, "is how you caught up to us. We must've had a week's head start on you. Did you get rides along the way?"

"I walked the whole time except once from the ferry to the farm.

"We stayed three days in Riedlingen when you were sick," Manfred said to Erich.

"You were sick?" Cort asked.

"Yes, but Mara nursed me back to health."

He still found it difficult to face her.

"Manfred's leg also slowed us down," Franz said.

"And my slow walking," the Scholar said.

"We've been here two days," Franz added. "So all those things gave you the chance to catch up."

"We've much to talk about," Erich said. "But you should rest now."

"You're right," he said, stretching. "I'm ready for a long sleep."

As Cort trudged to the shelter, Erich felt immense pride in Cort's accomplishments during his travels with the wolf, which outweighed his disappointment over his rash decision to leave the family. He looked forward to learning more about what he experienced during the next part of their journey.

The journey had become even more worthwhile to him now that he was together again with his son.

18.

The Swedes

Klaus chomped on a leg of mutton, swallowed it after a few bites, and washed it down with ale, some of which spilled down his face and goatee onto the collar of his gilded shirt and vest. He slammed the mug on the table, and stared bleary-eyed out the window of the farmhouse. A buxom woman wearing a low-cut blouse sat next to him. Her cheeks were puffed up with rouge, and cheap trinkets and copper jewelry adorned her arms and neck. She reached into his pants with a leering grin, but he grunted, pushed her hand away, and raised his mug.

"Hurry, dear!" the woman bellowed. "Don't keep my man waiting."

A frightened-looking girl dashed in from a back room carrying a pitcher and poured more ale with shaky hands. The wench stroked his chest as he drank. He set the mug down and groped and kissed her breasts as she laughed with haughty delight.

A knock at the door interrupted his pleasure. "Come in," he said with some annoyance.

A soldier entered, followed by Lothar and Sigi.

"Sorry to disturb you, sir," the sergeant said, "but a courier arrived from headquarters with an important dispatch."

He handed Klaus a rolled-up parchment tied with red cloth. As he read it, he broke into a smile.

"Ah, good news. The armies are assembling. We'll leave within a fortnight and unite with General von Werth at Ratisbon by the first of May. This will give us time to rid the surrounding towns of Protestant influence."

"But what of me?" the wench asked.

"I'll decide when the time comes. Now go to the bedchamber. I'll summon you later."

She gave him a wink, slapped her bottom to tease the other men, and left the room with a shrill laugh.

"Well, sergeant, I trust our men will be ready to march soon."

"Yes sir, they will."

"I want them to be the best fighting unit in the regiment. You're dismissed."

He turned to his men. "I took out a little from our treasury today." He reached into his pocket and set a pouch of coins on a table. "You know what this is for."

"For that *other matter*," Lothar said.

"We've known about Erich's relatives near Nördlingen," Sigi said. "They also might be in Nürnberg."

"Why there?"

"A shopkeeper told us that Erich was stationed there. He made friendships among some town officials, so he might've sent his family there."

"Search both places". He slid the pouch toward them. "There'll be more if you find them."

After they left, Klaus stood in front of a mirror, donned a richly plumed hat, tucked in his shirt, and smiled at his reflection. He adjusted the soft folds at the tops of his knee-high leather boots and then snipped a few stray hairs from his goatee with scissors. Even the eye patch suited his appearance, enhancing the image of a soldier who had sacrificed on the battlefield. He slipped on his officer's coat and walked outside.

He placed one foot on the porch railing and admired the scene before him. As the day drew to a close, most of the ninety men under his command rested around the numerous tents spread across the pasture. He scanned other areas of the encampment. Horses grazed at a trough within a fenced corral. Artillery cannons and other weapons were stored in a barn. Outside the barn stood the wagons carrying food and provisions for the soldiers. Everything appeared to be in order.

Soon, he'd be on the march again, not merely as a foot soldier but as an officer in the Imperial Army. During that time, he rose to the rank of sergeant and recalled the battles he fought under Wallenstein and Tilly, whose forces swept north and crushed all who stood before them. All that changed, however, when the apostate Gustavus Adolphus arrived with his barbaric horde and cut through the realm, dividing the people once more. But ever since Gustavus fell at Lützen, those cursed Swedish troops and their allies had been in disarray.

He knelt on the porch and recited a prayer of thanks to God for guiding him to his current position. He'd come such a long way from the humble beginnings of his youth when he and his family barely made enough to put food on the table, with no hope or means to improve their condition. Yes, things were going quite well in his life. As he went inside to the back room where the buxom wench awaited him, he couldn't imagine it going any better.

————

Peter carved a small block of wood in his workshop, shaping it into a bishop chess piece. Rudi stood beside him, watching his father with keen interest. He had been teaching his son how to smooth the pieces using a coarse-haired brush and thought he would soon be ready to learn how to use some basic carving tools.

After the family settled, he found work in a craft shop serving the rising mercantile class and landed gentry in Leipzig. His woodcarvings became the family's primary source of income. Thomas took on heavy labor jobs, such as hauling bricks for the many new structures built to replace those destroyed by the war. Agatha and Eva worked as midwives for some of the town's more tolerant Protestant and Catholic families.

Initially, they lived in wagons until Catherine's family settled them in one of their properties: a small place by the river, shielded from the street by a sturdy wooden fence. It took some effort to clean and furnish the rooms, but soon they were able to live comfortably in the house. They cleared a patch of vacant land behind the house and grew vegetables. Later, they acquired a rooster and more chickens, which they housed in a coop that Thomas built. Whenever their spirits sagged due to the hardships of their circumstances, Agatha always reminded them to be thankful for what they had, especially in comparison to so many others affected by the War, and that Erich and Cort would soon return.

Anna burst into the workroom. "Come on, you two, it's supper time!"

Rudi jumped off the stool and dashed out of the room.

"In a minute," Peter said as he carved the castle piece.

She walked up to him and held out her hand. "They told me not to come back unless you're with me. And I'm hungry! Aren't you too?"

He sniffed the air. "Yes, I am." He grasped her hand, and she led him out of the room.

Peter dipped a ladle into the pot, served himself more stew, and handed it to Thomas. Rudi was still working on his first bowl. Heloise clutched a spoon, trying to feed herself. She had turned one year old that month, and the family celebrated the occasion with a sumptuous meal. Agatha soaked up the juice on her plate with bread. Anna stared forlornly at the only empty chair at the table—her mother's.

"Oma," Anna said to Agatha, "will Mother be better soon?"

"Yes, dear. I checked on her today. It's only a minor ailment. Why don't you go into her room with a bowl of stew and keep her company? That will cheer her up."

"You too, Rudi," Peter said.

Eva made sure the children were out of the room before facing Agatha. "She's been this way far too long," she said in a lowered voice. "I wasn't that way when I was with child either time."

"Carrying a baby affects a woman differently," Agatha said. "None of mine were the same. And it's been many years since she's carried."

"I think it's more than that," Peter said. "Being separated from Erich and with Cort gone is weighing on her."

"And what happened to Gunther," Thomas said.

"You're right," Eva said. "She seemed better until we told her why Erich left and how long before he returns. She might be worried he won't come back before the birth. When did you say that would be?"

"No later than Mabon," Agatha answered. "Or earlier September."

"He'll be back before then," Peter said.

"And Cort too," Thomas said, nodding.

————

Cort walked with his father along the road by the Rhein, which meandered through a pleasant countryside dotted with small farms and villages. They'd been inseparable ever since their reunion three days prior. Mara now joined the others behind them. Manfred walked with her, still limping as he led Baldur. Franz guided his horse beside the Scholar.

During this time, Erich remained vigilant for highwaymen. On the second day, a group of ragged-looking horsemen watched them cautiously from a grove of trees as they passed. When this happened, he always told her to pull the hood of her coat over her head.

Manfred noted the various boats and barges of different sizes and shapes moving up and down the river. A few days earlier, he had asked Erich about riding on one of them during their trip through the town of Kehl, but he firmly declined, stating that they were all too small for him and the horses. After hearing this, and based on his tone, Mara suspected there might be other reasons for his reluctance to travel on the river.

About midday, the road branched off. One went east and the other, according to a crude sign, led north to the town of Baden. A short time later, Cort dashed into the woods. Mara had wanted to talk to Erich alone for some time, so she hurried up to be beside him.

"How soon before we get there?" she asked.

"Early tomorrow."

"You can leave me there to return to your family faster."

He shook his head. "I've thought about this, but it's out of the question. The roads aren't safe, as you've seen."

"I could get on a boat and—"

"A woman on a boat full of men is a bad idea. Besides, we're going north all the way to Mainz, so you might as well stay with us until then."

"If that's so," she said with a hopeful smile, "perhaps you can come to Eibingen since it's so close. And rest there before you venture east."

Cort emerged from the woods, tucking his shirt, and ran back to them.

"It's settled then," she said. "This pleases me very much."

"And I."

———

On the outskirts of Baden, they approached two tall posts erected on each side of the road with wheel-shaped objects on the top. Erich knew what they were before they could make out the bodies of two men on the wheels, their crushed limbs wrapped around the spokes. Mara averted her eyes as they went by. Their faces were streaked with dried blood streaming from their empty eye sockets, gorged out by the crows. The two men appeared dead, but Erich thought he detected a faint breathing movement within one of the torsos.

Erich maintained a firm grip on Baldur as they walked through the bustling streets of Baden, filled with chaotic activity. Two men burst out of the alehouse, grappling and fighting in the street. More drunken patrons stumbled out from the establishment and joined the brawl. The townsfolk cheered and jeered them on as the fight escalated. He guided Baldur around the melee, looking for a livery.

They came upon a noisy crowd in a market square, accompanied by drum beats.

"I'll find out what they're doing," Cort said.

On one side of the square, men gathered in front of a row of tables while a town crier read aloud from a pamphlet. Cort picked up a pamphlet from one of the tables and read it as he walked back.

He handed the pamphlet to his father. "You won't like this. They wanted me to join the Imperial Army."

Erich took a glance and gave it to the Scholar, who shook his head and threw it down.

Soon, they found a livery. As they waited for the proprietor, another pamphleteer greeted them smilingly and gave one to Erich. This one was a recruitment pamphlet from the Protestant Union. He handed it to the others. The Scholar crumpled it up and threw it down again.

"I wouldn't even use this piece of trash to wipe my arse," he said in a voice loud enough for the pamphleteer to hear.

"This looks like a good town to make money," Franz said. "I'm going to juggle here after we find a place to stay."

Erich now realized that the town was a mustering center, based on the pamphlets and raucous street activity. Once word spread that armies were recruiting in a town, the lawless and down-and-outers from the entire region flocked to sign up. The few pieces of copper and silver they received for signing were all the incentives they needed, but more often than not, they spent it all the same day, drinking and gambling. Some, of course, tried to escape their commitments by fleeing to other towns. Special squads from both armies hunted them down. Those captured were dealt with severely and used as examples to discourage other conscripts from taking similar action. Some ended up like those two men on the wheels.

After they had bought food and supplies, a wagon carrying several partially covered corpses raced by them on the street, some with dark lesions on their exposed limbs.

"The plague!" Mara said to Erich.

"We leave right away."

On their way out of town, they came upon a smaller market square with a few people milling around a tall, charred post erected on a platform. The remains of a human body were lashed to the post from a recent witch burning. They stared at it for a moment and went on. Mara stopped and glanced back to the square.

"Wait here," she said. "I won't be long."

She slipped the hood over her head and made her way toward the platform. A woman and two young men walked away as she approached. They observed her with suspicion from a distance as she knelt in front of the post. She closed her eyes and offered a silent prayer for the victim.

After the prayer, she looked up at the corpse: from the burnt remains of the feet and legs, still lashed to the post, and up to the charred body and arms. Slight protrusions of flesh still hung on the breast. She hesitated before viewing the head. Tufts of hair dangled from the skull, and the mouth was agape, revealing some teeth, in a pose of suffering indicative of her final agony.

She walked back to them, head down, hoping the woman's soul had a clearer path to the next world.

———

Erich and Cort sat together fishing in the Rhein. They hadn't talked much since they started, both absorbed in thought

"Father," he said. "I'm glad you told me why you rescued her. I only wish you said so before we left the farm."

"I had a lot on my mind and overlooked your feelings."

Cort cast his line into the water. "Well, I think you did a good thing."

Erich nodded. Those words meant much to him.

Cort got a nibble and reeled in a good-sized fish. As he unhooked it, another idea came to him.

"Can we practice with the Bow soon?"

———

The next day, he walked next to his father with a confident stride. He ate well again and enjoyed a restful sleep. He had also practiced shooting the Bow the day before, the first time he had done so since that cold winter day by the farm. This time, pulling the string back farther and keeping the arrow steady felt easier. He wanted to practice again, but his father advised that they needed to wait at least a week because learning to shoot should not be rushed.

The Scholar lagged far behind, so Erich stopped to wait for him. A thick cloud of dust appeared on the road much farther away, accompanied by the distant rumble of horses. He counted six—then nine—men approaching them. The sound faded as they vanished into a dip on the road. When the Scholar finally caught up with him, the riders reemerged into view once more.

Erich could tell they were soldiers by the numerous weapons they carried and those slung across the saddles of their battle horses. The lead horse carried a furled banner displaying distinctive blue and yellow colors.

As they rumbled by, one of them slowed down and circled back, keeping an eye on Erich. He didn't look as rough as the others and sported a well-groomed beard with a mustache curled at the ends. He whistled to the others ahead to stop, rode up, and spoke to the lead rider while pointing back at them.

"What do they want?" Cort asked.

"I'm not sure," Erich answered.

"They don't look like highwaymen to me," Manfred said.

"They're Swedes."

The horsemen rode up to them in two lines of four. The one with the banner on his saddle, likely their leader, rode between the two lines.

They stood with great unease as the soldiers approached.

"I don't like this," Manfred murmured, "Swedes or not."

The horseman with the curled mustache rode up to them and halted beside Erich. He reached for the Black Bow that was looped on Baldur's saddle, but Erich stopped him from taking it. The horseman pulled harder, and eventually, Erich relented. He rode away with the Bow to his group and handed it to the leader, a heavy-set man with reddish hair and a closely cropped beard. The leader withdrew the Bow from its sheath and inspected it.

"I've seen this bow," he said to Erich, his accent noticeable. "There's not another one like it. How did you get it?"

"It's been with my family for many years. My father owned it before me and his father before that. And so on for hundreds of years."

"What happened to your father, so it's now with you?"

"He died in battle three years ago. Some soldiers returned it to us."

The leader narrowed his eyes. "Which battle?"

"Lützen."

A few horsemen had to settle their horses, suddenly becoming restless.

"Your father's name?"

"Richard."

"And yours?"

"Erich."

"Where were you during those times?"

"Recovering from battle wounds. My sister was killed in Magdeburg when the Imperials sacked it, and so my father took a vow to avenge her death."

Mara shot him a surprised glance. He hadn't told her this.

"And where do you live?"

"At the time, in Ulm."

The leader relaxed his posture. "I knew your father well, as did others here. He died a warrior's death—" His voice dropped. "As did so many at Lützen. Your father was a man of means and property. And you, well, traveling on foot, don't look like someone from such a family. We thought the worst with the Bow on your saddle."

"Our family has come upon hard times. I'm on a pilgrimage now with friends."

"A pilgrimage, you say?" The leader studied each member, settling the longest on Mara. She raised her chin a bit and met his gaze without flinching.

"You travel with only two horses and one that should not be used for packing."

"Baldur has been with me in battles," he said, patting his neck, "before your men arrived."

"You know who we are?" the man with the curled mustache asked.

"By the colors on your banner. My father told me stories of the Swedish Yellow and Blue Brigades. Their courage and fighting skills. And what an honor it was to serve with them."

The other Swedes straightened their posture in acknowledgment of those words. The leader nodded. "Enough talk! We'll camp here and invite you to join us. We have much to discuss."

He held out the Bow toward Erich. "And so, Erich, son of Richard of Ulm, who fought and died with the Lion at Lützen. And the rightful holder of the Black Bow. Take back what is yours!"

Erich walked to the leader between the two lines of the horsemen, who regarded him with the respect of a fellow warrior. The leader gave it to him.

"My name is Ansgar," the leader said to Erich. "The one with the sharp eyes next to me is Helmar. You'll meet the others later."

Cort felt a surge of pride as his father strode back to them.

Mara couldn't shake the feeling of apprehension about being near them; yet, despite their formidable appearance, they seemed to be men of honor who could be trusted.

————

Cort strummed the lute while the others listened at the campsite. The Swedes pitched their camp downstream, where a sheep roasted on a spit. After he finished playing, he set the instrument down.

"Father, I want to get a lute like this."

"Maybe in Leipzig. But you'll have to work for it."

Helmar came by and invited them to their campsite. Erich walked back with him, followed by the others.

"I knew your father well," Helmar said. "We had contests with the Bow, and let me shoot it a few times. It filled me with amazement when I saw it and then rage when it was in different hands and perhaps stolen. And a greater rage when you let it go so fast. The true owner wouldn't do so without a fight."

"I'd challenge your best man to keep it."

"Soon you'll meet Valborg. He would've fought you. He's never been beaten by just one."

"I'd defeat him with the Bow at stake."

Ansgar greeted them at the camp. "Come, you'll meet my men now."

They came to a group of men sharpening their swords and conversing together.

"These are our pikemen and musketeers," Ansgar said. "The one sharpening his sword is Axel. The dark one is Nico. He keeps to himself but is a demon in battle."

Mara observed Nico's features, which were distinctly different from those of the fair-haired Swedes, particularly because of his ornate and colorful clothing. His crimson shirt contrasted sharply with his long black coat, which was embroidered with gold and silver thread. A piece of studded jewelry decorated one of his earlobes.

They headed to the raging campfire where two large and burly men turned the spit with the sheep.

"The hogget is almost ready," the one stoking the fire said with a grin.

"Our artillerymen—Magnus and Markus," Ansgar said. "They don't need horses to pull our cannons. They do it themselves. They're brothers, twins no less. Even after all these years, I can only tell the difference by their scars."

Both men had scars on their bodies, but one displayed a prominent gash along his cheek that extended to his eye, resulting in a half-closed lid.

Ansgar led them to the last group of three men.

"Here are our cavalrymen." He pointed to two of them. "Gunnar, Valborg, and I come from the same town."

Valborg turned toward Erich with arms akimbo.

"You don't look much like your father," Valborg said with a wild grin.

"But I fight like him," he said with an equally confident grin.

"If so, you are one of the few Germans who do," he scoffed.

Gunnar sized up Erich but said nothing. He was more fair-skinned than Ansgar, with short blondish hair, blue eyes, and eyebrows and lashes so light that it almost appeared he did not have any.

"And here's Mackenzie," Ansgar said. "His bunch from Scotland joined us at the beginning in Stralsund. Most of his countrymen have returned, but he's been staying with us for some reason."

"For some very good reasons," Mackenzie said, rubbing his thumb along his fingers on one hand.

"You'll have to tell us about your pilgrimage over the meal," he said to Erich, "as I'll tell you about our wanderings. Come, let's eat now."

———

They all sat on stones and logs around the campfire, feasting on the hogget. Ansgar had been recounting their exploits from the past two years.

"After the defeat at Nördlingen, our brigades disbanded, and the rest of the army scattered to the four winds. Some went back to Sweden. Others stayed and united with the German Protestants in the north. We were stationed in Bremen and Potsdam. But they couldn't pay us, so we left the army and went off alone."

"How long ago?" Erich asked.

"Almost two years."

"What've you been doing since then?"

"Selling our services to towns needing protection. Many towns became lawless places after the battles and fighting. The officials hired us to run out the riff-raff. An easy job that paid us more than we made as soldiers."

"It wasn't just because of the money, though," Gunnar said. "Our hearts weren't into fighting anymore."

"We felt invincible before Lützen," Helmar said. "But our spirits sank after Gustavus fell."

"We're mercenaries now," Ansgar said. "A far cry from when we first landed on those North Sea shores. Full of hope and confidence."

"But we can't return with nothing," Valborg said. "That's one reason we're doing this."

"Coming back alive to your families is something," Erich said.

"*Ja*," Ansgar added. "That day will come, but not yet."

"And now you fight for whoever pays you," Erich said, "Protestant, Calvinist . . . or Catholic."

"Never them!" Helmar exclaimed.

"We sell our services only when needed," Ansgar said. "We just came back from the Alsace and helped the Huguenots run off Cardinal Richelieu's troops."

"They paid us well," Helmar said. "But I fear Richelieu will send more men next time."

"Ay, they paid us so well," Mackenzie said. "I might have enough to head back home myself."

"Ah," Gunnar said, "we'll get rid of you at last."

Magnus carved out a section and gave it to Erich. "Good hogget, eh?"

"Yes. My favorite meat. We passed some sheep on a nearby farm but couldn't afford one."

"Neither could we," Valborg said, grinning. "So we took it."

Erich stopped chewing, glared at him a moment, and resumed eating.

Ansgar noticed his displeasure and changed the subject. "And so, we've told you about our journeys. Now tell us yours."

Erich cleared his throat. "I'm on a journey to return Mara to her home near Mainz. She was unjustly accused of certain crimes and about to be tortured and burned for them. I couldn't abide by that, so I freed her from prison in Ulm."

Everyone turned to her. She lowered her eyes before speaking.

"I was prepared to die. Then he came for me. The sacrifice he made is beyond words."

Valborg mumbled something, chuckling, to Gunnar.

"Manfred has been with me from the beginning," Erich said. "The rescue would've failed if not for him. The others joined us later, including my son."

"And the rest of your family?" Ansgar asked.

"I sent them to Leipzig. I'll go to them after Mara is safe."

"Leipzig, yes, so near Lützen," Ansgar said. "We've heard rumors that the War might be afoot again, and our forces are combining with the Germans in Saxony."

"Are you going there now?" Manfred asked.

"No. To Lauenburg," Helmut answered.

"That's well north of here," Erich noted. "Another mercenary mission?"

"Not quite," Ansgar answered. "We have business with a certain man who resides in the area."

The other Swedes nodded with grim expressions.

"So, Erich," Helmar said, "I'd like to see you shoot the Black Bow. I'll match mine against yours. Gunnar and Nico also have some skills."

Erich took one more bite and stood. "Let's go now."

———

Early the next morning, Erich and Manfred were stoking the fire.

"Too bad we'll be parting soon," Manfred said.

"They're much like the way my father described them. It's not easy to earn their favor, but once you do, they'll stick with you to the end."

"It sounds like Helmar knew your father well. Even with him on his deathbed."

"That surprised me. And that they mourned his death."

"How did he die?"

Erich set the last log on the flames

"After Gustavus Adolphus fell, several brigades regrouped and vowed to avenge his death. They mounted a series of furious charges, forcing the Imperials to retreat. It turned the tide of the battle. Father was one of those in the leading charge. A visiting Protestant officer said he cut down one of the main Imperial's officers, named von Pappenheim. But a volley of arrows and musket fire hit him. He died the next day."

Both men stared into the flames, musing about their days in battle. The sound of footsteps broke their reverie. Ansgar, Helmar, Valborg, and Gunnar strode toward them.

"We've been talking," Ansgar said to Erich. "And will join you on your pilgrimage since we're going the same way."

"You shouldn't trouble yourself."

"It's no trouble," Helmar said. "Besides, we've seen armed men on the road."

"How can we without horses?"

"That's why we're here," Ansgar said. "We'll get some for you."

The unexpected offer rendered Erich speechless for a moment. "I can't pay for them."

"Pay?" Valborg said. "We'll take them from the farms."

"No," Erich said. "People need their horses more than us. We'll just keep walking, thank you."

Ansgar hesitated a moment before responding. "We'll pay for them."

"What?" Valborg bellowed.

"You heard me!" Ansgar exclaimed. "Like we used to! Remember The Lion's orders? No looting or pillaging." He turned to Erich. "This is out of respect for your father and his sacrifice. What say you?"

"We accept your offer," Erich said.

Ansgar gave a pouch of coins to Valborg.

"Go to Phillipsburg with Gunnar and purchase four horses. We'll wait for you here."

————

Erich and the others sat by the campfire, eating pieces of the boar they had killed earlier in the day. Parts of the animal remained on the spit. The other Swedes sat beside them. Franz played the lute while Ansgar glanced at Baldur, who was tethered nearby.

"The Lion had a horse with the same build and features as yours. The sire came from a region in Spain."

"Andalusia," Erich said.

"That's right. He bred them to some of our local stock. He had the best. Almost eighteen hands tall with great strength and speed. The sight of his horse charging toward them put the Imperials in a rout."

"My father got Baldur for me as a yearling. It took a long time to break him, but he gradually took to me."

"How old is it?" Ansgar asked.

"This will be his thirteenth year."

"Not so old for such a strong horse. Some can live for over twenty years."

"If taken care of, which I do."

"I've been lucky with horses as well," Ansgar said. "I've seen what happens to men thrown during a charge. Sometimes, I don't know how I survived those battles. But when on the right horse, I felt nothing could touch me."

"I felt the same on mine until a cannon shell tore up my leg," Erich said.

Franz finished and set the lute down.

"Could you play that song again?" the Scholar asked, staring wistfully into the fire.

"*Ja*, I've had my share of wounds too," Ansgar said. "But nothing ever kept me down for more than a few days. Musket balls have whizzed past my ears. Seen men die next to me. My men, the Imperials, hundreds of them. I've lost count of the men I've killed. I see them at night, their faces. Or what was left of them."

"Soldiers dying in battle are one thing," Erich said. "But what the War has done to others is worse. The plundering and looting in the countryside. Families destroyed. People with nothing left, starving, diseased. Living in caves. Or fighting their neighbors."

Franz continued to play as everyone reflected on Erich's and Ansgar's words.

"Not long ago," the Scholar said, just above a whisper, "everyone got along and helped each other. I remember songs like this during those times. Peaceful, happy, gentle songs. But now there's so much suffering and cruelty." His voice trembled with emotion. "Even from my students. They pushed me back, you know."

"What do you mean?" Mara asked.

"They pushed me back. To the people who put the tar on me as I tried to flee. My students. My children. They laughed when they threw the feathers at me. But it wasn't real laughter. The opposite. It was a laughter full of anger and hatred! I still see their faces. Possessed. Demonic. I've seen the Devil in their faces. My students' faces."

He broke down and sobbed. Franz stopped playing.

"What's the matter with him?" Axel asked.

"People tarred and feathered him because he spoke out against injustices in his town," Manfred said. "We found him on the road, and Mara mended his scars. He is on his way to the Low Countries."

She placed her hand on his head. He closed his eyes and began to take deeper breaths.

"Yes," she said. "Sink into your feelings. And you'll be healed."

For some time, he moaned lowly and swayed back and forth. But then he jerked to a stop and opened his eyes. She removed her hand.

"I feel strange," he whispered. "Like I'm under a—"

His eyes darted to Mara and backed away from her.

"I'm better now," he said to no one in particular. He grasped his book lying next to him. "I take comfort from reading passages from the classics. That's my protection from the evil surrounding us."

He strode off to his shelter, prompting most everyone else to retire to theirs. Only Erich and Mara remained. She moved closer to him, and they exchanged smiles.

"Superstition runs deep in some people," he said. "Even among the learned."

"Especially among the learned. Their intelligence can turn small fears and superstitions into larger ones, which run deeper and are harder to root out."

Erich recalled his mother using similar words to explain why book knowledge was not the only form of knowledge. Once again, he was struck by how often Mara's words echoed his mother's wisdom.

"I've wanted to ask you something," she said. "About what happened to your sister in Magdeburg. But if you don't want to—"

"No, I do. Beata married a teacher there. They had two children. The Imperials sacked and burned the town. My mother spent a week grieving alone in her room. They sometimes had a difficult relationship. Mother tried to guide her in her beliefs and practices, but Beata was more traditional. And they had disagreements."

"Still—"

"Yes, her only daughter. That was the beginning of hard times for us. First, my father left and was killed in battle. Soon after, Peter almost died of a cough that went deep into his chest. I reinjured my leg and couldn't walk without pain for a year. Later, we had to move out of our ancestral home to a smaller farm. But we pulled through it and managed to stay together."

"You and your family have much strength. You'll survive the War."

"Every time I hope the War might end, it starts anew. It's becoming harder to continue. For my family. For everyone."

He gazed into the campfire. The coals glowed brighter when stirred by gentle gusts of wind, pulsing in a steady bright-dark rhythm, resembling the beating of a heart.

"Someone has to end this," he said.

"It'll take more than one person."

"It has to begin somewhere."

Now she wanted to reach out and grasp his hands as they did in the prison cell.

He shook his head and looked up at her.

"What about you? You've told me about your life in the convent. But not the times before."

His question caught her off guard. "Oh, I'd like to share that with you but another time. I'm tired from another long day."

She bade him good night and went back to her shelter.

He wished she could have stayed because he wanted to say more to her. Above all, he wanted to confess his true feelings to her, but that would never happen. Within the month, they would be in Bingen, and she would no longer be in his life.

Once again, he mused about how quickly time had passed with her.

19.

Toward Bingen

They had been riding along the Rhine at a leisurely pace all day, passing farms and villages, observing boat traffic on the river, and enjoying views of castles on the slopes. Erich felt a strength in Baldur's gallop since much of the packing weight had been redistributed to the four horses provided by the Swedes two days before.

After the horses had arrived, Mara and the others gathered around to select which ones to ride. The decisions proved to be straightforward. She favored the gray horse because it reminded her of one she had in her youth, both in appearance and temperament. Manfred and Cort haggled a bit over two of the largest and strongest horses, but Cort eventually conceded to Manfred's choice. The Scholar ended up with the oldest and calmest horse. This eased Erich's concern about finances since he had planned to buy two horses for Cort and Manfred for their journey to Leipzig. Now he'd have plenty left for food, supplies, and occasional lodging during the long trip east.

They attracted considerable attention as they rode through the streets of Mannheim, particularly at the only woman in the group riding a striking gray horse. They set out for the market from the livery while Erich and Cort went to shops for flint, fishing supplies, and clothing. The three cavalrymen—Gunnar, Valborg, Mackenzie— and the twins headed straight to the nearest inn.

A pack of children dressed in rags dashed up to them from one of the abandoned buildings. Some held out their hands for food or coins.

"Look at the poor souls," Axel said. "We should give them something."

"If you do," the Scholar said, "every beggar in the town will be on us."

Nico glared at him and tossed a loaf of bread to them. Axel did the same. The older children snatched the loaves after a scramble. Mara and Manfred each threw a loaf as well. They scampered back to the building, clutching the small loaves—except for one young girl with long dark hair braided in the back. She stood empty-handed but forced a brave smile instead of holding out her hand.

"Sorry, little girl," Manfred said. "Get some from your friends."

They walked away, but Mara stayed, taken in by her plight. "Wait!" she declared. "I want to talk to her first."

She knelt on one knee. "Hello. My name is Mara. What's yours?"

The girl averted her eyes, head down.

"That's alright. I have food in my bag. Would you like some?"

She barely nodded

"Let's go find a shady spot and eat together."

They walked to a building on a quiet side street and sat on some old wooden planks. The others waited in the nearby shade. Mara offered her a piece of bread. She stared at it with hungry eyes, took a small bite, and then devoured it like a starved animal.

"I see you're hungry. Here's some cheese. Try to chew slower if you can."

"Thank you," she said, with a full mouth.

"She brushed her hand through the girl's dusty hair. "You're a very pretty girl. Can you tell me your name now?"

"Adele."

"Tell me, Adele. When did you last eat?"

She continued to chew without responding.

"Does your mother or father give you enough food?"

Still no answer.

"Adele . . . do you have a mother or father?"

She grimaced as she ate.

"Do grown-ups take care of you? Does anyone?"

Adele pointed to a building where the same children huddled in a corner, casting furtive glances at them.

"Do you like being with your friends?"

"Sometimes," she said, staring back at them.

"Do you find shelter with them?"

"We sleep in buildings no one else lives in," she replied more confidently.

"How often do you eat?"

"People in the market give us food if we clean their stalls."

"Do you ever get in trouble?"

"No. I mean, yes. Some people chase us away and throw things at us."

Mara had heard enough. Adele was doomed to a hopeless and bleak future.

"Adele. Would you like to come with me?"

Adele backed away in surprise.

"I don't think you're safe here. With no mother or father and with no place to stay. Not knowing when you'll eat next."

Mara reached out her hand.

Adele glanced at her friends, who were still watching her, then back at Mara with hopeful, trusting eyes—and grasped her hand.

"Good! Let's go where you can wash up and get new clothes. And then have more food and talk."

Mara learned a bit more about Adele during the meal. She grew up in a village near the town but remembered little about her mother, who died from the plague when Adele was three. She had no brothers or sisters. Her father had died two years earlier after falling through the ice while fishing. She stayed in the town's only orphanage until it closed. Afterward, she lived a hand-to-mouth existence with her friends and their relatives.

————

Cort finished loading Baldur and his horse at the livery. His father left to join the Swedes for "a drink or two" at a tavern. Across the street, Franz juggled in front of a crowd. Ansgar, Helmar, and the twins stood by the stable, waiting to leave.

"I think I hear them," Markus said.

The Swedes and Erich strolled around a corner, singing and shouting drunkenly. Mackenzie and Gunnar tried to support Valborg on each side as he stumbled along. Erich draped his arm over Gunnar's shoulder. The townsfolk observed them with bemused expressions.

They staggered toward Ansgar. Gunnar and Mackenzie let go of Valborg, who swayed slightly before regaining his balance.

"Can you ride?" Ansgar asked.

"*Ja*! I'm ready to get out of this piss pot of a town." He burped. "Nothing worth staying for. Ugliest hags I've ever seen. Speaking of piss—"

He unbuttoned his fly and shuffled to the stable wall.

"We should do this again," Gunnar said as he slapped Erich's back.

"Yes, in the next town," Erich said with a laugh as he slapped his back in return. "And the town after that."

Cort took note of his father's merry behavior, which often happened after he drank much ale.

Valborg continued pissing against the wall.

"He's right about the hags in the place," Mackenzie said. "No amount of ale could make me want to poke them."

"Good ale, though," Gunnar said.

"The best I've had in a long time," Mackenzie said.

"What would you rather have?" Helmar asked. "Good ale with stale women? Or stale ale with good women?"

Gunner shrugged. "A tough choice. You tell me."

"Not tough for me," Helmar said, twirling his mustache. "A good woman trumps all by far."

"Here they come," Cort said.

Mara, holding a young girl's hand, walked toward them with the others. She tried to remain as nonchalant as possible while loading the food onto her horse, with Adele by her side. The girl clutched Mara's dress with frightened eyes as the men stared at her.

"Look, Adele," Mara said. "This is the horse we're going to ride on. You can hold on to my waist. It'll be fun."

"What did you say?" Erich asked.

"This is Adele. She's coming with me."

"She will not."

His abrupt manner caught her off guard. "Her parents are dead. She has no one taking care of her. We found her begging for food with other children."

"She doesn't look like a beggar," Erich said.

She detected that he'd been drinking, so she chose her words carefully. "I cleaned her up and bought her newer clothes."

"You can't be snatching every unfortunate child from the streets. All towns have them. They survive somehow. She must have relatives here."

"She has no one. I'm not talking about every unfortunate child. I'm talking about this *one little girl.*"

He looked down at Adele. She looked apprehensively at him with her big brown eyes, much like Anna's.

"Very well," he said begrudgingly, "but she's your responsibility."

"Thank you," she said with deference. "She'll be no trouble."

———

Mara returned from the river with Adele, carrying a bucket of water. Along the way, as Cort watched, Erich and Helmar took turns shooting the Black Bow. The twins and the cavalrymen were engaged in an axe-throwing contest on the other side of the clearing. They cheered when Magnus's throw landed inside a target marked on a tree trunk.

They stayed at an abandoned farm for two days. A day's journey from

Mannheim, a heavy rainstorm drenched them, forcing them to camp in the leaky old barn. Although the storm passed the next morning, the roads remained impassable due to mud, so they stayed another day.

Mara set the bucket down and listened to Franz playing the lute while Nico accompanied him on the flute. She and Adele clapped after they finished, eliciting a smile from Nico—the first time she had seen him do so. She glanced inside the barn, where Ansgar tended to the shoes on his horse.

"Stay here, Adele," she whispered. "I'll be right back."

Ansgar halted his shoeing as she approached.

"Ansgar, I've wanted to ask you about one of your men—Nico. Is he from your country?"

"They're all from Sweden. Except for that lout Mackenzie." He chuckled to himself. "Why?"

"He looks different from the rest of you."

"I suppose he does. His people came from the south before the War started. From what I understand, others persecuted them for some reason. The Gypsy people, you know."

"Yes, I know. I didn't think they'd been driven so far north."

"Our rulers then let them settle in the Finnish frontier after they arrived. They didn't bother anyone, and we didn't bother them as long as they paid their taxes. But we needed men for the War and recruited them. They turned out to be some of the best fighters in the army. King Gustav recognized that and promoted them. They often volunteered for dangerous missions, but many were killed. Nico is one of the few left. He keeps to himself and talks mostly to Axel, another loner type."

Mackenzie galloped into the barn and dismounted beside Ansgar.

"The road looks ready for travel," Mackenzie said.

"We leave tomorrow," Ansgar said.

———

The next day, the sound of distant musket fire disrupted the tranquility of the ride. The Swedes formed a perimeter around the others as they rode ahead to an elevated spot along the road. Below, a group of ten highwaymen on horseback attacked six wagons. An equal number of men occupied the wagons, but the highwaymen wielded superior weapons—swords, clubs, and knives. One of the men in the wagon fired a musket at them, but two highwaymen quickly descended upon him. Women and children screamed as the marauders charged into the wagons.

"That's no good," Mackenzie said.

"Let's take them," Helmar said.

Ansgar nodded, tight-lipped. "Get your weapons out."

"I'll join you," Erich said.

"I'm ready," Manfred said.

"You should stay with the others," Erich said. "Just in case."

"Mackenzie, you too," Ansgar said. "Keep an eye out for trouble."

He bellowed a protest but complied as well. Ansar pushed his fist forward, and they thundered down the hill.

Ansgar cut down one of the wounded highwaymen who struggled to mount his horse. Axel dispatched the next one with a thrust of his pike. Nico finished off another with a flurry of furious blows from his sword.

The seven remaining highwaymen attempted to regroup. Helmar charged into a wagon, but three highwaymen confronted him. Helmar struck one but struggled to defend himself against the other two. Valborg and Gunnar rushed to his aid. The men from the wagons retreated from the battle, bewildered by the sudden turn of events.

The fight centered on the two captured wagons, where Helmar, Valborg, and Gunnar confronted four highwaymen. Magnus and Markus approached them, wielding clubs and axes, while Nico followed the twins into battle. Magnus incapacitated a highwayman with a single strike from his club, and Markus did the same to another. An enraged Valborg, with blood streaming down his face, killed another highwayman with his sword. Ansgar took down yet another who was trying to flee while Erich guarded the perimeter, waiting for a skirmish that required his attention.

Two highwaymen managed to gallop away. One went into the woods while the other headed in Erich's direction. He took a feeble swing at Erich with his sword, which Erich deflected, and then cut him down with two more swings.

The fight was over. The bodies of nine highwaymen lay scattered before the wagons. Helmar and Valborg bore the most wounds, with blood flowing from their heads and arms. Gunnar had lesser wounds on his shoulder. Nico's shirt was stained with blood, but none of it was his. Erich, Ansgar, and Axel remained on their horses while Magnus and Markus calmly wiped the blood off their axes.

A few men from the wagons dropped their weapons and went to check on the women and children, still wailing from the attack. The others helped a fallen man to his feet. Another man lay dead from a head wound. A woman fell weeping beside him.

Two men came up to Ansgar. "We thank you," one of them said.

"We couldn't have held them off."

"We knew about the dangers on this road," the other one said, "but didn't expect so many."

"Look!" Magnus shouted, pointing up the hill. "One of them is getting away!"

The highwayman who dashed into the woods raced toward Manfred and Mackenzie.

Manfred drew out his sword. "He's mine."

"Go to it," Mackenzie said.

Manfred spurred his horse to intercept him. The sudden charge caught the highwayman by surprise. Both horses reared up at close quarters. Manfred remained saddled, but the highwayman fell to the ground, gasping for air, the wind knocked out of him. Manfred jumped off and plunged his sword into his chest. The highwayman shook spasmodically from the thrust. Blood burst forth from the area below his heart after he withdrew it.

"Nicely done, man," Mackenzie said matter-of-factly. "Quick and clean."

Mara turned Adele's head away from the sight. Erich and the Swedes raced toward them.

"You got one!" Cort said to his father. "Manfred killed one, too!"

"It's good you did," Ansgar said to Manfred. "He might've alerted others."

"You think there's more?" Erich asked.

"Maybe," Ansgar said. "They looked more like soldiers than ordinary highwaymen."

"They might be part of one of the armies," Helmar said.

"Marauders," Gunnar said.

"We call them thief-heads," Erich said.

Ansgar grunted in agreement.

"Father, what are thief-heads?" Cort asked.

"Men with the army who do bad things. Their commanders tell them to go into towns and villages and take anything of value. The thief-heads give some of what they find to them and keep the rest."

Erich observed the wagon's occupants. Some wandered in a daze, bruised and bloodied, while others tended to the injured or gathered their scattered belongings. Wailing children clutched their elders. The fact that such a large group could be attacked like this made him realize he had underestimated the dangers on the road for his family.

The wagon group traveled with them until they arrived in Darmstadt two days later. After replenishing their supplies, they headed toward Mainz the next day. Those in the wagons stayed in the town, waiting for another group to join.

————

Cort sat with his father by the campfire, eating the fish they had caught that day. The sun had set behind the hills above the Rhein, and the sky glowed with deep orange and purple hues. On one side of the camp, Manfred arm-wrestled with Magnus, while Franz and the Scholar exchanged stories away from the others. Mara brushed Adele's hair as she did every evening; they had become inseparable since she joined them in Mannheim.

Cort stood and stretched. "I'm going to miss everyone after we take Mara home. Where do you think they'll go?"

"Of course, Adele will stay with Mara. The Scholar will go to the Low Countries. Who knows about Franz? The Swedes have some business to attend to in Lauenburg. Manfred will ride with us to Leipzig."

"I like the Swedes. They're good fighters, aren't they?"

"What you must remember is that they're part of an invading force and have caused much destruction in this country. Almost as much as the Imperials."

Cort stretched once more before heading to his shelter. Erich joined Mara and Adele.

"My daughter is about your age, you know," Erich said to Adele.

"What's her name?"

"Anna."

"Hmm. Maybe she can play with me in my new home."

Mara and Erich exchanged smiles.

"We'll be in Mainz tomorrow," he said to Mara. "And another two days to Bingen."

"We should be there before the first of May, then. We always celebrate at the monastery for the occasion. People from all around the countryside come for it. I hope that hasn't changed. So much could've happened since I left. Anyway," she sighed, "I'll find out soon."

————

Erich stood with the others on the banks of the Rhein, watching a slow-moving ferry approach from Mainz as strong gusts of wind blew in from the north. The skies began to darken, and the waters grew choppy. He made his way to one of the ferrymen as the people and wagons disembarked.

"Should we wait until the storm passes?" Erich asked.

"Oh no," the ferryman said. "I've crossed in worse."

Halfway across, the wind picked up, and rain pelted down on them. The ferrymen struggled to maintain their course. Waves lapped onto the deck, and the Swedes' horses grew restless, needing a firm hold. Mara noted Erich's withdrawn posture as he huddled next to Baldur on the rocking ferry.

"What a crazy ride," Manfred said as they guided their horses off.

"I thought we were going to swim to town," Gunnar said.

"Perhaps the singing of a beautiful Lorelei maiden enchanted them," Franz said. "Their spirits reside in this part of the river, I'm told."

"Ah yes," Helmar said. "I'd love to meet this enchanting Lorelei. I'd do some things to make her sing."

"I heard strange sounds during the storm," the Scholar said. "Like a woman's voice. Did anyone else?"

No one answered.

"It's just a fable," Franz said.

"Fables are based on truth!" the Scholar shot back. "There are demons in the world of spirits that exist in a hidden realm. It's why so many boats sink in the river around here."

"I'm sure it was only the wind," Mara said.

The Scholar glared at her. "It's not only the wind that lures men to death." He turned and walked away.

The townsfolk in Mainz paid little attention to them as they rode down the street. The town reminded Erich of Ulm before the War. He recognized some of the larger buildings and landmarks from his childhood visit to Mainz, particularly the grand church with a tall steeple resembling the one in Ulm. He also remembered the statues and monuments along the roads, some of which were built by the people who first settled the region many centuries earlier—the Romans, as his father had told him.

Erich, Mara, and Adele sat together in the dining hall of an inn. They decided to stay an extra day due to the good food and clean rooms. The Swedes went directly to some less-than-respectable inns to drink their fill and try their luck with women. Erich joined them for a short time but later returned to spend more time with Mara.

Adele gazed out the window overlooking the Rhein while Erich and Mara discussed the upcoming May Day festivities and shared their travel experiences. Sunlight filtered through the trees, casting shade from the hot afternoon sun. In the morning, Cort left with Franz for the town square, accompanied by Manfred and the Scholar.

Cort barged into the room in high spirits.

"Father!" he exclaimed breathlessly, sweat beading his forehead. He guzzled water from Erich's cup. "I played the lute! In front of people while Franz juggled! They liked my playing because some put coins in *my* hat too!"

He reached into his pocket and showed them a handful of coins.

"You must've played well," Mara said.

"The coins are nice. But it was more than that." He stared out of the window. "Now I see why Franz travels so much and plays in front of crowds. At first, I couldn't understand why he lived that way. Never settled down and always on the road. But now I do. It's a good life, I think."

Franz, Manfred, and the Scholar entered with another man who had a pack strapped on his back. They sat down at the next table.

"I told them how we played in the square," Cort told Franz.

"I think they liked your playing more than my juggling. Especially the maidens."

"I see you brought a guest," Mara said.

"Oh, yes," Franz said. "This is Christian. He was selling his sketches in the market square. So I asked him to draw one of me."

"Franz said you might want to peruse some of them," Christian said.

"We'd love to," Mara said. She couldn't take her eyes off his long and curly brown hair. She guessed that he was in his late twenties, with gray-green eyes, a clear complexion, and no signs of facial hair.

"First, I want to show you the one he did for me," Franz said.

He pulled a small roll of parchment from his sack and showed it to them, revealing a sketch drawn in black and shades of gray. The sketch captured the joy on his face as he juggled.

Christian then took out a thick leather book-like portfolio. He unclasped a ribbon and unfolded the drawings, some depicting buildings and scenic vistas of nature.

"These are all quite exceptional," Erich said as he examined one in particular.

The Scholar also studied them. "I've never seen drawings like this. They look like engravings of some kind."

"They're done with charcoal," Christian said. "A type of art I learned when studying in France. You can draw faster than in other ways."

"I've read of this technique," the Scholar said. "How did you draw so much detail using this method?"

"A good question." He reached into his pack and pulled out several markers in different shapes and sizes, each tightly wrapped in sheepskin around the charcoal and bound with strings. "Some are condensed and hard, which I use for the details. The others are softer and used for shading."

"Where did you purchase them?" the Scholar asked.

"In Amsterdam."

"Tell me what it's like there! I must know!"

"It's a town bustling with activity. Both in commerce and in art."

"So I've read."

"I've seen paintings done in oil and watercolors that left me breathless," Christian said. "Especially one by a master named Rembrandt. A simple portrait of a girl on a chair looking out a window. He captured every quality of her face, body, and clothes. Most remarkable was how he portrayed the light filtering into the room from outside."

"I think it would be wonderful if you could draw some of us as you did for Franz," Mara said. "If you have the time." She shot a glance at Erich. "They would make such good . . . remembrances."

"How many do you want?"

"I'd like one of myself and one with Adele," she answered.

"And one of Cort and one of me," Erich said. "We can pay you."

"And me," Manfred said.

"I'd like one, alone," the Scholar said.

"Even if we start now, it'll take another day to complete them."

"But we plan to leave tomorrow for Bingen," Erich said.

"Alas, I'm on my way to Heidelberg so—" He noted their disappointment. "Still, I've wanted to visit Bingen. Because of a castle that I could capture in a sketch."

"Others are traveling with us who might make it worth your time as well," Franz said.

"You mean the Swedes?" Cort asked.

"Of course," Franz answered.

"That's true," Erich said to Christian. "I think you'll be busy drawing much of the time with us."

"It's settled then!" Christian said. "Let's start now while there's still light!"

"Father, do you think the Swedes will want to be drawn?"

"Yes, I think so," Erich answered. He suppressed a grin as he thought more about it. "In fact, I'm almost sure of it."

20

Journey's End

A band of soldiers led a group of frightened people through the streets of Geislingen, brandishing swords and other weapons. The children and women wept as they stumbled along. The townsfolk witnessed the scene with a mute and fearful resignation. Other soldiers emerged from stores carrying sacks of goods piled into a supply wagon. The shopkeepers watched them with utter contempt.

Further down the street on the outskirts of town, Klaus stood next to Father Wilhelm, an older Jesuit priest sent by Father Helmut to monitor Klaus's progress. They both regarded the evicted people passing by with cold detachment. Wilhelm had accompanied Klaus since they began banishing unrepentant Protestants in the region the previous month and plundering the store owners who had "protected" them. The soldiers directed them to another wagon. The women, trying to muffle their sobs, huddled beside the men. Children clutched their mothers' arms. The wagon slowly pulled away.

"Our God is merciful," Father Wilhelm said. "They refused to convert. Perhaps the poor souls will discover the true light of His spirit another time."

"By choice or by force," Klaus said. "They might think they'll be free in the north, but soon our forces will be there. And they'll have to make the same decision as today. But with nowhere else to flee."

"Some might try to cross the Baltic to Sweden," Wilhelm said.

"We'll conquer those lands too," Klaus said.

Sigi rolled up with a wagon full of the town's plunder.

"Shall I divide the spoils among our men now?" Sigi asked Klaus.

"Do so. Give them what clothing and supplies they need, but leave the rest for us. Afterward, unload the wagon in the same building."

Initially, Klaus kept a record of all the loot they had gathered since they began pacifying the region, but he soon gave up on the task due to its rapid accumulation. He hoped that once the war concluded, he would have enough wealth to live comfortably and easily.

———

They rode leisurely along the Rhine toward Bingen, now on their third day out of Mainz. The slowdowns were due to Christian's sketches for everyone, which caused them to start their travels later and end each day earlier.

On the first day, during the midday rest, Christian drew a portrait of Mara posed on an outcropping of rocks overlooking the Rhine. Without any extra charge, he cut pieces of thin leather from a roll and stitched a simple cover for it to protect it from smudging. She then showed it to Erich.

"I wonder what the Scholar will think if I show this to him," she said.

"What do you mean?"

"He might think of me as a Lorelei maiden since I'm sitting on a hill over the river with boats below."

They laughed at the thought of it.

That evening, Christian sketched Erich. Ansgar wandered over to watch but left without a word. Later, Helmar did the same. Erich suspected that perhaps Cort was right about the Swedes; they didn't seem interested.

The following day, during the midday meal, Ansgar took Christian to a spot near the camp that overlooked a vista of the Rhein. He stood with one arm akimbo at his hip and the other raised, gripping his sword. He then began sketching Ansgar in his warrior pose while the other Swedes watched intently as he drew.

After Christian finished, he handed the drawing to Ansgar. He stared at it without expression for a moment and then broke into a wide smile.

"This . . . is me!" he bellowed while showing it to the others.

The Swedes gathered around Christian, eager to be drawn as well.

Valborg stood in a pose similar to Ansgar's, except he grasped a club in one hand and a sword in the other. Helmar posed with both hands folded on his chest, staring defiantly ahead. Gunnar flashed his sword in one hand and held a knife in the other. The next day, Magnus and Markus stood together, each holding an axe with rolled-up sleeves to showcase their muscular arms. Mackenzie held his sword out, with the point turned down into the ground. Nico clutched a bow, with his sword hanging at his side. Axel proudly displayed his pike.

The slow pace allowed Mara to take in the scenery, and she recognized more landmarks as they got closer to Bingen. The road meandered along the river, passing several villages and abandoned farms.

Many castles dotted the steep hillsides on the opposite side of the river. The boat traffic appeared busier than she remembered.

Later in the morning, they paused at the crest of a hill overlooking Bingen. The most striking feature of the area was a massive, castle-like stone building, partially in ruins, towering above the town where another river flowed into the Rhein.

"Is this your home?" Magnus asked Mara.

"It used to be. But we had to move across the river in a smaller convent beyond those hills."

"Remember this town?" Marcus asked his brother.

"Now I do. Because of the castle."

"What?" Ansgar asked the twins. "You were here?"

"Ja, during the first winter with The Lion," Magnus answered. "We camped near Cologne, and General Hanna needed artillery to break a siege, so they ordered us here. It took almost a fortnight before we broke them." He squinted at the castle and grinned. "I see some of my cannon marks on those walls by the tower."

"We had some good times here," Markus said. He made a lewd gesture.

"At least you were humane enough to let us move our belongings," Mara said. "But I don't understand why you destroyed it afterward."

"The rules of war," Ansgar said. "So it couldn't be used as a fortification against us."

"Ah, yes, the rules of war," she said. "So easy to say when it isn't your country being destroyed."

The Swedes exchanged nervous glances.

She yanked the reins and rode down the hill. Adele looked back with a worried expression until they all trailed behind her.

———

They rested by the dock, waiting for the ferry to arrive. An unending layer of light gray clouds covered the sky. It was a warm, muggy day with hardly any wind. Erich and the others sat together while the Swedes formed another group. No one spoke much. Franz plucked a soft melody on the lute, enhancing everyone's reflective mood.

"Christian," Erich said. "Can you do one more sketch of me before it arrives?"

"Of course," Christian said. He shielded his eyes, gazed toward the distant ferry, and then down to Erich for some time, as if a thought or inspiration had just occurred to him. He set up his easel and began to draw.

Mara spotted a bird soaring above them, believing it was an eagle or a hawk. As the bird drifted closer, a chill of regret washed over her when she realized it was a raven. It swooped down and perched on a nearby tree branch, looking down at them.

Christian gave the sketch to Erich. Just as he was about to pay, Christian raised his hand.

"Not this time. My purse is full enough. This one should have no price."

The ferry landed at the dock, and wagons and passengers moved off.

Mara walked over to the Swedes and spoke to Ansgar.

"We're grateful to you and your men for helping us and for the horses. Our journey would've been more difficult without you."

"It's been an honor."

"Again, you can join us in our May Day celebrations."

"We'll think about it," Ansgar said. "We might stay here another day or two."

"Maybe we'll find our old friends here," Magnus said to his brother with a wink.

"You can have your old friends," Mackenzie said. "I'll take those younger ones we passed along the road."

"*Ja,*" Helmar said. "Sometimes, the smaller towns have the fairest maidens."

"And the most willing," Valborg added, chuckling.

"You'll like our May Day celebration then," Mara said. "People from all over the region come to it. From what I remember, there were always more women than men during the occasion."

"When will that be?" Helmar asked, suddenly interested.

"In two days. There'll be plenty of food and drink too."

"I like the sound of that," Valborg said.

"Ask anyone in Rudersheim for directions to the Eibingen convent."

"I'll also stay here," Christian said. "I want to draw this grand castle. Perhaps I can transcribe it into an oil painting." He gazed up at it again. "So mighty and eternal. And yet, so damaged. A likeness of how the War has ravaged our country."

Erich glanced back at Ansgar and acknowledged him with a nod—there was no reason to do more. He felt a kinship in their company, but he knew they would have to part at some point.

As he settled on the ferry, which was smaller than the one to Mainz, he became gripped by a familiar unease. His fears diminished as the other passengers loaded around him; however, they returned as soon as they lunged off the dock.

He tried to distract himself by thinking about the journey, now nearing its end. He had succeeded in everything he set out to achieve: the rescue, the escape, and guiding Mara to her convent. Soon, they would part ways, and he would head back to his family. Still, he couldn't shake his conflicting feelings about leaving her, and he hoped the sorrow of their parting would lessen on the way to Leipzig.

Mara also reflected on the journey as she steadied her horse and how she owed her life to Erich. She'd prepared herself for the farewell, but now realized more than ever how unhappy she'd be without him. He stood with a stooped and withdrawn posture, but she didn't want him to endure this alone—no, not this time. She gave the reins to Franz and made her way to Erich. Once beside him, she slipped her arm inside his as unobtrusively as possible, hoping to allay his fears.

Upon her touch, the apprehension that had gripped him moments before vanished almost entirely. A profound emotion surged within him as she rested her head on his shoulder. He closed his eyes and began to imagine her presence. Soon, every nuance of her face became vivid. She gazed into his eyes with the faintest hint of a smile. A wave of confidence and strength pulsed through his entire being.

She reached inside her bag and gave him one of Christian's drawings. "For you," she said. "A keepsake."

He opened a portrait of Mara sitting on a log with the Rhein and the orb of the setting sun in the background. The half-smile Christian captured was strikingly similar to the one he'd just visualized of her.

He withdrew the sketch Christian had just done of him, folded back the cover, and handed it to her.

"And one for you," he whispered.

It depicted a stoic strength in his posture and a melancholy expression. Unlike his other drawings, Christian included more detail in the landscape: the surrounding hills, the river currents, and the approaching ferry. She found it unusual that, even with other people and wagons on the ferry, he drew only the silhouetted image of a single ferryman rowing toward them.

She closed the cover and placed it into her bag. Once more, she rested her head on his shoulder and tightened her grip on his arm as the ferry glided across the river.

Of all the moments they had shared on their journey, he knew that his most vivid memory would be the one he was living right now: arm-in-arm with her on this ferry, between both shores of the Rhein.

BOOK TWO

21.

May Day

Erich held a firm grip on Baldur's bridle as he led the others up a steep, narrow path above Rudesheim. After reaching the top, they rested to take in the sight of the Eibingen monastery in the distance. While not as large as Rupertsberg Castle, it was still an impressive structure that stood out prominently against the sloping countryside of low grasses and shrubs. The main building was constructed of stone, rising two stories high with a steeple on one side. Fences surrounded the barn that contained goats, sheep, pigs, and cows. A large stream flowed nearby, meandering toward the Rhein.

She felt both relieved and impressed by the sight. The monastery appeared to be in better condition than when she had left, judging by the increased size of the cultivated grounds and the numerous people involved in their maintenance.

Along the way, a hooded monk sat in the shade of a tree a short distance from the path. He stood with his staff in hand, observing them as they passed. Erich nodded to the monk and continued, but Mara kept her gaze fixed on him.

"Wait," she said and broke into a smile. "Gottfried!"

The hooded figure relaxed his pose. "Mara? *Mein Gott in Himmel.*" He pulled down his hood, revealing his shaven head. "You're back!"

"I hoped you'd still be here," she said.

"I had a strange premonition this morning and came here to meditate. I was reminiscing on the times in Rupertsberg when you were there. And you now appear! As if my meditations have been answered."

He faced the others.

"These are my friends who guided me along the way," she said.

"You're welcome here," Gottfried said. "We'll tend to your horses and arrange quarters for you."

The people in the fields halted their work and stared at them as they approached. Some of the younger ones eagerly rushed into the smaller buildings.

———

Inside the abbey, Gottfried led them to the dining hall. He stepped aside to speak with another monk, who then directed the servants.

"Please make yourselves comfortable. Food and drink will arrive soon."

"Is the Priestess Ursula here?" Mara asked.

"Yes. I'll inform her of your return after her midday prayers."

As they ate, three young maidens near the entrance whispered to each other while glancing at Cort. They quickly dashed across the hall to another room. One of them, with long, fair hair styled in braids, turned back and gave him a shy smile.

"Looks like you already have some admirers," Franz said to Cort.

Cort shook his head and resumed eating.

Erich and Mara exchanged glances, both thinking the same thing: their time together was nearing an end.

"This is an interesting place," the Scholar said to Mara. "There are monks and nuns of different orders here by their vestments."

"People from many faiths reside here. They come to teach and learn the wisdom and philosophy of Hildegard, who founded the convent here centuries ago."

"Ah, yes, Hildegard. I've read her writings on medicine. For a woman, she was quite intelligent."

She was about to offer a rebuke but refrained from doing so.

"Mara!" a voice proclaimed.

A tall, regal woman in her early forties walked down the stairway with a broad smile. She wore a long, flowing dress, and an ornate headband held back her light brown hair.

They clasped hands as they met.

"So wonderful to see you again," Ursula said. "It filled me with joy when Gottfried told me of your arrival." She examined Mara's features. "You look the same as when you left. Yet inwardly so different. More composed and wise."

"Much of the country has fallen into a barbaric and violent state. It's been difficult for me." She turned to the others. "These two men guided me here from Ulm—Erich and Manfred."

Ursula fixed her gaze on Erich, a half-smile on her lips. Her eyes drifted to the Black Bow resting in its sheath on the table beside him. She stared at it for some time.

"Ulm is so far away," she finally said to Mara. "The last letter we received from you was from Heilbronn." She directed her attention to the others.

"This is Erich's son, Cort," Mara said, "who found us along the way. And here is Adele, whom I found along the way. We were also blessed to have a minstrel and a scholar join us."

"You're welcome to stay in our guest quarters," Ursula said. "We'll have a meal to celebrate Mara's return after you're settled."

The servants led them away, but Mara stayed with Ursula. They sat down in a small alcove beside a window overlooking the monastery grounds.

"Much has changed since I left," Mara said. "New buildings and more people."

"Many have come here for sanctuary in recent years. We've granted most of them protection and security. They provide us with some means of support through their labor or some form of their wealth. They work on tasks to help keep the place in order." She took a sip of water. "We've become nearly self-sufficient. We still make trips to Bingen or Mainz for foodstuffs or supplies. I try to visit the Bishop whenever we go to Mainz. He's been very supportive and has pledged to send troops to protect us if the War flared up again. If so, I worry how we'll provide for refugees."

"I've seen signs of warfare in my recent travels. I wouldn't have made it back on my own after the rescue if they—"

"The rescue, you say? Tell me more, my child."

Mara sighed. "A long story. Perhaps tonight after I've rested."

"I assume those two men were instrumental in this *rescue*."

"Yes. They both possess the most honorable of natures."

"One of them, Erich, emanates a rare and defined aura. I've also detected something from the object beside him covered in a sheath. I can only describe it as being related to a kind of strongly earth-based power. Similar to those I've associated with certain stones. It is a bow of some type. Am I correct?"

"It's a long black bow. And there are some stones embedded on the surface." She glanced back at the doorway. "Are the servants and teachers still here?"

"Most, but not all."

"What about Lucinda?"

"She's still here. But she fell into dark and fitful moods after you left. She's been better lately. Although some days she regresses. She should be meditating in the garden now. But be warned if you go there because she's in high vapors. So take care when entering."

Mara strolled down a narrow corridor, guided by Lucinda's chanting voice ahead, which reminded her of the times when they first met. They took the same classes and soon became best friends, playing imaginary games together in the fields and woods around the castle and later sharing their deepest thoughts at night before falling asleep. As the years passed, Lucinda withdrew from others and grew increasingly dependent on Mara for comfort and companionship—almost oppressively so. Ultimately, it became too overwhelming, contributing to her decision to leave.

The corridor opened into a spacious garden. She stopped beside a column as Lucinda chanted in front of a small, trickling fountain. Sitting cross-legged with her eyes closed and arms extended, she chanted words she recalled, composed by Hildegard.

> *"...O cruor sanguinas*
> *qui in alto sonuisti*
> *cum omnia elementa se implicuerunt*
> *in lamentabilem vocem cum tremore,*
> *quia sanguis Creatoris sui illa tetigit,*
> *unge nos de languoribus nostris..."* [*1]

Lucinda sat still for a moment before snapping her head to Mara as if awakening from a trance. She opened her mouth in surprise, rose, and staggered toward Mara with a disturbed and intense expression.

"No . . . no. The visions . . . the cruel visions," she stammered.

Mara hardly recognized her as she approached. She looked gaunt, with a wild shock of reddish hair that was uncombed and carelessly cut. She halted and gently stroked Mara's cheek.

"You're here," she whispered. "Not a vision."

"Yes, I'm here."

She spoke with escalating joy. "I touch and hear you. The one I

----

[1] O bloodshed, with which the heights resounded, as all the elements unfolded themselves, in wailing voices, trembling, as the Creator's own blood touched them, soothe our ills, relieve our distress.

love." Her mood suddenly shifted, and her voice took on a darker tone. "But you left without a goodbye. . . Oh, I hate you! I hate you!"

She flailed her arms at Mara, who blocked them.

"I hate you," Lucinda mumbled and collapsed while sobbing on Mara's shoulder. "Why did you leave me? Why? I suffered so much."

Mara embraced her, which soothed her anger.

"It's wonderful to hold you again. Will you stay?"

Mara considered her words carefully. "For as long as I can."

"I'm happy now!"

Mara's gaze focused on her smile and the distinctive feature she had nearly forgotten—the small gap between her two front teeth. This somehow rekindled the warm and caring feelings she had for her before she left.

Lucinda held her close again. Mara felt a stirring warmth and returned her embrace with both compassion and desire.

———

The following morning, Ursula and Mara guided Erich, with the Bow slung over his shoulder, and Manfred along a path outside the monastery. They crossed a small footbridge over a stream and sat on wooden benches under the shade of an alder tree.

"This place is so peaceful," Manfred said, scanning the countryside. "It seems so far away from all the suffering below."

"We hope to stay and not be roused from our perch again," Ursula said.

They sat silently for a while, captivated by the vista of land sloping down to the Rhein, the vibrant wildflowers, and the sounds of chirping birds and buzzing insects.

"Mara told me of the circumstances of her rescue," Ursula said. "You acted with great chivalry and valor to guide her here." She turned her attention to the Bow. "I would like to examine this bow of yours now."

He removed the Bow from the sheath and handed it to her.

"My, it's so large."

She gently brushed her fingertips against its surface and examined each animal etching.

"Some things Mara recounted about this are quite fantastical," she said. "Notably, the power that emanates from it."

"It took some time to learn how to use it. I finally realized that I'd been overthinking when shooting it and not letting myself *feel* it. It's hard to explain. Now I'm teaching my son"

"You explained it very well," Ursula said. "Too much thought often interferes with feelings." She shot a knowing glance to Mara and stood up with the Bow. "I want to try it now."

Ursula nocked the arrow and slowly drew it back. She paused in her pull, holding it momentarily, then jerked back as if jabbed with a stick.

"Strange . . ." she whispered.

"What happened?" Mara asked.

"When I pulled it, I felt a surge within my body, which emanated from below my feet—from the earth. I felt a similar sensation emanating from my hand where I gripped the Bow. Something quite disturbing."

"This same happens to me," Erich said. "I feel a strength from it when pulling. Afterward though, if I pull back too far . . . I feel weak for a short time."

Ursula's eyes narrowed. "So, it seems this occurs when you pull beyond the point of balance between yourself and the Bow. It provides the power that you summon but leaves you weakened afterward. The Bow both giveth and taketh away." She shot another knowing glance at Mara. "Such are the fundamental truths and laws of nature."

"I think this power comes from something within the wood," Erich said

"Perhaps not only the wood," Ursula said. "Some of what I felt emanated from the center of the Bow. Where the stones are." She examined them closely. "They are quite unusual. The kind of which I've never seen."

"What do you mean?"

"I mean they are *un-natural*. They've been cut and shaped in precise patterns. Only a highly skilled craftsman could do this." She continued to examine them. "Two are so bright and clear. Whereas the other two are a greenish yellow."

"I always thought they were for adornment."

"I believe they were placed for a purpose. They seem to act as a focus to draw on the power of the earth and somehow provide it to the holder. Of course, this is mere conjecture on my part. In any case, I'll peruse our library to see if I can learn more about these stones."

She handed him the Bow. He studied the stones with renewed interest before putting it back in the sheath.

"I'm pleased you and your companions can stay for our Beltane celebrations," Ursula said. "Most churches have forbidden such ceremonies. Fortunately, our Bishop has permitted us to continue it. People come from near and far for the celebration." She removed a folded piece of thick parchment from her pocket and began to fan herself. "But alas, the festivities have not been quite as joyous since so many men have been carried off by war and disease. Despite that, we'll celebrate as best we can."

Manfred and Erich exchanged glances.

"Ah . . . we know where there might be other men who'd enjoy the celebration," Erich said. "They joined us along the way. There are nine of them, all Swedish soldiers. Except for one from Scotland. Some of them are a little rough in manner, but I can vouch for their character."

"As can I," Mara said.

"And I," Manfred added.

"An artist we met might be amongst them as well," Erich said.

"Oh? Ursula asked. "Where are they now?"

"We parted ways at Bingen. They might still be there."

"Since you can vouch for them, they're welcome."

"I'll go check on them," Manfred said.

————

Manfred stumbled toward a table and grasped it with both hands, dizzy from dancing and spinning amidst so many locked arms. He reached for a mug of ale, took a long swig, and surveyed the scene before him.

The field was bustling with people of all ages, laughing, dancing, drinking, and eating. He tried to identify some he recognized. Erich and Christian danced with one group, all holding hands, moving in a circle, and switching positions with formal steps. Mara danced arm in arm with a woman he didn't recognize but who had been by her side all day. The Swedes sat at the tables, eating and drinking alongside a woman or two.

Franz played his flute alongside other musicians. Cort sat next to him, tapping on a small cowhide drum resting between his legs in rhythm with the music. Adele found other children her age to play with. The Scholar stood beside Gottfried and other monks, watching the dancers and clapping along with the beat. Ursula sat under a beech tree with the other nuns, taking in the festivities with a pleased and satisfied expression.

Manfred guessed there were five or six hundred people in the field. They began to arrive early in the morning when he helped put up the maypoles. They came from all directions, some on foot, on horses, or in wagons. Most attendees arrived laden with food and supplies for the celebration, many dressed in traditional costumes for such occasions.

The women wore dirndls with colorful bodices and long skirts, complemented by aprons. The men were dressed in shades of brown and gray, some in suspenders holding up their lederhosen and bright white shirts. Everyone cheered—the Swedes loudest of all—when five carts packed with barrels of ale arrived from the nearby breweries.

Four men performed a lively rendition of the *schuhplattler* dance, whooping, clapping, and stomping as they tapped their shoes with each jump, much to the audience's delight. Some younger women twirled around the male dancers, lifting their dresses just enough to reveal their ankles.

Several monks, including Gottfried, carried torches and ignited shallow piles of kindling near the maypoles. The music quieted, and the dancing stopped. All eyes turned to Ursula. She stood and raised her arms.

"The fires are lit!" Ursula declared. "It's the time to cleanse and purify yourself of all the ills and troubles that may have befallen you. A time to celebrate the fortune to come your way. Now, off to the maypoles!"

"Now *there's* a woman," Helmar remarked.

Everyone cheered and headed toward them. Manfred raced out to join Erich. Cort, Christian, Mara, and Lucinda stood with them. Each person grabbed a ribbon tied to the top of the maypole. First, they took formal steps toward and away from the pole but later pranced around it in opposite directions. They sang and laughed with reckless abandon, occasionally bumping into each other. The ribbons grew shorter and tighter as they wove around. Their laughter and joy escalated as they all became intertwined.

One of the men raced to the small bonfire, calling out cheerful, merry words as he leaped over it. Cort followed suit, accompanied by Mara, Lucinda, Erich, Manfred, Christian, and the others.

Later, more people took turns at the maypole. Some women pulled the Swedes away from the tables. After a few steps, Valborg and Gunnar carried the laughing women toward the poles.

That night, the brightly lit banquet hall was alive with revelers' activity. Erich sat beside Ansgar, gripping a mug of ale and watching the festivities with great pleasure. The dancers swayed to the rhythm of the music and the beat of the drums. Cort tapped on a small drum. Manfred danced there, along with Christian and a few Swedes, each partnered with one or more women.

When the music paused, Mara headed outside into the cooler air. On the way, she passed by alcoves where others took part in quieter activities. In one, Franz juggled tumblers before an enthusiastic audience. Ursula played the harp in a larger room.

She paused to listen to the Scholar reading verses from one of his books to the gathered monks and nuns. They listened with rapt attention as he read one of her favorite passages from the English cleric who had befriended him.

". . . the Church is catholic, universal, and so are all her actions; all that she does belongs to all. When she baptizes a child, that action concerns me, for that child is thereby connected to the body which is my head too, and ingrated into that body whereof I am a member. And when she buries a man, that action concerns me: all mankind is of one author and is one volume; when one man dies, one chapter is not torn out of the book, but translated into a better language, and every chapter must be so translated. God employs several translators; some pieces are translated by age, some by sickness, some by war,"

He took out a cloth to wipe beads of sweat from his forehead.

"and some by justice, but God's hand is in every translation, and his hand shall bind up all our scattered leaves again for that library where every book shall lie open to one another. And therefore that bell rings to a sermon calls not upon the preacher only, but upon the congregation to come, and so this bell calls us all . . ."

She left before he finished to step out into the cool night air.

Three maidens, including the blonde one with braids, watched Cort as he performed, all smitten by his handsome features and the bold manner of his drumming while his head bobbed up and down to the beat. Mara sauntered over to Erich and extended her hand with an inviting smile. He set down the mug and followed her to the dance floor.

Several maidens, including Lucinda, stood aside by a wall observing the festivities.

"Those Swedes look so wild and uncouth," one of them said. "But they also possess manners and grace."

"It's so rare for a man to have both," another one said.

"And so unlike too many German men," Lucinda said, "who are all rough and ill-tempered. Or over-civilized simpletons."

"How would you know?" the other maiden said with a smirk. "You never venture out beyond these walls."

"I know about German men," Lucinda said. "More than you think!"

"So tell us," another one said, "what do you know about German men?"

The maidens laughed. Lucinda clammed up in anger.

"Not all German men are so bad," the first maiden said. "Like the man dancing with Mara. Did you hear the story of how he rescued her? Such nobility!"

"Look at him!" the other one said. "What a strong and handsome man. He can rescue me from danger anytime. Oh, I feel like I'm in danger now." She began to fan herself. "Rescue me now, oh, handsome knight!"

The maidens laughed once more. Lucinda's mood soured further as Mara continued dancing with Erich. She stormed toward them, pushed through the other dancers, inserted herself between Mara and Erich, and placed her hands on Mara's shoulders.

Mara noted Erich's displeasure at the intervention and improvised steps and movements so that she stayed between them, touching first one and then the other. The music from the lutes and drums grew more intense. Now she twirled and spun her body around, arms extended, staring up at the ceiling while spinning, beaming with joy and pleasure, in a kind of rapture. Erich and Lucinda stood transfixed as she did so.

The music stopped, and the dancers slowed down. Mara halted her spin, still staring up with arms extended, and began to fall back. Erich and Lucinda lunged to catch her. They exchanged smiles as they cradled her in their arms.

———

Later in the night, most of the revelers had retired for the evening. Those still present sat in groups, enjoying the leftover food. Manfred had been relishing the company of a buxom servant woman. Franz played a soft melody on his lute while Lucinda sang a quiet chant to the tune before a small audience, including Erich, with a mug in hand, and Mara.

Christian stood in an alcove with Gottfried and the other monks, sharing his portfolio of sketches.

Helmar stayed in Ursula's company and plucked the harp while listening to Lucinda's chanting.

It's been a day and night to remember," Helmar said.

"Yes, but the night is not over yet," Ursula said.

"I must tell you," he said, searching for the right words, "that I respect your position here. Above all, I honor the vows you've taken."

Pleased by his sincere humility, she returned his gaze. "They are vows I take seriously. But I also believe there are times of the year when a certain *latitude* is allowed by Him, so we can more fully understand and celebrate God's spirit. Tonight is one of those times."

She held out her hand. He grasped it briefly, understanding the need for discretion.

"Alas, it is time for me to retire from the festivities for the night. My servant will meet you in the back garden and direct you to my quarters. So you can view my collection of . . . reliquaries."

Helmar bowed as she departed.

Erich staggered back to the tables. Mara took him by the arm and guided him along. Once he sat down, he tried to focus on the double image of Mara as she walked away.

The young maiden smitten with Cort padded back into the banquet hall. She paused in the shadows between the torches, close enough for him to see her while he played the flute.

He blew out a sour note when he saw her. Her long, unclasped hair cascaded halfway down her waist. She wore a short-sleeved blouse that exposed the soft white skin below her neck. Enchanted, he approached her. She guided him away as discreetly as possible.

Erich had been watching them from the other side of the hall. He smiled, took one last swig, and dropped his head onto his arms on the table. Soon, he was softly snoring.

22

A Change of Plans

The family strolled along the river road on their way to the Botanical Gardens, which featured many unusual plants from various parts of Europe and even some from the far-off Middle East.

They enjoyed spending early evenings exploring Leipzig, which was larger than Ulm. On some days, they visited the Thomaskirche or the Paulinerkirche and relaxed on the benches as people strolled by. A few times, Peter treated them to a meal at Auerbach's Cellar when he earned extra money from his carvings.

On their way home, Peter and Eva waved to one of their friendly neighbors. Thomas and Rudi tossed stones into the water. Max barked at a squirrel scurrying up a tree. Heloise had just learned to walk on her own and held Anna's hand as she toddled along. Agatha walked with Catherine, who was now in her fourth month of pregnancy. Her patient guidance helped Catherine come out of her shell, allowing her to interact more with the family again.

Mounted soldiers galloped by, a familiar sight during their walks. They discussed the issue over evening meals and agreed that the presence of friendly troops provided them with a greater sense of security, especially after reading pamphlets about disturbances and unrest in other areas, including the Ulm region. However, this did not ease their emptiness without Erich and Cort. They prayed before each meal for their safe return.

The next morning, Erich woke up, wincing from a throbbing headache and the bright light. A few people slept at the tables, and nearby, Magnus—or was it Markus?—snored like a bull.

Cort stared wide-eyed and alert at the glowing coals in the fireplace, holding a cup of water. He glanced back and saw his father awake, then bounded toward him.

"Good morning!" he said in a loud and cheery voice, causing Erich to flinch.

He grabbed Cort's cup and guzzled the contents in large gulps.

"Your eyes look a little red," Cort said.

"It will pass. I drank too much. As I've told you, you pay the price the next day whenever this happens. You'll find out soon enough, I'm sure."

"How will I know when I've drunk too much?"

"Like I said, you'll know the next day."

"How do I know when to stop so I won't feel so bad later?"

"It comes with experience. You'll make mistakes along the way. Hopefully not too often."

"Like you did last night."

He sighed. "Yes, like I did last night. It's alright to drink during certain occasions like this, but not too often. It'll ruin you."

"What do you mean?"

"It drains your strength, and you'll end up like the men you've seen lying in the streets by the alehouses."

"I still don't understand how I know when to stop."

"It's all about a sense of moderation and balance. Knowing when you've gone too far."

"Sounds like what you've been telling me about the Bow. Like when you pull it far and are weakened later."

"Huh?" Erich responded, surprised at the connection. "I suppose it does."

"So, do you feel the same way when you pull the Bow back a lot as you do now?"

He tried to laugh. "No, it's different." He shut his eyes and held his throbbing head.

Cort examined his father's muscular arms and shoulders. Would he ever be as strong? For the first time, he noticed a few gray hairs in his beard in the bright morning light and even a hint of wrinkles around his eyes.

He didn't want to press him on the drinking matter anymore so he changed the subject. "Quite a celebration yesterday."

Erich opened his eyes and nodded.

"I like playing the drums. I must get one when we're in Leipzig."

"First you want a flute, then a lute, and now the drums. You should make up your mind."

"I want to learn to play all three. Maybe I'll study music at the university."

He regarded him tight-lipped. "I studied to become an officer. A much more practical profession. Besides, you need to catch up on your studies." He scanned the hall for Mara. "How was your evening?"

"Fine. Why do you ask?"

"I saw you going off with the girl and—"

"I thought you were asleep."

"Not quite."

"We walked together in the garden. Her name is Sophie. She wanted to know where I learned to play. And then, well, we started kissing and—"

"We can talk more when my head clears," he interjected. "Come, let's go outside to wash up in the stream."

———

That afternoon, Ursula examined the scene in the banquet hall, where the residents sat at their usual tables. At one end of her table, Erich was conversing with Cort, who kept glancing at Sophie, several tables away. The Scholar, Franz, Christian, Manfred, Mara, and Lucinda also joined them. Ursula focused the longest on an adjacent table with most of the Swedes, including Helmar.

"Well, I must confess that this has been quite a joyous Beltane," she said to Mara. "One of the best I can remember."

"Yes," she answered, somewhat absentmindedly. "Like the ones we used to have." She glanced at Erich again, still talking to Cort.

"Much better, actually," Ursula said, still gazing at Helmar. "I never expected such a . . . *vigorous* celebration."

"I tell you what," Manfred said, keeping his eye on the buxom servant woman heading to the table with a pitcher in hand. "It was worth the long walk from Ulm for this." He held out his cup when the servant arrived and gave her a wink as she poured. She blushed and suppressed a smile.

"I'm pleased you think so," Ursula said. She noticed that Erich had finished talking to Cort. "Erich," she said in a louder voice. "I understand you'll be traveling across the heartland to Leipzig."

Everyone stopped to listen.

"Yes, where my family is. It's safer there for them than in Ulm."

Gottfried faced Erich from the next table. "That may be for now. But not for long, I fear. There've been reports that the War is moving north. Duke Maximilian has organized a force under General von Werth and plans to march to Saxony."

"What of the truce from the Peace of Prague?" Erich asked, suddenly alarmed.

"No more. The Duke claimed that Protestant uprisings earlier in the year had broken it."

"What uprisings? Where?"

"They said it started in the Ulm and Augsburg areas."

"Who told you this?"

"Rumors have abounded for months from local pamphleteers, most unreliable," Gottfried answered. "But another monk from Mainz gave this to me yesterday." He reached into his pocket and gave Erich a pamphlet. "It comes from the office of the Bishop. Now I fear it's more than rumors."

Erich read the pamphlet, which confirmed what he had heard from others along the way.

"What's worse," Gottfried added, "is that the Swedes have re-armed to meet von Werth's forces. Prince Bernhard is raising an army to unite with them. I'm sure that scoundrel Richelieu is funding both sides against each other." He shook his head. "It seems this War will never end."

"What's that?" Ansgar said. "The Swedish army is reorganizing? Who's leading them?"

"It says," Gottfried answered, "a General Horn and a General—"

He snatched the pamphlet from his hands and read it. "Horn is back!" he said to Valborg across from him. "And Baner!"

Ansgar pounded his fist on the table with such force that the water cups toppled, spilling their contents. The loud and jarring noise made everyone in the hall stop and stare at him with shocked and troubled expressions.

Mara, seated directly behind him, held her head in pain, grimacing as her skull throbbed from the reverberations. She closed her eyes and became overwhelmed by a series of startling visions: smoke, fire, screaming, and blood falling to the earth.

"*Ja!*" Valborg exclaimed. "To rejoin our countrymen in battle!" He raised his fist, as did Gunnar and the twins.

Everyone kept staring at them. The Swedes realized they had disrupted the peace and tranquility of the place, so they went back to eating in silence.

"Alas, and so it seems as if our little run of fun is done," Franz remarked loudly to the Scholar.

Erich realized that the Imperial army moving north could soon enter Saxony. "We must leave for Leipzig immediately," he said to Manfred and Cort.

Mara gradually recovered from the disorienting visions, but then a sudden fear gripped her, as she sensed it was connected to what she had foreseen while reading his hands in the prison cell. Other fragmented visions also emerged. She hoped to gain a better understanding after her meditations.

"I humbly seek your advice and counsel on a most important matter," she whispered to Ursula.

———

That evening, they gathered in Ursula's quarters. The walls were adorned with artwork and engravings, and statues of human and animal figures stood on shelves and pedestals throughout the room. A beam of light from the setting sun illuminated the interior.

"I remember when you were here before you left," Ursula told Mara. "Or, more accurately, ran off. You spoke out of rebellion, impatience, and anger. Now you sit here with wisdom and experience." She took a sip of water. "This is about Erich—is it not?"

"Yes. I know he must return to his family, but there's something else. It's what I sensed about him when he first entered my cell. It's related to—"

"The aura."

"More than that. It's what I discerned from a reading of his hands. He's a man with a pronounced destiny, like Samson's."

"And you saw this from his hands?"

"Yes. Hildegard wrote on this but I also studied more on my own. My people use such methods."

"I recall some passages from Hildegard on the subject of chiromancy," Ursula said. "I thought it rather esoteric yet with a grain of truth. She wrote that it can be used as a way of illuminating aspects of our nature."

"The signs are unmistakable. His fate line comes so close to his lifeline and radiates out in many directions from one spot. But preceding and intersecting that point, there's a deep and crooked travel line, which indicates a perilous path. Now with the news of the War moving north to the region he is going, I fear the worst could happen, unless—" She paused to gather her thoughts.

"And so you're undecided whether to stay here or go with him."

"I feel I can guide him through this fateful period in his life. And believe events will soon occur that will elevate his status amongst others. But it will also put him in great danger. I want to be with him when this happens."

"You must examine if this calling is one of the spirit. Or more . . . of the flesh."

Mara sighed. "I'm aware of my feelings for him. But my calling hasn't wavered from the beginning. And so, with your blessing, I ask permission to accompany him. If he allows it."

Once again, she considered everything Mara had recounted to her, along with her impressions of Erich.

"You should meditate and pray on this matter tonight. You have my permission if you feel the same in the morning."

"Thank you, Priestess Ursula."

"There will always be more to study within the safety of these walls," Ursula said. "Yet there's also a time when one must venture forth into the outside world and act on the knowledge they've acquired. Perhaps you left early last time. Now you're ready." She sensed something else on her mind. "I see you found an orphan along the way."

"Yes, little Adele. She was living in a hopeless condition, so I took her with me."

"I remember when we picked up another girl," Ursula mused. "Years ago, at the destroyed Romany camp. She was a bit older than Adele at the time." She laughed at the memory of it. "Even at such a young age, you were so bold as to walk right up and ask if you could come with us. Everyone said no because the Romany people cannot be trusted and will steal from us and all that. But there was something *bright* about you, so I convinced them to take you in."

"I sense the same in Adele. I hope you can take her in as a student. She can already read and write a little."

"We can arrange it, but some sacrifices must be made to provide for her room and food."

"This means a lot to me. I've seen so much hardship and suffering in my travels. It's fulfilling to know I've given hope to at least *one person*."

The next day, Mara walked between the buildings with her eyes lowered, absorbed in thought. She had spent the entire evening meditating on which direction to take in her life. Several times, she had nearly decided against following Erich back to Leipzig. After all, he had fulfilled his mission to return her to the monastery, and now his future lay with his family; however, these doubts vanished when she reflected on the reading of his hands, which was confirmed in a strange way by her visions in the banquet hall.

The monastery residents carried out their chores in the area. Most of the May Day celebrants had left, except for the Swedes and those with Erich. She guessed he would be at the stables, so she headed there.

He was busy with Baldur's shoes when she entered. Some Swedes were doing likewise.

Somewhat surprised, Erich stood, and they clasped hands together.

"I searched for you last night to bid farewell," he said. "But Ursula said you were in meditation."

"I was. But maybe you don't have to . . . bid farewell."

"What do you mean?"

She took a deep breath. "I've decided to join you on the way to Leipzig. If you'll have me."

Erich straightened his posture and stepped back. "I don't understand."

"Events may befall you soon that could put your life in peril. So I want to be there to help when—"

"The War is coming north, but I'm prepared for that. I don't know what more you can do."

"It's something else," she said, feeling unsure of herself.

"What then?"

"It has to do with what I detected in your hands. I've tried dismissing those thoughts, but yesterday's news changed everything. I had a sudden vision that made me realize these events could occur sooner than I expected. Perhaps sometime between now and when you arrive in Leipzig. When it does, I want to help and guide you. As you did for me."

"We should be safe traveling with the Swedes," he said annoyedly.

"It has less to do with danger befalling you than . . ."

"What? Speak your mind!"

"Your family."

"You saw them in danger?"

"Only that something might happen that I could help with. Both to you and them."

His manner softened. "Your words affect me deeply. Forgive my moment of anger. But I left my family to bring you all this way to safety. And now you want to plunge back into danger again."

"I'm immensely grateful for the sacrifices you've made."

"We'll be riding long and hard each day. We won't rest or refresh ourselves as often as before."

"The Swedes gave me a strong horse. I won't slow you down."

Erich shook his head, unable to decide.

"I've dwelt on these matters all night," she added. "And feel that perhaps our time together . . . is not yet destined to end."

Erich weighed her words. "You speak from your heart and have insights which contain much truth. And so I will accept your decision to join us."

They clasped hands again, feeling grateful and relieved that they would stay together, while understanding that the next part of the journey would be quite different.

23

Crossroads

The monastery residents milled about in small groups, conversing amongst themselves in the banquet hall. Mara approached Christian as he spoke with several monks.

"Well, Christian, Gottfried told me you'll teach here."

"Yes, the offer filled me with great joy. He showed me the engraving press, which I'd like to know more about."

"I'm glad you'll find your time here worthwhile."

"It's the best of both worlds for me. To teach as well as to learn."

Later, she sat down at the front table in the banquet hall with Priestess Ursula, Lucinda, Gottfried, and Christian. A servant gave Ursula a small, ornate box. She examined its contents and closed it. The room fell into a hushed silence.

"As most of you know," Ursula said, "Mara will be departing on a journey into the heartland of our realm to perform a role of the highest order. As a spiritual guide to the man who showed much valor to bring her back here from a point of immense danger. She believes this man possesses a strong destiny. With a mission in life as yet unfulfilled but whose path is fraught with peril. Based on my brief acquaintance with him and discussing this with Mara, I agree with her insights."

She turned to her. "I only wish you could've stayed longer. But we'll all pray you have a safe journey and return soon. Because of the nature of your travels, I now offer you something to protect you along the way. And also balance the forces of light and dark, and life and death that may confront you."

She slid the ornate box to Mara. She pulled out a necklace with a white stone attached to a silver chain and examined it with wonder and surprise.

"This is beautiful. And with a moonstone pendant! I'll cherish it and always wear it with all my heart." She faced the audience. "You're all a source of strength for me. I'll recite a prayer in your honor every day."

———

The next morning, Mara walked with Ursula, Gottfried, and Lucinda to the entrance of the monastery. Two servants awaited her, carrying the supplies and clothing she had packed. Before departing, she bid farewell to those closest to her: Ursula, Gottfried, Lucinda, and the servants. She had spent the night with Lucinda and sensed a newfound confidence in her bearing.

Mara knelt and stroked Adele's hair, who appeared close to tears. "Goodbye, for now, dear Adele. Remember, you're safe here."

Adele burst into tears and hugged her.

"There now, I'll be back. And when I do, you can show me how smart you've become."

Adele stifled her tears. One of the maidens took her hand and guided her away. Before they reached the doorway, Adele glanced back at Mara, who waved at her. Adele returned the wave with a smile—so reminiscent of the brave smile Mara remembered seeing on Adele when she first saw her dressed in rags on that Mannheim street.

———

They had ridden hard for most of the day since leaving Eibingen, traveling along a road that wound through lightly forested terrain before rising to a plateau of tall grasses and scrub brush. They halted upon reaching a crossroads near the base of a massive oak tree. Ansgar pulled out a travel guide map and studied it, comparing it to the signposts. They were in a remote and desolate region, yet it appeared to be an important junction. One road continued north, another branched east, and a third headed northwest. Each road was visible for great distances along the flat plateau, which was mostly devoid of vegetation except for a few trees. In fact, the tallest tree in the entire area stood directly before them at the crossroads.

Mara focused her attention on the tree, which appeared to be centuries old. Above the thick, gnarled trunk, the lower branches spread wide enough to provide shade for everyone. A long fissure extended down the trunk, a clear sign of a lightning strike. One half of the tree looked dead or dying, while the other half was healthy and blooming. She spotted two hawks perched on the top branches. One of them scanned the northeastern horizon while the other hawk gazed down at her. She shut her eyes and visualized the hawk looking down at them from high above.

Ansgar put away the map and pointed east. "We take this road."

"But not I," said Mackenzie.

"What's that you say"? Ansgar asked.

"I know where this road goes," he answered, pointing in the north-western direction. "Straight to the Low Countries. From there, I'll catch a boat and return to Scotland."

"Aw," Gunnar said, "just when we were getting to like you."

"Liar."

"Why so sudden?" Ansgar asked.

"I've been thinking about this for some time but kept it to myself. If I told anyone, you'd have convinced me to stay. No, this way is best. To go now, from this spot. Clean and quick, like a good kill in battle."

"*Ja!* A good kill in battle!" Valborg said, raising his fist.

Mackenzie's demeanor softened briefly as he regarded each of the Swedes. But then he urged his horse forward and galloped away.

The Scholar rode to the front as they watched Mackenzie ride down the long and flat northwesterly road.

"If this road goes to the Low Countries, I'm going on it too. To the Dutch states! Where true freedom resides. The last bastion of civilization in this realm."

"We wish you well," Erich said.

"Yes," Mara said. "You must follow the direction of your freedom."

The Scholar showed a brief display of emotion, recollecting the memory of the flower he picked on the first day of Spring above the Rhein.

"I thank you all for how you've helped me. You've given me the strength to go forth to the west. Perhaps I'll even venture to the distant shores of the new lands in America, where a man can live at one with nature and the noble savage. Not there," he said, pointing east and shaking with emotion. "That road leads to a hellscape. Ravaged by death. Pestilence. Misery. Cruelty and barbarism. That's what our country is now—a hellscape! I turn my back on you! Never to return!"

He rode down the northwest road, waving his hand. "Goodbye!"

"Goodbye," Markus said and turned to his brother. "What's his name?" Magnus shrugged. "Does anyone know his name?"

No one spoke.

The Swedes continued to watch Mackenzie galloping away.

Franz rode next to Erich. "I think it's time for me also to part ways."

"Not you, too!" Cort said.

"But why?" Manfred asked.

"For one thing, I don't want to go to hell," he answered with a mirthful voice. "At least not yet, since I have so many more fine tales to tell. And so I will head west. The West—which is the best. Not the East, wherein doth lie . . . a strange and terrible *beast*!" He made a gruesome face, causing some to chuckle. "Now I'm off to catch up with my friend."

"Alas, we won't be able to sleep so restfully," Helmar said, "without your peaceful melodies on the lute."

Cort seemed the most disappointed. "Goodbye, Franz."

"Farewell, my young musical friend. Be sure to keep up your interest in it. You have much talent."

Others murmured their goodbyes.

"Oh, the scholar's name is Ludwig," Franz said, with a wink

He pulled out his flute as he rode away and began to sing. *"Yes, I will go west, which is the best. Not the east, the land of beasts."* He played a few notes on the flute and then repeated the words. *"The west, which is the best. Not the east . . ."* His voice faded as he rode away.

They all stared silently down the road. Mackenzie was barely visible on the horizon. Ludwig paused to wait for Franz. After their meeting, they shook hands and rode off together.

Once Mackenzie vanished from sight, Ansgar and Erich turned their horses eastward, leading the group along the road into the German heartland.

24.

Heartland

Klaus sat in his tent sipping ale while his henchmen partook of food and drink, all in a festive mood and chatting about the plunder they'd acquired from the "heretical" shopkeepers in towns they had pacified the previous fortnight. They had performed their duties enthusiastically, knowing they could keep portions of the plunder. Horst and Ernst worked with the soldiers to help store everything in an organized manner. Sigi did the same after returning from Ulm. Dieter and Joachim, both young and strong, assisted in enforcing his commands on the populace.

He'd been waiting for Lothar to arrive ever since Sigi mentioned seeing him riding into the camp earlier that day. Lothar was his last hope for obtaining information about Erich.

Eventually, Lothar barged in, snatched a mug, and filled it from the spigot of a barrel of ale at the end of the table. He then reached for a loaf of bread and a chunk of meat.

"No trace of them," he said, swigging more ale.

Klaus sighed. This confirmed what he expected.

"They were there at one time, though. The owner of an inn said a family matching their description stayed there for three days during a snowstorm. And then went north."

"They could've gone anywhere from there," Klaus said. "To Hesse, Thuringer, or Saxony."

"Saxony, you say?" Sigi asked.

"That's right. What of it?"

"It's just that . . . a town official in Ulm showed me a scroll with records of his wife's relatives there."

"Where in Saxony?"

"Leipzig."

"My God, man!" Klaus bellowed while briefly lifting his eye patch.

"Why didn't you tell me this before?"

His harsh response left Sigi momentarily speechless. "It seemed too far away for—"

"Leipzig is full of heretical disbelievers like them," Klaus said. "As is most of Saxony." He pondered his next move.

"What do we do now?" Lothar asked.

Klaus faced Sigi. "I'll send you there to search for them. I hope I won't be disappointed this time."

————

It took them nearly a week to reach Frankfurt because the weather had become oppressively hot. They needed to stop several times each day to rest and cool the horses in the waters of the Main. Erich was relieved to see that Mara could maintain the faster pace without showing any signs of fatigue.

They spent a day in Frankfurt to restock their food and supplies. Erich obtained a pamphlet from a town crier that contained news of events related to the War and shared it with the Swedes. The Imperial commander, General von Werth, was still stationed in Ratisbon, waiting for the arrival of additional Croatian, Slavic, and Polish troops. This alleviated his concerns about the urgency to be in Leipzig before hostilities began; however, it also meant that von Werth's army would become a larger and more formidable force when it moved north.

From Frankfurt, they traveled through a rural countryside, much of which had fallen into a state of devastation, the land eroded and barren. Every day, they passed abandoned villages, whose only inhabitants were wild-looking refugees and emaciated dogs. Broken wagons, rotting waterwheels, collapsed fences, and burned-out barns and farmhouses cluttered the once-fertile and thriving farms, with the bones of horses and livestock scattered across the fields. High grasses and lifeless brush had overtaken their neglected pastures. The small bridges over the tributaries flowing into the Main were impassable, forcing them to ford the waters.

————

"It seemed cooler today," Manfred said as he ate his fish before the campfire.

"Not by much," Axel said.

"Ah hell," Valborg said. "At least the eating is good."

"Strength for the battles to come!" Markus said.

"*Ja* to that," Magnus said.

"And put an end to this War," Ansgar said.

"And go home like Mackenzie," Manfred said.

The Swedes exchanged glances.

"Easier for him than us," Helmar said.

"Why is that?" Manfred asked.

"It's an oath we took," Ansgar answered. "To avenge a death."

"We took it four years ago," Helmar said. "Mackenzie wasn't part of the brigade and so not held to it like us."

"Whose death is it that you've taken an oath to avenge?" Erich asked.

Ansgar stared at him before answering. "The Lion. King Gustav."

"What? How can such an oath be taken? They avenged his death. The Protestants were victorious."

"Yes, he died in battle," Helmar said. "But as a result of treachery. Killed by one of our own. Someone we took in who turned against us."

"Shot in the back and hacked down by the Imperials," Valborg said.

"Are you certain of this?" Erich asked.

"Some of our men saw it from a distance," Valborg said.

"The man who did this fled to the other side and joined the Imperials," Gunnar said. "They welcomed him and gave him a fat reward."

"Who is the traitor?" Erich asked.

"His name is Franz Albert," Ansgar answered. "The Duke of Lauenburg."

"Prince Bernhard didn't trust the man," Helmar said. "And counseled The Lion not to bring him in. But our forces needed the Duke's men, so we allied."

"During the battle, King Gustav's horse raced across the front without a rider," Ansgar said. "So we searched for him." His expression tightened. "I was one of those who found the body. That's when we first heard about the treachery from witnesses."

"We took the oath to avenge his death," Helmar said. "We couldn't do much about it the first year with battles still being fought. After the defeat at Nördlingen, the brigades disbanded. That's when we went out to find him."

"We went straight up to Lauenburg, but the bastard might've received word and fled a few days before," Gunnar said. "We've been chasing him ever since."

"What will you do when you get him?" Manfred asked.

The Swedes laughed sardonically.

"Oh, we'll give him a chance to tell us his side of the story," Gunnar said.

"And then we'll start with the toes," Nico interjected with a grin as he tapped his index finger on the tip of his knife. "And work our way up."

"You've been gone all this time and still haven't found him," Mara said. "He must know that you're after him and probably hasn't slept well since. Unable to stay anywhere too long. Such a fearful way to live."

"And maybe we're not the only ones after him," Ansgar said, nodding. "Yes. I'll think more about this. I, for one, am getting weary of tramping around these lands, chasing ghosts." He paused to think some more. "But an oath is an oath."

———

During the next few days, they passed more areas of ruin and devastation: unburied bodies, salted fields, wells poisoned by corpses, and people looking insane with grief in the villages.

About a week after leaving Frankfurt, Ansgar stopped the group at a point where the road turned sharply south along the river's course. He studied an itinerary map while Helmar and Erich paused beside him. The others rested in a grove of trees.

"We'll lose many days if we follow the road along this part of the river," Ansgar said to them.

"I see what you mean," Helmar said. "It runs south, then turns north again. We can cut across those hills and get back on the same road going north."

"That's what I'm thinking," Ansgar said.

"But there's no road that way," Erich said.

"It could save us a week of traveling," Helmar said.

Erich scanned the eastern horizon toward the rolling hills rising from the flat terrain. "We should do it then."

———

Two days later, they paused near the ridge's summit, where a view of the Main stretched toward the distant east. A thick ribbon of green vegetation twisted along a gully leading down toward the Main—a clear indication of a creek or small stream—so they made their way toward it.

They soon entered an area with makeshift wooden shelters scattered across the hills above the creek, yet there was no sign of people. A short distance away, Helmar pointed to the hillside where shepherds tended to a flock of sheep. Later, they encountered additional habitats and some partially cultivated land on the other side of the stream. People scrambled in and out of the dwellings, alarmed by their approaching presence. The Swedes drew their swords.

They approached a large settlement of tattered tents, crude sod structures, and hillside caves. The inhabitants wore torn and ragged clothing. Some of the men stood in front of their habitats, clutching makeshift weapons: wooden rakes and pitchforks, threshing rods, and flails. The women and children peered at them from within the shelters with anxious eyes.

Erich estimated that several hundred people lived there. He had encountered individuals living in such primitive conditions before, but never so many in one place. He wondered if more wretched encampments like this existed in the hinterlands, settled by people with nowhere else to go, who once engaged in honest and useful work in their now-destroyed communities: farmers, cobblers, bakers, and smiths. He could see that Mara and Cort were also disturbed by the sight.

The next day, they passed two more abandoned villages, both flattened and marked by burned-out structures. The following day, they rode through a small town, also in ruins. People shuffled in the street, staring at them with vacant, hopeless expressions. Later, they passed the remnants of an apple orchard, where blackened, gnarled trees stood in rows among dead and fallen branches.

Erich could now see that the damage from the War was far worse than he had imagined. The devastated landscape and destroyed villages served as painful reminders of his time as an officer a decade earlier, when he had participated in the destruction that left the countryside in ruins. Initially, he didn't question the orders to burn the farms and crops his company encountered because he believed that doing so would deny the pursuing Imperials any resources to salvage. Eventually, however, he reached a point where he could no longer partake in the carnage and allowed the troops under his command to carry out the orders while he watched them, which was almost worse in a way. After those campaigns, he vowed to make amends to the people whose lives he had ruined—a vow that remained unfulfilled.

———

They entered the town of Lohr, which seemed less damaged from the War, despite the presence of refugees and beggars on the side streets. They rested there for the night and bought more supplies.

They gathered around Ansgar at an inn, examining a new travel guide he had purchased from a storekeeper.

"We'll be coming across larger towns soon," Ansgar said. He ran his finger along the road on the map. "Ah, and this one I remember."

"Würzburg," Helmar said. "A rich, fat town."

"But we couldn't stay there long," Ansgar said. "Because we had General Tilly on the run. King Gustav wanted to make him pay for what he did at Magdeburg."

"And that we did," Gunnar said.

"The days of glory," Helmar said.

"With more to come!" Valborg bellowed.

"We'll follow the river to Bamberg," Ansgar said. "And then cut to Bayreuth and take this road north through some mountains to Leipzig." He glanced at Erich, who nodded in approval. "From there to Brandenburg. That's where our armies should be."

Erich examined the map more closely after everyone had left. He recognized the names of some towns from his time as an officer. He remembered his commanders calling the region "priest's alley" because so many were under Catholic rule, all well-fortified to defend against an attack from the Protestants in the north. He wondered if the Catholics still held those towns. He would find out soon enough, as Würzburg was one of them.

Mara walked back toward the campsite after bathing in the river, a routine she followed almost daily. The men always maintained a respectful distance until her return. Along the way, Erich showed Cort how to use the Black Bow. Cort's shot struck the center of a tree trunk across the grove.

When she arrived at her shelter, she began preparing the potatoes, turnips, and carrots she bought in Lohr for a stew. As she did so, she reminisced once again about the people from her journey before Eibingen—especially Adele. She also missed the jovial Franz, who played his music at the campfires. She even had fond memories of the often cranky Scholar. How different things were now.

Erich and Cort walked by her as she cut the vegetables.

"I can prepare more for you to put in the stew," she said to them.

Cort made a face and shook his head.

"Thank you but another day," Erich said. "We'll finish the deer meat tonight."

Those were the first words he'd spoken to her all day—like so many other days. Because of that, she sometimes wondered if she'd made the right decision to rejoin him. As always, when her doubts grew, she visualized their first meeting in the cell and how strongly she felt about his destiny.

After cutting the last vegetable, she reflected on the upcoming time of year. Ever since leaving Lohr, she had been checking the sundial. Each day, the shadows from the stick grew shorter, indicating that the Summer Solstice would soon arrive—the time when light triumphs but begins its decline into darkness.

She attempted to remember the words from the summer rituals she experienced while in the monastery:

The Sun King embraces the Queen of the Summer in the love that is death because it is so complete. The Lord of Light dies to himself and sets sail across the dark seas of time. We turn the Wheel and share his fate, and we must now accept even the passing of the sun.

She gazed at the men by the campfire. They had endured a wilderness of despair and devastation for far too long. Soon, however, they would find themselves in a *place* of transformation, surrounded by larger towns. She also sensed that it would be a *time* of change—a shifting like the coming Solstice—for her, Erich, and others in the group. And when that occurred, she would be there to guide him.

———

After taking another overland shortcut, they encountered the familiar sight of downtrodden people living in partially destroyed structures on the outskirts of Karlstad. The town's residents regarded them with curiosity and suspicion. Beggars scrambled out from their makeshift shelters, pleading for handouts.

Erich, Mara, Manfred, and Cort walked down a street after buying food at the marketplace. Most of the Swedes went to the taverns. Soon, a raucous crowd approached them from a distance, taunting people huddled together in the street who were trying to protect themselves from objects thrown at them: sticks, rotting vegetables, and rocks. Young children clung to their mothers and fathers. A few soldiers and town officials followed them. A black-robed priest with a calm and peaceful countenance strolled alongside the officials. He stood out from the rest due to his regal attire, complemented by his contrasting silvery-gray hair and beard.

Erich stopped and gripped his staff, focusing on the priest. He had seen families like these evicted from towns because of their religious beliefs by Church authorities like him far too often. He stepped into the street to get the priest's attention and show his disapproval. The priest noted him with casual indifference. Amid his simmering rage, Erich took another step toward him, feeling an increasing urge to strike him down with his staff. Just then, he felt a hand on his shoulder—Mara's hand, which tempered his rage.

The priest no longer regarded Erich with mild indifference. He glared at this man—with a long bow slung across his chest—and the woman behind him, who had her hand on his shoulder, with growing outrage. It seemed these two strangers were casting a silent judgment on him. *How dare they!* With a scowl, he turned away as he walked past.

Mara removed her hand from his shoulder. "Thank you," he said.

For the first time since they left the monastery, she felt a sense of worth to him again.

25

Würzburg

They paused on the crest of a ridge, gazing at the distant view of Würzburg, defined by its tall steeples and imposing central fortress. The sky had just cleared after a rain squall, the latest in a series of downpours since their departure from Karlstadt two days earlier. A blanket of misty fog covered the rain-drenched plain along the river, making the town appear as if it were floating above a layer of clouds.

Ansgar reflected on his time there four years ago. So much had changed since they rode with The Lion, and their mission had been clear: pursue Count Tilly's Imperial troops to the south. Now, here he was again, but this time facing north—the direction of his homeland. Once more, he recalled Mara's words about the oath and how long they had been fulfilling it.

They descended from the ridge into the foggy valley that led to the town.

———

Erich sensed that he had been in the town before as he trotted along the main street, even though he couldn't remember passing through Würzburg either before or during his time in the army. Yet, there was something strangely familiar about everything he noticed. It also seemed that people were staring at him with a knowing expectation, including a group of shiftless, sullen-looking men loitering around one of the rundown inns. One man wearing a red headband caught Erich's attention and stood out from the rest. He appeared down on his luck like the others, but looked less beaten down. His posture was strong as he regarded the group with an expression of defiance, curiosity, and respect.

After stabling their horses, they headed to an inn recommended by the owner. On the way, they encountered a noisy crowd gathered in the town square, observing some spectacle, judging by the clamor of voices and steady drumbeats. A tall wooden pole packed at the base with straw and kindling stood on a makeshift platform in the square. The drums increased in frequency after soldiers emerged from the entrance of a nearby building. Two men escorted a thin, weeping woman with a shaved head toward the platform. A priest and the hooded executioner followed behind. The men dragged her up the stairs. One of them lifted her above the kindling and pushed her against the pole while the others bound her hands and body to it. The priest began to administer the rites as she wept.

Mara noticed the executioner holding a loop of leather in one hand, indicating that the woman had confessed to being a witch. Because of that, she would be "mercifully" strangled before the burning. She recited a silent prayer and walked away, deeply troubled by the incident. The Swedes accompanied her.

"Go with Mara," Erich said to Cort. "I'll join you later."

"But I want to stay and—"

"Go now!" he demanded.

He complied, knowing not to cross his father when he used that tone. Manfred remained with Erich.

Erich closed his eyes, striving to manage his growing anger. The sounds blended together in his mind: the boisterous crowd, the relentless, heavy drumbeats, and the tolling of church bells. Gradually, the chaos diminished, and a little boy's pleading voice resonated above the others.

"No, no Mother, make it stop . . . make it stop!"

He shook his head and opened his eyes in a daze.

"But she's not a witch! She didn't do anything wrong!"

He had heard that voice and those words before—and then it struck him. It happened during his childhood with his mother at the beginning of a witch burning in the town square, a painful memory he had suppressed until this moment.

It was *his* voice

The executioner walked toward the victim after the final bell rang. The woman's sobs became more pronounced as the crowd quieted to a whisper.

No! Erich commanded himself.

He plunged forward, pushing aside the people in his way. A soldier attempted to block his path, but he knocked him down with his staff. Two other soldiers rushed to the scene, and he drew his sword to confront them.

The townsfolk nearest the fight shouted alarmingly and scattered away from the melee. The executioner stopped to check on it.

Manfred stayed behind when Erich left him, thinking he wanted to get a better view. But he knew he was in trouble after he struck down the first soldier and was now fighting two more.

"My God," he whispered and hurried to his aid.

Erich struggled to fend them off when Manfred approached with his sword raised. Three more soldiers surged forward, and swiftly, all five surrounded them, closing in. They crouched back-to-back to defend against the attackers.

Mara glanced back at the sudden clamor, expecting to see flames engulfing the victim. Instead, she found the victim still alive, with the executioner staring down at the crowd. Now she thought of Erich and what had happened in Karlstadt, realizing she shouldn't have left this scene without him.

"Can you see what's going on there?" she asked Cort. Cort jumped onto a bench and stiffened with shock. "It's Father and Manfred fighting soldiers!"

"Ansgar! Ansgar!" she screamed. "Come now!"

She pointed toward the platform as they rushed up to her.

"Soldiers are fighting Erich and Manfred!"

"Get your weapons out," he commanded.

They formed two lines and jogged as a unit to the square.

Erich and Manfred were barely fending them off when the Swedes arrived. Both had cuts and bruises on their arms and heads. Two soldiers lay sprawled on the ground, battered and bleeding.

Gunnar and Valborg felled two soldiers with their swords and clubs. The other three retreated. At a signal from Ansgar, the Swedes established a perimeter around the platform, holding back the crowd. Ansgar turned to Erich, who was still dazed and panting heavily.

"What now?" he asked.

Erich tried to gather his senses. Upon hearing the sobbing victim, the fire came back into his eyes. He pointed to the executioner.

"Free this woman!"

The townsfolk erupted, and some pushed forward. The Swedes kept them back.

He strode up the platform, staff in hand. The executioner awaited him, clutching a club, but he pushed him back with his staff. The executioner swung wildly at him but missed. The momentum from the swing carried him past Erich, who kicked him in the back, sending him tumbling down the stairs. He landed with a thud on the ground. Enraged, he charged back up, but Magnus blocked him.

"Walk away," Magnus warned.

The executioner stood his ground.

Magnus lifted his axe. "While you still can."

The executioner's eyes narrowed through the slits in his hood. He turned and retreated into the crowd.

Erich cut the bindings off the woman's hands and body.

"You're free now," he said.

She cowered against the pole and shook her head.

"No one will hurt you. Come, take my hand. We'll go together."

"Stop this heresy!" a voice shouted within the crowd.

A tall man in black robes stepped out from a group of clergymen and marched up the steps to the platform.

"What in God's name are you doing?" the man shrieked to Erich.

"In God's name, I'm setting this woman free."

"She's a condemned witch!"

Erich sized up the man as he spoke. He wore no religious artifacts and seemed more akin to one of the Witch Hunter or Inquisitor types.

"No! I say she's innocent! Like others, you and your kind have burned. And so I set her free."

"People of Würzburg!" the Witch Hunter shouted. "Don't let this heathen stranger snatch the witch away! You can stop him. Lest your town be condemned in the eyes of God!"

The crowd erupted once more. Additional soldiers advanced, but Axel, Nico, and Gunnar obstructed their path.

"This will end now," Erich said. "The pole will come down first!"

He nodded to Markus and Magnus. Both ascended the stairs with axes in hand and took positions on opposite sides of the pole. The twins each delivered two powerful swings, and the pole toppled off the platform and crashed to the ground. The townsfolk gasped—and some cheered—once it landed.

"You're an agent of the Devil!" the Witch Hunter screamed. "People of Würzburg! Stop him! God is on your side."

Erich advanced toward the Witch Hunter, who cringed away from him.

"You kill and torture the innocents in the name of God," Erich said with increased fury. "What God?" He faced the crowd. "Not the God I worshipped. When people freely worshipped differently from their neighbors. Without fear of reprisals. Not so long ago."

This time, the townsfolk remained subdued, taken in by his words.

"But men like this came into your town," he said, pointing to the Witch Hunter. "Men who've poisoned your minds and made you turn against your neighbors. Make you watch while they are tortured and killed. Like this girl here. Some of you may know her but are afraid to speak up out of fear you'll be next. Is that the way you want to live?"

"No! No! He twists the truth!"

Erich glared at him. "The truth? How many others have you sent to burn—*in the name of God*?"

The Witch Hunter glared back at him with reddish, glazed eyes.

"And how many more will there be?" He faced the crowd. "You can stop this! What do you say?"

Some in the crowd yelled, "No more!" and "Stop it now!"

Cort couldn't believe his eyes. He had never heard his father speak with such power and eloquence, in a voice he hardly recognized.

Mara stood beside him, recognizing that his actions were integral to his unfolding destiny.

Erich raised his hand to quiet the crowd.

"First, you must rid yourself of these men. If not, the pole will come up again. Is that what you want?"

He waited for the shouting to subside.

"It's up to you! You can't let this happen again!"

Some in the crowd shouted, "Get the Witch Hunter!" and "Kill the Witch Hunter!" and surged forward to the platform. The Swedes tried to hold them back, but some got by and rushed up the stairs.

Erich blocked them. "No! Not this way! Let him go. So he can tell others that they're not welcome here. Ever again! The soldiers will take him away."

He signaled for them to come.

The soldier in charge turned to the town officials for guidance. One of them nodded in agreement. The soldiers moved to the platform and escorted him away.

"Remember this sight!" Erich said. "Do not allow his kind to return. If they do, stand together and turn them away. Show them your pitchforks!" he commanded, raising his fist.

The townsfolk now responded with sustained shouts of approval.

Amidst the crowd, a young man with thick, curly brown hair observed the proceedings with a bewildered smile. He wore an assortment of mismatched clothing, highlighted by a vibrant scarf around his neck.

Nearby, the group of men who had initially seen Erich ride into town— including the one wearing a red headband—also watched the unfolding events with keen interest.

He turned to the woman and reached out his hand. "Come with me."

She broke down again. "My sister . . . is in prison."

"Are there more like her?" he shouted to the crowd.

"Yes!" a voice exclaimed.

A well-dressed man stepped forward from the town officials with a disturbed, conflicted expression. He hesitated before speaking. "Follow me," the official said.

Others rushed ahead, including the young man with the colorful scarf. The Swedes cleared a way to the door.

Mara stood next to Cort, Manfred, and the Swedes as Erich approached. Their eyes met briefly, but his expression of steadfast determination remained unchanged.

Helmar smiled at Ansgar after Erich passed. "The spirit of The Lion is in that one."

Ansgar nodded. This affirmed what he already knew

The man with the colorful scarf came up to the bruised and bloodied Manfred. "Who is that man? And where is he from?"

Manfred regarded him with mild suspicion. "He's from the south, on his way east to be with his family."

"I'd like to speak with him."

"For what purpose?"

At that moment, the town official and Erich emerged from the building, accompanied by other prisoners. A few people shouted and rushed toward the prisoners, some of whom were bandaged and limping. When they met, they embraced, weeping with joy.

Many curious townsfolk followed as they made their way to the inn. Manfred noticed a man with a colorful scarf rushing toward Erich, wielding what appeared to be a weapon. He knocked the man down and raised his sword.

The man covered his head. "Don't strike! I mean no harm!"

"What's in your hand?" Manfred asked.

"What? Oh—". He extended his hand, which held a long wooden cylinder. "One of my scrolls."

"He asked about you earlier," Manfred said to Erich. "And now he rushed you."

"I just want a chance to talk to you," the man said.

"So talk."

"My name is Friedrich," he said, trying to catch his breath. "I'm a scribe by trade and have been chronicling the events of the War. One day, I'll put them in a book. So people will know what happened."

Friedrich's forthright and confident manner impressed Erich and reminded him of one of his university friends. "Tell me more while we walk to the inn."

"Which one?" Friedrich asked.

"At the end of this road."

"I know a better one. Where I'm staying. With clean beds, strong drink, and"—he glanced at the Swedes—"the best wenches in town."

"Lead the way!" Valborg bellowed.

"I've been north and south, east and west," Friedrich said to Erich. "So here I am in Würzburg on this fair and pleasant day to witness yet another witch burning. Then you came along, and everything changed. You acted courageously and spoke with words reaching the people's hearts."

"Like you, I think, I've seen too many witch burnings and killings."

"Your comrade in arms," Friedrich said half-jokingly, "told me you were going east. I'd like to join you. When the times are right, perhaps we can talk so I can chronicle your story in my humble book."

"There's not so much to say, but you can come along if you want. We leave in two days."

———

The following day, Erich sat with some Swedes at the inn when two men approached their table. Erich recognized one of them as the town official who had guided them through the prison.

"Good day to you," he said to Erich. "My name is Leopold Holtz, the Vice Mayor of Würzburg. I'd like to discuss something with you now."

Erich nodded and motioned for him to sit.

"I'd offer you a drink," Leopold said, "but can see you're being well-fortified with Würzburg's finest ale."

"And fine ale it is," Valborg said as he wiped the froth clinging to his beard.

"What would you like to talk about?" Erich asked.

"An employment opportunity," he said, pouring himself a drink. "For you."

"What do you mean?"

"Most people here are Protestants, but the Catholics have ruled the town for many years. They've set up a garrison, supported by the Church. Of course, they've enforced laws favoring the Catholics."

"The same thing happened in my town, Ulm."

"What you did yesterday tipped the scales of power here," Leopold said. "People have turned against the Catholics and run off their clerics. Moreover, the garrison soldiers have abandoned their posts. I witnessed both events this morning."

"What does that have to do with me?"

"Our sheriff is a lackey of the Church. Or I should say *was*. He resigned this morning. We'd like to offer this position to you."

"This is too much to ask. I can't decide now."

"Take as long as you want."

"I'm on my way to meet my family in Leipzig."

"We can offer housing for all of you," the other official said. "And a generous salary."

Erich took a swig and set the mug down. "I'll consider it. But it's unlikely I'll accept."

"The position will always be open to you as long as I'm here."

———

Erich and the Swedes loaded their horses at the livery the next morning. A crowd of curious townsfolk watched them from across the street.

A group of about thirty men ambled toward them, all dressed shabbily and armed with simple, crude weapons, resembling peasant soldiers. The peasants stopped, but three continued on. Nico and Axel intercepted them.

"What's your business here?" Axel asked.

Erich recognized one of the men wearing a red headband as a member of the group he'd seen in front of an inn when they first entered the town. Another man was much younger, nearly Cort's age. The third man had long, unruly black hair and a scruffy beard.

The man with the headband hesitated before answering. "We hear you're going east to fight the Imperials," he blurted out to Erich. "We want to join you."

"Whatever gave you that idea?"

"It's all over the town."

"I'm going east, but not to fight the Imperials. The War hasn't started and perhaps never will."

"Everyone knows it will. Both sides are arming."

"Why don't you join the army?"

"There are no Protestant forces here."

Erich sized up the three peasants and the men behind them, who all looked fit and healthy despite their shabby clothing.

"Have you ever fought in battle before?"

"No."

"What were you doing during the War?"

"I, and most others with me, lived off the land as farmers. Some of us were craftsmen. Then the Imperials came and burned everything down. Our houses, crops. Everything."

"Your family?"

His expression darkened. "Taken away. Like others here. We've nothing left except what we have on us now. And our horses."

Erich shook his head. "What's your name?"

"Jürgen."

"Mine is Hans," the young man next to him said.

"I'm Georg," the man with the long black hair added.

"Look at you. You have no armor, and your weapons are useless against pikemen and cavalry. You'll be cut to pieces in battle. Most of all, you must learn tactics and how to fight as a unit. The opposition will rout you on the first charge. No, I think you should go back to your farms."

"We've done that and starved!" Hans said with rising desperation. "We even tried being highwaymen. But that's no way to live."

"We came here a year ago to scratch out a living but can't go on like this!" Jürgen pleaded. "Slowly rotting away! We must do something! If we die in battle, so be it. At least we'll go down fighting."

Erich sized up Jürgen a little closer. Deep bruises stood out on his face and the knuckles of both hands as if he'd been in tavern brawls. Georg looked like a man you didn't want to turn your back on, ever.

"I don't know," Erich said, shaking his head.

"Just a moment here," Ansgar said. "We've trained men with little or no experience but with a willingness to fight. A fighting spirit—that's the key to a strong army. From what I've seen," he said to Jürgen, Hans, and Georg, "you have it. And maybe your men do too. But if we take you in, it won't be easy. The training is hard, and my men will put you to the test. Some of you might back off. Those who stay will make good soldiers. What say you?"

"I will not back off on this," Jürgen said, emboldened by his words. "I wager that no one else will either. It's our chance to make amends for what happened to us."

"Are your horses in shape to take a long ride?" Erich asked.

"They are," Jürgen answered. "They're the last thing most of us have left. I, for one, have missed a few meals to feed mine."

That was enough to convince Erich. "All right, but understand this. No looting or pillaging. You feed and shelter yourself."

"Understood!" Jürgen said.

"We leave by the next bell," Erich said.

26.

Interlude

Peter stood behind the counter in the shop, waiting for the last lingering customers to leave before he closed it down. After they left and he locked the door, an older couple nodded to him as they strolled by. He was becoming a respected member of the community, earning a reputation as a skilled wood carver and an assistant in one of the town's most prestigious shops.

A beggar with a double-pointed beard, wearing a shabby brown cap, sat hunched over across the street, munching on a bone. He had noticed the beggar earlier in the day, who turned his head away as Peter passed.

The setting sun shimmered on the horizon as Peter walked along the river road. A neighbor couple with two children waved at him from a bench. One of them, a young boy, sneaked up behind him with a mischievous grin and let out a loud "Boo!" He jumped and pretended to be frightened, which made the boy laugh and scurry back to his parents. Further down, he spotted the same beggar walking furtively beside the road before ducking behind some shrubs.

He arrived home at dusk. Max greeted him with friendly barks, prompting him to kneel and pet the dog. As he did this, a figure shuffled along the darkening road before fading into the shadows. He stared at the area for a while until Rudi ran out to meet him.

———

Two days later, Peter carved toys and figurines from small blocks of wood in his shop as Rudi watched him intently. Eva had left with Thomas earlier in the morning to buy food at the market. Catherine rested in the bedroom. Her mood and health had improved, but on some days, she rarely ventured out of bed.

He'd been annoyed by Max's constant barking and was about to investigate before it stopped. After Eva and Thomas entered the house, the barking started again.

"What's the matter with Max?" Peter asked.

"He might be barking at the man across the road," Eva said.

"What man?"

"He's behind a hedge."

"What's he doing?"

"Just sitting there. Staring at the river."

"And chewing on something," Thomas added.

"What's he look like?"

"He has a funny beard and hat," Eva answered.

This brought to mind the beggar a few days before. "Show me."

As soon as he opened the gate, Max bolted toward a row of hedges, circled the area with nose to the ground, and sniffed longest beside piles of empty nutshells and bones.

"Anyone there?" Agatha asked Peter.

"No. Just scraps of food by a bush."

"That's odd, don't you think?"

He considered telling her his concern, but didn't want to cause worry since he wasn't sure.

"Yes, but he's gone now. We'll check again if he barks."

"Next time I'll run him off with this," Thomas said, holding up a club of wood discarded from Peter's shop.

————

Rudi dangled a bone for Max while the family ate supper, but he pulled it away as the dog jumped for it.

"Don't tease Max," Anna said. "Give it to him."

"When I feel like it!"

"Drop it—now!" Peter declared.

He tossed it to the dog.

"At least he isn't barking so much anymore," Eva said. "I guess the man is gone."

"Whenever I hear Max bark," Anna said barely above a whisper, "I think that Father is back. Each time he barks, I think of him. And Cort, too."

Anna's simple, heartfelt words struck everyone by surprise.

"Me too," Rudi said. "They'll be here soon—right Father?"

"Yes," he answered, patting Rudi's head. "Very soon."

"I've been meditating on this for some time," Agatha said. "And sense they're together now and on the way here."

Catherine sighed with relief, knowing she wouldn't say such a thing unless she were sure. "It must be true then."

"Let's pray," Agatha said, "for their safety the rest of the way."

Mara sat with Friedrich by a small lake near the camp, recounting her experiences with Erich. Since they had left Würzburg a week earlier, Friedrich had already spoken to Erich and Manfred about their journey. He informed them that these events and the people he met along the way would be included in the book about the War. His easygoing and friendly nature made them happy to oblige.

Afterward, they visited a meadow where the Swedes trained peasant soldiers. Their contingent had grown as more volunteers joined from the villages and towns they passed. News of their actions traveled quickly along the road, with the inhabitants of each place eagerly awaiting their arrival.

"I've talked to some of them, and they seem to be good fellows," Friedrich said. "But I fear what will happen to them if they go into battle."

"Erich has told me about the battles he was in. I can tell it still disturbs him. Even after so many years."

"I've seen friends come back from the War. Once happy and carefree, now moody or violent. Drinking ale all day."

"Such harsh experiences affect people in different ways."

"My father wanted me to have a military career. I spent a year as a cadet, training to be an officer. I tried to learn how to fight, shoot, and work a sword. Can you believe it?"

Mara glanced at him, observing his tousled hair and vibrant, mismatched attire.

"You don't look like the military type to me."

"I'm not. When I told my father of my plans to be a scribe, he stopped supporting my education. So I went off alone to write my thoughts and observations."

"How long have you been doing this?"

"Almost three years. Sometimes, I have doubts, though. Since I've nothing to show for it."

"Except your scrolls."

"That's something, I suppose."

"You shouldn't doubt yourself. Besides, there are far too many men in the army today. What this country needs now are more writers and fewer soldiers."

Jürgen sat against a tree with one pant leg rolled up and rubbing his knee, so they walked over to him.

"What happened?" Friedrich asked.

"I took a hard thump from Gunnar," Jürgen said, "and slipped on a rock."

"I'll fetch some things for it," she said, noticing the swelling. "So it can heal properly."

––––––––––

Jürgen had dozed off when Mara returned. She was about to nudge him awake when he suddenly opened his eyes as if waking from a bad dream.

She noticed the numerous bruises on his face, arms, and one on his upper cheekbone beneath his eye as he pulled up the leg of his pants.

"Did you get those from training with the Swedes?" she asked.

"Oh no. There's no hitting allowed around the head. I got these before I joined them." He took note of her concern. "I wear the marks with pride. But alas, they all soon fade, so I get new ones."

"You get into fights on purpose to have more bruises?"

"Not on purpose. For money. I'm a barn fighter. Others call it stable fighting. We go into a town, settle in a tavern, and after a few drinks, I brag about what a strong fighter I am. Someone always thinks he's tougher, and we end up in a barn or stable to fight. The money comes from betting. My men take care of that. I win most of the time, but not always. One fellow from Windsheim beat me pretty good. Georg's a good fighter, too."

She shook her head. "Let's check this now. I want you to bend your knee."

He grimaced as he bent it.

"You couldn't do that if you had broken bones." She reached into her bag and brought out some cloth strips and two lengths of thin, flat wood. "Hold the wood on each side of your knee while I wrap the cloth around it. This way, you won't disturb the healing with too much movement. Try to keep weight off your leg for a few days."

He stared at her as she wrapped it. "My woman practiced these arts. A midwife."

She was about to ask him about her, but remembered what he had said about his family in Würzburg.

"The man you're with—Erich. Have you known him long?"

"We met this year. He helped me when I got into a bad situation. Now I'm doing the same for him until he reaches Leipzig."

"Hmm," he murmured, gazing across the pasture. "There's

something about him. When his group first rode into the town, he stood out amongst the others, and I sensed something was about to happen because of him. So it didn't surprise me when he freed that woman and spoke to the people. He's given us much hope when he took us in."

Hans and Georg came up behind them.

"Are you going to live?" Hans asked with a laugh.

"You should make him a crutch to keep the weight off his leg," she said.

As they helped Jürgen to camp, she began to better understand how the destiny she had foreseen connected to his actions in Würzburg.

————

They arrived in Schweinfurt three days later, the largest town since Würzburg. As in other places, people were already lined up along the street to greet them. Baldur's prancing gait was another aspect that entertained the crowd. The horse had begun doing this on its own in the previous towns with large welcoming crowds like this one, perhaps sensing, Erich surmised, that it was in a military parade where the horse had been trained to prance in such a manner. Erich could have halted this with a terse command, but he let Baldur continue since the townsfolk enjoyed it so much.

Erich, Mara, Manfred, and Cort sat together at an inn, finishing their meal and discussing their recent experiences during the journey. The other patrons stared at them, whispering as they did so. Friedrich engaged in conversation with the patrons at the counter.

"Do you think the War will start again soon?" Cort asked his father.

"When both armies mass as they're doing now, it's only a matter of time."

"Where will it happen?"

"From what I heard, somewhere near Brandenburg or Saxony."

"Near the family."

"I'll tell you one thing," Erich said. "If I find out the Imperials are on the march, we'll break off from the Swedes and head to Leipzig. If they want to train soldiers along the way, it's their business."

"Why not now?" Manfred asked.

"I've thought about it, but the road isn't safe. Still, I'd go if I had to."

Friedrich sat down at their table with a mug of ale in hand. "I've found out some rather interesting things from the patrons here. It seems word of your deeds in Würzburg has outraced us."

"We've seen that in other places," Erich said.

"It's more than that. One of them recounted a tale about a man—a *Prince from the South* he told me—leading a force of soldiers who liberated Würzburg from the Imperials. An Imperial garrison here fled when they learned that some of them were from the Swedish brigades." He took a sip and set the mug down. "And so, you're regarded as a liberator of sorts. Feared by some, welcomed by others."

"I didn't want this," Erich said. "I just want to be with my family."

"But things are different now because of what you've done," Friedrich said, trying to be cheerful. "Look at all the men following us. Their numbers grow each day."

"I didn't want this!" Erich repeated in a louder voice. He slammed his fist on the table and stormed out of the room. Cort and Mara followed. Friedrich stared at Manfred, wondering how his words could've caused such a reaction.

———

Klaus sat brooding in the darkest corner of an inn near the Ratisbon camp, drinking ale alone. For weeks, he had been unable to tolerate the sight and presence of other people and had shunned the company of even the most eager wenches. He felt trapped and confined in his quarters ever since the march north had been delayed due to rumors of a truce or peace on the horizon. If true, it meant the army would disband, and he would likely return to his previous life: maintaining order in some small town among the local populace. He chafed at the thought of it. He took another swig and lifted the patch from his eye to relieve the pressure.

Each night, he placed the patch on a bedside table before retiring, and put it on the first thing in the morning. Sometimes, however, he forced himself to examine his disfigurement in the mirror first. The apothecary in Augsburg instructed him to do this to check for infections and any signs of improvement. Each time, however, it looked the same: smashed back in the socket, bruised along the edges, the lid half open—a darkened, lifeless mass staring out into nothingness.

The effects of the ale began to ease his anguish. Things weren't so bad for him. After all, he was now in a position of power and commanded much respect. In fact, his new status might not have occurred if not for the fight in the square. God had already tested and rewarded his strength of spirit, so he realized that he must remain patient and not waver in his faith.

The innkeeper approached with a pitcher in hand, but Klaus waved him away. His thoughts had brought him a sense of peace on this night, and more drink would likely shift him into a darker mood once again. He was about to leave when Sigi and another man entered the inn.

"Sorry to disturb you, sire," Sigi said, "but the men said you might be here. I have information that might interest you," he said with a grin. "Some news from the north."

"Sit down," he said, eyeing the bearded man with a brown cap beside him.

Klaus waved to the innkeeper for more mugs and ale. "I take it the news is good."

"Yes, it is," Sigi said as he poured himself some ale. "His family is in Leipzig."

Klaus tried to cover his elation. "Are you sure?"

"We found out where his brother, Peter, worked, so I told Emil to follow him to his house."

He cast another glance at Emil, who nodded meekly in response.

"I went there the next day and spotted most of his family. But not Erich. I waited two days and left to tell you."

"I want you to go back and tell me when he returns. I'll give you another pouch before you leave tomorrow."

Klaus walked back to his quarters with uplifted spirits but also realized how far he was from Leipzig. He only hoped that when or if the army marched north, he would have a chance to capture Erich. After settling into his tent, he removed the Pear of Anguish—a gift from the Inquisitor (who had been unable to perform his duties anymore)—from his vest pocket, opened it to admire the intricate network of gears and blades, and began to contemplate how he could make this happen.

———

Mara washed her clothes by the riverbank on a warm, sunny day, pondering the future and how much time she and Erich had left together. The next day, they would be in Bamberg, and from there, according to him, it would only be a month to Leipzig. And then . . . for the first time, she considered what would happen once they arrived. He would be back with his family. What about her? How would she return to the monastery? Surely, he wouldn't let her travel back alone. Would she return with Manfred? Had Erich thought about this as well?

After washing the clothes, she lingered to watch the river flow by. A man and his dog herded a flock of sheep along a path on the opposite bank. Later, a small boat drifted by with a man dangling a fishing pole in the water.

Despite the tranquility of the place, her thoughts once again returned to the moment in Eibingen when Ansgar slammed his fist so close to her, unleashing visions of suffering, bloodshed, and death. Initially, she believed these might be linked to the escalating tensions of the War, but after her meditations, she sensed they were connected to Erich's perilous journey.

She regretted not taking the time to consult Gottfried and Ursula about this before leaving. Gottfried possessed a wealth of knowledge about the new science of astronomy and remembered the lectures he gave, which included the teachings of the Polish astronomer Copernicus. Additionally, Ursula could have provided insights on astrological matters.

She accepted the reality that she would need to rely on her general understanding of both matters. One thing she recalled reading was the belief that when certain alignments of the sun, moon, and stars took place, their *convergence* could significantly influence individuals born on a specific year and day.

Now, she surmised they were in an interlude of time and place, between what had happened in Würzburg and what was about to unfold on the way to Leipzig. Indeed, she also sensed significant events occurring beyond that point. She hoped to stay by his side throughout the fulfillment of his destiny.

The sound of loud, whooping voices interrupted her musings. Some peasant soldiers stopped at the riverbank, stripped off most—and in some cases all—of their clothes, and jumped into the water. She observed them from behind a hedge, strong and fit, with curiosity and interest. She gathered her washed clothes and left as unobtrusively as possible.

27.

Cleansed By Fire

They weren't sure what to expect when they approached the outskirts of Bamberg. The town was well-known for its strict Catholic rule and for the many witch burnings that took place, but they decided to go since they had run short on feed for their horses. They entered the town alert for signs of danger, but, as in other towns along the way, only the many curious people, expectant of their arrival, lined the streets. Later, more townsfolk cheered and waved at them. Once again, Baldur's prancing gait delighted the crowd, especially the children. Near one busy corner, a few bold maidens stepped onto the street to ensure the Swedes noticed them.

———

Two days later, Erich, Manfred, and Friedrich, along with some Swedes and peasant soldiers, sat in Bamberg's largest alehouse, drinking ale among the local revelers, who were all at various stages of drunkenness. The alehouse owner, a staunch Protestant, invited them to celebrate the "liberation" of their town. Like Würzburg and Schweinfurt, the Imperial garrisons and Church authorities fled upon hearing that "The Prince of the South" and his men were marching toward them. He treated them like royalty after their arrival, providing food, drink, and shelter at the best prices. The extra time allowed him to rest Baldur and for Mara to refresh herself after being on the road for so long. During their stay, they listened to many firsthand accounts of the widespread repressions from previous years. Most of the worst atrocities occurred in a particular building they referred to as the "Witch House."

The revelry escalated as the night progressed. More fights erupted, and chairs and cups flew across the room. Jürgen and the other peasant soldiers joined in the brawls while the Swedes cheered them on. Their cheers reached a crescendo after Georg delivered a head-butt to his opponent, sending him sprawling to the floor. When some local deputies attempted to restore order, the revelers pushed them away.

Soon, angry voices yelled, "Burn it down!" above the din and tumult. They charged out of the inn and into the streets, followed by Erich, the Swedes, and a few town officials.

"Where are they going?" Erich asked an official.

"To the Witch House. To burn it down."

The raucous crowd paused in front of the market square, some gripping torches as they listened to the leaders urging them on.

"Where's the Witch House?" Erich asked.

"There," an official said, pointing to an imposing wood and stone frame building along the square.

The sheriff and his deputies came up to the officials.

"Sheriff," one of the officials said. "You must stop them! They'll burn down the town."

The sheriff and his deputies rushed toward the mob.

Erich now realized that Mara and Cort were at a nearby inn. "Manfred," he said. "Bring Cort and Mara here."

"You see what's going to happen?" he asked Ansgar.

"Yes. And our horses are stabled close by."

"I'll stop them," Erich said. "But need your help."

Erich and Ansgar hurried away, closely followed by the other Swedes. The revelers overtook the sheriff's men as they stepped in front of the torchbearers, blocking their path. The Swedes formed a line between them.

"Move away!" the lead torchbearer shouted.

"You must not do this!" Erich demanded.

"This isn't your fight!" another torchbearer exclaimed.

The crowd surged ahead. The Swedes resisted their advance.

"Wait!" Erich said. "Other buildings will catch fire if you do this!"

"He's right!" someone shouted.

"We shouldn't do it!" another voice cried.

"They tortured and killed my wife here!" the lead torchbearer said, his face contorted with rage. "We have to destroy it!"

"I agree!" Erich said. "But not this way."

"But how?" another one asked.

"With your axes and hammers or anything else. You say this isn't my fight. You're right. But I've seen what goes on in places like this. More than you know. So go forth and drag those instruments of torture into the square and set them ablaze! What say you to this?"

The lead torchbearer nodded and signaled for the others to follow. The crowd hastily made their way to the Witch House, carrying tools and clubs. Manfred, Mara, and Cort came up to Erich.

"Father, what's happening?" Cort asked.

"They're destroying that building."

"Why?"

"People were tortured there."

Soon, men dragged broken furniture out the door, and later the rack and strappado apparatus, the implements used to cut and slice the flesh and to crush the bones, a casket studded with spikes, ropes, and clamps. As the pile increased, beggars and street urchins carried off whatever items of use or value they could grab.

The Swedes and peasant soldiers helped drag more pieces out of the building and into the square. Erich, Cort, Manfred, and Friedrich joined them in this effort. Eventually, the townsfolk set the pile ablaze. Initially, they cheered as the flames soared higher, but later, they watched the fire consume the heap in calm and subdued silence.

Mara now realized the fire's cleansing and healing effect upon the people.

"I wonder," she said to Erich, "if this is a place where other burnings happened."

He nodded in affirmation.

Friedrich stood nearby, watching Erich and Mara together, their faces illuminated by the throbbing firelight. Later in the evening, he unrolled a new scroll and noted his observations of the incident.

———

Klaus feared the worst when the generals summoned the officers to headquarters on a hot, humid afternoon. Rumors of peace had circulated ever since Pope Urban arrived in Cologne the previous month and called the leaders of the warring factions to a council. He also learned that Field Commander von Werth was to be sent to the western front with two brigades to suppress Huguenot uprisings in northern France at the request of Cardinal Richelieu.

He wiped the sweat from his brow as he walked to headquarters. It seemed that the campaign against the Swedes had become secondary in Vienna. Subordinate generals now led the army stationed in Ratisbon. Perhaps God had different plans for him. *Be patient*, he told himself again, *and things will unfold as God intends*.

The generals entered the room, but von Werth was not among them. All the commanders sat down except for one: General von Hatzfeldt. Klaus didn't care for his officious manner or the fact that he came from high nobility with limited battle experience. Now it seemed he had taken command following von Werth's departure.

"We've received news from the west," von Hatzfeldt said, adjusting his pince-nez spectacles to read a pamphlet.

Klaus thought the worst. *The Pope must have arranged a Peace in Cologne. That is why the rulers in Vienna sent von Werth to France. The northern campaign was no longer of importance to them.*

"It's been reported," von Hatzfeldt read, "that Protestant forces have stormed through towns along the Main and routed our garrisons. They appear to be marching east."

The news astounded Klaus and the other officers. They'd known about pockets of resistance in the area but never anything organized or supported by troops.

An officer raised his hand and stood. The general acknowledged him with a nod.

"How large is this force, Herr General?"

"Unknown at this time." He nodded to another officer.

"Which garrisons, Herr General?"

"Würzburg was the first last month. More reports followed. Schweinfurt for one and other smaller towns. Nürnberg is safe."

"What of Bamberg, Herr General?" an officer asked.

Von Hatzfeldt removed his pince-nez glasses, adjusted his collar, and stared back at them with a grave expression. "Sacked. Based on a report we received today."

The officers gasped at the news. "My God. The holiest of our towns," one of them said. "Has this been confirmed, Herr General?"

"We have reports of burning and looting in the streets."

"I fear this is revenge for what happened in Magdeburg," an officer said.

"I have family there," another one said in a shaky voice.

"We must send our forces immediately and defeat the aggressors!" an officer shouted.

"No." Von Hatzfeldt said. "Not until we gauge the size of their force. We can't divide our army. Gustavus used that strategy against us. We'll dispatch a company to investigate and report on the situation when they return."

"Herr General. Who's leading it?" an officer asked.

"Unknown. We think it may be an ally of that knave Prince Bernhard."

"Whoever the leader is, it appears they've united with a force of Swedish soldiers," another general said. "The reports from Bamberg indicated sightings displaying colors of the Blue and Yellow Brigade."

"But they disbanded after Nördlingen," an officer said.

"So we thought," von Hatzfeldt said.

The room fell into a hushed silence.

"We must do two things right away," von Hatzfeldt declared. "First, we'll send troops to these towns to assess the situation. Based on the reports, we'll dispatch an emissary to Vienna so they may consider giving the order to move north without further delay."

At last, Klaus thought, a bit of good news.

"It appears they've taken the initiative and caught us off guard," another general said. "We must react quickly and with force."

"We'll also dispatch a company of men to Dresden to protect our interests and allies there," von Hatzfeldt said. "The Elector of Saxony had pledged allegiance to our cause, but we must supply him with reinforcements if his position becomes endangered. Together we'll be an unstoppable and righteous host."

Klaus attempted to grasp the unexpected turn of events and came up with an idea. He raised his hand.

"Herr General. Have you decided which company will go to Dresden on this most urgent matter?"

"Not yet."

"I volunteer mine to do so."

"We'll consider your request and give the orders tomorrow."

"Oh, and one more question," Klaus said. "What of the talks of peace from Cologne?"

"Dashed," one of the generals said. "Few agreements of any consequence ever came from them."

Klaus clenched his jaw as he tried to suppress a smile.

The following day, he received orders to lead two cavalry companies to Dresden. Upon arrival, he would inform Elector John George of the situation and protect his interests until the main army arrived.

Back in his tent, he took a moment to kneel in prayer. His patience was once again rewarded. Soon, he would be in Dresden, serving as a guard to one of Vienna's most influential allies, an important mission that could position him for a promotion. He unrolled a map and examined the route to Dresden. As he did so, he realized how close Dresden was to Leipzig—a mere two-day ride away.

———

It took them a week to reach Bayreuth because the number of men who joined them in Bamberg had slowed their progress. They also needed to stop in a village for a day when several peasant soldiers fell ill from an unknown malady and were left behind. By Ansgar's latest count, there were almost seventy in the group. Additionally, he negotiated with a merchant in Bamberg to join them and drive two supply wagons loaded with food and grain for the rest of the journey. He joked that they were a real army now, "complete with a baggage train and all."

Erich and the Swedes sat at an inn in Bayreuth studying a travel guide of the region.

"The road to Zwickau goes through some hard country," Ansgar said. "Thick forests, hills, and mountains, with only a few towns or villages."

"How long to Leipzig?" Erich asked.

He studied the guide again. "A week through Zwickau and the mountains. Another week to Leipzig."

"That's interesting,' the innkeeper behind the counter said. "Imperial soldiers came through the town two days ago on their way north along the same road."

"How many?" Valborg asked.

"About fifty. They only stayed to buy supplies."

"Where are they going?" Ansgar asked.

"To Dresden, they told us."

"Perhaps an advance guard," Ansgar said.

"This might be a sign that their army will be marching north soon," Helmar said.

Erich took a long swig of ale and slammed the mug down. "I hope there won't be more delays before Leipzig."

———

Ernst leaned against a post, closely watching the livery across the road. He had learned the day before that the renegade soldiers were in town, but his interest in them went beyond idle curiosity. Klaus had ordered him to stay for a fortnight and learn more about the group if they passed through.

Around midday, a contingent of soldiers and two wagons entered the livery. Ernst tried to remain as inconspicuous as possible among the Bayreuth townsfolk as he counted them. About half were ill-equipped and appeared poor, while others looked like seasoned veterans, judging by their weaponry and the swagger of their gait. One of the veteran soldiers' horses carried a rolled-up banner displaying a Swedish brigade's blue and yellow colors.

He continued to circle the area to observe more of the group. A woman loaded a gray horse, likely a camp follower. Nearby, a teenage boy laughed with other young soldiers. Then, a sight that stopped him in his tracks—Erich, leading his horse toward the street.

His eyes glinted with pleasure as they rode down the road that Klaus and his company had taken three days earlier. Such valuable information would surely be worth a handsome reward.

28.

Convergence

Erich and Helmar stood by as Nico aimed his bow at a target etched on a tree across a clearing. Erich took note of how Nico's approach and stance were similar to his own; the way he arched his body back and held the position as if waiting until he *felt* the right time to shoot.

His shot soared over the clearing and landed on the target.

"That will be hard to beat," Helmar said.

Unlike Nico, Helmar aimed and shot without delay. The shot struck the trunk but fell short of the target.

"Not my day, I think. Maybe it's the heat."

Erich aimed, but a bead of sweat trickled down his brow an instant before he shot. It landed just outside the target

"I'll get your arrow," Helmar said, noticing Erich was lost in thought.

Erich turned back toward the camp. From his vantage point on a rise of land, he watched the men—about eighty now—milling around their tents. They were all there because of what had happened in Würzburg. He recalled the stories he'd heard second-hand about himself, most of which were so exaggerated. He shuddered at the thought of people referring to him as the "Prince of the South"—a title he never sought or anticipated.

But she did. When they first met in the prison cell.

He spotted Mara walking toward the stream, carrying a basket of clothes. The men halted their activities as she approached and continued to gaze at her as she passed. She was an object of adoration and desire, yet untouchable to all of them.

And to him as well.

Almost every night, she filled his thoughts and dreams. He imagined what it would be like to be with her, but he knew it would never happen. Soon they'd be in Leipzig, and—it hit him with a jolt. How could he arrange for her return? Why hadn't he thought about this earlier? He found himself not wanting to dwell on it any longer.

———

Mara experienced an odd sensation as she walked through the woods. The scenery felt familiar, as if she had traversed this path before. Then it struck her—a recent dream . . .

She walked in a meadow with Erich on a sunny day. Everything was so vivid: the bright blue sky, the sounds of chirping birds and buzzing insects, the breeze on her face, and the soft, moist ground beneath her bare feet. His strong and resolute presence made her feel safe, protected—and aroused. As they headed toward a grove of woods, he touched her shoulder and drew her close. Then she felt a sudden chill when they entered the woods; he wasn't at her side. She continued to walk, now alone, following a rustic path. When she emerged into a clearing by a river, clouds swirled in the sky as if a storm were brewing, growing darker . . .

Cort knelt by the riverbank, splashed water on his face, and gazed sleepily at some peasant soldiers swimming nearby. His reverie was disrupted when Mara came by with a basket in hand.

"Remember what I told you about only drinking flowing water," she said. "The still waters along the banks collect harmful elements that can make you ill. You should stir it before you drink."

"Sometimes I forget."

"Cort, I want to ask you something about your father." She paused for a moment. "I've detected a certain fear in him whenever we cross a river. Did something happen to cause this?"

"Why do you want to know?"

"It's just something I've noticed. If you don't want to talk about it—"

"It's alright." He stirred the water and took another drink. "Grandmother told me that when he was a boy on a boat on the Danube, his grandfather fell into the river and drowned." He tossed a rock into the water. "She said something else happened to him when fishing with friends in the mountains when he was about my age. He got stuck on a rock in a river for a whole night and almost drowned. Maybe that's why he never taught me how to swim. Peter did."

She nodded thoughtfully.

"You care a lot about him, don't you?"

"Of course. He saved my life."

"He told me you're coming with him this time because you think you can help him somehow."

"I felt something important would happen to him on the journey and wanted to guide him on the way."

"You're right. Those men are following him because of what he did in Würzburg. I feel proud to be his son and ride beside him." He stared across the stream. "But also worry."

"What do you mean?"

"Some thoughts I have. Mostly at night."

"Like dreams?"

"Yes. Like dreams, I think."

He stood but wobbled slightly to regain his balance. "Whew. I think I need to rest now."

———

The next morning, Mara had just hung a kettle full of water on a spit to boil potatoes and turnips when Erich rushed up to her.

"It's Cort," he said, ashen with concern. "He's very sick."

Cort moaned on a bed of straw with his eyes closed as they entered the tent. Manfred stood beside him.

She leaned down and placed her hand on his forehead. "Cort, open your mouth, please."

She tilted his head toward the light and noticed the red and white spots on his throat.

"He picked up poisons from the water or from something he ate," she said. "We need to act fast. First, make sure he drinks fresh, clean water. Also, soups with vegetable and meat broth."

Ansgar and Friedrich came into the tent. "Others are sick," Ansgar said.

"Like the two last week?"

"I don't know. It started yesterday with a few of them. And now more. Including Gunnar."

"We must separate those who are ill," she said decisively. "And wash our clothes and scrub the cooking pots."

"I can attend to them," Friedrich said. "I've had some apothecary training."

"I'll help too," Manfred said

"We rode by an abandoned farmhouse yesterday," she said. "We should care for the sick there. A creek flows next to it."

She reached into her bag and pulled out a pouch of roots and herbs she had collected along the way. She placed them all on a table and organized them into groups.

"These will soothe his fever," she said to Erich. "Boil them in a pot until the water turns a greenish brown. Give some to Cort and make him drink as much soup as possible." She turned to Friedrich and Manfred. "You can do the same to the others after they're moved."

"Will you stay with Cort?" he asked.

"Yes, but first, I must get other plants to drain off his poisons. We passed by a marsh close by where they might grow. I'll search for them now."

"I'll send men to go with you," Ansgar said.

"Give him the brew right away," Mara said to Erich. "And make sure everyone washes up in the stream before they leave."

———

She returned to the abandoned farm with Nico and Axel at dusk. Tents and shelters were set up along a line of trees bordering the pasture. The old farmhouse and the surrounding landscape, bathed in the soft light of the setting sun, reminded her of a place she had once visited. A distant memory. Or perhaps a vision fragment.

Friedrich stood outside the barn when Mara rode up.

"The sick are inside," he said. "We made them drink your potion and much water. They're all weak and feverish."

"Any new ones today?"

"Six more since you left, which makes almost twenty."

She tried to hide her concern. She reached into her saddlebags to fetch a pouch filled with leafy plants. "Did everyone wash up as I instructed?"

"Yes. For some, it was their first bath in a long time. The sickness scared them into it. Did you find what you were looking for?"

I did. Thanks to these two gentlemen," she said, turning to Nico and Axel, "who helped me across the marsh to get what I needed."

"Honored to be of service," Nico said with a broad smile.

"How is Gunnar?" Axel asked.

"Same as the others," Friedrich said.

"And Cort?" she asked.

"Erich and Manfred are with him now."

Mara entered a small room at the back of the farmhouse, where Cort tossed and turned on a bed of straw. Erich sat beside him, applying a cold cloth to his forehead.

"You found what will cure this?" Erich asked.

"I found what can help. How is he?"

"Still fighting it. He can't hear my voice. He's of another mind."

"It would be worse if he were quiet and not moving before the fever broke. Then he'd be lost to us. He's trying to fight off the harmful poisons, which is good."

She reached into her pouch and laid out a variety of leaves and roots on the table.

"I need more boiled water. Did he have more soup?"

"A little," Erich said. "But fell sick again."

Her expression tightened. "You must awaken him and make him drink it. Now."

Manfred lifted Cort, and Erich held a cup to his mouth. "Cort," he said, "drink this."

Despite being weakened and delirious, he managed to take in some of it.

"The water is boiling now," Manfred said. "I'll help Friedrich with the others."

"The brew is bitter, she said. "I'll mix it with some soup. Afterward, he'll have some discomfort in his stomach, but it will pass."

"It sounds like what you gave me at Riedlingen."

"They're alike but not the same."

Later in the evening, both Mara and Erich stood by the bed, watching Cort. He remembered the times as a soldier when pestilences overtook the camps he'd been in. One type blackened and disfigured the skin, lingering for weeks before causing death. The other type that Cort and the others had, with high fever and delirium, often proved fatal much quicker.

––––––

The first morning light illuminated the room, so Erich blew out the candle. Mara woke up to the sound and checked on Cort, who was still asleep.

"Did he take fluids?" she whispered.

"Both the potion and some water."

She touched his forehead and rubbed her moist fingertips with her thumb

"What is it?"

"The fever has broken. The roots and plants are working. But the illness has drained much strength from him. There's little more we can do. He's in God's hands now."

"Does he have a chance?"

"He's young and strong. I'm hopeful."

He slumped back in the chair.

"You should rest now," she said. "I'll attend to him."

When Erich awoke, Manfred sat in the next room talking to Mara.

"Still the same?" he asked them.

"No change," she said. "Sleep is the best cure now."

"What about the others?"

"Four died last night," Manfred answered, taking note of Erich's pained expression. "But they were older. The younger ones are holding on. Gunnar too. Friedrich is attending to them."

"How many are ill now?" she asked.

"Almost twenty. No new ones all day."

Erich spent the rest of the day shuttling between Cort's bedside and the barn. All the healthy men had at least one sick friend present. Mara checked on them whenever she could. Toward evening, one of the ailing men awoke and seemed to have recovered; a hopeful sign.

Mara sipped her tea infused with herbs and grasses she knew would help keep her awake. Erich slept in a chair beside her. Just then, Cort began to moan. She watched him closely and went into the next room for more tea. He was in the same position when she returned, but his eyes were now open, staring at the ceiling. She nearly dropped her cup.

"Cort?" she whispered, creeping toward him.

Erich woke up from her voice. He jumped out of the chair and leaned over the bed.

"Cort! How are you?"

"Father?" he answered in a raspy voice. "Where am I? Where have I been?"

"You've been very sick," she said.

"For how long?"

"Almost three days," Erich answered.

He shook his head. "I feel strange."

"You've lost much strength," she said. "It'll take some time for you to recover."

"I'm thirsty."

Erich helped him sit up. Mara gave the cup to Cort, who held it with shaky hands as he drank.

"That's all for now," she said. "Open your mouth so I can check your throat.".

With a candle in hand, she noted that most of the lesions had shrunk or disappeared.

"Have any discomfort?" she asked.

"A little in my throat. I'd like some soup."

After he'd finished his third bowl, he flopped down in the cot. "That's so good. What's in it?"

"Some chicken broth, with potatoes, onions, sage, and parsley," she answered.

"Maybe I'll dream of swimming in the soup," he said, chuckling to himself with droopy eyes. "More funny dreams—"

"What dreams?" she asked.

"Funny dreams . . . Floating up above the ground. Looking down at people pointing at me. Like I was a bird, drifting along . . . I wanted to go higher, but something kept me from going up anymore . . . Something tugging in my stomach, like a string or something. I wanted to go into the clouds . . . but couldn't because the string held me back."

Later in the day, Mara and Manfred checked on the sick men in the barn. They acknowledged her with respectful nods as she walked by. She stopped at Gunnar's bedside, where he was chewing on a piece of meat. Ansgar, Helmar, and Friedrich stood next to him.

"I'm glad you and others have recovered," she said.

"Thanks to your potions," Gunnar said. "But oh, what bitter stuff. It was like someone had smashed me in the stomach. Before I fell asleep, I thought: *So this is death*."

"I've seen what this sickness does to camps," Ansgar told her. "You saved many lives."

Afterward, Erich, Friedrich, Manfred, and Mara ate stew in a farmhouse room, exhausted from lack of sleep.

"When can we ride again?" Erich asked her.

"About a week. If you go too soon, they may fall sick again."

"We're so close to Leipzig," he said with some disappointment. He turned to Manfred. "I'd like for you to ride there and tell my family where I am and that Cort and I will join them soon."

"I can make it in three days if all goes well."

"Yes. Three days there, three back, and one to stay with them. I'll give you directions to Catherine's family's house. They'll tell you where they settled. Cort and the other sick men should be ready to travel when you return." He extended his hand. "This means much to me."

Manfred shook it. "I'll leave right away. There's still half a day of riding left."

———

Mara had finished adding more ingredients to the stew and watched the sunset through the kitchen window. Erich had departed to the Swedes and Cort was fast asleep in the back room. A subtle shift of light on the wall beside the window caught her attention. Someone had entered.

Erich set a candle down and stood beside her. They admired the western sky, illuminated by the last remnants of a vibrant orange-purple sunset.

"Maybe this is what you meant," he said, searching for words. "When you said you wanted to be with me on this part of the journey. Because something might happen to my family. He wouldn't have made it if it weren't for you."

He placed his hand on hers, resting on the windowsill. His touch stirred a wave of emotion within her.

"I don't know how I can thank you," he said in a broken, shaky voice.

They faced each other. The opposing glows from the setting sun and the candle illuminated their faces. He glanced down at her heaving chest and then cupped his hand under her chin, taken in by the faint scent of wildflowers in her silken hair.

She turned her head away, torn by conflicting emotions. And yet, as she felt his breath on her neck, her desire grew stronger as he stroked her shoulders and breasts. She lowered her eyes and sighed. It was time to yield to those desires—to yield to him. Her whole body thrilled from his caress.

He placed a hand on the curve of her lower back, drawing her closer until their faces were mere inches apart.

Their kiss was deep and long. His hands explored the curvature of her hips and slender waist and the softness of her breasts. She loosened the lacing on her bodice. He pulled off his shirt and lowered her onto the table, almost knocking off some candles in the process. She gently pushed him back, gripped his hand, and guided him toward the adjacent bedroom. He lifted her, carried her across the room as she held his shoulders, and set her down on a straw bed. He retrieved the candle from the kitchen and closed the door behind him.

———

The family had finished their morning meal and settled into different areas of the house. Agatha was giving reading lessons to Anna while little Heloise played nearby with Bertina. Eva was cleaning the pots and pans in the kitchen, and Peter carved wooden figurines in the workshop as Rudi watched. Thomas chopped larger pieces of wood into smaller ones for Peter. Catherine rested in a bedroom, heavy with child and less than two months away from birth, according to Agatha.

Peter emerged from the shop. "I'm going to drop off my carvings in town. Who wants to join me? It's a nice morning for a walk. I'll bring some bread along for the ducks."

"Me! Me!" Anna exclaimed.

"Not now, dear," Agatha said. "We have to finish this section of the book first."

"I'll do it afterward."

"We've already started. Remember our agreement about your studies."

"I'll go with you," Eva said. "With Heloise and Rudi."

Rudi yelled for joy.

"Aww, I want to go," Anna said.

"I tell you what," Agatha said. "We'll go after you finish. Your mother can join us too."

———

Peter and Eva sat on a log by the river while Rudi tossed bread to the ducks.

"Don't you think we should've heard from him by now?" she asked.

"It should be any day. Perhaps the next knock on the door will be his."

"And Cort's."

He sighed. "And Cort's." Despite Agatha's encouraging words a fortnight before, he still had doubts about his safety.

"If not?" she asked.

"Maybe he made it to the Bingen monastery."

"How will we know?"

He shook his head.

A group of riders rumbled past, led by a man wearing a long black cape.

———

Max barked outside while Agatha read to Anna in the main room, but stopped abruptly after a loud yelp. Suddenly, someone pounded on the door. Thomas came out of the shop to investigate. The heavy pounding intensified with such force that the door broke free and crashed to the floor.

Lothar, Ernst, Horst, and Joachim burst in, brandishing swords and clubs. Thomas backed away as Anna screamed. Agatha pulled her away from them. Bertina scampered to the corner of the room. The men scanned the area with wild eyes as if searching for something. Catherine emerged from the bedroom, stifled a scream, and ran to Thomas.

"Who are you?" Agatha asked. "We're poor folk with nothing of value."

The men remained silent, holding their positions in a tense and uneasy stillness.

A long shadow stretched across the floor, illuminated by sunlight streaming through the doorway on the other side of the room. Bertina hissed, her back arched, at the figure. As the man in the dark cape entered, his features became clear. He removed his gloves and surveyed the room with haughty disdain.

Agatha recognized Klaus right away, even with the eye patch.

"So this is where his brood is hiding," Klaus said. "Where is he?"

No one responded.

"Look around," he commanded his men.

Lothar and Ernst shoved Thomas out of the way and stormed to the workshop. Catherine hurried away to join Agatha and Anna. Horst and Joachim searched the other rooms.

"No sign of him," Ernst said. "None of his clothes or weapons either."

"So he's not here now," he said to Agatha. "But you must know where he is."

Agatha narrowed her eyes as she sensed his hateful aura.

"I think you should answer me. Otherwise, it won't go well with you." He glanced around the room. "Any of you."

"He hasn't returned from his journey along the Rhein," Agatha said.

"We know about that. And who he took with him. But he must've given word to you by now since he is so close."

"What do you mean *so close?*" Catherine asked.

"Don't play games with me. My men spotted him not far from here, less than a fortnight ago. You can't tell me he hasn't returned or sent a message yet."

"I told you we don't know," Agatha said. "And that is that."

"I find *that* hard to believe," he said, mockingly. "I think he's already been here and is somewhere in or near the town. With that lawless bunch riding with him. Perhaps his wife, with child I see, can tell us since you refuse to do so." He motioned to Lothar.

Lothar pulled out his knife, pushed her to the wall, and held the blade to her throat.

Catherine's eyes bulged in terror.

Well?" Klaus asked her

"Mama!" Anna screamed, still in Agatha's arms.

"Please," Catherine whimpered. "I don't know."

"My God," Agatha said. "You must believe us."

"Don't hurt mama!" Anna pleaded.

Thomas backed into the shop and grabbed a piece of wood. With sudden fury, he leaped into the room, screaming, with the club raised. Before Lothar could react, Thomas struck him squarely in the ribs. Lothar fell, groaning. The others rushed at him. Thomas took down Ernst with another swing. Horst grasped him around the shoulders and waist while Joachim circled him with a knife. Thomas slammed Horst against the wall, forcing him to release his grip. Joachim lunged at him but missed.

Agatha tried to escape through the door with Anna, but Klaus blocked their way. They fell back behind a table at the far end of the room. Catherine huddled in a corner, paralyzed by fear.

They came at him once more. Thomas knocked Ernst to the ground with his club, but Joachim and Horst succeeded in pinning his arms back. He attempted to shake them off and slammed them against the wall again, but both men maintained their grip. Lothar approached him with a knife, but Thomas kicked it away.

Klaus pulled out his sword and lunged toward Thomas, who couldn't block it with his pinned arm. With a vicious thrust, he plunged it into his midsection and stepped back. Joachim and Horst relaxed their hold, but somehow Thomas found the strength to keep on his feet. He took another few swings with his club at them, knocking down Horst and Lothar. They backed off but came at him with a rage, angered by all the blows from him. Thomas crumpled to the floor as they continued to beat and stab him with their clubs and knives.

The sight of her brother being beaten so brutally was overwhelming for Catherine. Still in shock, she rushed toward him.

"Thomas!" she screamed.

As Catherine ran to him, she bumped into Lothar who, thinking he was being attacked, blindly swung his knife at her. It plunged deep into her upper chest, below her throat. Blood poured from the cut. She fell in a heap, holding her neck.

"Mama! Mama!" Anna cried, still in Agatha's arms.

Klaus and his men stood over Thomas's lifeless body. Joachim kicked him for good measure.

"My God, what an ox of a man," Klaus said and then faced Agatha. "That was most unnecessary, don't you think?"

Agatha stared at the two bodies, unable to answer.

"This could play into my hands," he went on. "Now he can't ignore me."

"Help . . . please," Catherine pleaded.

She raised her hand as blood gushed from her wound onto the floor.

"Mama!" Anna shrieked. She twisted away from Agatha and ran toward her mother. Agatha chased her, but Klaus pushed her back into the chair.

Anna sank to her knees in front of her mother, more distraught than ever at the sight of all the blood.

"Mama! Wake up!" she screamed. "Mama! Mama!"

"Someone shut her up!" Klaus yelled.

Lothar snatched her and covered her mouth, muffling her screams.

He adjusted his eye patch and glared at Agatha. "Still don't know where he is?"

"I told you no," she answered, trembling at the thought of what could happen next.

He nodded again at Lothar, who pressed down on Anna's nose and mouth. She twisted her head, struggling for breath. Klaus nodded, and Lothar removed his hand. Anna gasped for air between her frightened sobs.

"Are you sure?" he asked her.

"Not the little girl," Agatha pleaded. "I beg of you!"

He sneered and signaled Lothar again.

Agatha turned to Klaus, who continued to stare at the scene with a cold, blue eye.

Something surged forth from deep within her, radiating with increased force to her hands and feet, a sensation she hadn't felt in years—the power of the hex. The few times she'd ever used it, the hex emerged gradually due to meditations and rituals lasting many days. This time, it burst out unexpectedly, uncontrolled, thus more powerful and dangerous, for her as well. Her hands trembled from the surge, and she summoned all her strength to try and transform its energy.

Her eyes glazed over, and her lids drooped as she focused on Klaus, willing the hex to transform into something less intense that could penetrate the aura in a different way. Now, it had shifted into something new and more familiar, akin to a vision, yet undefined.

"Still no?" Klaus asked.

She barely distinguished the words since all sounds now echoed around her, including Anna's muffled screams.

The aura stopped shimmering and began to settle. Agatha's gaze fixed on his features, still blurry and indistinct. Her concentration was so intense that even the sound of a young, lifeless body hitting the floor did not distract her.

The vision became clear: a dark spot centered on his upper chest, the size of a button, shiny, reddish, and expanding. Another voice echoed throughout the room. The spot glowed with intensity, pulsating like a heartbeat.

A hand obscured the spot, disrupting the vision. The aura had faded, and Klaus's blurred image came into focus.

"Eh?" Klaus said, breathing hard and somewhat disconcerted. He slid his hand away from his chest.

"I said the deed is done," Lothar said to him. "She's gone."

"Aren't you well?" Ernst asked.

"I'm thinking,"

"What about the hag?" Lothar asked.

Klaus glanced at Agatha, who stared at him unflinchingly.

"What's the matter?" Joachim asked.

"I'm trying to figure out what to do next. I didn't plan on this."

"I say we kill her now," Lothar said. "No witnesses."

The others murmured in agreement. Lothar took out his knife and strode toward Agatha.

Klaus held up his hand. "No! I want her kept alive."

"Why?" Lothar hissed.

"For one thing, so that she can suffer from this sight." He turned to Agatha with a scowl. "And you will suffer from this sight. Will you not?"

Agatha stared at the three bodies on the floor and shook from emotion. "Yes, I will. You should feel satisfied with that." She faced Klaus. *"But not as much as you will suffer on your way to hell!"*

Lothar struck her cheek. She reeled from the blow. Her hair became unclasped and fell over her face. Brushing it back, she glared at him. He was about to strike her again when a sharp pain cut across his neck.

"I still say we kill her," he growled, rubbing his neck.

"I say no!" Klaus said. "I want her to tell that vermin son of hers who did this. If she's gone, he won't know."

"But what if she speaks to others of this?" Horst asked. "To the authorities about what we've done."

"She won't," Klaus said. "If she tries to implicate us, questions will be asked, and they'll find out about her son. A notorious criminal in the eyes of the law who has caused much destruction in the countryside. Yes, we were doing our duty, and they fought us."

He put on his officer's gloves and started to walk out of the room. "Come, let's go now. We have nothing to be concerned about."

Agatha staggered toward the bodies on the floor after they departed. She took a tablecloth from a shelf and spread it over Thomas. Anna lay curled up. She fell to her knees to check for any signs of life and heaved with sorrow at the confirmation of Anna's death. She placed a towel over her body.

On the other side of the room, Catherine lay on her back, her ashen face surrounded by pools of blood beside her shoulders and neck. Agatha stood above her and detected a movement around her torso. She knelt, felt a faint breath from her nose, and then checked her pulse. She was alive! Catherine's hand gripped hers, but only for a moment. She rechecked her pulse and shook her head. Catherine had held on for as long as she could because . . . there was another life within her!

She focused on what needed to be done. First, she dragged Catherine's body to the kitchen and attempted to lift it onto the table, but didn't have the strength to do so. She paused to catch her breath and then sprang into action. She placed a pot of water on the stove, selected a few carving tools from Peter's workshop, and dropped them into the water.

She recalled all the steps for this procedure as the water heated. She took one with the sharpest blade, took a deep breath, settled on the floor, and made the first cut.

She began to feel faint but continued. She reached into the womb, opened the placenta, and pulled out the newborn, who appeared well-formed—a girl. She lifted the baby by her feet and slapped her once on the back; there was no sound. Her heart sank, knowing that infants born so early often didn't survive. She slapped her again—and out came a beautiful, healthy wail! Tears of joy streamed down her cheeks. She washed the tiny infant in warm water and swaddled her in a blanket. She dipped a cloth in a bowl of milk and placed it in the infant's mouth.

And so, Agatha thought—as the infant suckled on the milk-soaked cloth—amid the horrific slaughter of three bloodied, murdered bodies, a new life was born.

———

Peter and Eva laughed joyfully as they approached the house. They had bought extra food at the market due to a generous payment Peter received for his carvings. Their merriment halted when they noticed that the front door had been broken down. Then came a more disturbing sight; the crumpled body of Max lying motionless against the wall.

"What happened to Max?" Rudi asked.

They exchanged worried glances.

"Come next to me," Eva said to Rudi.

Peter walked cautiously ahead of them. He surveyed the damage to the door and peered into the room. Agatha sat on a chair, cradling a tiny infant wrapped in a blanket. Eva stood beside him, shocked by Agatha's condition; her hair was so disheveled, and there was an ugly bruise on her mouth. Agatha shook her head as she dipped a small cloth into a bowl of milk. Three bodies lay on the floor, partially covered by blankets. Eva turned Heloise and Rudi away. Peter's face contorted with horror as he realized what had happened.

29.

A Time to Grieve

Erich and Ansgar leaned against a rickety fence, watching the peasant soldiers training with the Swedes in an abandoned pasture. More men joined them in Bayreuth, but since then, their numbers remained the same—around eighty.

Mara walked along a nearby path, carrying a bucket to the river. She waved at them and glanced at Erich before turning her gaze away.

Ansgar stifled a smile at their silent exchange, aware of the change in their relationship.

They both tried to be as discreet as possible around others, but when in private, they became as intimate as the circumstances allowed: sometimes for just a moment to steal a kiss, a touch, a quick embrace, or to share playful words and laughter. They spent much more time together in the evenings, always in each other's arms. Most nights, they were alone in the farmhouse, while Cort had befriended some younger peasant soldiers and often spent the night in their camp.

———

Manfred rode along the river road and stopped at the house that matched the description of where Erich's family lived. Catherine's family had given him directions earlier, but he needed to reread them because the house looked almost deserted. He thought he recognized one of the horses and walked toward it.

He knocked on the propped-up door, waited, and knocked again.

The door opened a crack, and a face peered out. "What do you want?" a man asked.

"Peter? It's Manfred."

"Go away!" He's not here!" He started to push the door shut.

"Wait! I helped Erich escape. I've been with him all this time."

"My God," Peter said, opening the door wider. "Why did you come?"

"I have news about Erich. He's not far from here. Only a few days away."

"Why isn't he with you?"

"He's been delayed. He sent me to tell you that he'll be coming soon."

"What about Cort?"

"He's with his father. He met us before we came upon the Rhein. Now he's recovering from an illness."

"All this time," Peter said with much relief. "And now we know."

Agatha emerged from another room, cradling a tiny infant. Eva held the hand of a small girl while a little boy stood beside her, staring at him with frightened eyes.

"Come in," Peter said. "There's much we need to tell you. And even more to ask."

————

Cort strolled alongside some younger peasant soldiers returning from a dip in the stream. He had been feeling better each day, eating and sleeping more than usual. Across the way, he spotted Manfred galloping toward the barn on his horse. He jumped off and raced to meet him.

"Manfred!" he yelled, waving his hands.

He acknowledged him but kept riding.

Cort ran to the farmhouse, where Erich was conversing with Friedrich. "Father! Look!" he said, pointing to the barn. "Manfred's back!"

Erich broke off the conversation and headed over to him. Friedrich and Cort followed.

Manfred stood beside his horse, brushing himself off, when Erich approached.

"Good to see you," Erich said. "A day sooner than expected. Did you find my family?"

He nodded.

"How are they doing?"

He tried to cover up his troubled emotions. "They were relieved that you'll be coming soon. And more so when I told them Cort was with you."

"I bet his mother most of all."

He couldn't go on, at least not in front of the others.

"The ride must've taken a lot out of you," Erich said. "We should go inside and talk."

Manfred sat at a table opposite Erich while Cort and Friedrich stood nearby. Mara handed him a cup of water, and he stared into it after he finished.

"I fear it's more than a long ride weighing on you," Erich said.

He summoned his composure. "Yes, it's more than that. It's better if we're alone."

Erich nodded to Cort and Friedrich. Cort turned, tight-lipped, and walked away.

"I want you to stay," Erich said to Mara.

She stood beside him and rested a hand on his shoulder.

"Go ahead," he said to Manfred.

"Some men came looking for you," he answered, carefully choosing his words. "A few days before I arrived. They asked where you were. Your family told them they didn't know. The men didn't believe them, so they threatened your wife. Her brother Thomas tried to protect her and came at them with a club. He took down some of them, but not all. They finished him."

It took Erich a moment to understand this because he was primarily concerned about who might be searching for them. When he finally comprehended, he shook his head and sighed. He sensed that Manfred had more to say.

"Anything else?"

Mara refilled Manfred's water cup. He took a long swig.

"Your wife rushed to his aid, not thinking. One of the men swung his knife at her. She died."

Erich stared at him in shock, shaking. "No . . ." He closed his eyes and lowered his head. "I should've been there. How did they know?"

"Peter said a man followed him from the town a fortnight before. At first, he didn't think much about it but later figured he was a spy to find out where you live."

He opened his eyes. "A spy? From—?" And then he knew.

"The men were part of Klaus's outfit. Klaus was with them."

"The rest of the family?" he asked.

"Peter and his wife were in town with their children when it happened. They're safe."

"What about . . . Anna?"

This would be the hardest one. "She became distraught. One of the men muffled her cries and held on too long. She fell from a lack of breath and expired."

"Oh no!" Mara uttered.

Erich covered his eyes with one hand.

"And mother?" he asked after a long silence.

"They spared her. There's one more thing." He took another swig of water. "She was with child. After they left, your mother managed, through her midwifery skills, to bring the infant out of the womb. A girl."

He stood and staggered away. Mara followed him into a back room. He slumped into a chair next to a small table, holding his head with both hands.

"I'll be outside for whatever you need," she said.

"Please tell Cort there's been a loss in the family," he said. "I'll talk to him about it soon."

She closed the door and sat across from Manfred. "He'll be inside for some time, I fear," she said.

———

Mara wiped the cooking pots in the kitchen, lost in grief. She gazed out the window—the same one where they had watched the sunset together before falling into each other's arms. That night and what followed was such bliss, but now, such despair. She wondered if her visions at the monastery had foretold what had happened to his family or something else entirely. She reaffirmed her pledge to remain by his side and guide him through all the events leading toward his destiny, just as she did now.

She entered the room several times a day to refill his water pitcher and leave food, which he barely touched. Each time, he stayed in the same position: hunched over the table with his back to the door.

Cort, Friedrich, Manfred, and Mara shared their evening meals in the farmhouse, conversing in hushed tones. No one wanted to disturb Erich behind the door on the other side of the room.

———

On the morning of the second day, Ansgar came into the kitchen as Mara prepared ingredients for a stew.

"Good day. How is Erich faring?"

"There's been no change."

"Can you guess when he'll recover?"

"It might be today, or tomorrow, or the day after."

"It would help if we knew so we can prepare to leave."

"If you're in such a hurry to plunge back into the War, you can go anytime," she answered with some impatience. "When he's ready, maybe he'll catch up with you. He has much grief to bear."

Her firm response took Ansgar aback. "Yes, I understand bearing grief. Manfred told me what happened for my ears only. I'll tell my men we'll wait for as long as it takes. It would be a dishonor to do otherwise. Forgive the intrusion. Thank you for your time. And again, I bid you a good day."

That afternoon, the sound of a door opening roused her from a nap. She sprang to her feet when Erich emerged.

"Thank you," he said.

They clasped hands.

He saw his son outside, speaking with Friedrich. "I'll talk with Cort now."

After he left the room, she noticed that his usual strong and confident voice had returned. The healing process had begun. Of course, the tragedy would always be a profound source of pain, but because he took the time to grieve, it wouldn't consume or destroy him from within.

From the window, she watched as Erich placed his hand on Cort's shoulder while they walked together along the path into the woods.

———

Erich had just told Cort what had happened to the family. Even though he tried to avoid the details of the atrocity recounted by Manfred, it did not alleviate his son's anguish. After the first words, he listened to the explanation with his head bowed and his eyes tightly closed, shaking his head. Once Erich finished, Cort glared at his father and began to weep, his chest heaving.

"You should've been there!" he bellowed.

Gut-punch words that hit Erich hard and rendered him speechless.

Aware of his father's distress, he ceased weeping and took a deep breath.

"I should've been there," Cort said, barely above a whisper.

"We should've been there," Erich replied.

And then he embraced his son.

30.

Lützen

They paused to rest at the edge of a plateau overlooking a vast expanse of rolling hills, intersected by a winding river flowing toward Leipzig. The journey had been slow for the past three days due to the mountainous terrain and poor road conditions, which necessitated stopping to repair the wheels on both supply wagons.

The Swedes gathered around Ansgar to examine a crude map they had purchased from a local innkeeper. Ansgar called for Friedrich, and they studied the map for a while. Afterward, Friedrich rode back to Erich.

"What were they talking about?" Erich asked.

"They want to go somewhere before Leipzig. So I showed them how to get there on the map."

He grimaced at the news; it was yet another delay. "Where?"

"By a village south of Leipzig. Named Lützen."

The mention of the word Lützen evoked a sudden flood of memories—of his father. As they trotted on, he began to embrace the slight delay in reuniting with his family, as it provided him the opportunity to visit the place where his father died in battle.

After they broke off from the road, they followed a crude path cutting through endless fields of tall grass and hills, often passing rundown buildings and broken fences from abandoned farms. The path deteriorated in some areas into little more than faint wagon tracks.

Later in the day, Ansgar and Helmar halted the group and rode to the top of a hill. They immediately signaled for Erich and the other Swedes to join them. The landscape ahead resembled everything around it, except for a few more trees growing along a stream that flowed from one of the small lakes in the area. The only notable landmarks were several old windmills in the fields beyond the lakes.

"This is it," Ansgar said to Erich. "We'll camp here and pay homage to the fallen tomorrow."

The Swedes remained on the hilltop, gazing at the vista below. Erich regarded the scene similarly. At times, he focused on a particular spot, such as the area in the field where the grasses were sparser and shorter. Was that where his father fought his final battle? Or perhaps it was in the open area closer to the lake. He felt his eyes droop; however, his mind and senses remained alert. The colors and hues of the ground before him—shades of yellow, green, and brown—became more vivid and intense. Now he imagined his father in the fields below . . .

amid the tumult of the battle, cutting down his adversary, and afterward taking all those strikes from a hail of arrows—as the Swedes described— retreating to safety but mortally wounded.

He emerged from this semi-trance, still preoccupied with the memory of his father's death. He glanced at the Swedes, who remained subdued and solemn, whispering amongst themselves.

Cort, Manfred, Friedrich, and Mara rode up and silently stood beside Erich.

"So this is it," Friedrich said in a boisterous tone. "Lützen—a field of light. So peaceful now. But not then, to be sure. A ground soaked red with the blood of all the dead and wounded. As the story goes."

Valborg and Helmar glared at him. Friedrich said no more.

"Is this where Grandfather died?" he whispered to his father.

He nodded. "The Swedes want to conduct a ceremony here tomorrow. Then we leave for Leipzig."

More reflective silence amongst the group.

"I'm glad we came here," Cort said.

He detected a ray of hope and joy in his son's eyes for the first time since he told him about what had happened to the family. The news hit Cort hard for the same reasons it affected him; they both suffered from grief over the losses and guilt for not being there to protect them.

Friedrich gazed down at the terrain. He'd read extensively about the battle while at the university: the ebb and flow of assaults, the loss of many men, including military leaders on both sides: King Gustavus for the Protestants and von Pappenheim for the Imperials. Now, being at the actual site of the events made everything he had read seem empty by comparison.

At that moment, he had an idea about what else to add to his book. How could he not have thought of it before? What a perfect ending! He wanted to shout this out with all his might, but dared not disturb the tranquil reflections of the others again. He decided to discuss this with Erich during the evening campfire.

————

The next day, Erich sat with Manfred atop a hill, watching Cort wash up in a stream. He focused on a spot at one end of the lake where the Swedes were digging into the ground. Later, Markus and Magnus carried a long wooden pole and pushed it beneath a huge boulder embedded near the bank. Eventually, they dislodged it. Gunnar and Valborg looped a thick rope around it while the other Swedes pulled on the opposite end.

"Why are they moving it?" Erich asked.

"They talked over the campfire last night," Manfred answered. "And want to put something in the field to honor where their leader, King Gustavus, had fallen. Maybe that's it."

The Swedes continued dragging the boulder as Jürgen and other peasant soldiers joined in to assist with the rope.

Cort ran up the hill toward his father, shirtless. Erich was pleased to see that he had regained much of the weight he lost after his illness.

"What are they doing?" he asked his father.

"Manfred said they're going to move the rock to the middle of the field to honor their leader and countrymen killed in the battle."

"And Grandfather."

They exchanged glances, both thinking the same thing.

"Let's join them!" Cort said.

Mara rested on a log between the wagons, watching Erich as he pulled, taking in the musculature of his arms and the strength of his grip. She felt a rush of desire at the memory of his hands embracing her when they were together in the farmhouse and his look of pleasure in the dim candlelight when they consummated the lovemaking.

Erich glanced at her as they passed. Her expression resembled the one he had envisioned of her on the ferry when they crossed the Rhein from Bingen; so dreamlike and pensive, as if she were searching for something deep within his soul and spirit. He felt infused with renewed strength as he progressed onward.

————

In the afternoon, Erich sat on a hill overlooking the terrain with Ansgar, Manfred, Friedrich, and Mara, while Gunnar and Valborg knelt below in the field, bowing their heads before the rock.

Earlier in the day, Ansgar spoke to his men about what the rock meant to him. Afterward, he knelt and placed his hands on it in silent prayer. Magnus and Markus joined him, while the other Swedes awaited their turn. Some touched the rock briefly before leaving, while others lingered longer, as Gunnar and Valborg did.

"So perfect, so simple," Friedrich whispered. "A massive stone dragged across a field to mark the spot where their leader fell. The Swedish King, on German soil; a stone . . . *the stone of the Swede.*" Hmm, he thought, I must write this down, lest I forget. He walked away, muttering more words to himself.

"There's stew in the pot," Mara said to them.

"I'll have some later," Erich said.

"All that pulling made me hungry!" Manfred said, patting his stomach.

Mara and Manfred headed back to the camp. Ansgar stayed with Erich.

"They have burnings in our country too," Ansgar said. "Not as many as here, but I've seen some. I didn't like them but was never moved enough to stop it. But I will, by God, when we return."

"When will that be?"

"When will what be?"

"When will *you* return?"

"Soon."

"Soon—meaning?"

"When the time is right."

"How long has it been?"

"Five, six years. I've lost track of the time."

"A long time to be away from your homeland and families."

"Too long." He shook his head. "I've been thinking more about this. Ever since she said those words about what's kept us here."

"The oath."

"Some of us think we've fulfilled it. As she said, we've given the man hell knowing we're after him. It's more than that, though. Somewhere along the way, we've gotten lost. Forgot why we came here and where we came from."

"Chasing ghosts."

"Yes, chasing ghosts. But no more, by God." He gazed toward the northerly horizon—the direction of his homeland. "After these next battles, it's back home for us. No more chasing ghosts." He glanced at Erich and back at the stone. "That's what the rock has told us."

31

Reunited

The group rested in a grove of trees outside Leipzig, observing the traffic going in and out of the town.

"We'll camp here and enter in groups," Ansgar said to Erich. "To not attract attention in case of hostile troops."

"And rest before your campaign ahead," Erich said.

"And you? Are you ready now?"

He glanced back at Mara, Manfred, and Cort and nodded.

"Some of my men will go with you. Once you reach your family, one of them will return and tell me if you're safe. If no one returns by the next day, we'll go in with our swords high to find you."

———

Valborg, Helmar, Gunnar, Axel, and Nico rode into town with them. They bought food at the market, where Mara also purchased some vibrant flowers. There was no sign of Imperial troops. She tried not to dwell on her situation during the ride, as the thought of leaving Erich distressed her greatly. Manfred stopped in front of the house, and they dismounted.

Erich and Cort led the way as the others followed.

Cort took a deep breath, knocked on the door, and waited with his head bowed. The door opened slowly. When Peter recognized them, he threw the door open, overwhelmed with emotion.

"Oh, my God! They're here!"

"Who?" Eva asked.

"Cort and Erich!"

They went into the house. The Swedes stayed outside.

"Good to see you again, brother," Erich said.

"And you, brother."

Peter cast his gaze at Cort. "Manfred told me about your journey. You must tell us more."

"I will!" Cort said, with both joy and sadness.

Peter glanced at the others in the room but was briefly surprised when he saw Mara.

"If I knew you were coming," he said, "we would've prepared a meal."

"We brought plenty from the market today," Erich said. "For us and our friends outside."

Rudi ran up and hugged Cort. "I missed you!"

"And I missed you. You've gotten so *big* since we left."

Agatha embraced her son. Tears streamed down her cheeks. "My sons. Together with my sons again." She faced Cort and noted how much he'd changed in stature. "I knew you'd make it."

"I followed your advice."

"So I heard. Your father taught you well."

"Of course, you know Manfred," Erich said. "Next to him is Friedrich, a scribe who we met along the way. And this is Mara. The prisoner I freed in Ulm."

All eyes turned to her as she stood alone against the back wall, apart from everyone else, with flowers in hand.

Agatha gazed intently at her. Their eyes met and locked. She detected a kindred soul.

Mara sensed the same and felt her spirit strengthen.

"I brought some flowers," Mara said as she strode to them. "A humble gift for your house."

"How nice," Eva said as she took them. "Such pretty colors, too."

"Very pretty indeed," Agatha said with a half-smile. "And perfect for the occasion."

They both knew that the types of flowers and colors she chose were those used in the ceremonies to celebrate the reunion of family and friends.

"I'll tell the Swedes we're safe," Friedrich said.

"And tell them they're invited to join us this evening," Erich said.

Peter walked to the door. "Come on," he said to the men. "Let's unload the horses."

Erich stayed in the room.

"What about the little one?" he asked Agatha.

"She's sleeping with Heloise. We tucked them in before you arrived. Come, I'll show you."

He stared at the infant for some time. Next to Heloise, a baby no bigger than a rag doll lay swaddled in a blanket. He had almost forgotten how small newborns could be; this one was the smallest he had ever seen.

"How's she doing?" he whispered.

"We hired a nursemaid. She's healthy, with a good skin color, and alert. She has a strong life force."

"Have you named her?" he asked.

"Not yet," Eva answered. "We thought it best if you did."

"I'll announce a name during the meal."

He stepped out of the room to join the men outside. Agatha rested a hand on Mara's shoulder.

"Come, let's go to the kitchen and talk while Eva and I prepare the food."

"I can help," Mara said.

"Good," she said as they left the room. "You must tell me what cure you used to heal Cort and the others."

Although they had just met, she felt as if she had known Agatha for a long time.

———

Sigi trudged toward the family house, stroking his scraggly beard. He had grown it to avoid being recognized if they saw him. He made his usual detour off the road and walked around a thicket of shrubs where he could observe the house undetected. This time, many new horses stood by the shed near the back wall. He decided to stay another day in case Erich came out. If not by then, he would sneak closer to the house at night and peer inside.

———

That evening, everyone gathered in the main room to enjoy a sumptuous meal with plenty of food and drink: chicken, goat meat, bread, potatoes, carrots, various other vegetables, cheeses, and sausages.

As they ate, Friedrich recounted a journey he took after completing his studies to lands beyond the southern sea, where people rode camels. He also described the strange and terrifying beasts he encountered: crocodiles, elephants, zebras, tigers, and lions.

"Horses with stripes," Axel said with a laugh. "That I'd like to see."

"You saw a lion?" Helmar asked.

"Not one, but many."

"By God, man," Valborg said. "Are they as fearsome as they say?"

"I saw them from a distance on a boat with missionaries and slavers on a big river. That was close enough for me."

The merriment at the table was a welcome relief to Erich. Before the meal, he went to a side room with Agatha and Peter to learn more about what happened that day. Her voice was strained at times as she recalled the events. It disturbed him to learn that Klaus was likely camped in the region. She also told him how they conducted the burial and ceremony for Catherine, Thomas, and little Anna in a nearby cemetery.

Near the end of the meal, the little one began to cry, so Eva brought her out.

"And here she is," Eva said, handing her to Erich.

"My God," he said, "She's like a feather."

"She? She?" Gunnar asked jokingly. "Does *she* have a name?"

Erich stood, holding his daughter in his outstretched arms. "In honor of my friends and family here, I therefore name my child Catherine Hildegard." He paused to gather his thoughts. "Hildegard is a name that symbolizes women's wisdom. And Catherine's is . . ." He bowed his head, unable to continue.

Agatha raised her cup. "To Catherine Hildegard." Everyone raised their cups and repeated her name.

Hildegard's little eyes twinkled brighter in the candlelight at the ovation, as if pleased with her newly given name.

———

Afterward, the men gathered in Peter's workshop while the women tidied up in the kitchen. Peter displayed his carving tools to the Swedes, who examined them with great interest.

Helmar pulled a pamphlet from his pocket and handed it to Erich. "I found this in town today. It's the latest news on the War."

The pamphlet reported that most of the Imperial forces were heading north from Upper Bavaria. Another branch of the army, comprised of mercenary troops from Croatia and Poland recruited by John George I, the Elector of Saxony, was moving west from Dresden. Forces led by the Protestant Prince Bernhard were marching toward the Swedes in the Mecklenburg region.

"This means the Imperials might arrive any time now," Erich said.

"If so, I think they'll just pass through here," Helmar said. "The battles will be fought elsewhere. This is a free town."

"Even so," Erich said, "the Imperials might keep a garrison to occupy it."

He now began to consider *who* would be responsible for occupying—likely Klaus and his men returning to finish the job. He couldn't expect the Swedes to stay with him since their obligation was to reunite with their forces in the north.

"What are you thinking?" Helmar asked.

"It may not be safe for the family with me here."

Friedrich finished reading the pamphlet and shook his head. "Those Croats. The atrocities they committed in Magdeburg."

That settled it. He decided to wait until the next day to announce his decision, giving himself time to reflect on the implications.

———

The family gathered around the table the next morning. Axel had left earlier to inform Ansgar about the army movements on both sides. Friedrich and the Swedes attended to the horses in the barn.

"We found out last night that the Imperial troops are coming this way," Erich told them. "Some of them may occupy the town while the rest of their forces head toward the Protestant armies. What worries me is if they do this, *who* will do the occupying."

He paused for a moment to ensure everyone grasped his concern. Peter and Agatha shared worried glances.

"By now, Klaus might already know I've come back. Or if he doesn't, he will soon. And when he does, he'll return. He's after me, but none of you are safe as long as I'm here. After the Swedes leave, we'll be unprotected."

"What are our choices?" Peter asked.

"I thought about leaving the family here and joining the Swedes. But I worry what else Klaus might do to you when he returns. And he will"

"I don't like that idea either," Peter said. "What he did—" He shook his head.

"The only other choice would be for us to go with the Swedes for now. That way, we'd be under their protection." He took a swig of water to gather his thoughts. "Somewhere along the way, we'll find a place to live for a short time until the fighting ends. Then return."

"Traveling with an army going into battle is a big risk," Peter said.

"I agree. We'll leave them before it happens."

"How soon do we depart?" Peter asked.

"The next two or three days."

"What about the children?" Eva asked.

"We'll travel in one of the wagons." Erich faced Peter. "How are the horses faring?"

"They're strong and healthy. I'll go into town to get supplies. And tell the people in the shop my situation."

"What of the house and our possessions here?" Agatha asked. "We should inform Catherine's family."

"I'll tell them. To pay my respects and to share in our mutual loss." He fell silent for a moment but regained his sense of urgency. "Alright, it's settled." He noticed their concerns. "There's one more thing you should know. From now on, I'll always be with you. I'll not leave the family again."

Mara had been listening with much on her mind. Just when it seemed there would be some peace in his life, everything became uncertain. This was a troubling confirmation of what she had sensed from the beginning. The events in his destiny were still unfolding and had not yet reached their ultimate fruition stage.

"And what of me?" she asked.

Before Erich could answer, Agatha spoke. "Of course, you'll stay with us. Once it's safer, we'll see how things work out for you."

He nodded in agreement.

————

Later in the evening, the front door burst open while everyone was packing. Nico seized Sigi by the scruff of his neck and threw him to the floor. He cowered as they all loomed above him.

"I spotted this man hiding in the bushes in front of the house," Nico said. "When he came closer, I snatched him."

"I'm lost and looking for directions," Sigi stammered.

Erich recognized him right away.

"I know you!" He grabbed his staff from the wall. "You're here to spy on me and let him know I'm back."

"No, no."

He slammed the staff into Sigi's midsection, causing him to gasp for breath

"I warn you," he said, stamping the staff hard onto the floor. "Do not lie to me. How did you find this place? Have you been here before?"

He nodded meekly.

"When?"

"When Klaus came with other men. But I stayed outside to keep watch."

"Did he come inside with the others?" he asked Agatha.

"No," she said. "But I'm sure he knows what happened here."

"Is that so?" Erich asked

"No! No! I had nothing to do with that!"

"To do with *that,* you say? So you know what *that* is."

Sigi shook his head but then quickly nodded up and down.

"Take him into the workshop," Erich said.

Helmar and Valborg hauled him to the shop, and Cort joined them. Erich glanced back at Mara and shut the door.

"Sit him in the chair by the table," Erich said to the Swedes.

"Now, a few questions," Erich said. "If you answer them to my satisfaction, we might let you go without harm. But if you lie, I'll know it." He picked out one of Peter's carving tools and flashed it in front of Sigi. "No lies. Understand?"

He nodded with wide, frightened eyes.

"Now tell me about your master, Klaus. First, about his status in the army."

He gulped before answering. "He's a captain now."

"How did that happen?"

"He went to München after pursuing you. He petitioned Duke Maximilian for more men to put down an uprising in Ulm. They believed him and made him an officer to do so."

"What uprising?"

"He told them what happened in the square and said it was part of a growing rebellion."

"Where is he now?"

"In Dresden. I'm to inform him when you return."

"How did he know where my family lived?"

"He learned you have relatives here, so he sent men to find where you live."

"The beggar spy," Peter said.

"Were you one of those men?" Erich asked.

He shook his head.

Erich recognized the lie. He struck the knife blade against the palm of his hand and slammed it onto the table, mere inches from Sigi's hand. Startled, he jerked back in fright.

"You've told me enough," Erich said. "Before we let you go, tell your master I'll be heading north with other soldiers. If he's going to pursue me, we can face each other with swords and settle our differences. Can you tell him that?"

Sigi nodded.

"One more thing." He faced Friedrich. "Get your quill and parchment out."

"This will be a message to your master. Be sure to give it to him."

"Of course," Sigi said, thinking he'd be free soon.

"Good. You can deliver it to him . . . with your one remaining hand."

He glared, terrified, at Erich. "What do you mean?" When it hit him, he wrapped his arms around his torso. "No—"

Valborg grasped Sigi's hands. "Which one do we take?"

"It doesn't matter."

Erich turned to Helmar. "The ax."

Helmar unfastened the small hand ax from his belt and handed it to him.

"I sharpened it a few days ago."

Sigi struggled and begged for mercy.

"Keep still damn you," Valborg said. "Choose which hand!"

Sigi continued to struggle. Valborg grabbed the knife Erich jabbed into the table and slammed it through his right hand, impaling it on the table. He let out an agonizing scream.

"Come on now," Valborg said with a grin. "Soon you won't feel pain in that hand."

Sigi turned away when Erich raised the ax.

He pounded the ax with a thud, severing the hand from the arm.

Sigi's body shook as he stifled a long, loud groan.

Valborg examined the severed hand with the same wild grin. "A good clean cut!"

Erich picked up a rag from the workbench and gave it to Manfred.

"Put this on the cut to stop his filthy bleeding."

As he pressed the rag against his wrist, Helmar created a simple tourniquet and wrapped it around Sigi's forearm, causing him to flinch.

"Now listen to me," Erich said to Sigi.

Sigi looked up to him, ashen-faced.

"I'll tell you why I did this. One reason is the lie you told. And you did lie to me about spying on the family here. Remember the truth. If you want to keep your other hand."

"Yes. I was here before Klaus came," he answered in a weak, raspy voice. "We took turns watching the house."

Erich regarded him with contempt. "And now the message. Friedrich, are you ready?"

Friedrich nodded, quill in hand at the other end of the table.

"To my old friend Klaus," Erich began, in a slow, deliberate voice. "When we meet again, and after I defeat you in battle, it will not be a fight to the death. Rather, I'll keep you alive so you can choose which *one* of your four limbs to keep." He paused until Friedrich signaled for him to continue. "As you see, I gave your Sigi the same choice for his hands. In your case, the choice will also include your feet. One for each life you took from my family."

"Ha!" Valborg bellowed. "The kind of justice I like."

"The choice will be yours when we meet again," Erich said. "To keep a foot or a hand."

He turned to Sigi. "Are you sure you'll deliver this message to your master?"

He hesitated before answering.

"I don't think he will," Friedrich said. "It's a waste of parchment."

"I think you're right," Erich said. "I'll deliver it to him myself after I catch him. So he can read it—with his one good eye."

That evoked cold laughter from the Swedes.

"That's all," Erich said dismissively to Sigi. "Will you remember to tell him what I told you?"

He nodded.

"Be gone with you!"

He struggled to his feet and staggered away, cradling his bandaged wrist.

"Wait!" Helmar shouted.

Sigi fell to his knees. "Mercy, please. I'll do all you say. Mercy!"

Helmar pulled the knife from the table, picked up the severed hand, and carried it to Sigi between his thumb and index finger, like a piece of trash.

"Before you leave," he said, "let me give you a hand."

He dangled the hand before Sigi, who gaped at it incredulously. "Go ahead and take it. It's yours."

Out of habit, Sigi reached for it with his right arm. But there was no hand on that arm to grasp anything anymore—it dangled in front of him. More cruel laughter erupted from the Swedes. Even Cort couldn't suppress a grin. When he realized his mistake, he withdrew the dead stump of his right arm and clutched it with his left hand.

Sigi stood, tucked the severed hand into his coat pocket, and shuffled out of the room with his head down.

———

Everyone gathered in the yard of the house two days later, ready to depart. The Swedes assisted Cort, Manfred, and Friedrich to finish packing the wagon while Peter made final arrangements with the servants from Catherine's family to watch over the house. Erich had visited her family the day before to pay his respects and inform them of their plans.

Peter urged the horses onward. Agatha sat beside him. Inside,

Eva, Heloise, Rudi, and Mara were comfortably seated, holding little Hildegard. Her gray horse was tied to the wagon.

They stopped at a cemetery on the outskirts of town. Erich helped Agatha down from the wagon. Mara handed him a bouquet she had picked from the gardens near the house. Peter and Cort joined them as they walked toward the cemetery. The other men dismounted and waited under a tree.

They stood before three wooden grave markers. Erich fell to his knees and placed the flowers at the base of each marker. He bowed his head in prayer before he finally stood up and headed back. The family walked beside him with downcast eyes.

His expression of grief remained unchanged as he approached Mara, who was leaning against the wagon with her arms crossed, gazing at him intently.

32.

In the Woods

Klaus stood outside his tent near the banks of the Elbe near Dresden, pleased at the sight before him. The united Imperial Army—almost 40,000 men—was camped along the bank. Wagons comprising the baggage train were interspersed amongst the troops, along with the horse traders, armorers, cobblers, cooks, carpenters, tanners, and the whores and strumpets. It was a powerful and unstoppable force, reminiscent of the times when he fought with the great armies under Wallenstein and Tilly. They'd been given orders to march north and engage the Swedish and German Protestant forces forming somewhere in the Brandenburg Pomerania region

He couldn't pull away from the sight, feeling part of something monumental and glorious. Now, he was participating in a military movement that would finally end the War and unify the German states under the one true faith once more. Everything was going as planned—well, almost everything.

He still hadn't heard about Erich. He had been expecting a report from Sigi, but it mattered less now because he was about to find out for himself. Through his influence with Elector John George, he received orders to lead a company to Leipzig and establish a garrison there. Then, he would capture Erich and take charge of the interrogations.

———

The next morning, Klaus sat in his tent, studying a map with his henchmen when Sigi entered, stooped and cowering.

"And so, back at last," Klaus said, taking note of the bandage on his wrist. "I expected you before now."

"Erich arrived two days ago," he answered in a weak and raspy voice, slumping onto a chair.

"Finally!"

"Yes, but—" he stammered.

"But what?"

"He might leave soon."

"How would you know that?"

"Because . . . he told me."

"He told you? You were with him? Explain yourself!"

He tried to regain his composure. "One morning, I spotted new horses there but didn't see him, so I snuck closer for a better look. But they snatched me."

"They?"

"The men with him. Some Swedish soldiers."

Klaus exchanged glances with the others. "How many?"

"Three. The rest are camped outside town."

"The same bunch that sacked those towns," Lothar said.

"So, he's still with them. Who else?"

"Members of his family. And the man who helped him escape. Manfred. Also the witch he rescued."

"Ha! Tell me more. Like how you know he's leaving."

"He wanted me to give you a message." He gulped. "He said to tell you that he's going with the Swedes. If you want to chase him, go ahead because he'll defeat you in battle."

"Unlikely," he scoffed. "Anything else?"

"Ah, that's the gist of it."

"I think they tortured more information out of you. Judging from your missing hand. Am I right?"

He took a deep breath. "They threatened me with knives. And . . . chopped off my hand with an ax."

"Who did?"

"Erich. He said he'd take off more limbs so . . . I told him you were stationed in Dresden."

"What?" he bellowed, livid with anger. "No wonder he's leaving! I've lost the element of surprise!" He glared at the petrified Sigi. "Get out of my sight! I'll decide later if I'll keep you in my service."

After he had slunk away, Klaus studied the map.

"Poor Sigi," Ernst said. "What Erich did—"

"That's what happens when you're with those Swedes," Horst said. "Such barbaric people."

"Moose riders," Lothar sneered.

"Maybe we can catch him before he flees," Joachim said.

"He's probably gone by now," Klaus said. And then an idea came to him. He slammed his fist onto the table. "Yes!" he bellowed out with a grin.

His abrupt change bewildered his men.

"We received some useful information. The Swedes are camped near Leipzig. With Erich likely with them. This could work in our favor."

"What do you mean?" Horst asked.

"It means we have a chance to pursue them. And defeat them with our forces."

"But our orders are to secure Leipzig and rejoin the army," a soldier said.

"Listen, corporal. Those orders can be changed when I tell them about this."

"The report from Ernst indicated they're about seventy strong," the corporal said. "We'll be outnumbered."

"I'll get reinforcements. The generals will accept my plan. That ragtag bunch has been a thorn in our side for too long."

The sudden shift in plans rendered them speechless.

"Men!" he declared. "This is our chance for glory. If we're victorious, promotions and spoils will be had by all."

They nodded affirmatively after considering that aspect of it.

The sergeant returned and saluted Klaus. "We're ready to depart."

"Tell them our plans have changed. We need another company to join us. I'll give new orders after I speak to the general."

He poured himself another cup of water after they departed. Yes, that's how it should be, he mused. There would be no honor in capturing Erich in such relative obscurity in the middle of the night. No, capturing him after defeating those notorious renegades would bestow far more prestige.

He set the cup down with a smile. *God works in mysterious ways.*

————

Mara walked up a hill in the woods above the campsite toward Erich, who stood halfway up the slope waiting for her. They had managed these rendezvous every evening since leaving Leipzig three days earlier—the only time of day they could be alone together. For some time, they sat there holding hands and savoring the moment. The setting sun filtered through the trees, and birds chirped throughout the forest.

"Another day," she said.

"Another day," he repeated. "On the run."

"At least the family is protected."

"For now."

"You don't like running."

"I don't mind running from battles. But I do mind running from *him.*" He turned to her. "I realize this must be hard on you. Not knowing where we're going. Or when you'll return to Eibingen."

"I miss some things about the monastery. But what I'd miss most is if. . . we were apart."

He clasped her hands. "I feel the same. I want to say . . . once we settle down, in Leipzig or Ulm, we could make plans to stay together. Forever."

His words took her by surprise and unlocked her most ardent desires.

"In Leipzig, I considered asking Manfred to take you back. I couldn't do it. I miss my Catherine, but I felt empty when I thought about my life without you."

"And I, without you."

They talked more about their plans before heading back at dusk.

————

Klaus and twenty of his soldiers galloped along the river road in Leipzig. They halted and dismounted in front of the house where Erich's family had lived.

Manfred had been fishing nearby but paused to observe them. Erich had instructed him to remain there if Klaus and his men arrived and to follow them to gauge their activity. He pulled a hood over his head and crawled closer for a better look. He recognized Klaus immediately. Two soldiers pushed a man, a servant from Catherine's family, out of the house toward Klaus, who interrogated him. Klaus strode away in anger, remounted, and galloped off with his men.

Manfred trailed at a safe distance, trying to blend in with the other travelers on the bustling road. Eventually, they arrived at an encampment housing approximately one hundred soldiers and artillery pieces. Shortly after, they dismantled the camp and departed.

Manfred followed them until they camped near the location where the Swedes had set up their bivouac. At dusk, he settled in for the night on a wooded ridge overlooking the camp.

The next morning, soldiers led three peasants into Klaus's tent. Later, they broke camp again and traveled north until they halted at a crossroads. He climbed to some high ground overlooking the group. The peasants gathered around Klaus, pointing toward one branch of the road—the same one he knew Erich and the others had taken two days earlier. They continued along the road, leaving the peasants behind.

Manfred examined a rough travel guide. He chose an alternate route to avoid them. Then, he would ride swiftly to catch up with Erich and inform him that Klaus was in pursuit with a contingent of soldiers and artillery.

———

He rode into Dessau nearly exhausted after two full days of riding, rising with the first morning light and not settling until dark. At an inn, he discovered that Erich's group was camped across the river. After finishing his meal, he headed toward them.

———

Erich, Cort, and young Rudi fished together on the banks of the Elbe. Cort was teaching Rudi how to bait a hook and cast the line.

"They're not biting much anymore," Cort told his father.

"We'll leave soon. Doubt we'll catch any more today."

"I'd rather stay. I like thinking about things when I'm fishing. Sometimes it doesn't matter if I catch anything or not."

"What have you been thinking about now?"

"About all the big rivers in our land."

"We've been traveling along four of the longest ones: the Danube, the Rhein, the Main, and now the Elbe. They help nourish the farmlands and are one reason the country was so prosperous. There are only a few places with bridges where armies can cross, like the one in this town. An important battle happened here over this bridge."

"I remember you and Grandfather talking about it. And how you hurt your leg here."

"This is the place," he replied, recalling those times. He cast his line and gazed across the river at the town. He recognized many landmarks and buildings from the time he spent there recovering from his injury. During those years, Imperial forces had defeated the Protestants in every battle. Now, ten years later, he stood in the same town, his family in a worsening condition and the War still raging. He shook his head at the thought.

"Where do you think we'll settle?" Cort asked. "After we leave the Swedes."

"Somewhere towards the Danish frontier. Perhaps Hamburg. It's never been attacked because factories provide arms and munitions for both armies."

"What about her?"

"She stays with us until it's safer."

As he fished, Cort glanced at the road across the river leading to the bridge and thought he recognized a rider galloping along it. He shielded his eyes from the sun.

"Isn't that Manfred riding across the bridge now?" he asked.

Erich turned and spotted him as well. "Let's go."

———

Manfred sat in the tent, sipping his second cup of water, his eyes red and droopy. Erich, Ansgar, Gunnar, and Helmar stood nearby.

"One hundred men, you say?" Ansgar said.

"Close to it," Manfred said.

"When did you pass them?" Erich asked.

"Two days ago."

"The artillery and baggage wagons will slow them down," Helmar said.

"This means they're likely a day behind us now," Gunnar said.

"I don't like the idea of someone chasing us," Helmar said.

"And they might've sent scouts out to report on our position," Ansgar said.

"We should do the same to them," Gunnar said.

"We will," Ansgar said. "We'll break camp today. A few of us can ride back to size them up for ourselves." He turned to Helmar. "It'll be two days of hard riding. You'll be in charge until we return."

"I'll go with you," Erich said, realizing there might be an opportunity to deal with Klaus if the conditions were right.

———

Erich, Ansgar, and Gunnar waited in the forest on an elevated spot that overlooked the road ahead. Gunnar had returned earlier to inform them that Klaus's men were approaching.

Klaus's men appeared from a distant curve in the road, with the artillery cart and baggage train wagons trailing behind.

"I counted ninety," Ansgar whispered. "I say we take off now so we can catch up with our men tomorrow."

"I'm for that," Gunnar said. "We'll scout them after we're back."

Erich paid little attention to the talk. He now recognized Klaus, trotting with other officers beside him in the lead; the first time he'd seen him with an eye patch.

"Watch Baldur," Erich said to them. "I'll join you soon."

He drew the Black Bow and crept along the ridge. Ahead, a cluster of rocks jutted from the ridge, offering a better vantage point for a shot. He took off running, crouching the whole way. He huddled behind the rocks, peered at the soldiers, and nocked an arrow.

Now, he doubted his ability to make the shot due to the gusty wind and a sudden rain squall. He would also need to shoot between a line of trees as Klaus came into view. Furthermore, two other officers rode beside him, obstructing the shot.

He aimed, but another gust of wind blew in. He lowered the Bow, realizing he couldn't succeed under those conditions. Then, he had an idea: he noticed a large tree along the road that would serve as an easier target.

He pulled the string back, felt the power of the Bow surge through his body, and, at just the right moment, released the arrow. It whistled through the air and struck the trunk with a loud thwack. The impact caused the horse in front of Klaus to rear up, throwing the cavalryman to the ground. Another soldier shouted and pointed at a hooded figure holding a longbow, standing between an outcropping of rocks in the distance.

No, it couldn't be, Klaus thought. His worst suspicions were confirmed when Erich pulled back his hood and pointed at them. But Klaus knew he was pointing at *him*.

"After him!" he ordered. "We're under attack!"

Ten soldiers galloped away but had difficulty maneuvering in the rugged terrain.

Erich took Friedrich's message from Leipzig, placed it on the outcropping, weighted it down with a rock, and dashed back to the Swedes.

———

As he waited for his men, he asked himself *how* and *why*. How did he find them? And why did he take such a risk? A short time later, the soldiers returned.

"No sign of him," one of them said. "He must've had a horse nearby."

"I think you could've searched longer."

Maybe," the sergeant said. "But we feared a trap. An old peasant trick. Lure soldiers into the woods and jump them with more men."

"Pretty fancy arrow for a peasant," the first lieutenant said as he examined it. "I've never seen one with a tip like this. Or with such fletchings."

"We found this," the sergeant said as he handed Klaus a rolled-up parchment. "With writing on it."

"Did you read it?" Klaus asked.

"Ah. . . I can't read, sir."

"Just as well," he said as he read it. He had a mighty urge to crumple it and throw it on the ground, but he knew he needed to maintain his composure in front of them.

"What does it say?" the second lieutenant asked.

"Some mindless scribbling. If anything, some crude prayer to Satan." He faced the soldiers. "Get back in formation. We need to be in Dessau by day's end."

"We should be alert for an attack," the first lieutenant said. "The bunch we're chasing might be waiting for us."

So that was it, Klaus thought. *A game of cat and mouse. Trying to put fear in me, thinking he is the hunter. Pretending he is now the cat when the opposite is true. Proven by the fact that he ran away. No. He has failed in his little game. I am still the hunter, and he is still the hunted.*

Klaus felt relieved when they emerged from the forest near the end of the day, as he had been wary of another arrow coming at him from the woods. He stayed close to his men instead of exposing himself alone at the front and remained alert to every sound. Once, a high-pitched whistle made him flinch until he realized it came from a bird.

They camped along the Elbe, just outside Dessau. He intended to stay only long enough to buy food and supplies. After that, he would push his men harder to pursue that lawless mob.

————

They caught up with the group early the next day. During the ride, Baldur's strength and stamina continued to impress him. Despite the fast pace, Baldur managed to keep up with the Swede's younger horses, showing no signs of fatigue.

He felt a surge of pride when his son galloped toward them with the stature and bearing of a confident young man.

"Did you get him?" Cort asked his father as he eased beside him.

"I'll tell you later. How's the family?"

"I think Eva is tired of riding in the wagon. And Grandmother too. But they don't complain."

Cort yelled to Peter that Erich was back. Peter alerted everyone inside.

Eva and Heloise poked their heads out from the back of the wagon and waved at him. Agatha followed suit. Rudi grinned, revealing the gap in his front teeth where the new ones had just begun to grow. A smiling Mara held up Hildegard, moving one of her little arms up and down as if she were waving too. Dust got into their eyes, so they ducked back inside.

The sight moved him deeply. There they were, he thought, putting on brave faces despite such difficult circumstances, far from home and on the road for so long. Their situation couldn't continue like this. It had to stop, and soon.

———

The next morning, Erich huddled with the Swedes as they studied a regional map. Heavy rain pelted the tent.

"We should take this road branching north," Helmar said. "It'll take us closer to our armies."

"What about Valborg?" Gunnar asked.

"He'll find us. He should be back from Magdeburg any time now."

"I hope he finds out something," Helmar said. "It's one thing to be chased like this. Almost worse than not knowing where we're going."

A short time later, Valborg burst in. He shook himself off, spattering the others as he did so.

"If you're going to shake yourself like a dog," Ansgar muttered, "stand away."

Valborg ignored him, removed his coat, and rubbed his hands to keep warm. Magnus threw him a loaf of bread.

"Did you find out anything?" Ansgar asked.

Valborg grunted affirmatively as he munched away.

"Well?" Ansgar asked. "Speak up!"

"They read me a pamphlet saying the Imperial army is camped outside Potsdam."

"Sooner than we expected," Helmar said.

"What about our forces?" Erich asked.

"General Baner's men are north of Brandenburg."

"Now we know for sure!" Gunnar exclaimed.

"But the Germans aren't with them," Valborg said. "Prince Bernhard's troops were dispatched to Baner, but their whereabouts are unknown."

"This means the Protestant armies are split," Erich said. "And the Imperials are united. What do we do now?"

"We go to our countrymen," Ansgar declared. "We leave tomorrow for the north road."

Erich continued studying the map. The road headed north, away from the Elbe and toward the Brandenburg region. It passed through a sparsely populated area with few roads branching off. If something occurred along the way, there would be no escape route, with the Imperials to the northeast and Klaus's men pursuing from the south. It seemed as though he were being pushed into an unavoidable trap.

He focused on the area around Brandenburg, which featured a series of long lakes and rivers flowing from east to west. The map ended to the north of it. He sensed that the final battles would take place somewhere in that uncharted territory.

33.

A Twist of Fate on a Lonely Road

Klaus watched with helpless agitation as his men struggled to pull one of the cannons out of the mud. He cursed his luck. He'd been driving them hard for days, and just when it seemed like they were gaining on Erich, the conditions bogged them down.

Based on reports from his fastest scouts, he felt somewhat relieved that they were on the same road as the other group. At times, he considered breaking away from his baggage train and artillery to ride swiftly toward them, but he dismissed the idea as too risky since they only had a partial advantage in numbers. He chose to wait until they could engage with their cannons, which would surely turn any battle in their favor.

At last, the soldiers dislodged the wagon from the mud and rolled it onto firmer ground.

"Shall we proceed or camp here?" the first lieutenant asked Klaus. "The men need a rest."

Klaus noted the orb of the sun behind the clouds on the horizon. "They've rested enough today. We ride until dark."

———

Erich stood by the roadside as Peter guided the wagon over a bypass cleared by the Swedes next to a muddy stretch. His family huddled nearby in the cool, damp air while the wagon bumped along. Eva chatted with Mara, the first to warm to her since they both shared a role in caring for Hildegard. Later, Peter and Cort began to engage with her more as well. Of course, her bond with Agatha remained as strong as ever.

Mara turned back to him with a faint smile. Oh, how he loved her.

———

The next day, the scout Klaus sent two days earlier galloped hard toward them.

Lothar rode alongside him. He had grown weary of traveling at such a slow pace and longed to ride on the open road as he had during his early years as a cavalryman in the War. He often reminisced about the time when he was younger, stronger, and in his prime—before the musket ball had torn through his leg. If only he could go on a scouting mission, he mused.

The scout brought his winded horse to a stop in front of them.

"They're still a day away," the scout said. "But they took a different road yesterday. Heading north away from the river."

"Interesting", the first lieutenant said. "That one branches to Brandenburg."

"There have been reports of Swedish troops in the area," the second lieutenant said.

Klaus turned to his second lieutenant. "Go with two of our fastest riders to the army in Potsdam. Tell them the renegade bunch we're chasing is on the road to Brandenburg. You must state in the strongest possible terms that they must send a company or more to block their route north. And that we'll be behind to finish them off."

"Right away, sir."

"The generals know our mission. This is our chance to trap them."

Lothar decided it was time to make his request. "I want to take a turn on a scouting mission. "What say you?"

"Why so?"

"My horse needs a hard gallop. This slow going is making him lazy."

He was about to reject him but recognized his eagerness. "I think you want to go for other reasons."

"True. I'm also getting lazy in spirit. I want to ride as I did when in the cavalry."

"Such glorious times. You were our most fearless cavalrymen. But this is a risky mission."

"I won't take any chances."

"You can go when we arrive at the crossroads then."

They arrived at the crossroads in the afternoon and stopped to regroup.

Lothar sat next to Klaus. "I'm ready."

He was about to extend his hand to Lothar but withdrew it, not wanting to show favoritism in front of others.

"It's doubtful you'll spot them today, but should tomorrow."

Lothar nodded with a tight grin and spurred his horse on.

Godspeed, my friend, he told himself as Lothar rode away.

As Klaus settled in for the night, he realized that if they could trap them, he would need to instruct his men to try to capture Erich and the witch he had rescued alive. He imagined a trial, in Leipzig or Dresden, followed by the executions, perhaps both of them together; she by the flame, and he by the wheel. He held onto that divine vision until he drifted off to sleep.

————

Erich rode along a desolate stretch of road through dense woods. He volunteered for this scouting mission because Valborg and Gunnar needed to rest their horses. He also did it in the off chance of getting another shot at Klaus with the Bow.

He paused to offer Baldur a drink from a small stream while keeping an eye on the road ahead. A movement in the trees captured his attention, followed by hoofbeats. He mounted Baldur as the horse and rider emerged.

The rider slowed his pace when he spotted Erich and halted.

Erich focused on the rider, sitting upright in his saddle as he trotted along—and then he recognized Lothar.

Both men sat motionless in their saddles, strategizing their attack. Erich reached back for the Black Bow, but it was too late. Lothar began his charge, sword raised. Erich drew his sword and spurred Baldur on, recognizing he was at a disadvantage with Lothar closing in quickly. Lothar swung at him; he managed to block it, but the force of the blow nearly knocked him off his horse.

They charged back in the opposite direction. This time, Erich surprised him. He feinted as if he would strike Lothar on the head but then shifted his swing toward Lothar's midsection. Lothar blocked it just in time.

Once again, both men turned their horses, circling each other before lunging forward. They flailed away in close quarters, inflicting cuts and blows on each other's arms and bodies. When Lothar's horse reared up from the activity, leaving him momentarily defenseless, Erich struck a blow to his midsection that knocked him to the ground.

He jumped off Baldur as Lothar lunged for the sword that had fallen away. He kicked it aside, ready to strike, but then recalled what Agatha had told him about what happened in the house. No, ending it this way would be too quick. With his sword pressed against Lothar's chest, he called for Baldur and retrieved his staff.

"Get up," he said to Lothar.

Erich circled him, clutching his staff.

"I've nothing to fight you with," Lothar growled.

"Yes, you do," he said, glancing at the knife on his belt. "The knife you used on my wife."

Lothar turned pale at the memory. He whipped out the knife, but Erich smashed his wrist with the staff before he could throw it. Lothar lunged at Erich, who sidestepped him and struck his knee with another hard blow, causing Lothar to crumple.

Erich took out his knife and grabbed Lothar's hair. At the same time, he pushed his knee into his back and pressed the flat part of the blade on his neck. He struggled to escape, but Erich kept a firm hold on his hair and forced his knee harder into his back. Lothar's eyes bulged with terror as Erich turned the blade—and then slit his throat. With a scowl, he watched Lothar gurgle for breath as the color drained from his face until his eyes fluttered to a close. He dropped his head with much disdain as blood gushed out of the wound.

Before he left, he had an idea. He dragged Lothar's body and propped it against a log facing the road. He shot an arrow into Lothar's chest and covered his body with leaves and branches. He planned to remove them on his way back so that, perhaps, Klaus's men would notice it.

————

Klaus drove his men hard along the road as dusk approached. One of the supply wagons had broken down earlier in the day, causing a delay that infuriated him. For days, they had only stopped to rest their exhausted horses, often eating while riding in the saddle. He could think of nothing else but charging down on the blocked group and defeating them with his superior forces and artillery.

Two officers rode up to him as they came upon a vast meadow.

"Sir," the first lieutenant said. "This is a good place to camp. And with a stream nearby."

Klaus scanned the terrain. "Very well. But I fear we've lost ground today. So we ride harder tomorrow."

After giving the orders, the two officers trotted to the campsite.

"I used to admire that man for his strong and steady manner," the second lieutenant said. "But he seems to have gone a little mad ever since we started chasing this bunch of renegades."

"There's a reason for it," the first lieutenant said. "Remember the note the sergeant brought back after the man who shot at us in the woods?"

"Yes. What about it?"

"It wasn't some local peasant."

"Who then?"

"The man he's pursuing."

"How do you know?"

"Before they returned, the sergeant showed it to a corporal, who could read a little. A few days later, the corporal told me what it said. I'll tell you more in camp."

———

Erich came across Klaus's men encamped in a meadow near the end of the day. With the dwindling light, he crept to the edge of the woods but couldn't spot Klaus. He spent the night there and had been watching the camp since early morning. Soldiers milled around the area, but there was still no sign of Klaus. Finally, he decided to leave because he needed to inform the Swedes of their position without delay. He uncovered Lothar's body along the way.

He caught up with them in the late afternoon.

Cort saw his father first. "He's back!" he shouted to the family.

Mara came up to him first after he dismounted and took note of his blood-stained shoulder.

"What happened?" Peter asked, also noticing the bruises on his face and body.

"I'll tell you later. I need to report to Ansgar first."

The Swedes were eating the remains of a deer when Erich entered. Valborg handed him a slab of meat.

"Looks like you slept in a den of bears last night," Valborg said

"I ran into one of their men on the road. A scout. I finished him."

"Looks like he got a piece of you first," Magnus said.

"I wasn't a clean kill. I took him out after his horse reared."

"How far away are they?" Ansgar asked.

"Still a day."

"We celebrate a kill like this with ale at day's end," Valborg said. "We have some left for this—what say you?"

"That I will," Erich said, "but only one. I need to be with the family."

———

Erich sat with the family around the campfire, telling them about the incident on the road.

"... I recognized him when he got closer. It was Lothar."

The news surprised them, and Agatha most of all.

"How did you kill him?" Agatha asked.

"I slit his throat," he answered, somewhat surprised by the question. She lowered her eyes. *Just as I envisioned.*

"I remember him," Cort said. "Oh, I forgot to tell you. He rode past me with three others after I jumped off the ferry."

"You never told me that!" Erich exclaimed.

"I turned my hat down so he wouldn't recognize me."

"My God," he muttered, shaking his head.

"He and Klaus were good friends," Manfred said. "But now he'll never find out what happened to him."

"He might. I made sure they'd see his body by the road. I shot an arrow in his chest. I think Klaus knows what my arrows look like now," he added with a wry smile.

————

Before retiring for the evening, Agatha and Mara discussed the events recounted by Erich.

"And now it appears one of your visions has been realized," Mara said.

"At first," Agatha said, "I interpreted the fates of Lothar and Klaus occurring at the same time and place."

"Perhaps what happened on the road was a twist of fate," Mara said. "Klaus will meet his end later."

"And that's what troubles me now. I felt a disturbance when he told us this." She paused to stare into the fire. "I fear there may be unforeseen consequences for him if he kills Klaus. I must meditate on this tonight."

————

Klaus worried about Lothar, who was still overdue to return, as he rode his men through the woods. He tried to reassure himself, knowing he was an able horseman, and expected him back any time.

Later in the morning, he noticed his lead cavalrymen looking down at something along the side of the road. They cast troubled glances at Klaus as he approached. It took him a moment to grasp the sight of Lothar's body propped against a log, a dark gash across his neck. The arrow in his chest looked all too familiar.

It was him.

"Looks like someone took the trouble to kill him twice," the first lieutenant said.

"Cursed peasants," the sergeant said. "They must have killed him for his horse."

"We should search the nearest village," the second lieutenant said to Klaus. "Bet we'll find it there."

"There's no time," Klaus said.

"I don't understand why they left him here," the sergeant said. "Where anybody can see him,"

The second lieutenant dismounted and examined the body. "That's odd," he said, stroking the arrow's fletching. "This looks like—" Now he recalled what the first lieutenant had mentioned about the note and realized who might have committed the killing. With some difficulty, he looked up at Klaus. "The body, sir?"

"Give him a proper burial."

As the soldiers dragged the body away, he asked himself once again—how and why? How did he know that Lothar was on the road then? Was there a spy among his men relaying information to Erich? After burying his old friend, the sergeant made a crude cross and pounded it into the ground with a heavy rock. With each strike of the rock against the cross, his desire for revenge grew stronger. Nothing else mattered anymore: not the outcome of the War, enriching himself with plunder, or even gaining military promotions. No, the only thing that mattered to him now was *to send that man to Hell.*

34.

A Recollection

"Lord and Lady watch over us," Agatha recited to the family as they sat with heads bowed around a makeshift table beside their wagon. "Bless us as we eat. And bless this food, this bounty of the earth. We thank you. So will it be."

They poured water into their cups and placed the bread, sausages, and cheese on their plates. Despite the harsh conditions, there was always plenty of food available. Catherine's family had given them a generous amount of coins before they left Leipzig, allowing them to restock in each town they passed through.

"The brown horse started favoring his right leg today," Peter said. "We've been pushing them too hard."

They remained silent because this addressed a subject they were hesitant to discuss. They needed to move forward, but where? Somewhere farther north was all they knew.

"I'll check their shoes after the meal," Erich finally said.

———

Friedrich sat in the woods beside a stream and took out his writing supplies from his knapsack: a smooth wooden board to write on, a roll of parchment, a jar of ink, a quill and sharpener, and, lastly, a small bag of fine sand to dry the excess ink off the page. He shut his eyes and listened to the wind rustling through the branches, the flowing water, and all the other sounds of the forest blending into a beautiful harmony that evoked feelings so difficult to capture in words. He had never experienced this before while writing but came to expect it whenever he sat alone to absorb the great mystery of nature.

Erich and Mara strolled hand in hand through the woods, alive with buzzing insects and chirping birds, all softly illuminated by the setting sun. As they walked, they encountered Friedrich sitting beside a stream.

"We missed you at the meal," she said.

"Oh," he said, a bit startled by their arrival. "I forgot the time."

"More writing about the War?" Erich asked.

"No. Just idle nonsense. Of my thoughts only. Nothing of importance."

"A person's thoughts are not idle nonsense," she said.

"But not as important as my accounts of the War." He faced Erich. "Only the final chapter left." He sprang up and patted his stomach. "But now to eat and then to sleep. With more to write tomorrow!" He rolled up the parchment and bounded away.

"What about the final chapter?" she asked as they walked away.

"He told me that he's never seen an actual battle. And how he wants to be in one and write about it in the last chapter. I've tried to talk him out of it and about the danger he'd be in." He paused to laugh. "That only made his resolve stronger. He wanted to be as close as he could, he said, because *'it's the only way to know for sure.'*"

They sat by the stream, watching the sunset and enjoying the simple pleasure of being alone together.

"And you?" she asked. "What will you do when the battles start?"

"I'll know when the time comes. The most important thing is to keep the family safe."

His gaze landed on her partially unbuttoned blouse. Her smooth, glistening skin shimmered in the light. He pulled her close, led her to a spot where they lay down, and made love on a bed of grass.

As they strolled back, they paused to embrace and kiss after every few steps, reminiscent of their youth when love first struck them. By the time they reached camp, everyone had already retired. They shared one last kiss and embrace before heading to the family wagon.

———

The next morning, they passed by a recently burnt-down farm. Later in the day, they entered a small village with more smoldering structures. Bodies were sprawled in the street, some charred beyond recognition. A few inhabitants wandered among the ruins in a daze. They found out from one of them that the Imperials had attacked them the day before. Ansgar ordered his men to set up a guard around the camp at night.

During their evening meal, Gunnar and Valborg charged into the camp and rushed into Ansgar's tent, so Erich left to investigate.

The Swedes huddled over a map when he entered. "Tell him," Ansgar said to Gunnar.

"They're gaining on us. Less than a day behind."

"How far are we from Brandenburg?" Erich asked.

"About two days," Gunnar said

"We should send someone ahead," Helmar said, "to make sure we know what's in front of us."

"Nico and I will go," Axel said.

On the way back to the family, Erich worried even more about being trapped between two groups of soldiers.

———

After the meal, Mara and Erich met in the woods again, just outside the camp. He brought the Black Bow along because she mentioned that she wanted to shoot it the day before. They found a spot to settle by a small meadow, where the grasses and wildflowers were still blooming. She reclined against a tree and brushed her hair back with a smile, aware that such a posture often aroused him; however, she could tell by his troubled expression that other thoughts occupied his mind.

"I think the news today has troubled you," she said.

"Imperials are sacking villages ahead of us. We might be in trouble if we run into them with Klaus's men behind us."

They sat in silence for some time before he handed her the Bow and an arrow.

She pulled back, struck by a strange sensation radiating through her arms and feet, emanating from the area below the center of her rib cage. She closed her eyes and held the pull. Then a flood of memories poured forth: her experiences with Erich, her time as a young woman in the monastery, childhood memories in Alsace, and even further back in time, followed by a series of intense and startling visions—until Erich's hand touched her shoulder.

"That's enough for now," he whispered.

His liquid gray-green eyes appeared to her like the rarest of gemstones, deep and mysterious.

"I've never seen anyone hold it back so long," he said.

"I felt energies emanating from the Bow and the earth. Both of them converged here." She placed her hand on her stomach, below the rib cage."

"That's what Ursula said. But she withdrew sooner."

"I reached a balance and held it there. Yes," she said, almost to herself. "I've held the Bow before. In another life."

He stared at her in wonder. "I don't understand."

"Maybe it's like the vision you had at Lützen. About the death of your father."

"That was different."

"But also the same. I believe people can access worlds beyond what we can see, hear, and touch. We can gain deeper insights about ourselves and our connections when we're in those realms. It reminds me of the words the Scholar read to me by the campfires from the poet he met in England. Sometimes, people enter these worlds through prayer and meditation. Other times, it happens because of a sudden life experience, like what occurred to me now and to you at Lützen."

She gazed across the meadow and up to the darkening sky, focusing on a prominent star on the horizon in the twilight. And then it all became clear to her.

"You've told me much about the Bow," she said. "About the stones, the animal inscriptions, and where and when it was first made. In the Holy Land during the time of the Crusades. My people resided there at that time."

"How do you know this?"

"The elders in our family read from parchments about our heritage. Our people came from a land far to the east. Over time, they migrated west. One of the places they settled was the region where the Crusades took place. From there, they fled west again. We've always been on the move because people feared or mistrusted us." She shook her head and frowned. "Despite that, my people are skilled artists and craftsmen. So it occurred to me that some of them could've crafted such a Bow as this. That's part of what I felt . . . I've held *this* Bow before."

"Only part of what you felt?"

She gazed up at the same bright star.

"When I held it, I sensed we were together then, too." She grasped his hands. "As we're together now."

Her words and touch made Erich sense something new and wondrous about her, evoking a feeling of transcendence beyond all earthly passion.

They stayed there until dusk, discussing the vision before heading back to camp.

———

Near the end of the day, Axel and Nico raced down the road toward them.

"Imperials are sacking another village," Axel said. "Not far ahead."

"How many?" Ansgar asked.

"Maybe thirty. Less than a company," Nico answered.

"I say we take them out," Valborg said. "Our men need fighting experience."

Erich was about to dissuade them but waited for Ansgar to speak.

"They're no threat to us yet," Ansgar said. "We'll make camp now and watch for them tomorrow."

———

They walked through the sacked village the next morning. People wandered the streets around the charred and smoking buildings. Dozens of bodies lay strewn on the ground. Children wailed forlornly beside them, looking up at the passing group with piteous expressions.

Later, they spotted a man limping along the side of the road with a bandaged head and saddlebags slung over his shoulder. The man turned and stood his ground with stoic resignation as they approached.

"What say you?" Ansgar asked. "Do you know what happened back there?"

"*Ja*, I do," the soldier answered with a thick accent while examining the banner propped on Ansgar's saddle. "It's where I fought those cursed Imperials."

"You're Swedish!" Helmar exclaimed.

"I am. And you as well from the banner you carry."

"What's your name, and what town are you from?" Ansgar asked.

"My name is Sven, from Göteborg. A shipbuilder by trade. Gustav needed men so I joined three years ago. I fought at Nördlingen with many of your men."

"How did you fall onto this place?" Ansgar asked.

"They sent me forward to spy on the Imperials in Brandenburg. A large force left there a few days ago heading north."

"How large?" Erich asked.

"Hundreds of men. But not a full battalion."

"The advance guard," Helmar said. "The main army can't be far behind."

"I went around them and came to this village to rest. I was about to report back when the Imperials came. The poor folks didn't have a chance. One of the soldiers shot out my horse as I fled. I hid in the forest until they left."

"Where is your unit now?" Ansgar asked.

"With Major Tortensson. His men are grouping near Wittstock."

"By God, that's where we're going!" Valborg said.

"Hop in the wagon," Ansgar said. "We'll get you a horse in Brandenburg."

The next day, the road branched off, one going east to Brandenburg and the other northwest along a large lake.

"Take the wagon to the town," Ansgar said to Gunnar and Valborg. "We need feed and grain for our horses the most. We'll camp along the lake and wait for you."

———

The family sat outside for their evening meal, weary from another long ride. Agatha noted that today was the Fall equinox. In previous years, they would always begin their Mabon meals with a prayer of gratitude to nature for providing the food and sustenance that was about to be harvested. Given their situation, they instead recited different prayers before the meal. No one spoke much as they ate; everyone was lost in thoughts about the unknown dangers ahead.

Mara listened to the sounds of the forest as she tried to fall asleep. She reflected once more on the time of year when night and day were equal and perfectly balanced, yet moving toward renewed darkness. It was the season when the Sun King followed a predetermined destiny and became the Lord of Shadows.

———

Klaus sat in his tent at the end of the day, simmering with rage. He had been informed that they had gained little ground on Erich and his men, despite riding hard for days. He also expected that the soldiers sent from Potsdam would have blocked Erich's path by now. He knew that headquarters had dispatched a company to intercept Erich's group, based on the report conveyed to him by the lieutenant he had sent on the mission. If that was the case, what happened to them?

When they came upon the first plundered village, he thought it was an isolated incident. After passing through another village the next day, he wondered if those soldiers might have deviated from their orders and were the ones who had sacked it. He had seen such things happen all too often: out-of-control soldiers plundering the countryside. He vowed to investigate the situation when the opportunity arose.

The thought of Erich slipping away again tormented him. He recalled how close he had come during the pursuit after the escape and again in Leipzig. Once more, he reminded himself to be patient. That evening, he prayed for His guidance on the matter. Afterward, he took out the Pear of Anguish and examined the gears in the device, which always calmed his spirit.

Unable to sleep, Erich sat by the lakeshore, leaning against a tree and seeking a moment of quiet reflection to soothe his mind. He brought the Black Bow in hopes of shooting one of the deer seen grazing in a nearby meadow. He gazed at the lake, where the moon cast a long trail of silvery light on the tranquil waters.

His thoughts drifted back to the not-so-distant past when his family resided in their ancestral home, then to the smaller farm, and finally on this road to an unknown destination. He reflected more on his decisions and what he could have done to help the family. He should have known the extent of Klaus's wrath. Were it not for him, they would still be in Leipzig, as the Imperials would have pursued the Swedes instead of him.

He wrapped a scarf around his neck as a bank of clouds rolled down to the water from the hills on the other side of the lake. Now, he began to think more about Klaus. The time for reconciliation between them had long passed, along with a tolerance for each other's differences, which had grown significantly over the years. They used to be such good friends among the boys he always played with. Some of them lived on smaller farms, while others, like Klaus, resided on the land owned by his family. Whether his friends came from richer or poorer families, Catholic or Protestant, didn't matter. They simply wanted to have fun together.

Things began to change during their early teens due to Klaus's growing resentment towards Erich's privileged situation compared to his own. Nevertheless, they maintained their friendship until the moment he left Erich on that rock in the raging Iller River. He never forgot Klaus's cold sneer as he walked away—"to get help," he said—acting almost out of revenge, fully aware of Erich's peril. But revenge for what?

He felt strangely comforted in the milky, silent darkness of the fog that completely enveloped him. He sensed he was nearing an important realization about Klaus until a shadow drifted by in the mist. A deer! He reached for the Bow, but knocked it over in haste, causing the deer to bolt away.

A sharp prick struck his fingertips as he picked it up. Then, a startling image of Klaus's face flashed before his eyes; it was from a time when he was younger, wearing a disturbed and hurt expression. The image remained vivid in his mind as he tried to remember where and when he had seen it.

It came to him with a jolt—the archery contest!

The archery contests, held during the local fairs, were always a time of such merriment for him. His father had won another competition, and everyone at the fair celebrated the occasion. He felt so proud to be his son, especially when his father handed him the Bow; however, his memory of the event became hazy after that. It was only now that he recalled Klaus asking him to hold the Bow too. But before he could, his father rushed up to the scene with swift and sudden anger. He pulled the Bow away from Klaus and spoke forcefully enough for everyone to hear: *"That is not for you!"* That's when he saw the same expression on Klaus's face as the one he'd just visualized; so utterly mortified and stunned, unable to speak because of the words that cut so deep—a memory long forgotten and recollected only now.

How could he have forgotten that? Now, he understood why Klaus had left him alone in the river, as it had happened right after the archery contest. Another memory surfaced of Klaus's father walking away from the scene with one hand on his son's shoulder, their heads bowed.

That had to be it then—when their split cut deepest and began to widen the most. The harsh rebuke of his father's words, forbidding Klaus from laying hands on the Bow, and the pain and shame Klaus felt afterward. Nothing was ever the same between them after that.

35.

Battle

The supply wagon from Brandenburg hadn't arrived by mid-morning, so Erich and Cort went fishing. They approached Jürgen and the peasant soldiers who were attending to the weapons and battle gear they had acquired in towns along the way.

"Good day, Erich," Jürgen said.

"And to you. Looks like your knee is healing."

"Yes, I heeded Mara's advice."

He sized up the others in the group. "Ansgar told me that you've worked hard to become able soldiers. I'll be confident to fight by your side if we go into battle."

"And we'll be honored to fight by yours!" the grizzled Georg declared.

The other men voiced their agreement.

Cort glanced up at his father with a troubled expression but remained silent.

"Father," Cort said as they ambled to the lake. "I thought you said you'd never leave us again."

"And I won't."

"But you said that you'll go to battle with them, so why—"

"Ah, but I said *if*."

"It sounded like you will."

"Know this, my son. I won't leave the family just to fight the Imperials. But there might be another one to go on."

"With Klaus."

"We'll never be safe until I finish him. If I need to go through his little army, I will."

Cort nodded in tight-lipped agreement.

The supply wagon entered the camp later in the morning, prompting them to head back. The peasant soldiers were already unloading the feedbags upon their arrival. He paused to listen to Ansgar speaking to Axel, who told him that Klaus's men were less than half a day away from town.

"That's too close," Helmar added.

Ansgar and Erich exchanged glances.

"We ride now," Ansgar said. "We'll divide the feed later."

They trotted through a landscape of meadows and farmland, interspersed with small streams and lakes. All the farms along the way appeared well-kept and vibrant. The people in the fields were busy with their harvests and barely noticed them. Near the end of the day, they passed a village of cheerful, contented people who waved at them as they went by.

Mara rode her horse instead of staying in the wagon, as she often did. The picturesque countryside reminded her of places she had visited in her childhood in Alsace before Ursula took her in. In fact, the entire area seemed untouched by the War.

———

They camped beside a wide stream. After the evening meal, Erich and Mara held hands as they walked through the woods and made themselves comfortable by the stream. They would begin their lovemaking on other evenings like this, but different thoughts occupied his mind.

"How are you now?" she asked.

"Calm and at peace with you. But troubled. Like the times just before I went into battle years ago."

"Will you?"

"That's not my plan, but I might have to. To get Klaus. I fear I won't sleep well tonight."

"Perhaps that's why you feel this way. Facing the unknown."

"I also worry for my family if I don't survive. Do you think . . .I will? From my hands." He turned up his palms. "Can you tell?"

She held his hand and studied the palm; it was the first time she'd done so since the prison cell. She recognized the same pattern of lines as before. Still, she now noticed something different: how the lifeline extended beyond the spot of many intersecting lines, although it faded past that point. She wondered how she could have missed that.

"Will I make it?"

"Yes," she answered. "Your hands tell me that you will survive the perils on your path and your spirit will live on afterward."

He broke into a broad smile. "I think I'll sleep very well tonight!"

———

The next day, they came upon a long, narrow lake stretching far to the north. Erich slowed Baldur and stared at the glistening waters, which seemed to calm him. The rising sun shone on the western hills. It reminded him of a place in the Alps where his father had taken him fishing. Or perhaps it was just a memory or a dream of a lake that resembled this one. He closed his eyes briefly but couldn't remember when or where he had seen it.

Later that morning, they passed through a town bustling with activity, many boats making their way to the western shore. Soon after, the distant rumble of cannon fire halted their advance. Gunnar and Valborg raced toward them.

"There's a battle ahead!" Valborg said.

"How many?" Ansgar asked.

"A few hundred on both sides," Gunnar said. "The Imperials have our forces pinned against the shore."

"You can see it from up there," Valborg said, pointing to a hill.

Erich, Manfred, and Sven accompanied the Swedes to the crest. From their vantage point, they watched in dismay as the Imperials on the higher ground unleashed artillery rounds upon the Swedes.

"Those are our men!" Sven declared.

"That must be the advance guard you saw," Ansgar said to him.

"They're getting butchered," Helmar said.

"We can change that," Valborg said.

"And we will," Ansgar said.

Ansgar and Erich exchanged looks. Now was the time for Erich to choose whether to stay with his family or to fight alongside them. Ansgar rode over to the peasant soldiers to inform them of the situation. Erich and Manfred rode towards the family.

He had figured out how to get them to safety but hadn't decided what to do afterward. Once again, it came down to Klaus. Even if he went with his family, he would always worry about when and if Klaus would find him. That was it then. He had to deal with him now. He and his men were less than half a day's ride away, so he hoped they could turn the fight in the Swede's favor and rout the Imperials. If so, he would then face Klaus's pursuing army with a superior force and take Klaus out with his sword. Or the Black Bow.

The family watched him ride up with concerned expressions.

"We're going back to the town," he said to them.

"Will you stay with us then?" Peter asked.

"I'm going with you to make sure you'll be safe. And then go back. If we win this battle, we'll face Klaus's group with more men. And I'll finish him."

The family stoically accepted his decision.

Erich surveyed the area as they entered the town. Most of the boats could accommodate only a few people; however, some larger ones were moored along the wharves.

"You know the situation," Erich said to Peter

"We can't go forward, and we can't go back. So we stay here."

"Troops might overrun the town soon. That's why so many are fleeing. So cross the lake with them."

"What about the horses and wagon?"

"Find a stable to watch the wagon and care for the horses. Then cross on one of those large boats on the wharf."

Erich pulled a chainmail vest from one of the storage trunks and put it on. Afterward, he lifted a battle helmet from the same trunk. He stared at it momentarily, recalling the last time he wore it during the War—almost ten years ago.

"Leave as soon as you get a boat," he said to Peter.

"May God be with you," Agatha said.

"When will you return to us?" Mara asked.

They held each other's hands and embraced while the family watched in silence. It was the first time they had shown a sign of affection in front of them.

"I'll see you on the other side," he said.

He secured the Bow and staff beside his saddle and galloped off with Manfred.

————

The soldiers waited for them as they rode up the hill.

"Our plan," Ansgar said to Erich, "is to take out as much of their near flank as possible and unite with our forces. And then we counter-strike before they regroup."

Friedrich trotted over to Erich. Someone handed him an ill-fitting helmet and equipped him with a stubby, nearly useless sword.

"I'm ready," he said with a grin.

"You're courting certain death if you go down there like that. Watch from here."

"It's not the same."

Erich faced Manfred. "Go with him, but keep away from the fighting." He turned to Friedrich. "Do you agree?"

He nodded, tight-lipped.

Helmar unfurled the Brigade banner. Ansgar thrust his sword forward with a mighty yell, and they thundered down the hill.

The Imperials on the near flank had no time to mount a defense against the charge. Ansgar took down the first Imperial. Valborg and Gunnar felled two more before they could load their muskets. The peasant soldiers spread out to inflict as many casualties as possible. Magnus and Markus rushed toward the nearest cannon, taking out an artillery crew with their axes and swords.

Manfred and Friedrich brought up the rear. Manfred guided him away from the battle until they stopped at a safe distance.

Erich rode alongside Helmar, who had secured the banner in a holder on his saddle. Axel and Nico confronted the Imperials with their pikes. Erich dashed toward a soldier aiming a crossbow at Nico and took him out with his sword.

The Imperials eventually reorganized to confront the attackers. Many peasant soldiers had fallen victim to the Imperial muskets and swords. Witnessing this, Ansgar ordered a retreat toward the lake.

———

The besieged Swedes opened their makeshift barricades to allow entry. An officer welcomed them in front of a small building that served as their headquarters.

"My God," the officer said to Helmar and Ansgar. "Who the hell are you? And where did you come from?"

"We've come from hell to help," Ansgar said.

"From hell indeed," the officer said, staring at the banner. "Back from the dead. We thought the Brigade had been disbanded."

"What happened?" Sven asked.

"So there you are, you bastard," another soldier said.

"The Imperials killed my horse. These men found me. Where is Tortensson?"

"He and a few others left to fetch reinforcements," the first officer answered.

"You wouldn't have lasted the day," Ansgar said.

"Enough talk!" Erich exclaimed. All eyes turned to him. "We must counterattack now while they're unorganized. You can't let those cannons start firing down here again."

"He's right!" Ansgar said. "We'll charge up one flank. You take your men," he said to the officers, "up the other one. Together, we'll squeeze them and force a retreat."

———

Klaus's men passed by a sleepy fishing village when another scout raced up to them.

"The renegade army is beyond the next town," the rider said. "They're fighting with Swedes that our advance guard has pinned against the lake."

"How goes the battle?" Klaus asked.

"Our forces have the high ground. We can finish them off if we leave right away."

"And so we will!" Klaus declared. "We'll ride straight to it." He faced the second lieutenant. "Take some men to escort our artillery crew while the cavalry rides ahead. We can't be slowed down by them now."

As they approached the larger town, Klaus noticed the many boats crossing the lake. He suspected that Erich was likely with the Swedes, but he might also be with his family waiting to depart on one of them. He had to find out.

———

Peter stood with his family beside one of the boats at the wharf. They had made arrangements to cross and were waiting for the crew to arrive. During this time, Imperial soldiers stormed down the road and then came to a halt. After a brief deliberation, they galloped towards the battle, except for a contingent of ten who rode into the town. The soldiers in the contingent scanned the area and made their way toward them. He recognized Klaus as they drew near.

Klaus immediately spotted Agatha standing with the family next to a boat. He paused in front of them, avoiding Agatha's baleful gaze as he assessed the situation. Mara stood beside her, holding a swaddled infant. The rest of the family stared defiantly at him.

"Search the boat," he commanded his men.

More townsfolk gathered around them, while the family stared at Klaus in silence as the search continued until the soldiers emerged from the lower decks and shook their heads.

"Where is he?" Klaus asked.

"He's waiting for you in the battle," Agatha said. "If you dare to face him."

Her words triggered the same unsettling pressure in his chest as when they were in the Leipzig house after they killed the young girl. He spun his horse around and galloped away.

"He's changed so much," Peter said. "So thin and gaunt."

"With such whitish skin," Eva added.

Agatha took Mara aside as the family waited for the boatmen to arrive.

"One of them will die today," Agatha said.

"It's his fate to reach this point," Mara said.

"And one of them will live on."

"You know something," she said, taking note of Agatha's faint smile and the sparkle in her eyes. "About the vision."

"I've meditated on this every day. From what just happened, it gives me hope."

She clutched Agatha's hands. "Tell me!"

They sat down on a log and began to talk.

The besieged Swedes and Ansgar's men charged up the hill on both flanks. Artillery shells exploded around Erich, but Baldur never flinched or faltered. Much to his dismay, he saw young Hans—Jürgen's companion and one of Cort's closest friends—collapse from a musket shot to the head.

The Swedes concentrated their assault on Imperial artillery batteries, eliminating them one by one. The Imperials were thrown into disarray and surrendered more ground. The tide was turning.

Another group of Imperials stormed over the hill. He maneuvered Baldur away from hostilities for a better look and grimaced when he recognized the banner from Klaus's forces. He was still too far away for a decent shot, but halfway up the ridge across an open stretch of ground, there was a thicket of shrubs, so he rode toward it.

Klaus watched the battle while also keeping an eye out for Erich. A familiar-looking horse at the periphery of the conflict, with a rider crouched low in the saddle, caught his attention. When the rider emerged from the crouch to look up, Klaus immediately recognized Erich.

Seeing this, Erich halted, seized the Bow, nocked an arrow, and took aim.

Enraged, Klaus ducked behind his officers. Just then, his artillery detachment arrived, so he rushed to them.

"Quickly!" he yelled to the artillery sergeant. "Bring the cannons and shoot down on their left flank!"

Before they could set up, Erich galloped away toward the Swedes.

Manfred and Friedrich remained away from the hostilities. They'd been close enough to observe the gruesome bloodshed, but far enough to avoid danger. Initially, Friedrich enthusiastically shared his thoughts with Manfred. As time passed, he became more reserved and kept his opinions to himself.

"Let's move back now," he said to Friedrich.

"So many men," Friedrich murmured. "Being killed like this. For what? And why?"

A cannonball screamed down and exploded before them, sending deadly shards into the air. They both struggled to steady their horses. Friedrich let out a sharp yelp.

"I'm hit," Friedrich said with a surprised expression.

"Where?"

"Here," he said, placing his hand on his stomach. Blood from the wound was already soaking through his shirt. "Now I have something to write about!"

Manfred grimaced and gave him a rag from his backpack. "Press down on it to stop the flow."

"So this is what it's like," he whispered to himself, transfixed by the sight of his blood.

————

Ansgar had seen enough. Fresh artillery shells rained down on his men. The Swedes on the other flank were being pushed back with each barrage. Helmar sat beside him as he surveyed the scene.

"We put up a good fight," Ansgar said, "but they're pushing us back with their new artillery. We have to retreat. Pass the word to our men to meet here."

After Erich rode back to the Swedes, he noticed Friedrich hunched over and clutching his side with the rag.

"What happened?" he asked Manfred.

"A cannonball exploded near us. A shard hit his stomach."

"Can you ride?" Erich asked him.

Friedrich nodded with a grimace. Gunnar and Valborg rode up to them.

"The others are retreating north," Valborg said.

"Are you sure?" Ansgar asked.

"We heard the order ourselves," Gunnar said.

"Do we still unite with them?" Helmar asked.

Once more, Ansgar surveyed the scene. More shells exploded on the open ground between them and the other Swedes.

"No," Ansgar answered. "We go south and regroup in the town."

"Where's Axel?" Magnus asked

"There!" Nico said, pointing to where the fighting was heaviest, with Axel amongst them. The Imperials were storming down on them as the Swedes positioned themselves around some buildings.

"We must go to him!" Valborg said to Ansgar.

Ansgar understood that charging across the open ground and confronting such a large force would have little chance of success. Another barrage of shells erupted in front of them.

"No! We'll avenge his death in the next battle!"

"He will not die alone!" Nico proclaimed. He spurred his horse and raced toward him.

"Damn!" Ansgar muttered.

Cannonballs exploded around Nico, yet he managed to stay on his horse. He slashed away as he neared the fighting, taking out several Imperials. Soon, he and Axel fought alongside the outnumbered Swedes.

They watched the fight with helpless resignation until the Imperials overtook Nico and Axel. They wheeled their horses and charged down the road toward the town.

———

Klaus watched the developments with great satisfaction as the battle turned in their favor. His artillery barrages had split the Swedish forces, and soon they would be in full rout. Because of this, he expected to receive a medal—or a promotion—for his leadership; however, all that mattered less than Erich's whereabouts. He continued to focus on the flank where Erich had fought. He spotted him heading south with a retreating group on the road to town.

"Get all the men you can and bring them here," he commanded the first lieutenant. "We're going after the leaders of those renegades. They've retreated to the town. Make sure to take one of our cannons."

———

Erich glanced back to see if Klaus's men were pursuing them as they rushed down the road. The last rays of the sun were visible above the hills across the lake. He tried to remember the sunrise from that morning, but couldn't. It felt like a day that had lasted forever. A deep chill washed over him after the sun set behind the hills.

36.

On the Lake

Erich had expected his family to be on the other side of the lake as he raced into the town; however, he was aghast when they all stood smiling by the wharf.

"Did you kill him, Father?" Cort asked him after they halted.

Erich ignored him and spoke to Peter. "Why are you still here?"

"It took a while to find a crew. Once we did, we decided to wait because—"

"We knew you'd come back," Mara said.

Agatha nodded beside her.

"Klaus and his men are coming after us! You should've left before now!"

The news shocked Agatha and Mara. Erich had returned just as the vision foretold. How could Klaus still be alive?

"Everyone get on right now!"

"This is where we part," Erich said to Ansgar. "All I ask is that you take Baldur to a livery. I'll come back for him later."

Ansgar glanced at his men. "We'll stay until you're all safe."

"He's after me, not you."

"He'll have to come through us first."

"Gunnar," Ansgar said, "Get another man, string up the horses, and take them to the livery."

Manfred helped the wounded Friedrich off his horse.

"My God, Friedrich!" Mara exclaimed. "What happened?"

"He caught some cannon fragments," Manfred said.

"My scrolls," he rasped.

She retrieved the scrolls and looped them over his shoulder. Magnus and Markus guided him on the boat.

Mara, Manfred, some peasant soldiers, and the Swedes scrambled on. About half of the peasant soldiers began searching for other vessels because there wasn't enough room on the boat for all of them. Erich was lifting the plank from the wharf when a woman carrying a baby ran toward them.

"Wait for me!" she screamed.

Erich supported her across.

"Thank you," she said, gasping for breath. She joined the others on the crowded boat, clutching her infant.

"There they are!" Helmar shouted, pointing to the road. A force of Imperials stormed around a bend toward the town.

Erich signaled for the oarsmen to push off. One of the boatmen unfurled a sail, which immediately caught a stiff breeze.

————

As he charged into the town, Klaus saw Erich with the soldiers on the departing boat. Once they reached the lake, he ordered his musketeers and archers to fire at them. Much to his dismay, the shots either missed or fell short as the boat drifted away. The artillerymen urged their horses to pull the heavy cannon closer to the shore.

————

Erich went to the family after noticing the cannon.

"Better take the family below," he said to Peter and Cort.

At the far end of the boat, Mara watched over Friedrich. Manfred and Jürgen stood beside him. Friedrich's eyes were glazed and droopy, and his skin was a deathly white.

The first round of cannon fire erupted from the shore. The ball landed with a heavy splash in front of them. Everyone waited in tense silence as it drifted away. Another blast followed, with the ball whistling overhead before landing in the water on the other side of the boat. Erich and Ansgar exchanged glances; the artillerymen were adjusting their aim. The next shell would be closer.

Ansgar paced across the deck, noticing how only a slight breeze furled into the sails.

"Magnus! Markus!" he shouted. "Give the oarsmen a hand."

Another explosion, followed by a louder whistle. The mast shattered from the impact, sending chunks of wood crashing down onto the deck.

Erich rushed to Mara, where a section of the mast had collapsed. Parts of it had fallen onto Friedrich's chest. Manfred lifted them off, but blood now flowed from Friedrich's mouth. Mara placed her hand on his forehead, which calmed him slightly. His eyes began to droop, and his breathing grew shallower.

My scrolls," he whispered to her. "Take care of them . . . so they won't forget."

He settled back into the blankets and took a deep breath, staring upward at the clouds still bright from the setting sun. Then, his head fell to one side.

She placed her fingertips on his neck and shook her head. She closed her eyes in silent prayer and draped a blanket over his body.

Another round struck the rear hull, knocking several off their feet. Ansgar examined the damage. The shell left a gaping hole in the hull just above the waterline.

Amid all the turmoil, Erich ran to the front of the ship and opened the hatch. The family clambered out of the dusty lower deck, with Eva carrying little Hildegard first, followed by Peter, who had Heloise and Rudi. Cort helped Agatha up as she cradled the young woman's crying infant.

"I fear the woman is dead," she said to Erich. "A beam fell on her head."

Magnus and Markus continued to row.

Klaus knew he had him; the last shell had nearly crippled the boat. He observed the darkening skies and saw a thick bank of fog drifting down from the hills across the lake. The artillerymen made another adjustment and fired. The shell struck the bow of the ship.

"Ha!" Klaus bellowed with much satisfaction, knowing the next shot would likely sink it.

The last shell shook the boat so violently that Valborg and three peasant soldiers tumbled into the water. Erich's family huddled on the opposite side. Jürgen and the Swedes attempted to assist those in the water. Valborg was the first to rise, cursing all the while. One of the peasant soldiers who had fallen did not resurface.

"We can't take another hit like that," Manfred said.

Erich nodded, staring at the activity along the shore. *There's no other choice now.* He reached back for the Bow, nocked one of his best arrows, and positioned his feet to aim. First, he flexed his knees to steady his body from the boat's rocking motion.

Helmar signaled for the rowers to stop. Everyone watched in rapt silence.

He pulled the string back, adjusting his stance while focusing on the target. As he began to shake from the effort, the Bow's power flowed into his arms and diffused throughout his body. With this added strength, he steadied himself and pulled back further.

"My God," Ansgar whispered. He'd never seen a bow bent so far without snapping.

As he focused on Klaus, Erich no longer felt any strain in his hands or arms. He raised the Bow slightly higher to achieve the right arc, which he visualized as . . . *a tight current of swirling air streaming up from the Bow and down to the target, that dark shape by the cannon.* He made the slightest adjustments, and then—at the exact moment he *felt* right—released the arrow with a resounding snap that hummed and vibrated in the air. The arrow followed his visualized arc, soaring over the lake and down to the shore.

———

Klaus awaited his crew's adjustment of the cannon; soon, his revenge would be fulfilled. He lifted his arm to signal the command to fire but paused when an unusual whizzing sound emanated from somewhere over the lake—transforming into a piercing, high-pitched whistle. He looked up and discerned a slender shape slicing through the air toward him.

No!

The arrow landed with a deep thud as it pierced his chest, knocking him backward with its force. He tried to keep his balance while flailing his arms but ended up on his back. Desperately, he pulled at the arrow, which had somehow penetrated his chainmail vest. He reached out to his men for help, but they all backed away, fearing another shot from the boat. The first lieutenant stepped toward him, paused, and then turned away.

He thrashed on the ground, gasping for breath. Blood trickled from the corners of his mouth. A deep crimson stain formed around the arrow. He glared at it in shock as the pulsing stain grew larger on his chest. Now choking on his blood, he stared up at the sky in horror as everything darkened until, at last, the darkness consumed him.

———

The cannon fire had ceased. Manfred, Helmar, and Ansgar stared at Klaus's distant figure, now fallen from the shot. The other soldiers stood with mouths agape, some shaking their heads in disbelief. Peter and Eva embraced, holding on to Heloise and Rudi. Mara cradled Hildegard with one hand and clutched Agatha's hand with the other. Cort watched his father intently, concerned about his condition.

Erich was only vaguely aware of the consequences of drawing so much power from the Bow as he continued to gaze at the scene on the shore, now devoid of soldiers. A faint wisp of smoke wafted from the cannon barrel. The only other movement came from a large, dark bird that had landed near Klaus, hopping closer to his torso.

He rose and slipped the Bow back into the sheath. Everything appeared detached and distant, yet close at the same time.

"Father, are you alright?"

Cort's voice snapped him from his semi-trance, making the people and objects regain a more familiar depth. Mara stood beside Cort, looking more wondrous and beautiful than ever before.

Mara noticed the faintest hue of an aura surrounding him in the dimming light. She glanced at Agatha, who regarded her son with the same eyes.

Everyone waited in silence for him to answer.

"Yes," he finally answered.

"I mean, because of the Bow," Cort said.

"I need to rest."

His knees wobbled after the first step. Cort handed him the staff. After a few steps, Manfred helped support him.

Erich took another step but halted. "Something's wrong with the boat."

Ansgar rushed to the side and peered down.

"It's taking in water!" he shouted. "Start rowing!"

The twins rowed with all their might, yet the boat barely progressed, now laden with water in the hull.

Ansgar looked desperately at the lake, where several small boats floated nearby, only big enough for two or three people. He turned to Jürgen.

"Do you see any of your men on the other boats?"

Jürgen scanned the lake in the fading light but shook his head.

"What about that one?" Helmar said, pointing in the opposite direction.

A large, flat, empty skiff approached them from the western shore, propelled by a boatman using a single rear oar. A torch was propped in front of it.

"Ahoy!" Ansgar yelled. "Our ship is sinking!"

The boatman regarded them suspiciously.

"There are children on board!" Manfred yelled.

He rowed to them and maneuvered the skiff next to the boat.

"We need to go to the other side," Ansgar said.

"Oh no, I can't—"

"We'll pay you," Ansgar said. He took a pouch of coins from his pocket and dangled it before him. "There's more here than you'll make in a fortnight of hauling."

Magnus threw him a line, which the boatman caught and secured around a cleat. Ansgar handed him the pouch. The boatman opened it and smiled at the contents.

Eva, Peter, Heloise, and Rudi navigated onto the skiff, followed by Agatha and Mara, both carrying infants. The oarsmen and soldiers trailed behind. They all huddled closely together.

"I thought you said women and children only," the boatman said to Ansgar.

"Do you want the coins or not?"

"There's too many—"

Ansgar's stare cut short his words.

After they clambered on the skiff, Manfred and Ansgar stood on either side of Erich—but there was no space for them.

"I told you!" the boatman said.

"I'll jump off to make room," Jürgen said. "And hang on the edge."

"And I," said Georg.

"No!" the boatman screamed in vain as the two men jumped off.

The sudden imbalance caused the overloaded skiff to rock back and forth, splashing water onto the surface. Rudi began to cry while Agatha and Mara clutched the infants tightly.

After the skiff settled, Ansgar stepped on. Manfred and Erich were the last ones left.

"Get on and help me across," Erich said.

Manfred stepped on and extended his hand.

"Help! My baby!" A woman's voice screamed from inside the boat. A hand reached up from the rear hatch.

Erich staggered toward the hatch and lifted the woman. She had a deep gash on her forehead, and dried blood streaked down one side of her face.

"Your baby's alive," he said. "On the other boat."

Agatha held up the infant.

They walked back together, and Erich guided her across.

"Thank you," she said as she gazed into his eyes. "Again."

The skiff tilted more when she stepped on it. Agatha handed the infant to the woman, who embraced and kissed it.

"Another one and we'll sink!" the boatman declared.

A fog began to drift around them. The boat creaked and listed more from the incoming water.

"He's right," Erich said. "I'll wait."

"No!" Mara blurted out.

"But father," Cort said. "The boat's sinking."

"I'll take your place," Manfred said.

"Let me give the Bow to Cort first."

After Cort slowly made his way to the front, he handed the Bow to his son. They held it together in a silent communion for a moment until Erich nodded to him. He then released his grip so that Cort could draw it in.

Erich quickly grasped his staff and pushed the skiff away with it.

"What?" Manfred asked.

"Father?"

"Come back after you reach the other side," Erich said as the skiff drifted away.

Helmar threw the torch to Erich.

"To see you when we return," Helmar said.

He picked up the torch and sat cross-legged on the deck.

All eyes were on Erich as he moved away. At first, the torch illuminated his features. Later, only his shape and silhouette could be seen in the mist and darkness. Further away, only the glowing torch remained visible.

"Hurry!" Jürgen yelled. "The water's cold." Georg nodded next to him, with chattering teeth.

The twins increased their pace, causing the water to churn behind them. The skiff moved along much faster.

As they approached the shore, night had fallen. Torches held by men on the wharf guided them to a landing place.

Mara looked back after they landed; the distant torchlight still shimmered through the mist.

"Your men told us what was happening," one of the torchbearers said to Ansgar, pointing to some peasant soldiers along the shore. "So we waited here for your arrival in case you needed help."

After she stepped off the skiff, Mara looked back again. This time, the torchlight moved to the side and vanished. She felt a sudden chill and gasped for air. Taking a deeper breath, she tried to summon her strength and courage. She shot a glance at Agatha, who noticed the same thing.

"Is everyone off?" a torchbearer asked.

"There's one man left," Ansgar answered. His expression changed when he saw that the torchlight was out. "We need another boat to get him off."

"I have one nearby," another torchbearer said. "Follow me."

Manfred, Ansgar, and Helmar went with him, along with Cort and Peter.

They rowed out into the darkness of the lake, with Ansgar and Helmar on each oar. Manfred, Cort, and Peter each held a torch. A heavy mist and fog swirled around them. They broke through the mist several times, revealing the moon and stars.

They stopped rowing in the area where they figured the sinking boat would be.

"Erich!" Peter shouted. "Call back if you hear us."

They listened for any sound in the water or a voice. After a period of silence, they rowed on.

They halted a short distance away.

"Father!" Cort called out. "Please answer us!"

Again, everyone listened for any sound above the waves lapping against the hull.

They rowed on in widening circles, stopping at intervals and, after hearing nothing, continued. When one of the torches burned out and the other two grew dim, they reluctantly headed back. This time, it seemed as though there were as many glistening torches on the shore as stars in the sky.

The townsfolk were waiting for them. Word had spread about the events on the lake, and they all gathered to see if they had rescued the man on the boat. It didn't take long for them to realize that they hadn't. Some bowed their heads in prayer.

Mara had resigned herself to the reality that Erich likely wouldn't be saved because of how she felt when the torchlight disappeared. Agatha also had little hope for his return because of the prolonged search. During that time, they discussed many things, including the implications of Agatha's vision on Erich's life.

Mara unfolded Christian's final sketch of Erich before they crossed the Rhein to Eibingen. They admired it in the soft glow of a nearby torch.

The soldiers trudged up the hill, their boots dragging against the ground, exhausted from the day's challenges. The woman with the baby cried softly, and Eva tried to comfort her.

Peter trudged toward town, carrying a sleeping Heloise and holding Rudi's hand. Eva cradled Catherine Hildegard next to him. Mara, carrying Friedrich's scrolls, and Agatha walked behind them. Cort headed to the Swedes gathered on the hill, with the Black Bow slung over his shoulder.

Mara paused to observe the soldiers kneeling on one knee with bowed heads, listening to Ansgar speak. Ansgar turned toward the lake and raised his sword. The others followed suit, holding their swords out for some time before withdrawing them and plodding away.

She turned back to the shore to conduct another ceremony.

Agatha wrapped a scarf around her neck and watched her step onto the wharf.

Mara stood at the end of the wharf, unclasping her necklace. The mist had cleared, and the moon shone brightly in the sky. She held the moonstone pendant in both hands for a moment before tossing it high into the air. It landed with a faint splash, sending ripples of concentric circles across the dark, placid waters.

When the first ripple reached the wharf near her feet, she visualized the necklace sinking into the waters . . .

slowly circling down, the moonlight still reflecting through the water on the stone, and circling deeper until it fell further down and disappeared into the blackness.

For an instant, a single glimmer of light shone in the blackness, followed by another.

They would be together in the next world.

Epilogue

The German and Swedish forces regrouped a fortnight later in the north and defeated the Imperial army at Wittstock. After the battle, the momentum of the War shifted as the Imperials' power and influence waned. For the next ten years, the War tapered off until it reached a point where the country's resources had become exhausted. The Peace of Westphalia concluded the Thirty Years War in 1648, restoring the lands and boundaries between Catholics and Protestants to what they were when the War began, thirty years earlier.

Witchcraft persecution gradually waned after that but persisted well into the next century.

Peter led the family back to Leipzig, where they had lived during the last years of the War. Following the Peace of Westphalia, the authorities restored their ancestral home and properties to the family name, and they returned to settle there.

Mara stayed with the family briefly in Leipzig before returning to the Eibingen monastery, accompanied by Manfred. There, she resumed her studies and taught classes to the students, including young Adele and, later, Catherine Hildegard. She recounted her experiences and lessons learned while touring the country, both before and during her time with Erich.

Manfred guided Mara and Catherine Hildegard across the heartland to the monastery, where he remained for three years. During this time, he worked various jobs, such as organizing a small defense force, assisting with the harvest and care of the animals, and cooking. He married the buxom maid he met during the May Day celebration, and together, they raised two children: a boy and a girl. Later, they left the monastery and settled in Mainz, where he opened a bakery.

Cort resumed his studies in Leipzig and later at Wittenberg University where, influenced by his father's implied wishes, he began training to become a military officer. He left two years later and adopted a nomadic lifestyle, traveling through the countryside with a lute, a flute, and a small set of drums—instruments he had learned to play at university. He visited family during his journeys before hitting the road again, with the Black Bow always by his side. During his last visit, the woman he married in a simple handfasting ceremony, Sophie, accompanied him, large with child.

After the battle at Wittstock, Ansgar and the Swedes honored the vows they had made at Lützen and returned to their homeland.

Jürgen and the surviving peasant soldiers remained with the army after Wittstock and reintegrated into the populace, strengthened by their experiences in the war and prepared to begin their lives anew.

Mara carried Friedrich's scrolls with her on the journey back to Eibingen and stored them in the monastery library. Both Ursula and Mara incorporated excerpts from his writings into the class curricula. They also ensured that the monastery made the scrolls available to outside scholars and others, so the truths of the War and its effects on the German people would never be forgotten.

www.ingramcontent.com/pod-product-compliance
Lightning Source LLC
Chambersburg PA
CBHW020237010826
48973CB00006B/1548